The French and Indian War Novels: 2

The French & Indian War Novels: 2

The Rulers of the Lakes

A Story of George & Champlain

•

The Masters of the Peaks

A Story of the Great North Woods

Joseph A. Altsheler

The French & Indian War Novels: 2
The Rulers of the Lakes & The Masters of the Peaks
by Joseph A. Altsheler

FIRST EDITION

Leonaur is an imprint of Oakpast Ltd

ISBN: 978-1-84677-588-8 (hardcover)
ISBN: 978-1-84677-587-1 (softcover)

http://www.leonaur.com

Publisher's Note

The views expressed in this book are not necessarily
those of the publisher.

Contents

THE FRENCH & INDIAN WAR NOVELS

The Rulers of the Lakes

A Story of George and Champlain

Foreword

The Rulers of the Lakes is a complete story, but it is also the third volume of the French and Indian War Series, following *The Hunters of the Hills* and *The Shadow of the North.* Robert Lennox, Tayoga, Willet, and all the important characters in the earlier romances reappear.

Characters in the French and Indian War Series

Robert Lennox	A lad of unknown origin
Tayoga	A young Onondaga warrior
David Willet	A hunter
Raymond Louis De St. Luc	A brilliant French officer
Aguste De Courcelles	A French officer
François De Jumonville	A French officer
Louis De Galisonnière	A young French officer
Jean De Mézy	A corrupt Frenchman
Armand Glandelet	A young Frenchman
Pierre Boucher	A bully and bravo
Philibert Drouillard	A French priest
The Marquis Duquesne	Governor-General of Canada
Marquis De Vaudreuil	Governor-General of Canada
François Bigot	Intendant of Canada
Marquis De Montcalm	French commander-in-chief
De Levis	A French general
Bourlamaque	A French general
Bougainville	A French general
Armand Dubois	A follower of St. Luc
M. De Chatillard	An old French Seigneur
Charles Langlade	A French partisan
The Dove	The Indian wife of Langlade
Tandakora	An Ojibway chief
Daganoweda	A young Mohawk chief

Hendrick	An old Mohawk chief
Braddock.	A British General
Abercrombie	A British general
Wolfe	A British general
Col. William Johnson	Anglo-American leader
Molly Brant	Col. Wm. Johnson's Indian wife
Joseph Brant	Young brother of Molly Brant; afterward the great Mohawk Chief Thayendanegea
Robert Dinwiddie	Lieutenant-Governor of Virginia
William Shirley	Governor of Massachusetts
Benjamin Franklin	Famous American patriot
James Colden	A young Philadelphia captain
William Wilton	A young Philadelphia lieutenant
Hugh Carson	A young Philadelphia lieutenant
Jacobus Huysman	An Albany burgher
Caterina	Jacobus Huysman's cook
Alexander Mclean	An Albany schoolmaster
Benjamin Hardy	A New York merchant
Johnathan Pillsbury	Clerk to Benjamin Hardy
Adrian Van Zoon	A New York merchant
The Slaver	A nameless rover
Achille Garay	A French spy
Alfred Grosvenor	A young English officer
James Cabell	A young Virginian
Walter Stuart	A young Virginian
Black Rifle	A famous "Indian fighter"
Elihu Strong	A Massachusetts colonel
Alan Hervey	A New York financier
Stuart Whyte	Captain of the British sloop Hawk
John Latham	Lieutenant of the British sloop Hawk
Edward Charteris	A young officer of the Royal Americans
Zebedee Crane	A young scout and forest runner
Robert Rogers	Famous Captain of American Rangers

Chapter 1

The Heralds of Peril

The three, the white youth, the red youth, and the white man, lay deep in the forest, watching the fire that burned on a low hill to the west, where black figures flitted now and then before the flame. They did not stir or speak for a long time, because a great horror was upon them. They had seen an army destroyed a few days before by a savage but invisible foe. They had heard continually for hours the fierce triumphant yells of the warriors and they had seen the soldiers dropping by hundreds, but the woods and thickets had hid the foe who sent forth such a rain of death.

Robert Lennox could not yet stop the quiver of his nerves when he recalled the spectacle, and Willet, the hunter, hardened though he was to war, shuddered in spite of himself at the memory of that terrible battle in the leafy wilderness. Nor was Tayoga, the young Onondaga, free from emotion when he thought of Braddock's defeat, and the blazing triumph it meant for the western tribes, the enemies of his people.

They had turned back, availing themselves of their roving commission, when they saw that the victors were not pursuing the remains of the beaten army, and now they were watching the French and Indians. Fort Duquesne was not many miles away, but the fire on the hill had been built by a party of Indians led by a Frenchman, his uniform showing when he passed between eye and flame, the warriors being naked save for the breech cloth.

"I hope it's not St. Luc," said Robert.

"Why?" asked Willet. "He was in the battle. We saw him leading on the Indian hosts."

"I know. That was fair combat, I suppose, and the French used the tools they had. The Chevalier could scarcely have been a loyal son of

France if he had not fought us then, but I don't like to think of him over there by the fire, leading a band of Indians who will kill and scalp women and children as well as men along the border."

"Nor I, either, though I'm not worried about it. I can't tell who the man is, but I know it's not St. Luc. Now I see him black against the blaze, and it's not the Chevalier's figure."

Robert suddenly drew a long breath, as if he had made a surprising recognition.

"I'm not sure," he said, "but I notice a trick of movement now and then reminding me of someone. I'm thinking it's the same Auguste de Courcelles, Colonel of France, whom we met first in the northern woods and again in Quebec. There was one memorable night, as you know, Dave, when we had occasion to mark him well."

"I think you're right, Robert," said the hunter. "It looks like De Courcelles."

"I know he is right," said Tayoga, speaking for the first time. "I have been watching him whenever he passed before the fire, and I cannot mistake him."

"I wonder what he's doing here," said Robert. "He may have been in the battle, or he may have come to Duquesne a day or two later."

"I think," said Willet, "that he's getting ready to lead a band against the border, now almost defenceless."

"He is a bad man," said Tayoga. "His soul is full of wickedness and cruelty, and it should be sent to the dwelling place of the evil minded. If Great Bear and Dagaeoga say the word I will creep through the thickets and kill him."

Robert glanced at him. The Onondaga had spoken in the gentle tones of one who felt grief rather than anger. Robert knew that his heart was soft, that in ordinary life none was kinder than Tayoga. And yet he was and always would be an Indian. De Courcelles had a bad mind, and he was also a danger that should be removed. Then why not remove him?

"No, Tayoga," said Willet. "We can't let you risk yourself that way. But we might go a little closer without any great danger. Ah, do you see that new figure passing before the blaze?"

"Tandakora!" exclaimed the white youth and the red youth together.

"Nobody who knows him could mistake him, even at this distance. I think he must be the biggest Indian in all the world."

"But a bullet would bring him crashing to earth as quickly as any other," said the Onondaga.

"Aye, so it would, Tayoga, but his time hasn't come yet, though it will come, and may we be present when your Manitou deals with him as he deserves. Suppose we curve to the right through these thick bushes, and from the slope there I think we can get a much better view of the band."

They advanced softly upon rising ground, and being able to approach two or three hundred yards, saw quite clearly all those around the fire. The white man was in truth De Courcelles, and the gigantic Indian, although there could have been no mistake about him, was Tandakora, the Ojibway.

The warriors, about thirty in number, were, Willet thought, a mingling of Ojibways, Pottawattomies and Ottawas. All were in war paint and were heavily armed, many of them carrying big muskets with bayonets on the end, taken from Braddock's fallen soldiers. Three had small swords belted to their naked waists, not as weapons, but rather as the visible emblems of triumph.

As he looked, Robert's head grew hot with the blood pumped up from his angry heart. It seemed to him that they swaggered and boasted, although they were but true to savage nature.

"Easy, lad," said Willet, putting a restraining hand upon his shoulder. "It's their hour. You can't deny that, and we'll have to bide a while."

"But will our hour ever come, Dave? Our army has been beaten, destroyed. The colonies and mother country alike are sluggish, and now have no plans, the whole border lies at the mercy of the tomahawk and the French power in Canada not only grows all the time, but is directed by able and daring men."

"Patience, lad, patience! Our strength is greater than that of the foe, although we may be slower in using it. But I tell you we'll see our day of triumph yet."

"They are getting ready to move," whispered the Onondaga. "The Frenchman and the band will march northward."

"And not back to Duquesne?" said Willet. "What makes you think so, Tayoga?"

"What is left for them to do at Duquesne? It will be many a day before the English and Americans come against it again."

"That, alas, is true, Tayoga. They're not needed longer here, nor are we. They've put out their fire, and now they're off toward the north, just as you said they would be. Tandakora and De Courcelles lead, marching side by side. A pretty pair, well met here in the forest. Now, I wish I knew where they were going!"

"Can't the Great Bear guess?" said the Onondaga.

"No, Tayoga. How should I?"

"Doesn't Great Bear remember the fort in the forest, the one called Refuge?"

"Of course I do, Tayoga! And the brave lads, Colden and Wilton and Carson and their comrades who defended it so long and so well. That's the most likely point of attack, and now, since Braddock's army is destroyed it's too far in the wilderness, too exposed, and should be abandoned. Suppose we carry a warning!"

Robert's eyes glistened. The idea made a strong appeal to him. He had mellow memories of those Philadelphia lads, and it would be pleasant to see them again. The three, in bearing the alarm, might achieve, too, a task that would lighten, in a measure, the terror along the border. It would be a relief at least to do something while the government disagreed and delayed.

"Let's start at once for Fort Refuge," he said, "and help them to get away before the storm breaks. What do you say, Tayoga?"

"It is what we ought to do," replied the Onondaga, in his precise English of the schools.

"Come," said Willet, leading the way, and the three, leaving the fire behind them, marched rapidly into the north and east. Two miles gone, and they stopped to study the sun, by which they meant to take their reckoning.

"The fort lies there," said Willet, pointing a long finger, "and by my calculations it will take us about five days and nights to reach it, that is, if nothing gets in our way."

"You think, then," asked Robert, "that the French and Indians are already spreading a net?"

"The Indians might stop, Robert, my lad, to exult over their victory and to celebrate it with songs and dances, but the French leaders, whose influence with them is now overwhelming, will push them on. They will want to reap all the fruits of their great triumph by the river. I've often told you about the quality of the French and you've seen for yourself. Ligneris, Contrecoeur, De Courcelles, St. Luc and the others will flame like torches along the border."

"And St. Luc will be the most daring, skilful and energetic of them all."

"It's a fact that all three of us know, Robert, and now, having fixed our course, we must push ahead with all speed. De Courcelles, Tandakora and the warriors are on the march, too, and we may see them again before we see Fort Refuge."

"The forest will be full of warriors," said Tayoga, speaking with great gravity. "The fort will be the first thought of the western barbarians, and of the tribes from Canada, and they will wish to avenge the defeat they suffered before it."

It was not long until they had ample proof that the Onondaga's words were true. They saw three trails in the course of the day, and all of them led toward the fort. Willet and Tayoga, with their wonderful knowledge of the forest, estimated that about thirty warriors made one trail, about twenty another, and fifteen the smallest.

"They're going fast, too," said the hunter, "but we must go faster."

"They will see our traces," said Tayoga, "and by signalling to one another they will tell all that we are in the woods. Then they will set a force to destroy us, while the greater bands go on to take the fort."

"But we'll pass 'em," said Robert confidently. "They can't stop us!"

Tayoga and the hunter glanced at him. Then they looked at each other and smiled. They knew Robert thoroughly, they understood his vivid and enthusiastic nature which, looking forward with so much confidence to success, was apt to consider it already won, a fact that perhaps contributed in no small measure to the triumph wished so ardently. At last, the horror of the great defeat in the forest and the slaughter of an army was passing. It was Robert's hopeful temperament and brilliant mind that gave him such a great charm for all who met him, a charm to which even the fifty wise old sachems in the vale of Onondaga had not been insensible.

"No, Robert," said the Great Bear gravely, "I don't think anything can stop us. I've a prevision that De Courcelles and Tandakora will stand in our way, but we'll just brush 'em out of it."

They had not ceased to march at speed, while they talked, and now Tayoga announced the presence of a river, an obstacle that might prove formidable to foresters less expert than they. It was lined on both sides with dense forest, and they walked along its bank about a mile until they came to a comparatively shallow place where they forded it in water above their knees. However, their leggings and moccasins dried fast in the midsummer sun, and, experiencing no discomfort, they pressed forward with unabated speed.

All the afternoon they continued their great journey to save those at the fort, fording another river and a half dozen creeks and leaping across many brooks. Twice they crossed trails leading to the east and twice other trails leading to the west, but they felt that all of them would presently turn and join in the general march converging upon Fort Refuge. They were sure, too, that De Courcelles, Tandakora and their band were marching on a line almost parallel with them, and that they would offer the greatest danger.

Night came, a beautiful, bright summer night with a silky blue sky in which multitudes of silver stars danced, and they sought a covert in a dense thicket where they lay on their blankets, ate venison, and talked a little before they slept.

Robert's brilliant and enthusiastic mood lasted. He could see nothing but success. With the fading of the great slaughter by the river came other pictures, deep of hue, intense and charged with pleasant memories. Life recently had been a great panorama to him, bright and full of changes. He could not keep from contrasting his present position, hid in a thicket to save himself from cruel savages, with those vivid days at Quebec, his gorgeous period in New York, and the gay time with sporting youth in the cosy little capital of Williamsburg.

But the contrast, so far from making him unhappy, merely expanded his spirit. He rejoiced in the pleasures that he had known and adapted himself to present conditions. Always influenced greatly by what lay just around him, he considered their thicket the best thicket in which he had ever been hidden. The leaves of last year, drifted into little heaps on which they lay, were uncommonly large and soft. The light breeze rustling the boughs over his head whispered only of peace and ease, and the two comrades, who lay on either side of him, were the finest comrades any lad ever had.

"Tayoga," he asked, and his voice was sincerely earnest, "can you see on his star Tododaho, the founder and protector of the great league of the Hodenosaunee?"

The young Onondaga, his face mystic and reverential, gazed toward the west where a star of great size and beauty quivered and blazed.

"I behold him," he replied. "His face is turned toward us, and the wise serpents lie, coil on coil, in his hair. There are wreaths of vapour about his eyes, but I can see them shining through, shining with kindness, as the mighty chief, who went away four hundred years ago, watches over us. His eyes say that so long as our deeds are just, so long as we walk in the path that Manitou wishes, we shall be victorious. Now a cloud passes before the star, and I cannot see the face of Tododaho, but he has spoken, and it will be well for us to remember his words."

He sank back on his blanket and closed his eyes as if he, too, in thought, had shot through space to some great star. Robert and Willet were silent, sharing perhaps in his emotion. The religion and beliefs of the Indian were real and vital to them, and if Tododaho promised success to Tayoga then the promise would be fulfilled.

"I think, Robert," said Willet, "that you'd better keep the first watch. Wake me a little while before midnight, and I'll take the second."

"Good enough," said Robert. "I think I can hear any footfall Tandakora may make, if he approaches."

"It is not enough to hear the footfall of the Ojibway," said Tayoga, opening his eyes and sitting up. "To be a great sentinel and forester worthy to be compared with the greatest, Dagaeoga must hear the whisper of the grass as it bends under the lightest wind, he must hear the sound made by the little leaf as it falls, he must hear the ripple in the brook that is flowing a hundred yards from us, and he must hear the wild flowers talking together in the night. Only then can Dagaeoga call himself a sentinel fit to watch over two such sleeping foresters as the Great Bear and myself."

"Close your eyes and go to sleep without fear," said Robert in the same vein. "I shall hear Tandakora breathing if he comes within a mile of us, at the same distance I shall hear the moccasin of De Courcelles, when it brushes against last year's fallen leaf, and at half a mile I shall see the look of revenge and cruelty upon the face of the Ojibway seeking for us."

Willet laughed softly, but with evident satisfaction.

"You two boys are surely the greatest talkers I've heard for a long time," he said. "You have happy thoughts and you put 'em into words. If I didn't know that you had a lot of deeds, too, to your credit, I'd call you boasters, but knowing it, I don't. Go ahead and spout language, because you're only lads and I can see that you enjoy it."

"I'm going to sleep now," said Tayoga, "but Dagaeoga can keep on talking and be happy, because he will talk to himself long after we have gone to the land of dreams."

"If I do talk to myself," said Robert, "it's because I like to talk to a bright fellow, and I like to have a bright fellow talk to me. Sleep as soundly as you please, you two, because while you're sleeping I can carry on an intellectual conversation."

The hunter laughed again.

"It's no use, Tayoga," he said. "You can't put him down. The fifty wise old *sachems* in the vale of Onondaga proclaimed him a great orator, and great orators must always have their way."

"It is so," said the Onondaga. "The voice of Dagaeoga is like a river. It flows on forever, and like the murmur of the stream it will soothe me to deeper slumbers. Now I sleep."

"And so do I," said the hunter.

It seemed marvellous that such formal announcements should be followed by fact, but within three minutes both went to that pleasant land of dreams of which they had been talking so lightly. Their breathing was long and regular and, beyond a doubt, they had put absolute faith in their sentinel. Robert's mind, so quick to respond to obvious confidence, glowed with resolve. There was no danger now that he would relax the needed vigilance a particle, and, rifle in the hollow of his arm, he began softly to patrol the bushes.

He was convinced that De Courcelles and Tandakora were not many miles away—they might even be within a mile—and memory of a former occasion, somewhat similar, when Tayoga had detected the presence of the Ojibway, roused his emulation. He was determined that, while he was on watch, no creeping savage should come near enough to strike.

Hand on the hammer and trigger of his rifle he walked in an ever widening circle about his sleeping comrades, searching the thickets with eyes, good naturally and trained highly, and stopping now and then to listen. Two or three times he put his ear to the earth that he might hear, as Tayoga had bade him, the rustle of leaves a mile away.

His eager spirit, always impatient for action, found relief in the continuous walking, and the steady enlargement of the circle in which he travelled, acquiring soon a radius of several hundred yards. On the western perimeter he was beyond the deep thicket, and within a magnificent wood, unchoked by undergrowth. Here the trees stood up in great, regular rows, ordered by nature, and the brilliant moonlight clothed every one of them in a veil of silver. On such a bright night in summer the wilderness always had for him an elusive though powerful beauty, but he felt its danger. Among the mighty trunks, with no concealing thickets, he could be seen easily, if prowling savages were near, and, as he made his circles, he always hastened through what he called to himself his park, until he came to the bushes, in the density of which he was well hidden from any eye fifty feet away.

It was an hour until midnight, and the radius of his circle had increased another fifty yards, when he came again to the great spaces among the oaks and beeches. Halfway through and he sank softly down behind the trunk of a huge oak. Either in fact or in a sort of mental illusion, he had heard a moccasin brush a dry leaf far away. The command of Tayoga, though spoken in jest, had been so impressive that his ear was obeying it. Firm in the belief that his own dark shadow blurred with the dark trunk, and that he was safe from the sight of a questing eye, he lay there a long time, listening.

In time, the sound, translated from fancy into fact, came again, and now he knew that it was near, perhaps not more than a hundred yards away, the rustling of a real moccasin against a real dry leaf. Twice and thrice his ear signalled to his brain. It could not be fancy. It was instead an alarming fact.

He was about to creep from the tree, and return to his comrades with word that the enemy was near, but he restrained his impulse, merely crouching a little lower that his dark shadow might blend with the dark earth as well as the dark trunk. Then he heard several rustlings and the very low murmur of voices.

Gradually the voices which had been blended together, detached themselves and Robert recognized those of Tandakora and De Courcelles. Presently they came into the moonlight, followed by the savage band, and they passed within fifty yards of the youth who lay in the shelter of the trunk, pressing himself into the earth.

The Frenchman and the Ojibway were talking with great earnestness and Robert's imagination, plumbing the distance, told him the words they said. Tandakora was stating with great emphasis that the three whose trail they had found had gone on very fast, obviously with the intention of warning the garrison at the fort, and if they were to be cut off the band must hasten, too. De Courcelles was replying that in his opinion Tandakora was right, but it would not be well to get too far ahead. They must throw out flankers as they marched, but there was no immediate need of them. If the band spread out before dawn it would be sufficient.

Robert's fancy was so intense and creative that, beginning by imagining these things so, he made them so. The band therefore was sure to go on without searching the thickets on either right or left at present, and all immediate apprehension disappeared from his mind. Tandakora and De Courcelles were in the centre of the moonlight, and although knowing them evil, he was surprised to see how very evil their faces looked, each in its own red or white way. He could remember nothing at that moment but their wickedness, and their treacherous attacks upon his life and those of his friends, and the memory clothed them about with a hideous veil through which only their cruel souls shone. It was characteristic of him that he should always see everything in extreme colours, and in his mind the good were always very good and the bad were very bad.

Hence it was to him an actual physical as well as mental relief, when the Frenchman, the Ojibway and their band, passing on, were blotted from his eyes by the forest. Then he turned back to the thicket in which his comrades lay, and bent over them for the purpose of awakening them. But before he could speak or lay a hand upon either, Tayoga sat up, his eyes wide open.

"You come with news that the enemy has been at hand!"

"Yes, but how did you know it?"

"I see it in your look, and, also when I slept, the Keeper of Dreams whispered it in my ear. An evil wind, too, blew upon my face and I knew it was the breath of De Courcelles and Tandakora. They have been near."

"They and their entire band passed not more than four hundred yards to the eastward of us. I lay in the bush and saw them distinctly. They're trying to beat us to Fort Refuge."

"But they won't do it, because we won't let 'em," said Willet, who had awakened at the talking. "We'll make a curve and get ahead of 'em again. You watched well, Robert."

"I obeyed the strict injunctions of Tayoga," said young Lennox, smiling faintly. "He bade me listen so intently that I should hear the rustle of a dry leaf when a moccasin touched it a mile away in the forest. Well, I heard it, and going whence the sound came I saw De Courcelles, Tandakora and their warriors pass by."

"You love to paint pictures with words, Robert. I see that well, but 'tis not likely that you exaggerate so much, after all. I'm sorry you won't get your share of sleep, but we must be up and away."

"I'll claim a double portion of it later on, Dave, but I agree with you that what we need most just now is silence and speed, and speed and silence."

The three, making a curve toward the east, travelled at high speed through the rest of the night, Tayoga now leading and showing all his inimitable skill as a forest trailer. In truth, the Onondaga was in his element. His spirits, like Robert's, rose as dangers grew thicker around them, and he had been affected less than either of his comrades by the terrible slaughter of Braddock's men. Mentally at least, he was more of a stoic, and woe to the vanquished was a part of the lore of all the Indian tribes. The French and their allies had struck a heavy blow and there was nothing left for the English and Americans to do but to strike back. It was all very simple.

Day came, and at the suggestion of Willet they rested again in the thickets. Robert was not really weary, at least the spirit uplifted him, though he knew that he must not over-task the body. His enthusiasm, based upon such a sanguine temperament, continued to rise. Again he foresaw glittering success. They would shake off all their foes, reach the fort in time, and lead the garrison and the people who had found refuge there safely out of the wilderness.

Where they lay the bushes were very dense. Before hiding there they had drunk abundantly at a little brook thirty or forty feet away, and now they ate with content the venison that formed their breakfast. Over the vast forest a brilliant sun was rising and here the leaves and grass were not burned much by summer heat. It looked fresh and green, and the wind sang pleasantly through its cool shadows. It appealed to Robert. With his plastic nature he was all for the town when he was in town, and now in the forest he was all for the forest.

"I can understand why you love it so well," he said to Tayoga, waving his hand at the verdant world that curved about them.

"My people and their ancestors have lived in it for more generations than anyone knows," said the Onondaga, his eyes glistening. "I have been in the white man's schools, and the white man's towns, and I have seen the good in them, but this is my real home. This is what I love best. My heart beats strongest for the forest."

"My own heart does a lot of beating for the woods," said Willet, thoughtfully, "and it ought to do so, I've spent so many years of my life in them—happy years, too. They say that no matter how great an evil may be some good will come out of it, and this war will achieve one good end."

"What is that, Great Bear?"

"It will delay the work of the axe. Men will be so busy with the rifle that they will have mighty little time for the axe. The trees will stop falling for a while, and the forest will cover again the places where it has been cleared away. Why, the game itself will increase!"

"How long do you think we'd better stay here?" asked Robert, his eager soul anxious to be on again.

"Patience! patience, my lad," replied Willet. "It's one thing that you'll have to practice. We don't want to run squarely into De Courcelles, Tandakora and their band, and meanwhile we're very comfortable here, gathering strength. Look at Tayoga there and learn from him. If need be he could lie in the same place a week and be happy."

"I hope the need will not come," laughed the Onondaga.

Robert felt the truth of Willet's words, and he put restraint upon himself, resolved that he would not be the first to propose the new start. He had finished breakfast and he lay on his elbow gazing up through the green tracery of the bushes at the sky. It was a wonderful sky, a deep, soft, velvet blue, and it tinted the woods with glorious and kindly hues. It seemed strange to Robert, at the moment, that a forest so beautiful should bristle with danger, but he knew it too well to allow its softness and air of innocence to deceive him.

It was almost the middle of the morning when Willet gave the word to renew the march, and they soon saw they had extreme need of caution. Evidence that warriors had passed was all about them. Now and then they saw the faint imprint of a moccasin. Twice they found little painted feathers that had fallen from a headdress or a scalplock, and once Tayoga saw a red bead lying in the grass where it had dropped, perhaps, from a legging.

"We shall have to pass by Tandakora's band and perhaps other bands in the night," said Tayoga.

"It's possible, too," said Willet, "that they know we're on our way to the fort, and may try to stop us. Our critical time will soon be at hand."

They listened throughout the afternoon for the signals that bands might make to one another, but heard nothing. Willet, in truth, was not surprised.

"Silence will serve them best," he said, "and they'll send runners from band to band. Still, if they do give signals we want to know it."

"There is a river, narrow but deep, about five miles ahead," said Tayoga, "and we'll have to cross it on our way to the fort. I think it is there that Tandakora will await us."

"It's pretty sure to be the place," said Willet. "Do you know where there's a ford, Tayoga?"

"There is none."

"Then we'll have to swim for it. That's bad. But you say it's a narrow stream?"

"Yes, Great Bear. Two minutes would carry us across it."

"Then we must find some place for the fording where the trees lean over from either side and the shadow is deep."

Tayoga nodded, and, after that, they advanced in silence, redoubling their caution as they drew near to the river. The night was not so bright as the one that had just gone before, but it furnished sufficient light for wary and watching warriors to see their figures at a considerable distance, and, now and then, they stopped to search the thickets with their own eyes. No wind blew, their footsteps made no sound and the intense stillness of the forest wove itself into the texture of Robert's mind. His extraordinary fancy peopled it with phantoms. There was a warrior in every bush, but, secure in the comradeship of his two great friends, he went on without fear.

"There is no signal," whispered Tayoga at last. "They do not even imitate the cry of bird or beast, and it proves one thing, Great Bear."

"So it does, Tayoga."

"You know as well as I do, Great Bear, that they make no sound because they have set the trap, and they do not wish to alarm the game which they expect to walk into it."

"Even so, Tayoga. Our minds travel in the same channel."

"But the game is suspicious, nevertheless," continued Tayoga in his precise school English, "and the trap will not fall."

"No, Tayoga, it won't fall, because the game won't walk into it."

"Tandakora will suffer great disappointment. He is a mighty hunter and he has hunted mighty game, but the game that he hunts now is more wary than the stag or the bear, and has greater power to strike back than either."

"Well spoken, Tayoga."

The hunter and the Onondaga looked at each other in the dark and laughed. Their spirits were as wild as the wilderness, and they were enjoying the prospect of the Ojibway's empty trap. Robert laughed with them. Already in his eager mind success was achieved and the crossing was made. After a while he saw dim silver through the trees, and he knew they had come to the river. Then the three sank down and approached inch by inch, sure that De Courcelles, Tandakora and their forces would be watching on the other side.

CHAPTER 2

The Kindly Bridge

The thicket in which the three lay was of low but dense bushes, with high grass growing wherever the sun could reach it. In the grass tiny wild flowers, purple, blue and white were in bloom, and Robert inhaled their faint odour as he crouched, watching for the enemy who sought his life. It was a forest scene, the beauty of which would have pleased him at any other time, nor was he wholly unconscious of it now. The river itself, as Tayoga had stated, was narrow. At some points it did not seem to be more than ten or fifteen yards across, but it flowed in a slow, heavy current, showing depths below. Nor could he see, looking up and down the stream, any prospect of a ford.

Robert's gaze moved in an eager quest along the far shore, but he detected no sign of Tandakora, the Frenchman or their men. Yet he felt that Tayoga and Willet were right and that foes were on watch there. It was inevitable, because it was just the place where they could wait best for the three. Nevertheless he asked, though it was merely to confirm his own belief.

"Do you think they're in the brush, Dave?"

"Not a doubt of it, Robert," the hunter whispered back. "They haven't seen us yet, but they hope to do so soon."

"And we also, who haven't seen them yet, hope to do so soon."

"Aye, Robert, that's the fact. Ah, I think I catch a glimpse of them now. Tayoga, wouldn't you say that the reflection in the big green bush across the river is caused by a moonbeam falling on a burnished rifle barrel?"

"Not a doubt of it, Great Bear. Now, I see the rifle itself! And now I see the hands that hold it. The hands belong to a live warrior, an Ojibway, or a Pottowattomie. He is kneeling, waiting for a shot, if he should find anything to shoot at."

"I see him, too, Tayoga, and there are three more warriors just beyond him. It's certainly the band of Tandakora and De Courcelles, and they've set a beautiful trap for three who will not come into it."

"It is so, Great Bear. One may build a splendid bear trap but of what use is it if the bear stays away?"

"But what are we to do?" asked Robert. "We can't cross in the face of such a force."

"We'll go down the stream," replied Willet, "keeping hidden, of course, in the thickets, and look for a chance to pass. Of course, they've sent men in both directions along the bank, but we may go farther than any of them."

He led the way, and they went cautiously through the thickets two or three miles, all the time intently watching the other shore. Twice they saw Indian sentinels on watch, and knew that they could not risk the passage. Finally they stopped and waited a full two hours in the thickets, the contest becoming one of patience.

Meanwhile the night was absolutely silent. The wind was dead, and the leaves hung straight down. The deep, slow current of the river, although flowing between narrow banks, made no noise, and Robert's mind, coloured by the conditions of the moment, began to believe that the enemy had gone away. It was impossible for them to wait so long for foresters whom they did not see and who might never come. Then he dismissed imagination and impression, and turned with a wrench to his judgment. He knew enough of the warriors of the wilderness to know that nobody could wait longer than they. Patience was one of the chief commodities of savage life, because their habits were not complex, and all the time in the world was theirs.

He took lessons, too, from Tayoga and Willet. The Onondaga, an Indian himself, had an illimitable patience, and Willet, from long practice, had acquired the ability to remain motionless for hours at a time. He looked at them as they crouched beside him, still and silent figures in the dusk, apparently growing from the earth like the bushes about them, and fixed as they were. The suggestion to go on that had risen to his lips never passed them and he settled into the same immobility.

Another hour, that was three to Robert, dragged by, and Tayoga led the way again down the stream, Robert and the hunter following without a word. They went a long distance and then the Onondaga uttered a whisper of surprise and satisfaction.

"A bridge!" he said.

"Where? I don't see it," said Robert.

"Look farther where the stream narrows. Behold the great tree that has been blown down and that has fallen from bank to bank?"

"I see it now, Tayoga. It hasn't been down long, because the leaves upon it are yet green."

"And they will hide us as we cross. Tododaho on his star has been watching over us, and has put the bridge here for our use in this crisis."

Tayoga's words were instinct with faith. He never doubted that the great Onondaga who had gone away four hundred years ago was serving them now in this, their utmost, need. Robert and Willet glanced at each other. They, too, believed. An electric current had passed from Tayoga to them, and, for the moment, their trust in Tododaho was almost as great as his. At the same time, a partial darkening of the night occurred, clouds floating up from the south and west, and dimming the moon and stars.

"How far would you say it is from one shore to the other?" asked Robert of Willet.

"About sixty feet," replied the hunter, "but it's a long tree, and it will easily bear the weight of the three of us all the way. We may be attacked while we're upon it, but if so we have our rifles."

"It is the one chance that Tododaho has offered to us, and we must take it," said Tayoga, as he led the way upon the natural bridge. Robert followed promptly and Willet brought up the rear.

The banks were high at that point, and the river flowed rather more swiftly than usual. Robert, ten feet beyond the southern shore, looked down at a dark and sullen current, seeming in the dim moonlight to have interminable depths. It was only about fifteen feet below him, but his imagination, heightened by time and place, made the distance three or fourfold greater.

He felt a momentary fear lest he slip and fall into the dark stream, and he clung tightly to an upthrust bough.

The fallen tree swayed a little with the weight of the three, but Robert knew that it was safe. It was not the bridge that they had to fear, but what awaited them on the farther shore. Tayoga stopped, and the tense manner in which he crouched among the boughs and leaves showed that he was listening with all his ears.

"Do you hear them?" Robert whispered.

"Not their footsteps," Tayoga whispered back, "but there was a soft call in the woods, the low cry of a night bird, and then the low cry of another night bird replying. It was the warriors signalling to one another, the first signal they have given."

"I heard the cries, too," said Willet, behind Robert, "and no doubt Tandakora and De Courcelles feel they are closing in on us. It's a good thing this tree was blown down but lately, and the leaves and boughs are so thick on it."

"It was so provided by Tododaho in our great need," said Tayoga.

"Do you mean that we're likely to be besieged while we're still on our bridge?" asked Robert, and despite himself he could not repress a shiver.

"Not a siege exactly," replied Willet, "but the warriors may pass on the farther shore, while we're still in the tree. That's the reason why I spoke so gratefully of the thick leaves still clinging to it."

"They come even now," said Tayoga, in the lowest of whispers, and the three, stopping, flattened themselves like climbing animals against the trunk of the tree, until the dark shadow of their bodies blurred against the dusk of its bark. They were about halfway across and the distance of the stream beneath them seemed to Robert to have increased. He saw it flowing black and swift, and, for a moment, he had a horrible fear lest he should fall, but he tightened his grasp on a bough and turning his eyes away from the water looked toward the woods.

"The warriors come," whispered Tayoga, and Robert, seeing, also flattened himself yet farther against the tree, until he seemed fairly to sink into the bark. Their likeness to climbing animals increased, and it would have required keen eyes to have seen the three as they lay along the trunk, deep among the leaves and boughs thirty feet from either shore.

Tandakora, De Courcelles and about twenty warriors appeared in the forest, walking a little distance back from the stream, where they could see on the farther bank, and yet not be seen from it. The moon was still obscured, but a portion of its light fell directly upon Tandakora, and Robert had never beheld a more sinister figure. The rays, feeble, were yet strong enough to show his gigantic figure, naked save for the breech cloth, and painted horribly. His eyes, moreover, were lighted up either in fact or in Robert's fancy with a most wicked gleam, as if he were already clutching the scalps of the three whom he was hunting so savagely.

"Now," whispered Tayoga, "Tododaho alone can save us. He holds our fate in the hollow of his hand, but he is merciful as well as just."

Robert knew their danger was of the uttermost, but often, in the extreme crises of life and death, one may not feel until afterward that fate has turned on a hair.

De Courcelles was just behind Tandakora, but the light did not fall so clearly upon him. The savage had a hideous fascination for Robert, and the moon's rays seemed to follow him. Every device and symbol painted upon the huge chest stood out like carving, and all the features of the heavy, cruel face were disclosed as if by day. But Robert noticed with extraordinary relief that the eyes so full of menace were seeking the three among the woods on the farther shore, and were paying little attention to the tree. It was likely that neither Tandakora nor De Courcelles would dream that they were upon it, but it was wholly possible that the entire band should seek to cross that way, and reach the southern shore in the quest of their prey.

The three in the depths of the boughs and leaves did not stir. The rising wind caused the foliage to rustle about them again. It made the tree sway a little, too, and as Robert could not resist the temptation to look downward once, the black surface of the river seemed to be dancing back and forth beneath him. But, save the single glance, his eyes all the while were for the Ojibway and the Frenchman.

Tandakora and De Courcelles came a little closer to the bank. Apparently they were satisfied that no one was on the farther shore, and that they were in no danger of a bullet, as presently they emerged fully into the open, and stood there, their eyes questing. Then they looked at the bridge, and, for a few instants, Robert was sure they would attempt the crossing upon it. But in a minute or so they walked beyond it, and then he concluded that the crisis had passed. After all, it would be their plan to hold their own shore, and prevent the passage of the three.

Yet Tandakora and De Courcelles were cruelly deliberate and slow. They walked not more than fifteen feet beyond the end of the tree, and then stood a while talking. Half of the warriors remained near them, standing stolidly in the background, and the others went on, searching among the woods and thickets. The two glanced at the tree as they talked. Was it possible that they would yet come back and attempt the crossing? Again Robert quivered when he realized that in truth the crisis had not passed, and that Tandakora and De Courcelles might reconsider. Once more, he pressed his body hard against the tree, and held tightly to a small bough which arched an abundant covering of leaves over his head. The wind rustled among those leaves, and sang almost in words, but whether they told him that Tandakora and De Courcelles would go on or come upon the bridge he did not know.

Five minutes of such intense waiting that seemed nearer to an hour, and the leaders, with the band, passed on, disappearing in the undergrowth that lined the stream. But for another five minutes the three among the boughs did not stir. Then Tayoga whispered over his shoulder:

"Great is the justice of Tododaho and also great is his mercy. I did not doubt that he would save us. I felt within me all the time that he would cause Tandakora and De Courcelles to leave the bridge and seek us elsewhere."

Robert was not one to question the belief of Tayoga, his sagacious friend. If it was not Tododaho who had sent their enemies away then it was some other spirit, known by another name, but in essence the same. His whole being was permeated by a sort of shining gratitude.

"At times," he said, "it seems that we are favoured by our God, who is your Manitou."

"Now is the time for us to finish the crossing," said Willet, alive to the needs of the moment. "Lead, Tayoga, and be sure, Robert, not to give any bough a shake that might catch the eye of a lurking savage in the forest."

The Onondaga resumed the slow advance, so guiding his movements that he might neither make the tree quiver nor bring his body from beneath the covering of leaves. Robert and the hunter followed him in close imitation. Thus they gained the bank, and the three drew long breaths of deep and intense relief, as they stepped upon firm ground. But they could not afford to linger. Tayoga still in front, they plunged into the depths of the forest, and advanced at speed a half hour, when they heard a single faint cry behind them.

"They've found our trail at the end of the natural bridge," said Willet.

"It is so," said Tayoga, in his precise school English.

"And they're mad, mad clean through," said the hunter. "That single cry shows it. If they hadn't been so mad they'd have followed our trail without a sound. I wish I could have seen the faces of the Ojibway and the Frenchman when they came back and noticed our trace at the end of the tree. They're mad in every nerve and fibre, because they did not conclude to go upon it. It was only one chance in a thousand that we'd be there, they let that one chance in a thousand go, and lost."

The great frame of the hunter shook with silent laughter. But Robert, in very truth, saw the chagrin upon the faces of Tandakora and De Courcelles. His extraordinary imagination was again up and leaping and the picture it created for him was as glowing and vivid as fact. They had gone some distance, and then they had come back, continually searching the thickets of the opposite shore with their powerful and trained eyesight. They had felt disappointed because they had seen no trace of the hunted, who had surely come by this time against the barrier of the river. Frenchman and Ojibway were in a state of angry wonder at the disappearance of the three who had vanished as if on wings in the air, leaving no trail. Then Tandakora had chanced to look down. His eye in the dusky moonlight had caught the faint imprint of a foot on the grass, perhaps

Robert's own, and the sudden shout had been wrenched from him by his anger and mortification. Now Robert, too, was convulsed by internal laughter.

"It was our great luck that they did not find us on the tree," he said.

"No, it was not luck," said Tayoga.

"How so?"

"They did not come upon the tree because Tododaho would not let them."

"I forgot. You're right, Tayoga," said Robert sincerely.

"We'll take fresh breath here for five minutes or so," said the hunter, "and then we'll push on at speed, because we have not only the band of Tandakora and De Courcelles to fear. There are others in the forest converging on Fort Refuge."

"Great Bear is right. He is nearly always right," said Tayoga. "We have passed one barrier, but we will meet many more. There is also danger behind us. Even now the band is coming fast."

They did not move until the allotted time had passed. Again Robert's mind painted a picture in glowing colours of the savage warriors, led by Tandakora and De Courcelles, coming at utmost speed upon their trail, and his muscles quivered, yet he made no outward sign. To the eye he was as calm as Tayoga or Willet.

An hour after the resumption of their flight they came to a shallow creek with a gravelly bed, a creek that obviously emptied into the river they had crossed, and they resorted to the commonest and most effective of all devices used by fugitives in the North American wilderness who wished to hide their trail. They waded in the stream, and, as it led in the general direction in which they wished to go, they did not leave the water until they had covered a distance of several miles. Then they emerged upon the bank and rested a long time.

"When Tandakora and De Courcelles see our traces disappear in the creek and fail to reappear on the other side," said Willet, "they'll divide their band and send half of it upstream, and half downstream, looking everywhere for our place of entry upon dry land, but it'll take 'em a long time to find it. Robert, you and Tayoga might spread your blankets, and if you're calm enough, take a nap. At any rate, it won't hurt you to stretch yourselves and rest. I can warn you in time, when an enemy comes."

The Onondaga obeyed without a word, and soon slept as if his will had merely to give an order to his five senses to seek oblivion. Robert did not think he could find slumber, but closing his eyes in order to rest better, he drifted easily into unconsciousness. Meanwhile Willet watched, and there was no better sentinel in all the northern wilderness. The wind was still blowing lightly, and the rustling of the leaves never ceased, but he would have detected instantly any strange note, jarring upon that musical sound.

The hunter looked upon the sleeping lads, the white and the red. Both had a powerful hold upon his affection. He felt that he stood to them almost in the relationship of a father, and he was proud, too, of their strength and skill, their courage and intelligence. Eager as he was to reach Fort Refuge and save the garrison and people there, he was even more eager to save the two youths from harm.

He let them sleep until the gold of the morning sun was gilding the eastern forest, when the three drew further upon their supplies of bread and venison and once more resumed the journey through the pathless woods towards their destination. There was no interruption that day, and they felt so much emboldened that near sundown Tayoga took his bow and arrows, which he carried as well as his rifle, and stalked and shot a deer, the forest being full of game. Then they lighted a fire and cooked delicate portions of the spoil in a sheltered hollow. But they did not eat supper there. Instead, they took portions of the cooked food and as much as they could conveniently carry of the uncooked, and, wading along the bed of a brook, did not stop until they were three or four miles from the place in which they had built the fire. Then they sat down and ate in great content.

"We will fare well enough," said Willet, "if it doesn't rain. 'Tis lucky for us that it's the time of year when but little rain falls."

"But rain would be as hard upon those who are hunting us as upon us," said Robert.

"'Tis true, lad, and I'm glad to see you always making the best of everything. It's a spirit that wins."

"And now, Great Bear," said Tayoga, his eyes twinkling, "you have talked enough. It is only Dagaeoga who can talk on forever."

"That's so about Robert, but what do you mean by saying I've talked enough?"

"It is time for you to sleep. You watched last night while we slept, and now your hour has come. While you slumber Dagaeoga and I will be sentinels who will see and hear everything."

"Why the two of you?"

"Because it takes both of us to be the equal of the Great Bear."

"Come, now, Tayoga, that's either flattery or irony, but whatever it is I'll let it pass. I'll own that I'm sleepy enough and you two can arrange the rest between you."

He was asleep very soon, his great figure lying motionless on his blanket, and the two wary lads watched, although they sat together, and, at times, talked. Both knew there was full need for vigilance. They had triumphed for the moment over Tandakora and De Courcelles, but they expected many other lions in the path that led to Fort Refuge. It was important also, not only that they should arrive there, but that they should arrive in time. It was true, too, that they considered the danger greater by night than by day. In the day it was much easier to see the approach of an enemy, but by night one must be very vigilant indeed to detect the approach of a foe so silent as the Indian.

The two did not yet mention a division of the watch. Neither was sleepy and they were content to remain awake much longer. Moreover, they had many things of interest to talk about and also they indulged in speculation.

"Do you think it possible, Tayoga," asked Robert, "that the garrison, hearing of the great cloud now overhanging the border, may have abandoned the fort and gone east with the refugees?"

"No, Dagaeoga, it is not likely. It is almost certain that the young men from Philadelphia have not heard of General Braddock's great defeat. French and savage runners could have reached them with the news, could have taunted them from the forest, but they would not wish to do so; they seek instead to gather their forces first, to have all the effect of surprise, to take the fort, its garrison and the people as one takes a ripe apple from a tree, just when it is ready to fall."

"That rout back there by Duquesne was a terrible affair for us, Tayoga, not alone because it uncovers the border, but because it heartens all our enemies. What joy the news must have caused in Quebec, and what joy it will cause in Paris, too, when it reaches the great French capital! The French will think themselves invincible and so will their red allies."

"They would be invincible, Dagaeoga, if they could take with them the Hodenosaunee."

"And may not this victory of the French and their tribes at Duquesne shake the faith of the Hodenosaunee?"

"No, Dagaeoga. The fifty sachems will never let the great League join Onontio. Champlain and Frontenac have been gone long, but their shadows still stand between the French and the Hodenosaunee, and there is Quebec, the lost Stadacona of the Ganegaono, whom you call the Mohawks. As long as the sun and stars stand in the heavens the Keepers of the Eastern Gate are the enemies of the French. Even now, as you know, they fight by the side of the Americans and the English."

"It is true. I was wrong to question the faith of the great nations of the Hodenosaunee. If none save the Mohawks fight for us it is at least certain that they will not fight against us, and even undecided, while we're at present suffering from disaster, they'll form a neutral barrier, in part, between the French and us. Ah, that defeat by Duquesne! I scarcely see yet how it happened!"

"A general who made war in a country that he did not know, with an enemy that he did not understand."

"Well, we'll learn from it. We were too sure. Pride, they say, goes before a fall, but they ought to add that those who fall can rise again. Perhaps our generals will be more cautious next time, and won't walk into any more traps. But I foresee now a long, a very long war. Nearly all of Europe, if what comes across the Atlantic be true, will be involved in it, and we Americans will be thrown mostly upon our own resources. Perhaps it will weld our colonies together and make of them a great nation, a nation great like the Hodenosaunee."

"I think it will come to pass, Dagaeoga. The mighty League was formed by hardship and self-denial. A people who have had to fight long and tenaciously for themselves grows strong. So it has been said often by the fifty *sachems* who are old and very wise, and who know all that it is given to men to know. Did you hear anything stirring in the thicket, Dagaeoga?"

"I did, Tayoga. I heard a rustling, the sound of very light footfalls, and I see the cause."

"A black bear, is it not, seeing what strangers have invaded the bush! Now, he steals away, knowing that we are the enemies most to be dreaded by him. Doubtless there are other animals among the bushes, watching us, but we neither see nor hear them. It is time to divide the watch, for we must save our strength, and it is not well for both to remain awake far into the night."

It was arranged that Robert should sleep first and the Onondaga gave his faithful promise to awaken him in four hours. The two lads meant to take the burden of the watch upon themselves, and, unless Willet awoke, of his own accord, he was to lie there until day.

Robert lay down upon his blanket, went to sleep in an instant, and the next instant Tayoga awakened him. At least it seemed but an instant, although the entire four hours had passed. Tayoga laughed at the dubious look on his face.

"The time is up. It really is," he said. "You made me give my faithful promise. Look at the moon, and it will tell you I am no teller of a falsehood."

"I never knew four hours to pass so quickly before. Has anything happened while I slept?"

"Much, Dagaeoga. Many things, things of vast importance."

"What, Tayoga! You astonish me. The forest seems quiet."

"And so it is. But the revolving earth has turned one-sixth of its way upon itself. It has also travelled thousands and thousands of miles in that vast circle through the pathless void that it makes about the sun. I did not know that such things happened until I went to the white man's school at Albany, but I know them now, and are they not important, hugely important?"

"They're among the main facts of the universe, but they happen every night."

"Then it would be more important if they did not happen?"

"There'd be a big smash of some kind, but as I don't know what the kind would be I'm not going to talk about it. Besides, I can see that you're making game of me, Tayoga. I've lived long enough with Indians to know that they love their joke."

"We are much like other people. I think perhaps that in all this great world, on all the continents and islands, people, whether white or red, brown or black, are the same."

"Not a doubt of it. Now, stop your philosophizing and go to sleep."

"I will obey you, Dagaeoga," said Tayoga, and in a minute he was fast asleep.

Robert watched his four hours through and then awakened the Onondaga, who was sentinel until day. When they talked they spoke only in whispers lest they wake Willet, whose slumbers were so deep that he never stirred. At daybreak Tayoga roused Robert, but the hunter still slept, his gigantic bulk disposed at ease upon his blanket. Then the two lads seized him by either shoulder and shook him violently.

"Awake! Awake, Great Bear!" Tayoga chanted in his ear. "Do you think you have gone into a cave for winter quarters? Lo, you have slept now, like the animal for which you take your name! We knew you were exhausted, and that your eyes ached for darkness and oblivion, but we did not know it would take two nights and a day to bring back your wakefulness. Dagaeoga and I were your true friends. We watched over you while you slept out your mighty sleep and kept away from you the bears and panthers that would have devoured you when you knew it not. They came more than once to look at you, and truly the Great Bear is so large that he would have made breakfast, dinner and supper for the hungriest bear or panther that ever roamed the woods."

Willet sat up, sleep still heavy on his eyelids, and, for a moment or two, looked dazed.

"What do you mean, you young rascals?" he asked. "You don't say that I've been sleeping here two nights and a day?"

"Of course you have," replied Robert, "and I've never seen anybody sleep so hard, either. Look under your blanket and see how your body has actually bored a hole into the ground."

Then Willet began to laugh.

"I see, it's a joke," he said, "though I don't mind. You're good lads, but it was your duty to have awakened me in the night and let me take my part in the watch."

"You were very tired," said Robert, "and we took pity on you. Moreover, the enemy is all about us, and we knew that the watch must be of the best. Tayoga felt that at such a time he could trust me alone, and I felt with equal force that I could trust him alone. We could not put our lives in the hands of a mere beginner."

Willet laughed again, and in the utmost good humour.

"As I repeat, you're sprightly lads," he said, "and I don't mind a jest that all three of us can enjoy. Now, for breakfast, and, truth to say, we must take it cold. It will not do to light another fire."

They ate deer meat, drank water from a brook, and then, refreshed greatly by their long rest, started at utmost speed for Fort Refuge, keeping in the deepest shadows of the wilderness, eager to carry the alarm to the garrison, and anxious to avoid any intervening foe. The day was fortunate, no enemy appearing in their path, and they travelled many miles, hope continually rising that they would reach the fort before a cloud of besiegers could arrive.

Thus they continued their journey night and day, seeing many signs of the foe, but not the foe himself, and the hope grew almost into conviction that they would pass all the Indian bands and gain the fort first.

Chapter 3

The Flight

They were within twenty-four hours of the fort, when they struck a new trail, one of the many they had seen in the forest, but Tayoga observed it with unusual attention.

"Why does it interest you so much?" asked Robert. "We've seen others like it and you didn't examine them so long."

"This is different, Dagaeoga. Wait a minute or two more that I may observe it more closely."

Young Lennox and Willet stood to one side, and the Onondaga, kneeling down in the grass, studied the imprints. It was late in the afternoon, and the light of the red sun fell upon his powerful body, and long, refined, aristocratic face. That it was refined and aristocratic Robert often felt, refined and aristocratic in the highest Indian way. In him flowed the blood of unnumbered chiefs, and, above all, he was in himself the very essence and spirit of a gentleman, one of the finest gentlemen either Robert or Willet had ever known. Tayoga, too, had matured greatly in the last year under the stern press of circumstance. Though but a youth in years he was now, in reality, a great Onondaga warrior, surpassed in skill, endurance and courage by none. Young Lennox and the hunter waited in supreme confidence that he would read the trail and read it right. Still on his knees, he looked up, and Robert saw the light of discovery in the dusky eyes.

"What do you read there, Tayoga?" he asked.

"Six men have passed here."

"Of what tribe were they?"

"That I do not know, save as it concerns one."

"I don't understand you."

"Five were of the Indian race, but of what tribe I cannot say, but the sixth was a white man."

"A Frenchman. It certainly can't be De Courcelles, because we've left him far behind, and I hope it's not St. Luc. Maybe it's Jumonville, De Courcelles' former comrade. Still, it doesn't seem likely that any of the Frenchmen would be with so small a band."

"It is not one of the Frenchmen, and the white man was not with the band."

"Now you're growing too complex for my simple mind, Tayoga. I don't understand you."

"It is one trail, but the Indians and the white man did not pass over it at the same time. The Indian imprints were made seven or eight hours ago, those of the white man but an hour or so since. Stoop down, Great Bear, and you will see that it is true."

"You're right, Tayoga," said Willet, after examining minutely.

"It follows, then," said the young Onondaga, in his precise tones, "that the white man was following the red men."

"It bears that look."

"And you will notice, Great Bear, and you, too, Dagaeoga, that the white man's moccasin has made a very large imprint. The owner of the foot is big. I know of none other in the forest so big except the Great Bear himself."

"Black Rifle!" exclaimed Robert, with a flash of insight.

"It can be none other."

"And he's following on the trail of these Indians, intending to ambush them when they camp tonight. He hunts them as we would hunt wolves."

Robert shuddered a little. It was a time when human life was held cheap in the wilderness, but he could not bring himself to slay except in self-defence.

"We need Black Rifle," said Willet, "and they'll need him more at the fort. We've an hour of fair sunlight left, and we must follow this trail as fast as we can and call him back. Lead the way, Tayoga."

The young Onondaga, without a word, set out at a running walk, and the others followed close behind. It was a plain trail. Evidently the warriors had no idea that they were followed, and the same was true of Black Rifle. Tayoga soon announced that both pursuers and pursued were going slowly, and, when the last sunlight was fading, they stopped at the crest of a hill and called, imitating first the cry of a wolf, and then the cry of an owl.

"He can't be more than three or four hundred yards away," said Willet, "and he may not understand either cry, but he's bound to know that they mean something."

"Suppose we stand out here where he can see us," said Robert. "He must be lurking in the thickets just ahead."

"The simplest way and so the right way," said Willet. "Come forth, you lads, where the eyes of Black Rifle may look upon you."

The three advanced from the shelter of the woods, and stood clearly outlined in an open space. A whistle came from a thicket scarce a hundred yards before them, and then they saw the striking figure of the great, swarthy man emerging. He came straight toward them, and, although he would not show it in his manner, Robert saw a gleam of gladness in the black eyes.

"What are you doing here, you three?" he asked.

"Following you," replied Robert in his usual role of spokesman.

"Why?"

"Tayoga saw the trail of the Indians overlaid by yours. We knew you were pursuing them, and we've come to stop you."

"By what right?"

"Because you're needed somewhere else. You're to go with us to Fort Refuge."

"What has happened?"

"Braddock's army was destroyed near Fort Duquesne. The general and many of his officers were killed. The rest are retreating far into the east. We're on our way to Fort Refuge to save the garrison and people if we can, and you're to go with us."

Black Rifle was silent a moment or two. Then he said: "I feared Braddock would walk into an ambush, but I hardly believed his army would be annihilated. I don't hold it against him, because he turned my men and me away. How could I when he died with his soldiers?"

"He was a brave man," said Robert.

"I'm glad you found me. I'll leave the five Indians, though I could have ambushed 'em within the hour. The whole border must be ablaze, and they'll need us bad at Fort Refuge."

The three, now four, slept but little that night and they pressed forward all the next day, their anxiety to reach the fort before an attack could be made, increasing. It did not matter now if they arrived exhausted. The burden of their task was to deliver the word, to carry the warning. At dusk, they were within a few miles of the fort. An hour later they noticed a thread of blue smoke across the clear sky.

"It comes from the fort," said Tayoga.

"It's not on fire?" said Robert, aghast.

"No, Dagaeoga, the fort is not burning. We have come in time. The smoke rises from the chimneys."

"I say so, too," said Willet. "Unless there's a siege on now, we're ahead of the savages."

"There is no siege," said Tayoga calmly. "Tododaho has held the warriors back. Having willed for us to arrive first, nothing could prevent it."

"Again, I think you're right, Tayoga," said Robert, "and now for the fort. Let our feet devour the space that lies between."

He was in a mood of high exaltation, and the others shared his enthusiasm. They went faster than ever, and soon they saw rising in the moonlight the strong palisade and the stout log houses within it. Smoke ascended from several chimneys, and, uniting, made the line across the sky that they had beheld from afar. From their distant point of view they could not yet see the sentinels, and it was hard to imagine a more peaceful forest spectacle.

"At any rate, we can save 'em," said Robert.

"Perhaps," said Willet gravely, "but we come as heralds of disaster occurred, and of hardships to come. It will be a task to persuade them to leave this comfortable place and plunge into the wilderness."

"It's fortunate," said Robert, "that we know Colden and Wilton and Carson and all of them. We warned 'em once when they were coming to the place where the fort now is, and they didn't believe us, but they soon learned better. This time they'll know that we're making no mistake."

As they drew near they saw the heads of four sentinels projecting above the walls, one on each side of the square. The forest within rifle shot had also been cleared away, and Black Rifle spoke words of approval.

"They've learned," he said. "The city lads with the white hands have become men."

"A fine crowd of boys," said Willet, with hearty emphasis. "You'll see 'em acting with promptness and courage. Now, we want to tell 'em we're here without getting a bullet for our pains."

"Suppose you let me hail 'em," said Robert. "I'll stand on the little hill there—a bullet from the palisades can't reach me—and sing 'em a song or two."

"Go ahead," said the hunter.

Standing at his full height, young Lennox began to shout:

"Awake! Awake! Up! Up! We're friends! We're friends!"

His musical voice had wonderful carrying power, and the forest, and the open space in which the fort stood, rang with the sound. Robert became so much intoxicated with his own chanting that he did not notice its effect, until Willet called upon him to stop.

"They've heard you!" exclaimed the hunter. "Many of them have heard you! All of them must have heard you! Look at the heads appearing above the palisade!"

The side of the palisade fronting them was lined with faces, some the faces of soldiers and others the faces of civilians. Robert uttered a joyful exclamation.

"There's Colden!" he exclaimed. "The moonlight fell on him just then, and I can't be mistaken."

"And if my eyes tell me true, that's young Wilton beside him," said the hunter. "But come, lads, hold up your hands to show that we're friends, and we'll go into the fort."

They advanced, their hands, though they grasped rifles, held on high, but Robert, exalted and irrepressible, began to sing out anew:

"Hey, you, Colden! And you, too, Wilton and Carson! It's fine to see you again, alive and well."

There was silence on the wall, and then a great shout of welcome.

"It's Lennox, Robert Lennox himself!" cried someone.

"And Willet, the big hunter!"

"And there's Black Rifle, too!"

"And Tayoga, the Onondaga!"

"Open the gate for 'em! Let 'em come in, in honour."

The great gate was thrown wide, and the four entered quickly, to be surrounded at once by a multitude, eager for news of the outside world, from which they had been shut off so long. Torches, held aloft, cast a flickering light over young soldiers in faded uniforms, men in deerskin, and women in home-made linsey. Colden, and his two lieutenants, Wilton and Carson, stood together. They were thin, and their faces brown, but they looked wiry and rugged. Colden shook Robert's hand with great energy.

"I'm tremendously glad to see you," he exclaimed, "and I'm equally glad to see Mr. Willet, the great Onondaga, and Black Rifle. You're the first messengers from the outside world in more than a month. What news of victory do you bring? We heard that a great army of ours was marching against Duquesne."

Robert did not answer. He could not, because the words choked in his throat, and a silence fell over the crowd gathered in the court, over soldiers and men and women and children alike. A sudden apprehension seized the young commander and his lips trembled.

"What is it, Lennox, man?" he exclaimed. "Why don't you speak? What is it that your eyes are telling me?"

"They don't tell of any victory," replied Robert slowly.

"Then what do they tell?"

"I'm sorry, Colden, that I have to be the bearer of such news. I would have told it to you privately, but all will have to know it anyhow, and know it soon. There has been a great battle, but we did not win it."

"You mean we had to fall back, or that we failed to advance? But our army will fight again soon, and then it will crush the French and Indian bands!"

"General Braddock's army exists no longer."

"What? It's some evil jest. Say it's not true, Lennox!"

"It's an evil jest, but it's not mine, Colden. It's the jest of fate. General Braddock walked into a trap—it's twice I've told the terrible tale, once to Black Rifle and now to you—and he and his army were destroyed, all but a fragment of it that is now fleeing from the woods."

The full horror of that dreadful scene in the forest returned to him for a moment, and, despite himself, he made tone and manner dramatic. A long, deep gasp, like a groan, came from the crowd, and then Robert heard the sound of a woman on the outskirts weeping.

"Our army destroyed!" repeated Colden mechanically.

"And the whole border is laid bare to the French and Indian hosts," said Robert. "Many bands are converging now upon Fort Refuge, and the place cannot be held against so many."

"You mean abandon Fort Refuge?"

"Aye, Colden, it's what wiser men than I say, Dave here, and Tayoga, and Black Rifle."

"The lad is speaking you true, Captain Colden," said Willet. "Not only must you and your garrison and people leave Fort Refuge, but you must leave it tomorrow, and you must burn it, too."

Again Robert heard the sound of a woman weeping in the outskirts of the crowd.

"We held it once against the enemy," protested Colden.

"I know," said Willet, "but you couldn't do it now. A thousand warriors, yes, more, would gather here for the siege, and the French themselves would come with cannon. The big guns would blow your palisades to splinters. Your only safety is in flight. I know it's a hard thing to destroy the fort that your own men built, but the responsibility of all these women and children is upon you, and it must be done."

"So it is, Mr. Willet. I'm not one to gainsay you. I think we can be ready by daylight. Meanwhile you four rest, and I'll have food served to you. You've warned us and we can count upon you now to help us, can't we?"

"To the very last," said Willet.

After the first grief among the refugees was over the work of preparation was carried on with rapidity and skill, and mostly in silence. There were enough men or well grown boys among the settlers to bring the fighting force up to a hundred. Colden and his assistants knew much of the forest now, and they were willing and anxious, too, to take the advice of older and far more experienced men like Black Rifle and Willet.

"The fighting spirit bottled up so long in our line has surely ample opportunity to break out in me," said Wilton to Robert toward morning. "As I've told you before, Lennox, if I have any soldierly quality it's no credit of mine. It's a valour suppressed in my Quaker ancestors, but not eradicated."

"That is, if you fight you fight with the sword of your fathers and not your own."

"You put it well, Lennox, better than I could have stated it myself. What has become of that wonderful red friend of yours?"

"Tayoga? He has gone into the forest to see how soon we can expect Tandakora, De Courcelles and the Indian host."

The Onondaga returned at dawn, saying that no attack need be feared before noon, as the Indian bands were gathering at an appointed place, and would then advance in great force.

"They'll find us gone by a good six hours," said Willet, "and we must make every minute of those six hours worth an ordinary day, because the warriors, wild at their disappointment, will follow, and at least we'll have to beat off their vanguard. It's lucky all these people are used to the forest."

Just as the first rim of the sun appeared they were ready. There were six wagons, drawn by stout horses, in which they put the spare ammunition and their most valuable possessions. Everybody but the drivers walked, the women and children in the centre of the column, the best of the scouts and skirmishers in the woods on the flanks. Then at the command of Colden the whole column moved into the forest, but Tayoga, Willet and a half dozen others ran about from house to house, setting them on fire with great torches, making fifty blazes which grew rapidly, because the timbers were now dry, uniting soon into one vast conflagration.

Robert and Colden, from the edge of the forest, watched the destruction of Fort Refuge. They saw the solid log structures fall in, sending up great masses of sparks as the burning timbers crashed together. They saw the strong blockhouse go, and then they saw the palisade itself flaming. Colden turned away with a sigh.

"It's almost like burning your own manor house which you built yourself, and in which you expected to spend the remainder of your life," he said. "It hurts all the more, too, because it's a sign that we've lost the border."

"But we'll come back," said Robert, who had the will to be cheerful.

"Aye, so we will," said Colden, brightening. "We'll sweep back these French and Indians, and we'll come here and rebuild Fort Refuge on this very spot. I'll see to it, myself. This *is* a splendid place for a fort, isn't it, Lennox?"

"So it is," replied Robert, smiling, "and I've no doubt, Colden, that you'll supervise the rebuilding of Fort Refuge."

And in time, though the interval was great, it did come to pass.

Colden was not one to be gloomy long, and there was too much work ahead for one to be morbid. Willet had spoken of the precious six hours and they were, in, truth, more precious than diamonds. The flight was pushed to the utmost, the old people or the little children who grew weary were put in the wagons, and the speed they made was amazing for the wilderness. Robert remained well in the rear with Tayoga, Willet and Black Rifle, and they continually watched the forest for the first appearance of the Indian pursuit. That, in time, it would appear they never doubted, and it was their plan to give the vanguard of the warriors such a hot reception that they would hesitate. Besides the hundred fighting men, including the soldiers and boys large enough to handle arms, there were about a hundred women and children. Colden marched with the main column, and Wilton and Carson were at the rear. Black Rifle presently went ahead to watch lest they walk into an ambush, while Tayoga, Robert and Willet remained behind, the point from which the greatest danger was apprehended.

"Isn't it likely," asked Robert, "that the Indians will see the light of the burning fort, and that it will cause them to hasten?"

"More probably it will set them to wondering," replied the hunter, "and they may hesitate. They may think a strong force has come to rescue the garrison and people."

"But whatever Tandakora and the officer of Onontio may surmise," said Tayoga, "our own course is plain, and that is to march as fast as we can."

"And hope that a body of Colonial troops and perhaps the Mohawks will come to help us," said Willet. "Colonel William Johnson, as we all know, is alert and vigorous, and it would be like him to push westward for the protection of settlers and refugees. 'Twould be great luck, Tayoga, if that bold young friend of yours, Daganoweda, the Mohawk chief, should be in this region."

"It is not probable," said the Onondaga. "The Keepers of the Eastern Gate are likely to remain in their own territory. They would not, without a strong motive, cross the lands of the other nations of the Hodenosaunee, but it is not impossible. They may have such a motive."

"Then let us hope that it exists!" exclaimed Robert fervently. "The sight of Daganoweda and a hundred of his brave Mohawks would lift a mighty load from my mind."

Tayoga smiled. A compliment to the Mohawks was a compliment to the entire Hodenosaunee, and therefore to the Onondagas as well. Moreover the fame and good name of the Mohawks meant almost as much to him as the fame and good name of the Onondagas.

"The coming of Daganoweda would be like the coming of light itself," he said.

They were joined by Wilton, who, as Robert saw, had become a fine forest soldier, alert, understanding and not conceited because of his knowledge. Robert noted the keen, wary look of this young man of Quaker blood, and he felt sure that in the event of an attack he would be among the very best of the defenders.

"The spirit of battle, bursting at last in you, Will, from its long confinement, is likely to have full chance for gratification," he said.

"So it will, Lennox, and I tremble to think of what that released spirit may do. If I achieve any deed of daring and valour bear in mind that it's not me, but the escaped spirit of previous ages taking violent and reckless charge of my weak and unwilling flesh."

"Suppose we form a curtain behind our retreating caravan," said Robert. "A small but picked force could keep back the warriors a long time, and permit our main column to continue its flight unhampered."

"A good idea! an idea most excellent!" exclaimed Willet.

As a matter of form, the three being entirely independent in their movements, the suggestion was made to Colden, and he agreed at once and with thorough approval. Thirty men, including Willet, Robert, Tayoga and Wilton, were chosen as a fighting rear guard, and the hunter himself took command of it. Spreading out in a rather long line to prevent being flanked, they dropped back and let the train pass out of sight on its eastern flight.

They were now about ten miles from the burned fort, and, evidences of pursuit not yet being visible, Robert became hopeful that the caution of Tandakora and De Courcelles would hold them back a long time. He and Tayoga kept together, but the thirty were stretched over a distance of several hundred yards, and now they retreated very slowly, watching continually for the appearance of hostile warriors.

"They have, of course, a plain trail to follow," Robert said. "One could not have a better trace than that made by wagon wheels. It's just a matter of choice with them whether they come fast or not."

"I think we are not likely to see them before the night," said Tayoga. "Knowing that the column has much strength, they will prefer the darkness and ambush."

"But they're not likely to suspect the screen that we have thrown out to cover the retreat."

"No, that is the surprise we have prepared for them. But even so, we, the screen, may not come into contact with them before the dark."

Tayoga's calculation was correct. The entire day passed while the rear guard retreated slowly, and all the aspects of the forest were peaceful. They saw no pursuing brown figures and they heard no war cry, nor the call of one band to another. Yet Robert felt that the night would bring a hostile appearance of some kind or other. Tandakora and De Courcelles when they came upon the site of the burned fort would not linger long there, but would soon pass on in eager pursuit, hoping to strike a fleeing multitude, disorganized by panic. But he smiled to himself at the thought that they would strike first against the curtain of fire and steel, that is, the thirty to whom he belonged.

When night came he and Tayoga were still together and Willet was a short distance away. He watched the last light of the sun die and then the dusk deepen, and he felt sure that the approach of the pursuing host could not be long delayed. His eyes continually searched the thickets and forest in front of them for a sight of the savage vanguard.

"Can you see Tododaho upon his star?" he asked Tayoga in all earnestness.

"The star is yet faint in the heavens," replied the Onondaga, "and I can only trace across its face the mists and vapours which are the snakes in the hair of the great chieftain, but Tododaho will not desert us. We, his children, the Onondagas, have done no harm, and I, Tayoga, am one of them. I feel that all the omens and presages are favourable."

The reply of the Onondaga gave Robert new strength. He had the deepest respect for the religion of the Hodenosaunee, which he felt was so closely akin to his own, and Tododaho was scarcely less real to him than to Tayoga. His veins thrilled with confidence that they would drive back, or at least hold Tandakora and De Courcelles, if they came.

The last and least doubt that they would come was dispelled within an hour when Tayoga suddenly put a hand upon his arm, and, in a whisper, told him to watch a bush not more than a hundred yards away.

"A warrior is in the thicket," he said. "I would not have seen him as he crept forward had not a darker shadow appeared upon the shadow of the night. But he is there, awaiting a chance to steal upon us and fire."

"And others are near, seeking the same opportunity."

"It is so, Dagaeoga. The attack will soon begin."

"Shall we warn Willet?"

"The Great Bear has seen already. His eyes pierce the dark and they have noted the warrior, and the other warriors. Lie down, Dagaeoga, the first warrior is going to fire."

Robert sank almost flat. There was a report in the bush, a flash of fire, and a bullet whistled high over their heads. From a point on their right came an answering report and flash, and the warrior in the bush uttered his death cry. Robert, who was watching him, saw him throw up his hands and fall.

"It was the bullet of the Great Bear that replied," said Tayoga. "It was rash to fire when such a marksman lay near. Now the battle begins."

The forest gave forth a great shout, penetrating and full of menace, coming in full volume, and indicating to the shrewd ears of Tayoga the presence of two or three hundred warriors. Robert knew, too, that a large force was now before them. How long could the thirty hold back the Indian hosts? Yet he had the word of Tayoga that Tododaho looked down upon them with benignity and that all the omens and presages were favourable. There was a flash at his elbow and a rifle sang its deadly song in his ear. Then Tayoga uttered a sigh of satisfaction.

"My bullet was not wasted," he said.

Robert waited his opportunity, and fired at a dusky figure which he saw fall. He was heart and soul averse to bloodshed, but in the heat of action, and in self-defence, he forgot his repugnance. He was as eager now for a shot as Tayoga, Willet, or any other of the thirty. Tayoga, who had reloaded, pulled trigger again and then a burst of firing came from the savage host. But the thirty, inured to the forest and forest warfare, were sheltered well, and they took no hurt. The Indians who were usually poor marksmen, fired many bullets after their fashion and wasted much lead.

"They make a great noise, inflict no wounds, and do not advance," whispered Tayoga to Robert.

"Doubtless they are surprised much at meeting our line in the forest, and think us many times more numerous than we are."

"And we may fill their minds with illusions," said Robert hopefully. "They may infer from our strong resistance that reinforcements have come, that the Mohawks are here, or that Colonel Johnson himself has arrived with Colonial troops."

"It may be that Waraiyageh will come in time," said Tayoga. "Ah, they are trying to pass around our right flank."

His comment was drawn by distant shots on their right. The reports, however, did not advance, and the two, reassured, settled back into their places. Three or four of the best scouts and skirmishers were at the threatened point, and they created the effect of at least a dozen. Robert knew that the illusion of a great force confronting them was growing in the Indian mind, and his heart glowed with satisfaction. While they held the savage host the fugitive train was putting fresh miles between them and pursuit. Suddenly he raised his own rifle and fired. Then he uttered a low cry of disappointment.

"It was Tandakora himself," he said. "I couldn't mistake his size, but it was only a glimpse, and I missed."

"The time of the Ojibway has not come," said Tayoga with conviction, "but it will come before this war is over."

"The sooner the better for our people and yours, Tayoga."

"That is so, Dagaeoga."

They did not talk much more for a long time because the combat in the forest and the dark deepened, and the thirty were so active that there was little time for question or answer. They crept back and forth from bush to bush and from log to log, firing whenever they saw a flitting form, and reloading with quick fingers. Now and then Willet, or some other, would reply with a defiant shout to the yells of the warriors, and thus, while the combat of the sharpshooters surged to and fro in the dim light, many hours passed.

But the thirty held the line. Robert knew that the illusion of at least a hundred, doubtless more, was created in the minds of the warriors, and, fighting with their proverbial caution, they would attempt no rush. He had a sanguine belief now that they could hold the entire host until day, and then the fleeing train would be at least twenty miles farther on. A few of the thirty had been wounded, though not badly enough to put them out of the combat, but Robert himself had not been touched. As usual with him in moments of success or triumph his spirits flamed high, and his occasional shout of defiance rose above the others.

"In another hour," said Tayoga, "we must retreat."

"Why?" asked Robert. "When we're holding 'em so well?"

"By day they will be able to discover how few we are, and then, although they may not be able to force our front, they will surely spread out and pass around our flanks. I do not see the Great Bear now, but I know he thinks so, too, and it will not be long before we hear from him."

Within five minutes Willet, who was about a hundred yards away, uttered a low whistle, which drew to him Robert, Tayoga and others, and then he passed the word by them to the whole line to withdraw swiftly, but in absolute silence, knowing that the longer Tandakora and De Courcelles thought the defenders were in their immediate front the better it was for their purpose. Seven of the thirty were wounded, but not one of them was put out of the combat. Their hurts merely stung them to renewed energy, and lighted higher in them the fire of battle.

Under the firm leadership of Willet they retreated as a group, wholly without noise, vanishing in the thickets, and following fast on the tracks left by the wagons. When the sun rose they stopped and Tayoga went back to see if the Indian host was yet coming. He returned in an hour saying there was no indication of pursuit, and Robert exulted.

"We've come away, and yet we are still there!" he exclaimed.

"What do you mean?" asked Willet.

"We abandoned our position, but we left the great illusion there for the warriors. They think we're still before 'em and so long as that illusion lasts it will hold 'em. So you see, Dave, an illusion is often fully as good as reality."

"It may be for a little while, but it doesn't last as long. Within another hour Tandakora and De Courcelles will surely find out that we've gone, and then, raging mad, they'll come on our trail."

"And we'll meet 'em with a second stand, I suppose?"

"If we can find a good place for defence."

One of the men, Oldham, who had been sent ahead, soon returned with news that the train had crossed a deep creek with rather high banks.

"It was a hard ford," he said, "but I followed the trail some distance on the other side, and they seem to have made the passage without any bad accident."

"Was the far bank of the creek thick with forest?" asked Willet.

"Trees and undergrowth are mighty dense there," replied Oldham.

"Then that's the place for our second stand. If we can hold the creek against 'em for three or four hours more it will be another tremendous advantage gained. With high banks and the woods and thickets on 'em so dense, we ought to create what Robert would call a second illusion."

"We will!" exclaimed Robert. "We can do it!"

"At least, we'll try," said Willet, and he led the little force at speed toward the creek.

Chapter 4

A Forest Concert

The deep creek with its high banks and interwoven forest and thickets on the other side formed an excellent second line of defence, and Willet, with the instinct of a true commander, made the most of it, again posting his men at wide intervals until they covered a distance of several hundred yards, at the same time instructing them to conceal themselves carefully, and let the enemy make the first move. He allowed Robert and Tayoga to remain together, knowing they were at their best when partners.

The two lay behind the huge trunk of a tree torn down by some old hurricane and now almost hidden by vegetation and trailing vines. They were very comfortable there, and, uplifted by their success of the night they were sanguine of an equal success by day.

To the right Robert caught occasional glimpses of Willet, moving about in the bushes, but save for these stray glances he watched the other side of the stream. Luckily it was rather open there, and no savage, however cunning, could come within fifty yards of it without being seen by the wary eyes in the thickets.

"How long do you think it will be before they come?" Robert asked of Tayoga, for whose forest lore he had an immense respect.

"Three hours, maybe four," replied the Onondaga. "Tandakora and De Courcelles may or may not know of this creek, but when they see it they are sure to advance with caution, fearing a trap."

"What a pity our own people don't show the same wisdom!"

"You are thinking of the great slaughter at Duquesne. Every people has its own ways, and the soldiers have not yet learned those of the forest, but they *will* learn."

"At a huge cost!"

"Perhaps there is no other way? You will notice the birds on the bushes on the far side of the stream, Dagaeoga?"

"Aye, I see 'em. They're in uncommon numbers. What a fine lot of fellows with glossy plumage! And some of 'em are singing away as if they lived for nothing else!"

"I see that Dagaeoga looks when he is told to look and sees when he is told to see. The birds are at peace and are enjoying themselves."

"That is, they're having a sunlight concert, purely for their own pleasure."

"It is so. They feel joy and know that danger is not present. They are protected by the instinct that Manitou, watching over the least of his creatures, has given to them."

"Why this dissertation on birds at such a time, Tayoga?"

"Dissertation is a very long word, but I am talking for Dagaeoga's own good. He has learned much of the forest, but he can learn more, and I am here to teach him."

"Wondrous good of you, Tayoga, and, in truth, your modesty also appeals to me. Proceed with your lesson in woodcraft, although it seems to me that you have chosen a critical time for it."

"The occasion is most fitting, because it comes out of our present danger. We wish to see the approach of our enemies who will lie down among the grass and bushes, and creep forward very silently. We will not see them, perhaps, but others will give warning."

"Oh, you mean that the birds, alarmed by the warriors, will fly away?"

"Nothing else, Dagaeoga."

"Then why so much circumlocution?"

"Circumlocution is another very long word, Dagaeoga. It is the first time that I have heard it used since we left the care of our teacher in Albany. But I came to the solution by a circular road, because I wished you to see it before I told it to you. You did see it, and so I feel encouraged over the progress of my pupil."

"Thanks, Tayoga, I appreciate the compliment, and, as I said before, your modesty also appeals to me."

"You waste words, Dagaeoga, but you have always been a great talker. Now, watch the birds."

Tayoga laughed softly. The Indian now and then, in his highest estate, used stately forms of rhetoric, and it pleased the young Onondaga, who had been so long in the white man's school, to employ sometimes the most orotund English. It enabled him to develop his vein of irony, with which he did not spare Robert, just as Robert did not spare him.

"I will watch the birds," said young Lennox. "They're intelligent, reasoning beings, and I'll lay a wager that while they're singing away there they're not singing any songs that make fun of their friends."

"Of that I'm not sure, Dagaeoga. Look at the bird with the red crest, perched on the topmost tip of the tall, green bush directly in front of us. I can distinguish his song from those of the others, and it seems that the note contains something saucy and ironic."

"I see him, Tayoga. He is an impudent little rascal, but I should call him a most sprightly and attractive bird, nevertheless. Observe how his head is turned on one side. If we were only near enough to see his eyes I'd lay another wager that he is winking."

"But his head is not on one side any longer, Dagaeoga. He has straightened up. If you watch one object a long time you will see it much more clearly, and so I am able to observe his actions even at this distance. He has ceased to sing. His position is that of a soldier at attention. He is suspicious and watchful."

"You're right, Tayoga. I can see, too, that the bird's senses are on the alert against something foreign in the forest. All the other birds, imitating the one who seems to be their leader, have ceased singing also."

"And the leader is unfolding his wings."

"So I see. He is about to fly away. There he goes like a flash of red flame!"

"And there go all the rest, too. It is enough. Tandakora, De Courcelles and the savages have come."

Robert and Tayoga crouched a little lower and stared over the fallen log. Presently the Onondaga touched the white youth on the arm. Robert, following his gaze, made out the figure of a warrior creeping slowly through a dense thicket toward the creek.

"It is likely that Great Bear sees him, too," said Tayoga, "but we will not fire. He will not come nearer than fifty yards, because good cover is lacking."

"I understand that the contest is to be one of patience. So they can loose their bullets first. I see the bushes moving in several places now, Tayoga."

"It is probable that their entire force has come up. They may wait at least an hour before they will try a ford."

"Like as not. Suppose we eat a little venison, Tayoga, and strengthen ourselves for the ordeal."

"You have spoken well, Dagaeoga."

They ate strips of venison contentedly, but did not neglect to keep a wary watch upon the creeping foe. Robert knew that Tandakora and De Courcelles were trying to discover whether or not the line of the creek was defended, and if Willet and his men remained well hidden it would take a long time for them to ascertain the fact. He enjoyed their perplexity, finding in the situation a certain sardonic humour.

"The Ojibway and the Frenchman would give a good deal to know just what is in the thickets here," he whispered to Tayoga. "But the longer they must take in finding out the better I like it."

"They will delay far into the afternoon," said Tayoga. "The warriors and the Frenchmen have great patience. It would be better for the Americans and the English if they, too, like the French, learned the patience of the Indians."

"The birds gave us a warning that they had come. You don't think it possible, Tayoga, that they will also give the savages warning that we are here?"

"No, Dagaeoga, we have been lying in the thickets so long now, and have been so quiet that the birds have grown used to us. They feel sure we are not going to do them any harm, and while they may have flown away when we first came they are back now, as you can see with your own eyes, and can hear with your own ears."

Almost over Robert's head a small brown bird on a small green bough was singing, pouring out a small sweet song that was nevertheless clear and penetrating. Within the radius of his sight a half dozen more were trilling and quavering, and he knew that others were pouring out their souls farther on, as the low hum of their many voices came to his ears. Now and then he saw a flash of blue or brown or grey, as some restless feathered being shot from one bough to another. The birds, unusual in number and sure that there was no hostile presence, were having a grand concert in honour of a most noble day.

Robert listened and the appeal to his imagination and higher side was strong. Overhead the chorus of small sweet voices went on, as if there were no such things as battle or danger. Tayoga also was moved by it.

"By the snakes in the hair of the wise Tododaho," he said, "it is pleasant to hear! May the wilderness endure always that the birds can sing in it, far from men, and in peace!"

"May it not be, Tayoga, that the warriors watching the thickets here will see the birds so thick, and will conclude from it that no defenders are lying in wait?"

"De Courcelles might, but Tandakora, who has lived his whole life in the forest, will conclude that the birds are here, unafraid, because we have been so long in the bushes."

Time went on very slowly and the forest on either side of the creek was silent, save for the singing of the birds among the bushes in which the defenders lay hidden. Robert, from whom the feeling of danger departed for the moment, was almost tempted into? a doze by the warmth of the thicket and the long peace. His impressions, the pictures that passed before his mental and physical eye, were confused but agreeable. He was lying on a soft bank of turf that sloped up to a huge fallen trunk, and warm, soothing winds stole about among the boughs, rustling the leaves musically. The birds were singing in increased volume, and, though his eyes were half veiled by drooping lids, he saw them on many boughs.

"'Tis not their daily concert," he said to Tayoga "In very truth it must be their grand, annual affair I believe that a great group on our right is singing against another equally great group on our left. I can't recall having heard ever before such a volume of song in the woods. It's in my mind that a contest is going on, for a prize, perhaps. Doubtless juicy worms are awaiting the winners."

Tayoga laughed.

"You are improving, Dagaeoga," he said in precise tones. "You do not merely fight and eat and sleep like the white man. You are developing a soul. You are beginning to understand the birds and animals that live in the woods. Almost I think you worthy to be an Onondaga."

"I know you can pay me what is to you no higher compliment, but I have a notion the end of the concert is not far away. It seems to me the volume of song from the group on the left is diminishing."

"And you notice no decrease on our right?"

"No, Tayoga. The grand chorus there is as strong as ever, and unless my ears go wrong, I detect in it a triumphant note."

"Then the test of song which you have created is finished, and the prize has been won by the group on the right. It is a fine conceit that you have about the birds, Dagaeoga. I like it, and we will see it to the end."

The song on their left died, the one on their right swelled anew, and then died in its turn. Soon the birds began to drift slowly away. Robert watched some of them as they disappeared among the green boughs farther on.

"I also am learning to read the signs, Tayoga," he said, "and, having observed 'em, I conclude that our foes are about to make an advance, or at least, have crept forward a little more. The birds, used to our presence, know we are neither dangerous nor hostile, but they do not know as much about those on the other side of the creek. While the advance of the warriors is not yet sufficient to threaten 'em, it's enough to make 'em suspicious, and so they are flying away slowly, ready to return if it be a false alarm."

"Good! Very good, Dagaeoga! I can believe that your conclusions are true, and I can say to you once more that almost you are worthy to be an Onondaga. If you will look now toward the spot where the banks shelve down, and the grass grows high you will see four warriors on their hands and knees approaching the creek. If they reach the water without being fired upon they will assume that we are not here. Then the entire force will rush across the stream and take up the trail."

"But the creeping four will be fired upon."

"I think so, too, Dagaeoga, because there is no longer any reason for us to delay, and the rifle of the Great Bear will speak the first word."

There was a report near them, and one of the warriors, sinking flat in the grass, lay quite still. Robert, through the bushes, saw Willet, smoking rifle in hand. The three savages who lived began a swift retreat, and the others behind them uttered a great cry of grief and rage. They fired a dozen shots or so, but the bullets merely clipped leaves and twigs in the thickets. Nobody among the defenders save Willet pulled trigger, but his single shot was a sufficient warning to Tandakora and De Courcelles. They knew that the creek was held strongly.

Now ensued another long combat in which the skill, courage and ingenuity of warriors and hunters were put to the supreme test. Many shots were fired, but faces and bodies were shown only for an instant. Nevertheless a bullet now and then went home. One of Willet's men was killed and three more sustained slight wounds. Several of the warriors were slain, and others were wounded, but Robert had no means of telling the exact number of their casualties, as it was an almost invisible combat, which Willet and Tayoga, as the leaders, used all their skill to prolong to the utmost with the smallest loss possible. What they wanted was time, time for the fugitive train, now far away among the hills.

So deftly did they manage the defence of the creek that the entire afternoon passed and Tandakora and De Courcelles were still held in front of it, not daring to make a rush, and Willet, Robert and Tayoga glowed with the triumph they were achieving at a cost relatively so small. Night arrived, fortunately for them thick and black, and Willet gathered up his little force. They would have taken away with them the body of the slain man, but that was impossible, and, covering it up with brush and stones, they left it. Then still uplifted and exulting, they slipped away on the trail of the wagons, knowing that the Indian horde might watch for hours at the creek before they discovered the departure of the defenders.

"You see, Dagaeoga," said Tayoga to Robert, "that there is more in war than fighting. Craft and cunning, wile and stratagem are often as profitable as the shock of conflict."

"So I know, Tayoga. I learned it well in the battle by Duquesne. What right had a force of French and Indians which must have been relatively small to destroy a fine army like ours!"

"No right at all," said Willet, "but it happened, nevertheless. We'll learn from it, though it's a tremendous price to pay for a lesson."

"Do we make a third stand somewhere, Dave?" asked Robert, "and delay them yet another time?"

"I scarcely see a chance for it," replied the hunter. "We must have favourable ground or they'd outflank us. How old does the trail of the wagons look, Tayoga?"

"They are many, many hours ahead," replied the Onondaga. "They have made good use of the time we have secured for them."

"Another day and night and they should be safe," said Willet. "Tandakora and De Courcelles will scarcely dare follow deep into the fringe of settlements. What is it, Tayoga?"

The Onondaga had stopped and, kneeling down, he was examining the trail as minutely as he could in the dusk.

"Others have come," he replied tersely.

"What do you mean by 'others'?" asked Willet.

"Those who belong neither to pursued nor pursuers, a new force, white men, fifteen, perhaps. They came down from the north, struck this trail, for which they were not looking, and have turned aside from whatever task they were undertaking to see what it means."

"And so they're following the fugitive train. Possibly it's a band of French."

"I do not think so, Great Bear. The French do not roam the forest alone. The warriors are always with them, and this party is composed wholly of white men."

"Then they must be ours, perhaps a body of hunters or scouts, and we need 'em. How long would you say it has been since they passed?"

"Not more than two hours."

"Then we must overtake 'em. Do you lead at speed, Tayoga, but on the bare possibility that they're French, look out for an ambush."

"The new people, whoever they are," said Robert, "are trailing the train, we're trailing them, and the French and Indians are trailing us. It's like a chain drawing its links through the forest."

"But the links are of different metals, Robert," said Willet.

They talked but little more, because they needed all their breath now for the pursuit, as Tayoga was leading at great speed, the broad trail in the moonlight being almost as plain as day. It was a pleasure to Robert to watch the Onondaga following like a hound on the scent. His head was bent forward a little, and now and then when the brightest rays fell across them, Robert could see that his eyes glittered. He was wholly the Indian, his white culture gone for the moment, following the wilderness trail as his ancestors had done for centuries before him.

"Do the traces of the new group grow warmer?" asked Robert.

"They do," replied Tayoga. "We are advancing just twice as fast as they. We will overtake them before midnight."

"White men, and only by the barest possibility French," said Robert. "So the chances are nine out of ten that they're our own people. Now, I wonder what they are and what they're doing here."

"Patience, Dagaeoga," said the young Onondaga. "We will learn by midnight. How often have I told you that you must cultivate patience before you are worthy to be an Onondaga?"

"I'll bear it in mind, O worthy teacher. Your great age and vast learning compel me to respect your commands."

The new trail, which was like a narrow current in the broad stream of that left by the flying train, was now rapidly growing warmer. The speed of the thirty was so great that it became evident to Tayoga that they would overtake the strange band long before midnight.

"They stopped here and talked together a little while," he said, when they had been following the trail about two hours. "They stood by the side of the path. Their footprints are gathered in a group. They knew by the wagon tracks that white settlers, fleeing, were ahead of them, and they may have thought of turning back to see who followed. That is why they drew up in a group, and talked. At last they concluded to keep on following the train, and they cannot be more than a half hour ahead now."

Willet knelt down for the first time, and examined the traces with the greatest care and attention.

"The leader stood here by this fallen log," he said, "He had big feet, as anybody can see, and I believe I can make a good guess at his identity. I hope to Heaven I'm right!"

"Whom do you mean?" exclaimed Robert eagerly.

"I won't say just yet, because if I'm wrong you won't know the mistake I've made. But come on, lads. 'Twill not take long to decide the question that interests us so much."

He led the way with confidence, and when they had gone about a mile he sank down in a thicket beside the trail, the others imitating him. Then the hunter emitted a sharp whistle.

"I think I'll soon get an answer to that," he said, "and it'll not come from French or Indian."

They waited a minute or two and then the whistling note, clear and distinct, rose from a point ahead of them. Willet whistled a second time, and the second reply soon came in similar fashion.

"Now, lads," he said, rising from the bush, "we'll up and join 'em. It's the one I expected, and right glad I am, too."

He led the way boldly, making no further effort at concealment. Robert saw outlined in the moonlight on a low hill in front of them a group of fifteen or sixteen white men, all in hunter's garb, all strong, resolute figures, armed heavily. One, a little in advance of the others, and whom the lad took at once to be the leader, was rather tall, with a very powerful figure and a bold, roving eye. He was looking keenly at the approaching group and as they drew near his eyes lighted up with recognition and pleasure.

"By all that's glorious, it's Dave Willet, the Great Bear himself, the greatest hunter and marksman in all the northern province! Of a certainty it's none other!"

"Yes, Rogers, it's Willet," said the hunter, extending his hand, "though you complimented me too prettily. But glad am I, too, to see you here. You're no beauty, but your face is a most welcome sight."

Then Robert understood. It was Robert Rogers from the New Hampshire grants, already known well, and destined to become famous as one of the great partisan leaders of the war, a wild and adventurous spirit who was fully a match for Dumas and Ligneris or St. Luc himself, a man whose battles and hairbreadth escapes surpassed fiction. Around him gathered spirits dauntless and kindred, and here already was the nucleus of the larger force that he was destined to lead in so many a daring deed. Now his fierce face showed pleasure, as he shook the hunter's powerful hand with his own hand almost as powerful.

"It's a joy to meet you in these woods, Dave," he said. "But who are the two likely lads with you? Lads, I call 'em because their faces are those of lads, though their figures have the stature and size of men."

"Rogers, this is Tayoga, of the clan of the Bear, of the nation Onondaga, of the great League of the Hodenosaunee, a friend of ours, and no braver or more valiant youth ever trod moccasin. Tayoga, this is Robert Rogers of the New Hampshire grants."

The sunburnt face of Rogers shone with pleasure.

"I've heard of the lad," he said, "and I know he's all that you claim for him, Dave."

"And the other youth," continued Willet, "is Robert Lennox, in a way a ward of mine, in truth almost a son to me. What Tayoga is among the Onondagas, he is among the white people of New York. I can say no more."

"That's surely enough," said Rogers, "and glad am I to meet you, Lennox. I've come from the north and the east, from Champlain and George, with my brave fellows, hearing of Braddock's defeat and thinking we might be needed, and by chance we struck this broad trail. It's plain enough that it's made by settlers withdrawing from the border, but whether 'tis a precaution or they're pursued closely we don't know. We thought once of turning back to see. But you know, Dave."

Willet explained rapidly and again the fierce face of Rogers shone with pleasure.

"'Twas in truth a fortunate chance that guided us down here," he said.

"It was Tododaho himself," said Tayoga with reverence.

Then Willet also called rapidly the names of his hunters and scouts, who had remained in a little group in the rear, while the leaders talked.

"Dave," said Rogers, "you and I will be joint leaders, if you say so. We've now nearly two score stout fellows ready for any fray, and since you've twice held back Tandakora, De Courcelles and their scalp hunters, our united bands should be able to do it a third time. I agree with you that the best way to save the train is to fight rear guard actions, and never let the train itself be attacked."

"If we had about twenty more good men," said Willet, "we might not only defend a line but push back the horde itself. What say you to sending Tayoga, our swiftest runner, to the wagons for a third force?"

"A good plan, a most excellent plan, Dave! And while he's about it, tell him to make it thirty instead of twenty. Then we'll burn the faces of these Indian warriors. Aye, Dave, we'll scorch 'em so well that they'll be glad to turn back!"

It was arranged in a minute or two and Tayoga disappeared like one of his own arrows in the forest and the darkness, while the others followed, but much more slowly. It would not escape the sharp eyes of the warriors that a reinforcement had come, but, confident in their numbers, they would continue the pursuit with unabated zeal.

The united bands of hunters and scouts fell back slowly, and for a long time. Robert looked with interest at Rogers' men. They were the picked survivors of the wilderness, the forest champions, young mostly, lean, tough of muscle, darkened by wind and weather, ready to follow wherever their leader led, ready to risk their lives in any enterprise, no matter how reckless. They affiliated readily with Willet's own band, and were not at all averse to being overtaken by the Indian horde.

After dawn they met Tayoga returning with thirty-five men, rather more than they had expected, and also with the news that the train was making great speed in its flight. Willet and Rogers looked over the seventy or more brave fellows, with glistening eyes, and Robert saw very well that, uplifted by their numbers, they were more than anxious for a third combat. In an hour or so they found a place suitable for an ambush, a long ravine, lined and filled with thickets which the wagons evidently had crossed with difficulty, and here they took their stand, all of the force hidden among the bushes and weeds. Robert, at the advice of Willet, lay down in a secure place and went to sleep.

"You're young, lad," he said, "and not as much seasoned in the bark as the rest of us who are older. I'll be sure to wake you when the battle begins, and then you'll be so much the better for a nap that you'll be a very Hercules in the combat."

Robert, trained in wilderness ways, knew that it was best, and he closed his eyes without further ado. When he opened them again it was because the hunter was shaking his shoulder, and he knew by the position of the sun that several hours had passed.

"Have they come?" he asked calmly.

"We've seen their skirmishers in the woods about two hundred yards away," replied the hunter. "I believe they suspect danger here merely because this is a place where danger is likely to be, but 'twill not keep them from attacking. You can hold your rifle ready, lad, but you'll have no use for it for a good quarter of an hour. They'll do a lot of scouting before they try to pass the ravine, but our fellows are happy in the knowledge that they'll try to pass it."

Robert suppressed as much as he could the excitement one was bound to feel at such a time, and ate a little venison to stay him for the combat, imitating the coolness and providence of Tayoga, who was also strengthening his body for the ordeal.

"About noon, isn't it?" he asked of the Onondaga.

"A little after it," Tayoga replied.

"When did they come up?"

"Just now. I too have slept, although my sleep was shorter than yours."

"Have you seen Tandakora or De Courcelles?"

"I caught one glimpse of Tandakora. My bullet will carry far, but alas! it will not carry far enough to reach the Ojibway. It is not the will of Tododaho that he should perish now. As I have said, his day will come, though it is yet far away."

"What will happen here, Tayoga?"

"The forces of Tandakora and De Courcelles will be burned worse than before. The man Rogers, whom some of the Mohawks call the Mountain Wolf, is like a Mohawk warrior himself, always eager to fight. He will want to push the battle and Great Bear, having so many men now, will be willing."

The words of Tayoga came to pass. After a long delay, accompanied by much scouting and attempts to feel out the defence, Tandakora and De Courcelles finally charged the ravine in force and suffered a bitter repulse. Seventy or eighty rifles, aimed by cool and experienced sharpshooters, poured in a fire which they could not withstand, and so many warriors were lost that the Ojibway and the Frenchman retreated. The Great Bear and the Mountain Wolf would not allow their eager men to follow, lest in their turn they fall into an ambush.

Later in the day the Indian horde returned a second time to the attack, with the same result, and when night came Tayoga and several others who went forward to scout reported that they had withdrawn several miles. The white leaders then decided in conference that they had done enough for their purpose, and, after a long rest on their arms, withdrew slowly in the path of the retreating train, ready for another combat, if pursued too closely, but feeling sure that Tandakora and De Courcelles would not risk a battle once more.

They overtook the train late that evening and their welcome was enough to warm their hearts and to repay them for all the hardships and dangers endured. Colden was the first to give them thanks, and his fine young face showed his emotion.

"I'm sorry I couldn't have been back there with you," he said, when he heard the report Robert made; "you had action, and you faced the enemy, while we have merely been running over the hills."

"In truth you've made a good run of it," said Robert, "and as I see it, it was just as necessary for you to run as it was for us to fight. We had great luck, too, in the coming of Rogers and his men."

That night the train, for the first time since it began its flight, made a real camp. Willet, Rogers and all the great foresters thought it safe, as they were coming now so near to the settled regions, and the faces of the pursuers had been scorched so thoroughly. Scouts and skirmishers were thrown out on all sides, and then fires were built of the fallen brushwood that lay everywhere in the forest. The ample supplies in the wagons were drawn upon freely, and the returning victors feasted at their leisure.

It was a happy time for Robert. His imaginative mind responded as usual to time and place. They had won one victory. It was no small triumph to protect the fugitive train, and so they would win many more. He already saw them through the flame of his sanguine temperament, and the glow of the leaping fires helped in the happy effect. All around him were cheerful faces and he heard the chatter of happy voices, their owners happy because they believed themselves released from a great and imminent danger.

"Has anything been heard of Black Rifle?" Robert asked of Tayoga.

"He has not come back," replied the Onondaga, "but they think he will be here in the morning."

The dawn brought instead fifty dusky figures bare to the waist and painted in all the terrible imagery of Indians who go to war. Some of the women cried out in fright, but Tayoga said:

"Have no fear. These be friends. The warriors of our great brother nation, the Ganeagaono, known to you as the Mohawks, have come to aid us."

The leader of the Mohawks was none other than the daring young chief, Daganoweda himself, flushed with pride that he had come to the help of his white brethren, and eager as always for war. He gravely saluted Robert, Willet and Tayoga.

"Dagaeoga is a storm bird," he said. "Wherever he goes battle follows."

"Either that," laughed Robert, "or because I follow battle. How could I keep from following it, when I have Willet on one side of me and Tayoga on the other, always dragging me to the point where the combat rages fiercest?"

"Did you meet Black Rifle?" asked Willet.

"It was he who told us of your great need," replied Daganoweda. "Then while we came on at the speed of runners to help you, he continued north and east in the hope that he would meet Waraiyageh and white troops."

"Do you know if Colonel William Johnson is in this region or near it?"

"He lay to the north with a considerable force, watching for the French and Indians who have been pouring down from Canada since their great taking of scalps by Duquesne. Black Rifle will find him and he will come, because Waraiyageh never deserts his people, but just when he will arrive I cannot say."

Ample food was given to the Mohawks and then, burning for battle, Daganoweda at their head, they went on the back trail in search of Tandakora, De Courcelles and their savage army.

"We could not have a better curtain between us and the enemy," said Willet. "War is their trade and those fifty Mohawks will sting and sting like so many hornets."

The train resumed its flight an hour after sunrise, although more slowly now and with less apprehension, and about the middle of the afternoon the uniforms of Colonial militia appeared in the forest ahead. All set up a great shout, because they believed them to be the vanguard of Johnson. They were not mistaken, as a force of a hundred men, better equipped and drilled than usual, met them, at their head Colonel William Johnson himself, with the fierce young Mohawk eagle, Joseph Brant, otherwise Thayendanegea, at his side. The sombre figure of Black Rifle, who had brought him, stood not far away.

Colonel Johnson was in great good humour, thoroughly delighted to find the train safe and to meet such warm friends of his again. He was first presented duly to Captain Colden and his young officers, paid them some compliments on their fine work, talked with them a while and then conversed more intimately with Tayoga, Robert and Willet.

"The train is now entirely safe," he said. "Even if Tandakora and De Courcelles could brush away the screen of the Mohawks, they dare not risk an encounter with such a force as we have here. They will turn aside for easier game."

"And there will be no battle!" exclaimed young Brant, in deep disappointment. "Ah! why did I not have the chance to go forward with my cousin, Daganoweda?"

Colonel Johnson laughed, half in pride and half in amusement, and patted his warlike young Mohawk brother-in-law on the shoulder.

"All in good time, Joseph, my lad," he said. "Remember that you are scarce twelve and you may have fifty years of fighting before you. No one knows how long this conflagration in America may last. As for you, Tayoga and Lennox, and you, Willet, your labours with the train are over. But there is a fierce fire burning in the north, and it is for us to put it out. You have lost one commander, Braddock, but you may find another. I can release you from your obligations to Governor Dinwiddie of Virginia. Will you go with me?"

The three assented gladly, and they saw that their service of danger was but taking a new form.

Chapter 5

Gathering Forces

The eyes of all the warlike young men now turned northward. The people whom they had rescued scattered among their relatives and friends, awaiting the time when they could return to the wilderness, and rebuild their homes there, but Colden, Wilton, Carson and their troop were eager for service with Colonel William Johnson. In time orders arrived from the Governor of Pennsylvania, directing them to join the force that was being raised in the province of New York to meet the onrush of the savages and the French, and they rejoiced. Meanwhile Robert, Tayoga and Willet made a short stay at Mount Johnson, and in the company of its hospitable owner and his wife refreshed themselves after their great hardships and dangers.

Colonel Johnson's activities as a host did not make him neglect his duties as a commander. Without military experience, save that recently acquired in border war, he nevertheless showed indomitable energy as a leader, and his bluff, hearty manner endeared him to Colonials and Mohawks alike. A great camp had been formed on the low grounds by Albany, and Robert and his comrades in time proceeded there, where a numerous force of men from New York and New England and many Mohawks were gathered. It was their plan to march against the great French fortress of Crown Point on Lake Champlain, which Robert heard would be defended by a formidable French and Indian army under Baron Dieskau, an elderly Saxon in the French service.

Robert also heard that St. Luc was with Dieskau, and that he was leading daring raids against little bands of militia on their way from New England to the camp near Albany. Two were practically destroyed, half of their numbers being killed, while the rest were sent as prisoners into Canada. Two more succeeded in beating off the Frenchman, though with large loss, but he was recognized by everybody as a great danger, and Daganoweda and the best of the Mohawks went forth to meet him.

Rogers with his partisan band and Black Rifle also disappeared in the wilderness, and Robert looked longingly after them, but he and his friends were still held at the Albany camp, as the march of the army was delayed, owing to the fact that five provincial governors, practically independent of one another, had a hand in its management, and they could not agree upon a plan. Braddock's great defeat had a potent influence in the north, and now they were all for caution.

While they delayed Robert went into Albany one bright morning to see Mynheer Jacobus Huysman, who showed much anxiety about him these days. The little Dutch city looked its best, a comfortable place on its hills, inhabited by comfortable people, but swarming now with soldiers and even with Mohawks, all of whom brought much business to the thrifty burghers. Albany had its profit out of everything, the river commerce, the fur trade, and war itself.

Robert, as he walked along, watched with interest the crowd which was, in truth, cosmopolitan, despite the smallness of the place. Some of the Colonials had uniforms of blue faced with red, of which they were very proud, but most of them were in the homespun attire of every day. They were armed with their own rifles. Only the English had bayonets so far. The Americans instead carried hatchets or tomahawks at their belts, and the hatchet had many uses. Every man also carried a big jack or clasp knife which, too, had its many uses.

The New Englanders, who were most numerous in the camp, were of pure British blood, a race that had become in the American climate tall, thin and very muscular, enduring of body and tenacious of spirit, religious, ambitious, thinking much of both worldly gain and the world hereafter. Among them moved the people of Dutch blood from the province of New York, generally short and fat like their ancestors, devoted to good living, cheerful in manner, but hard and unscrupulous in their dealing with the Indians, and hence a menace to the important alliance with the Hodenosaunee.

There were the Germans, also, most of them descendants of the fugitives from the Palatinate, after it had been ravaged by the generals of Louis XIV, a quiet, humble people, industrious, honest, sincerely religious, low at present in the social scale, and patronized by the older families of English or Dutch blood, perhaps not dreaming that their race would become some day the military terror of the world.

The Mohawks, who passed freely through the throng, were its

most picturesque feature. The world bred no more haughty savages than they. Tall men, with high cheek bones, and fierce eyes, they wore little clothing in the summer weather, save now and then a blanket of brilliant colour for the sake of adornment. There were also some Onondagas, as proud as the Mohawks, but not so fierce.

A few Virginians and Marylanders, come to cooperate with the northern forces, were present, and they, like the New Englanders, were of pure British blood. Now and then a Swede, broad of face, from the Jersey settlements could be seen, and there was scarcely a nation in western Europe that did not have at least one representative in the streets of Albany.

It pleased Robert to see the great variety of the throng. It made a deep impression upon his imaginative mind. Already he foresaw the greatness of America, when these races were blended in a land of infinite resources. But such thoughts were driven from his mind by a big figure that loomed before him and a hearty voice that saluted him.

"Day dreaming, Master Lennox?" said the voice. "One does not have much time for dreams now, when the world is so full of action."

It was none other than Master Benjamin Hardy, portly, rubicund, richly but quietly dressed in dark broadcloth, dark silk stockings and shoes of Spanish leather with large silver buckles. Robert was unaffectedly glad to see him, and they shook hands with warmth.

"I did not know that you were in Albany," said young Lennox.

"But I knew that you were here," said Master Hardy.

"I haven't your great resources for collecting knowledge."

"A story reached me in New York concerning the gallant conduct of one Robert Lennox on the retreat from Fort Refuge, and I wished to come here myself and see if it be true."

"I did no better than a hundred others. How is the wise Master Jonathan Pillsbury?"

"As wise as ever. He earnestly urged me, when I departed for this town, not to be deceived by the glamour of the military. 'Bear in mind, Master Benjamin,' he said, 'that you and I have been associates many years, and your true path is that of commerce and gain. The march and the battlefield are not for you any more than they are for me.' Wise words and true, and it was not for me to gainsay them. So I gave him my promise that I would not march with this brave expedition to the lakes."

The merchant's words were whimsical, but Robert felt that he was examining him with critical looks, and he felt, too, that a protecting influence was once more about him. He could not doubt that Master

Hardy was his sincere friend, deeply interested in him. He had given too many proofs of it, and a sudden curiosity about his birth, forgotten amid the excitement of continued action, rose anew. He was about to ask questions, but he remembered that they would not be answered, and so he held his peace, while the merchant walked on with him toward the house of Mynheer Jacobus Huysman.

"You are bent upon going with the army?" said Mr. Hardy. "Haven't you had enough of battle? There was a time, after the news of Braddock's defeat came, when I feared that you had fallen, but a message sent by the young Englishman, Grosvenor, told me you were safe, and I was very thankful. It is natural for the young to seek what they call adventure, and to serve their country, but you have done much already, Robert. You might go with me now to New York, and still feel that you are no shirker."

"You are most kind, Mr. Hardy. I believe that next to Willet and Tayoga you are the greatest and best of my friends. Why, I know not, nor do I ask now, but the fact is patent, and I thank you many times over, although I can't accept your offer. I'm committed to this expedition and there my heart lies, too. Willet and Tayoga go with it. So do Black Rifle and Rogers, I think, and Colonel Johnson, who is also my good friend, is to lead it. I couldn't stay behind and consider myself a true man."

Master Benjamin Hardy sighed.

"Doubtless you are right, Robert," he said, "and perhaps at your age I should have taken the same view, despite Jonathan's assertion that my true ways are the ways of commerce and gain. Nevertheless, my interest in this struggle is great. It is bound to be since it means vast changes in the colonies, whatever its result."

"What changes do you have in mind, Mr. Hardy?"

"Mental changes more than any other, Robert. The war in its sweep bids fair to take in almost all the civilized world we know. We are the outpost of Britain, Canada is the outpost of France, and in a long and desperate strife such as this promises to be we are sure to achieve greater mental stature, and to arrive at a more acute consciousness of our own strength and resources. Beyond that I don't care to predict. But come, lad, we'll not talk further of such grave matters, you and I. Instead we'll have a pleasant hour with Mynheer Jacobus Huysman, a man of no mean quality, as you know."

Mynheer Jacobus was at home, and he gave them a great welcome, glancing at one and at the other, and then back again, apparently rejoiced to see them together.

Then he ordered a huge repast, of which they ate bountifully, and upon which he made heavy inroads himself. When the demands of hospitality were somewhat satisfied, he put aside knife and fork, and said to Mr. Hardy:

"And now, old friend, it iss no impertinence on my part to ask what hass brought you to Albany."

Master Benjamin, who was gravely filling a pipe, lighted it, took one puff, and replied:

"No, Jacobus, it is no impertinence. No question that you might ask me could be an impertinence. You and I are old friends, and I think we understand each other. I have to say in reply that I have come here on a matter of army contracts, to get a clearer and better view of the war which is going to mean so much to all of us, and to attend to one or two matters personal to myself."

Robert, excusing himself, had risen and was looking out of a window at a passing company of soldiers. Mynheer Jacobus glanced at him and then glanced back at the merchant.

"It iss a good lad," he said, "und you watch over him as well as you can."

"Aye, I do my best," replied Hardy in the same subdued tones, "but he is bold of spirit, full of imagination and adventurous, and, though I would fain keep him out of the war, I cannot. Yet if I were his age I would go into it myself."

"It iss the way of youth. He lives in times troubled und full of danger, yet he hass in the hunter, Willet, and the Onondaga, Tayoga, friends who are a flaming sword on each side of him. Willet hass a great mind. He iss as brave as a lion und full of resource."

"Right well do I know it, Jacobus."

"And the young Onondaga, Tayoga, is of the antique mould. Do I not know it, I who haf taught him so long? Often I could think he was a young Greek or Roman of the best type, reincarnated und sent to the forest. He does haf the lofty nature, the noble character und simplicity of a young Roman of the republic, before it was corrupted by conquest. I tell you, Benjamin Hardy, that we do not value the red men at their true worth, especially those of the Hodenosaunee!"

"Right well do I know that, too, Jacobus. I had a fair reading in the classics, when I was a schoolboy, and I should call the lad, Tayoga, more Greek in spirit than Roman. I have found in him the spiritual quality, the love of beauty and the kindliness of soul which the books say the Greeks had and which the Romans lacked."

"It iss fairly put, Benjamin, und I bethink me you are right. But there iss one thing which you do not know, but which you ought to know, because it iss of much importance."

"What is it?" asked Hardy, impressed by the manner of Jacobus.

"It iss the fact that Adrian Van Zoon arrived in Albany this morning."

The merchant started slightly in surprise, and then his face became a mask.

"Adrian Van Zoon is a merchant like myself," he said. "He has a right to come to Albany. Perhaps he feels the necessity, too, as no doubt he is interested in large contracts for the army."

"It iss true, Benjamin, but you und I would rather he had not come. He arrived but this morning on his own sloop, the *Dirkhoeven*, und I feel that wherever Adrian Van Zoon iss the air becomes noxious, full of poisonous vapours und dangerous to those about him."

"You're right, Jacobus. I see that your faculties are as keen as ever. You can see through a mill stone, and you can put together much larger figures than two and two."

Mynheer Jacobus smiled complacently.

"I haf not yet reached my zenith," he said, "und I am very glad I am not yet an old man, because I am so full of curiosity."

"I don't take your meaning, Jacobus."

"I would not like to die before this great und long war iss ended because I wish to see how it does end. Und I want to see the nature of the mighty changes which I feel are coming in the world."

"What changes, for instance, Jacobus?"

"The action of the New World upon the Old, und the action of the old monarchies upon one another. All things change, Benjamin. You und I know that. The veil of majesty that wraps around kings und thrones iss not visible to us here in der American forest, und maybe for dot reason we see the changes coming in Europe better than those who are closer by. France is the oldest of all the old und great monarchies und for dot reason the French monarchy iss most overripe. Steeped in luxury und corruption, the day of its decay hass set in."

"But the French people are valiant and great, Jacobus. Think not that we have in them a weak antagonist."

"I said nothing of the French nation, Benjamin, *mein* friend. I spoke of the French throne. The French leaders in Canada are brave und enterprising. They will inflict on us many defeats, but the French throne will not give to them the support to which they as Frenchmen are entitled."

"You probably see the truth, Jacobus, and it's to our advantage. Perhaps 'tis better that the French throne should decay. But we'll return to affairs closer by. You've had Van Zoon watched?"

"My stable boy, Peter, hass not let him out of sight, since he landed from the *Dirkhoeven*. Peter is not a lad of brilliant appearance, which iss perhaps all the better for our purpose, but he will keep Van Zoon in sight, if it iss humanly possible, without being himself suspected."

"Well done, Jacobus, but I might have known that you would take all needful precautions."

Robert came back from the window, and they promptly changed the current of the talk, speaking now of the army, its equipment, and the probable time of its march to meet Dieskau. Presently they left Mynheer Huysman's house, and Robert and the merchant went toward the camp on the flats. Here they beheld a scene of great activity and of enormous interest to Robert.

Few stranger armies have ever been gathered than that which Colonel William Johnson was preparing to lead against Crown Point. The New Englanders brought with them all their characteristics, their independence, their love of individualism and their piety. Despite this piety it was an army that swore hugely, and, despite its huge swearing, it was an honest army. It survives in written testimony that the greatest swearers were from the provinces of New York and Rhode Island, and Colonel Ephraim Williams, an officer among them writing at the time, said that the language they most used was "the language of Hell." And, on the other hand, a New York officer testified that not a housewife in Albany or its suburbs could mourn the loss of a single chicken. Private property everywhere was absolutely safe, and, despite the oaths and rough appearance of the men, no woman was ever insulted.

"They're having prayer meeting now," said Mr. Hardy, as they came upon the flats. "I've learned they have sermons twice a week—their ministers came along with them—prayers every day, and the singing of songs many times. They often alternate the psalm singing with the military drill, but I'm not one to decry their observances. Religious fervour is a great thing in battle. It made the Ironsides of Cromwell invincible."

Five hundred voices, nearly all untrained, were chanting a hymn. They were the voices of farmers and frontiersmen, but the great chorus had volume and majesty, and Robert was not one to depreciate them. Instead he was impressed. He understood the character of both New Englanders and New Yorkers. Keen for their own, impatient of control, they were nevertheless capable of powerful collective effort. A group of Mohawks standing by were also watching with grave and serious attention. When they raised a chant to Manitou they demanded the utmost respect, and they gave it also, without the asking, to the white man when he sang in his own way to his own God.

It was when they turned back to the town that they were hailed in a joyous voice, and Robert beheld the young English officer, Grosvenor, whom he had known in New York, Grosvenor, a little thinner than of old, but more tanned and with an air of experience. His pleasure at meeting Robert again was great and unaffected. He shook hands with him warmly and exclaimed:

"When I last saw you, Lennox, it was at the terrible forest fight, where we learned our bitter lesson. I saw that you escaped, but I did not know what became of you afterward."

"I've had adventures, and I'll tell you of 'em later," said Robert. "Glad I am to see you, although I had not heard of your coming to Albany."

"I arrived but this morning. No British troops are here. I understand this army is to be composed wholly of Colonials—pardon the word, I use it for lack of a better—and of Mohawks. But I was able to secure in New York a detail on the staff of Colonel Johnson. My position perhaps will be rather that of an observer and representative of the regular troops, but I hope, nevertheless, to be of some service. I suppose I won't see as much of you as I would like, as you're likely to be off in the forest in front of the army with those scouting friends of yours."

"It's what we can do best," said Robert, "but if there's a victory ahead I hope we'll all be present when it's gained."

Jacobus Huysman insisted that all his old friends be quartered with him, while they were in Albany, and as there was little at present for Grosvenor to do, he was added by arrangement with Colonel Johnson to the group. They sat that evening on the portico in the summer dusk, and Master Alexander McLean, the schoolmaster, joined them, still regarding Robert and Tayoga as lads under his care, and soon including Grosvenor also. But the talk was pleasant, and they were deep in it when a man passed in the street and a shadow fell upon them all.

It was Adrian Van Zoon, heavy, dressed richly as usual, and carrying a large cane, with a gold head. To the casual eye he was a man of importance, aware of his dignity, and resolute in the maintenance of it. He bowed with formal politeness to the group upon the portico, and walked majestically on. Mynheer Jacobus watched him until he was out of sight, going presumably to his inn, and then his eyes began to search for another figure. Presently it appeared, lank, long and tow-headed, the boy, Peter, of whom he had spoken. Mynheer Huysman introduced him briefly to the others, and he responded, in every case, with a pull at a long lock on his forehead. His superficial appearance was that of a simpleton, but Robert noticed sharp, observant eyes under the thick eyebrows. Mynheer Jacobus, Willet and Master Hardy, excusing themselves for a few minutes, went into an inner room.

"What has Mynheer Van Zoon been doing, Peter?" asked Jacobus.

"He has talked with three contractors for the army," replied the lad. "He also had a short conversation with Colonel Ephraim Williams of the Massachusetts militia."

"Williams is a thoroughly honest man," said Mr. Hardy. "His talk with Van Zoon could only have been on legitimate business. We'll dismiss him. What more have you seen, Peter?"

"Late in the afternoon he went to his schooner, the *Dirkhoeven*, which is anchored in the river. I could not follow him there, but I saw him speaking on the deck to a man who did not look like a sailor. They were there only a minute, then they went into the cabin, and when Mynheer Van Zoon came ashore he came alone."

"And the man who did not look like a sailor was left on the ship. It may mean nothing, or it may mean anything, but my mind tells me it hath an unpleasant significance. Now, I wish I knew this man who is lying hid in the *Dirkhoeven*. Perhaps it would be better, Jacobus, to instruct Peter to follow the lad, Lennox, and give the alarm if any threat or menace appears."

"I think it is the wiser course, Benjamin, and I will even instruct Peter in such manner."

He spoke a few sentences to Peter, who listened with eagerness, apparently delighted with the task set for him. When Mynheer Huysman had finished the lad slipped out at a back door, and was gone like a shadow.

"An admirable youth for our purpose," said Mynheer Jacobus Huysman. "He likes not work, but if he is to watch or follow anyone he hangs on like a hound. In Albany he will become the second self of young Lennox, whose first self will not know that he has a second self."

They returned to the portico. Robert glanced curiously at them, but not one of the three offered any explanation. He knew, however, that their guarded talk with Peter had to do with himself, and he felt a great emotion of gratitude. If he was surrounded by dangers he was also surrounded by powerful friends. If chance had put him on the outskirts of the world it had also given him comrades who were an armour of steel about him.

Tayoga and he occupied their old bedroom at Mynheer Jacobus Huysman's that night, and once when Robert glanced out of the window he caught a glimpse of a dark figure lurking in the shrubbery. It was a man who did not look like a sailor, but as he did not know of the conversation in the inner room the shadow attracted little attention from him. It disappeared in an instant, and he thought no more about it.

Robert and his comrades were back in the camp next day, and now they saw Colonel Johnson at his best, a man of wonderful understanding and tact. He was soon able to break through the reserve of the New England citizen officers who were not wont to give their confidence in a hurry, and around great bowls of lemon punch they talked of the campaign. The Mohawks, as of old, told him all their grievances, which he remedied when just, and persuaded them into forgetting when unjust.

Robert, Tayoga and Willet, in their capacity of scouts and skirmishers, could go about practically as they pleased. Colonel Johnson trusted them absolutely and they talked of striking out into the wilderness on a new expedition to see what lay ahead of the army. Adrian Van Zoon, they learned definitely, had started for New York on the *Dirkhoeven*, and Robert felt relief. Yet the lank lad, Peter, still followed him, and, as had been predicted truly, was his second self, although his first self did not know it.

He had been at Albany several days when he returned alone from the flats to the town late one evening. At a dark turn in the road he heard a report, and a bullet whistled very near him. It was followed quickly by a second report, but not by the whistling of any bullet. He had a pair of pistols in his belt, and, taking out one and cocking it, he searched the woods, though he found nothing. He concluded then that it was a random bullet fired by some returning hunter, and that the second shot was doubtless of the same character. But the first hunter had been uncommonly careless and he hastened his steps from a locality which had been so dangerous, even accidentally.

Inured, however, as he was to risks, the incident soon passed entirely out of his mind. Yet an hour or two later the lad, Peter, sat in a back room with Mynheer Jacobus Huysman, and told him with relish of the occurrence at the dark turn of the road.

"I was fifty or sixty yards behind in the shadow of the trees," he said. "I could see Master Lennox very well, though he could not see me. The figure of a man appeared in the woods near me and aimed a pistol at Master Lennox. I could not see his face well, but I knew it was the man on the boat who was talking to Mynheer Van Zoon. I uttered a cry which did not reach Master Lennox, but which did reach the man with the pistol. It disturbed his aim, and his bullet flew wide. Then I fired at him, but if I touched him at all it was but lightly. He made off through the woods and I followed, but his speed was so great I could not overtake him."

"You haf done well, Peter. Doubtless you haf saved the life of young Master Lennox, which was the task set for you to do. But it iss not enough. You may haf to save it a second und yet a third time."

The pale blue eyes of Peter glistened. Obviously he liked his present task much better than the doing of chores.

"You can trust me, Mynheer Huysman," he said importantly. "I will guard him, and I will do more. Is there anybody you want killed?"

"No, no, you young savage! You are to shoot only in self-defence, or in defence of young Lennox whom you are to protect. Bear that in mind."

"Very well, Mynheer. Your orders are law to me."

Peter went out of the room and slid away in the darkness. Mynheer Jacobus Huysman watched his departure and sighed. He was a good man, averse to violence and bloodshed, and he murmured:

"The world iss in a fever. The nations fight among themselves und even the lads talk lightly of taking life."

Peter reported to him again the next night, when Robert was safely in bed.

"I followed Master Lennox to the parade ground again," he said. "The Onondaga, Tayoga, the hunter, Willet, and the Englishman, Grosvenor, were with him. They watched the drill for a while, and spoke with Colonel Johnson. Then Master Lennox wandered away alone to the north edge of the drill ground, where there are some woods. Since I have received your instructions, Mynheer, I always examine the woods, and I found in them a man who might have been in hiding, or who might have been lying there for the sake of the shade, only I am quite sure it was not the latter. Just when Master Lennox came into his view I spoke to him, and he seemed quite angry. He asked me impatiently to go away, but I stood by and talked to him until Master Lennox was far out of sight."

"You saw the man well, then, Peter?"

"I did, Mynheer Huysman, and I cannot be mistaken. It was the same that talked with Mynheer Van Zoon on the deck of the *Dirkkoeven*."

"I thought so. And what kind of a looking man was he, Peter?"

"About thirty, I should say, Mynheer, well built and strong, and foreign."

"Foreign! What mean you, Peter?"

"French."

"What? French of France or French of Canada?"

"That I cannot say with certainty, Mynheer, but French he was I do believe and maintain."

"Then he must be a spy as well as a threat to young Lennox. This goes deeper than I had thought, but you haf done your work well, Peter. Continue it."

He held out a gold coin, which Peter pocketed with thanks, and went forth the next morning to resume with a proud heart the task that he liked.

Robert, all unconscious that a faithful guardian was always at his heels, was passing days full of colour, variety and pleasure. Admission into the society of Albany was easy to one of his manner and appearance, who had also such powerful friends, and there were pleasant evenings in the solid Dutch houses. But he knew they could not last long. Daganoweda and a chosen group of his Mohawks came back, reporting the French and Indian force to be far larger than the one that had defeated Braddock by Duquesne, and that Baron Dieskau who led it was considered a fine general. Unless Waraiyageh made up his mind to strike quickly Dieskau would strike first.

The new French and Indian army, Daganoweda said, numbered eight thousand men, a great force for the time, and for the New World, and it would be both preceded and followed by clouds of skirmishers, savages from the regions of the Great Lakes and even from beyond. They were flushed with victory, with the mighty taking of scalps, at Braddock's defeat, and they expected here in the north a victory yet greater. They were already assuming control of Champlain and George, the two lakes which from time immemorial, long before the coming of the white man, had formed the line of march between what had become the French colonies and the British colonies. It was equally vital now to possess this passage. Whoever became the rulers of the lakes might determine in their favour the issue of the war in America, and the youths in Johnson's army were eager to go forward at once and fight for the coveted positions.

But further delay was necessary. The commander still had the difficult task of harmonizing the provincial governors and legislatures, and he also made many presents to the Indians to bind them to the cause. Five of the Six Nations, alarmed by the French successes and the slowness of the Americans and English, still held neutral, but the Mohawks were full of zeal, and the best of their young chiefs and warriors stood by Johnson, ready to march when he marched, and to cover his van with their skirmishers and patrols.

Meanwhile the army drilled incessantly. The little troop of Philadelphians under Colden, Wilton and Carson were an example. They had seen much hard service already, although they spoke modestly of the dangers over which they had triumphed in the forest. It was their pride, too, to keep their uniforms neat, and to be as soldierly in manner as possible. They had the look of regulars, and Grosvenor, the young Englishman who had been taken on Colonel Johnson's staff, spoke of them as such.

New York and the four New England Colonies, whatever their lack of cooperation, showed energy. The governors issued proclamations, and if not enough men came, more were drafted from the regiments of militia. Bounties of six dollars for every soldier were offered by Massachusetts, and that valiant colony, as usual, led the way in energy.

They were full days for Robert. He listened almost incessantly to the sound of drum and fife, the drill master's word of command, or to voices raised in prayer, preaching or the singing of psalms. Recruits were continually coming in, awkward ploughboys, but brave and enduring, waiting only to be taught. Master Benjamin Hardy was compelled to return to New York, departing with reluctance and holding an earnest conference with Mynheer Jacobus Huysman before he went.

"The man, who is most certainly a French spy, is somewhere about," said Mynheer Jacobus. "Peter haf seen him twice more, but he haf caught only glimpses. But you can trust Peter even as I do. His whole heart iss in the task I have set him. He wass born Dutch but hiss soul iss Iroquois! He iss by nature a taker of scalps."

Master Benjamin laughed.

"Just at present," he said, "'tis the nature that suits us best. Most urgent business calls me back to New York, and, after all, I can't do more here than you are doing, old friend."

When they had bidden each other good-by in the undemonstrative manner of elderly men who have long been friends, Master Jacobus strolled down the main street of Albany and took a long look at a substantial house standing in fine grounds. Then he shook his head several times, and, walking on, met its owner, whom he greeted with marked coolness, although the manner of the other toward him had been somewhat effusive.

"I gif you good day, Hendrik Martinus," he said, "und I hear that you are prospering. I am not one to notice fashions myself, but others haf spoken to me of the beautiful new shawls your daughters are wearing und of the brooches und necklaces they haf."

The face of Martinus, a man of about fifty, turned a deep red, but the excessive colour passed in a few moments, and he spoke carelessly.

In truth, his whole manner was lighter and more agile than that of the average man of Dutch blood.

"I am not so sure, Mynheer Jacobus, that you did not take notice yourself," he said. "Mynheer Jacobus is grave and dignified, but many a grave and dignified man has a wary eye for the ladies."

Mynheer Jacobus Huysman frowned.

"And as for shawls and brooches and necklaces," continued Martinus, "it is well known that war brings legitimate profits to many men. It makes trade in certain commodities brisk. Now I'd willingly wager that your friend, Master Benjamin Hardy, whom you have just seen on his way to New York, will be much the richer by this war."

"Master Hardy has ships upon the seas, and important contracts for the troops."

"I have no ships upon the seas, but I may have contracts, too."

"It may well be so, Hendrik," said Mynheer Jacobus, and without another word he passed on. When he had gone a hundred yards he shook himself violently, and when he had gone another hundred yards he gave himself a second shake of equal vigour. An hour later he was in the back room talking with the lad, Peter.

"Peter," he said, "you haf learned to take naps in the day und to keep awake all through the night?"

"Yes, Mynheer," replied Peter, proudly.

"Then, Peter, you vass an owl, a watcher in the dark."

"Yes, Mynheer."

"Und I gif you praise for watching well, Peter, und also gold, which iss much more solid than praise. Now I gif you by und by more praise und more gold which iss still more solid than praise. The lad, Robert Lennox, will be here early tonight to take supper with me, und I will see that he does not go out again before the morrow. Now, do you, Peter, watch the house of Hendrik Martinus all night und tell me if anyone comes out or goes in, und who und what he may be, as nearly as you can."

"Yes, Mynheer," said Peter, and a sudden light flickered in the pale blue eyes.

No further instructions were needed. He left the house in silence, and Mynheer Jacobus Huysman trusted him absolutely.

Chapter 6

The Dark Stranger

Robert arrived at the house of Jacobus Huysman about dark and Tayoga came with him. Willet was detained at the camp on the flats, where he had business with Colonel Johnson, who consulted him often. The two lads were in high good spirits, and Mynheer Jacobus, whatever he may have been under the surface, appeared to be so, too. Robert believed that the army would march very soon now. The New York and New England men alike were full of fire, eager to avenge Braddock's defeat and equally eager to drive back and punish the terrible clouds of savages which, under the leadership of the French, were ravaging the border, spreading devastation and terror on all sides.

"There has been trouble, Mynheer Huysman," said Robert, "between Governor Shirley of Massachusetts, who has been in camp several days, and Colonel Johnson. I saw Governor Shirley when he was in the council at Alexandria, in Virginia, and I know, from what I've heard, that he's the most active and energetic of all the governors, but they say he's very vain and pompous."

"Vanity and pomp comport ill with a wilderness campaign," said Mynheer Jacobus, soberly. "Of all the qualities needed to deal with the French und Indians I should say that they are needed least. It iss a shame that a man should demand obeisance from others when they are all in a great crisis."

"The Governor is eager to push the war," said Robert, "yet he demands more worship of the manner from Colonel Johnson than the colonel has time to give him. 'Tis said, too, that the delays he makes cause dissatisfaction among the Mohawks, who are eager to be on the great war trail. Daganoweda, I know, fairly burns with impatience."

Mynheer Jacobus sighed.

"We will not haf the advantage of surprise," he said. "Of that I am certain. I do believe that the French und Indians know of all our movements und of all we do."

"Spies?" said Robert.

"It may be," replied Mynheer Jacobus.

Robert was silent. His first thought was of St. Luc, who, he knew, would dare anything, and it was just the sort of adventure that would appeal to his bold and romantic spirit. But his thought passed on. He had no real feeling that St. Luc was in the camp. Mynheer Jacobus must be thinking of another or others. But Huysman volunteered no explanation. Presently he rose from his chair, went to a window and looked out. Tayoga observed him keenly.

The Onondaga, trained from his childhood to observe all kinds of manifestations, was a marvellous reader of the minds of men, and, merely because Mynheer Jacobus Huysman interrupted a conversation to look out into the dark, he knew that he expected something. And whatever it was it was important, as the momentary quiver of the big man's lip indicated.

The Indian, although he may hide it, has his full share of curiosity, and Tayoga wondered why Mynheer Jacobus watched. But he asked no question.

The Dutchman came back from the window, and asked the lads in to supper with him. His slight air of expectancy had disappeared wholly, but Tayoga was not deceived. "He has merely been convinced that he was gazing out too soon," he said to himself. "As surely as Tododaho on his star watches over the Onondagas, he will come back here after supper and look from this window, expecting to see something or somebody."

The supper of Mynheer Jacobus was, in reality, a large dinner, and, as it was probably the last the two lads would take with him before they went north, he had given to it a splendour and abundance even greater than usual. Tayoga and Robert, as became two such stout youths, ate bountifully, and Mynheer Jacobus Huysman, whatever his secret troubles may have been, wielded knife and fork with them, knife for knife and fork for fork.

But Tayoga was sure that Mynheer Jacobus was yet expectant, and still, without making it manifest, he watched him keenly. He noted that the big man hurried the latter part of the supper, something which the Onondaga had never known him to do before, and which, to the observant mind of the red youth, indicated an expectancy far greater than he had supposed at first.

Clearly Mynheer Jacobus was hastening, clearly he wished to be out of the room, and it was equally clear to Tayoga that he wanted to go back to his window, the one from which he could see over the grounds, and into the street beyond.

"Will you take a little wine?" he said to Robert, as he held up a bottle, through which the rich dark red colour shone.

"Thank you, sir, no," replied Robert.

"Und you, Tayoga?"

"I never touch the firewater of the white man, call they it wine or call they it whiskey."

"Good. Good for you both. I merely asked you for the sake of politeness, und I wass glad to hear you decline. But as for me, I am old enough to be your father, und I will take a little."

He poured a small glass, drank it, and rose.

"Your old room iss ready," he said, "und now, if you two lads will go to it, you can get a good und long night's sleep."

Robert was somewhat surprised. He felt that they were being dismissed, which was almost like the return of the old days when they were schoolboys, but Tayoga touched him on the elbow, and his declaration that he was not sleepy died on his lips. Instead, he said a polite good-night and he and Tayoga went away as they were bid.

"Now, what did he mean? Why was he so anxious to get rid of us?" asked Robert, when they were again in their room.

"Mynheer Jacobus expects something," replied the Onondaga, gravely. "He expects it to come out of the night, and appear at a window of the room in which we first sat, the window that looks over the garden, and to the street behind us."

"How do you know that?" asked Robert, astonished.

Tayoga explained what he had seen.

"I do not doubt you. It's convincing," said Robert, "but I'd not have noticed it."

"We of the red nations have had to notice everything in order that we might live. As surely as we sit here, Dagaeoga, Mynheer Jacobus is at the window, watching. When I lie down on the bed I shall keep my clothes on, and I shall not sleep. We may be called."

"I shall do the same, Tayoga."

Nevertheless, as time passed, young Lennox fell asleep, but the Onondaga did not close his eyes. What was time to him? The red race always had time to spare, and nature and training had produced in him illimitable patience. He had waited by a pool a whole day and night for a deer to come down to drink. He heard the tall clock standing on the floor in the corner strike ten, eleven, and then twelve, and a half hour later, when he was as wide awake as ever, there was a knock at the door. But he had first heard the approaching footsteps of the one who came and knocked, and he was already touching the shoulder of Robert, who sat up at once, sleep wholly gone from him.

"It is Mynheer Jacobus," said Tayoga, "and he wants us."

Then he opened the door and the large red face of Mynheer Huysman looked into the room, which was illuminated by the moonlight.

"Come, you lads," he said, in sharp, eager tones, "und bring your pistols with you."

Robert and Tayoga snatched up their weapons, and followed him into the sitting-room, where the tall lank youth, Peter, stood.

"You know Peter," he said, "und Peter knows you. Now, listen to what he hass to tell, but first pledge me that you will say nothing of it until I give you leave. Do you?"

"We do," they replied together.

"Then, Peter, tell them what you haf seen, but be brief, because it may be that we must act quickly."

"Obeying the instructions of Mynheer Jacobus Huysman, whom I serve," said Peter, smoothly, evidently enjoying his importance of the moment, "I watched tonight the house of Mynheer Hendrik Martinus, who is not trusted by my master. The building is large, and it stands on ground with much shrubbery that is now heavy with leaf. So it was difficult to watch all the approaches to it, but I went about it continuously, hour after hour. A half hour ago, I caught a glimpse of a man, strong, and, as well as I could tell in the night, of a dark complexion. He was on the lawn, among the shrubbery, hiding a little while and then going on again. He came to a side door of the house, but he did not knock, because there was no need. The door opened of itself, and he went in. Then the door closed of itself, and he did not come out again. I waited ten minutes and then hurried to the one whom I serve with the news."

Mynheer Jacobus turned to Tayoga and Robert.

"I haf long suspected," he said, "that Hendrik Martinus iss a spy in the service of France, a traitor for his own profit, because he loves nothing but himself und his. He has had remarkable prosperity of late, a prosperity for which no one can account, because he has had no increase of business. Believing that a Frenchman wass here, a spy who wished to communicate with him, I set Peter to watch his house, und the result you know."

"Then it is for us to go there and seize this spy," said Robert.

"It iss what I wish," said Mynheer Huysman, "und we may trap a traitor und a spy at the same time. It is well to haf money if you haf it honestly, but Hendrik Martinus loves money too well."

He took from a drawer a great double-barrelled horse pistol, put it under his coat, and the four, quietly leaving the house, went toward that of Hendrik Martinus. There was no light except that of the moon and, in the distance, they saw a watchman carrying a lantern and thumping upon the stones with a stout staff.

"It iss Andrius Tefft," said Mynheer Jacobus. "He hass a strong arm und a head with but little in it. It would be best that he know nothing of this, or he would surely muddle it."

They drew back behind some shrubbery, and Andrius Tefft, night watchman, passed by without a suspicion that one of Albany's most respected citizens was hiding from him. The light of his lantern faded in the distance, and the four proceeded rapidly towards the house of Hendrik Martinus, entering its grounds without hesitation and spreading in a circle about it. Robert, who lurked behind a small clipped pine in the rear saw a door open, and a figure slip quietly out. It was that of a man of medium height, and as he could see by the moonlight, of dark complexion. He had no doubt that it was a Frenchman, the fellow whom Peter had seen enter the house.

Robert acted with great promptness, running forward and crying to the fugitive to halt. The man, quick as a flash, drew a pistol and fired directly at him. The lad felt the bullet graze his scalp, and, for a moment, he thought he had been struck mortally. He staggered, but recovered himself, and raising his own pistol, fired at the flying figure which was now well beyond him. He saw the man halt a moment, and quiver, but in an instant he ran on again faster than ever, and disappeared in an alley. A little later a swift form followed in pursuit and Robert saw that it was Tayoga.

Young Lennox knew that it was useless for him to follow, as he felt a little dizzy and he was not yet sure of himself. He put his hand to his hair, where the bullet had struck, and, taking it away, looked anxiously at it. There was no blood upon either palm or finger, and then he realized, with great thankfulness, that he was merely suffering a brief weakness from the concussion caused by a heavy bullet passing so close to his skull. He heard a hasty footstep, and Mynheer Huysman, breathing heavily and anxious, stood before him. Other and lighter footsteps indicated that Peter also was coming to his aid.

"Haf you been shot?" exclaimed Mynheer Jacobus

"No, only shot at," replied Robert, whimsically, "though I don't believe the marksman could come so close to me again without finishing me. I think it was Peter's spy because I saw him come out of the house, and cried to him to halt, but he fired first. My own bullet, I'm sure, touched him, and Tayoga is in pursuit, though the fugitive has a long lead."

"We'll leave it to Tayoga, because we haf to," said Mynheer Jacobus. "If anybody can catch him the Onondaga can, though I think he will get away. But come now, we will talk to Hendrik Martinus und Andrius Tefft who hass heard the shots und who iss coming back. You lads, let me do all of the talking. Since the spy or messenger or whatever he iss hass got away, it iss best that we do not tell all we know."

The watchman was returning at speed, his staff pounding quick and hard on the stones, his lantern swinging wildly. The houses there were detached and nobody else seemed to have heard the shots, save Hendrik Martinus and his family. Martinus, fully dressed, was coming out of his house, his manner showing great indignation, and the heads of women in nightcaps appeared at the windows.

"What is this intrusion, Mynheer Huysman? Why are you in my grounds? And who fired those two pistol shots I heard?"

"Patience, Hendrik! Patience!" replied Mynheer Jacobus, in a smooth suave manner that surprised Robert. "My young friend, Master Lennox, here, saw a man running across your grounds, after having slipped surreptitiously out of your house. Suspecting that he had taken und carried from you that which he ought not to haf, Master Lennox called to him to stop. The reply wass a pistol bullet und Master Lennox, being young und like the young prone to swift anger, fired back. But the man hass escaped with hiss spoil, whatefer it iss, und you only, Hendrik, know what it iss."

Hendrik Martinus looked at Jacobus Huysman and Jacobus Huysman looked squarely back at him. The angry fire died out of the eyes of Martinus, and instead came a swift look of comprehension which passed in an instant. When he spoke again his tone was changed remarkably:

"Doubtless it was a robber," he said, "and I thank you, Mynheer Jacobus, and Master Lennox, and your boy Peter, for your attempt to catch him. But I fear that he has escaped."

"I will pursue him und capture him," exclaimed Mynheer Andrius Tefft, who stood by, listening to their words and puffing and blowing.

"I fear it iss too late, Andrius," said Mynheer Jacobus Huysman, shaking his head. "If anyone could do it, it would be you, but doubtless Mynheer Hendrik hass not lost anything that he cannot replace, und it would be better for you, Andrius, to watch well here und guard against future attempts."

"That would be wise, no doubt," said Martinus, and Robert thought he detected an uneasy note in his voice.

"Then I will go," said Andrius Tefft, and he walked on, swinging his lantern high and wide, until its beams fell on every house and tree and shrub.

"I will return to my house," said Mynheer Martinus. "My wife and daughters were alarmed by the shots, and I will tell them what has happened."

"It iss the wise thing to do," said Mynheer Huysman, gravely, "und I would caution you, Hendrik, to be on your guard against robbers who slip so silently into your house und then slip out again in the same silence. The times are troubled und the wicked take advantage of them to their own profit."

"It is true, Mynheer Jacobus," said Martinus somewhat hastily, and he walked back to his own house without looking Huysman in the eyes again.

Mynheer Huysman, Robert and Peter returned slowly.

"I think Hendrik understands me," said Mynheer Huysman; "I am sorry that we did not catch the go-between, but Hendrik hass had a warning, und he will be afraid. Our night's work iss not all in vain. Peter, you haf done well, but I knew you would. Now, we will haf some refreshment und await the return of Tayoga."

"I believe," said Robert, "that in Albany, when one is in doubt what to do one always eats. Is it not so?"

"It iss so," replied Mynheer Jacobus, smiling, "und what better could one do? While you wait, build up the body, because when you build up the body you build up the mind, too, und at the same time it iss a pleasure."

Robert and Peter ate nothing, but Mynheer Jacobus partook amply of cold beef and game, drank a great glass of home-made beer, and then smoked a long pipe with intense satisfaction. One o'clock in the morning came, then two, then three, and Mynheer Jacobus, taking the stem of his pipe from his mouth, said:

"I think it will not be long now before Tayoga iss here. Long ago he hass either caught hiss man or hiss man hass got away, und he iss returning. I see hiss shadow now in the shrubbery. Let him in, Peter."

Tayoga entered the room, breathing a little more quickly than usual, his dark eyes showing some disappointment.

"It wass not your fault that he got away, Tayoga," said Mynheer Jacobus soothingly. "He had too long a start, und doubtless he was fleet of foot. I think he iss the very kind of man who would be fleet of foot."

"I had to pick up his trail after he went through the alley," said Tayoga, "and I lost time in doing so. When I found it he was out of the main part of the town and in the outskirts, running towards the river. Even then I might have caught him, but he sprang into the stream and swam with great skill and speed. When I came upon the bank, he was too far away for a shot from my pistol, and he escaped into the thickets on the other shore."

"I wish we could have caught him," said Mynheer Jacobus. "Then we might have uncovered much that I would like to know. What iss it, Tayoga? You haf something more to tell!"

"Before he reached the river," said the Onondaga, "he tore in pieces a letter, a letter that must have been enclosed in an envelope. I saw the little white pieces drift away before the wind. I suppose he was afraid I might catch him, and so he destroyed the letter which must have had a tale to tell. When I came back I looked for the pieces, but I found only one large enough to bear anything that had meaning." He took from his tunic a fragment of white paper and held it up. It bore upon it two words in large letters: Achille Garay.

"That," said Robert, "is obviously the name of a Frenchman, and it seems to me it must have been the name of this fugitive spy or messenger to whom the letter was addressed. Achille Garay is the man whom we want. Don't you think so, Mynheer Huysman?"

"It iss truly the one we would like to capture," said Mynheer Jacobus, "but I fear that all present chance to do so hass passed. Still, we will remember. The opportunity may come again. Achille Garay! Achille Garay! We will bear that name in mind! Und now, lads, all of you go to bed. You haf done well, too, Tayoga. Nobody could haf done better."

Robert, when alone the next day, met Hendrik Martinus in the street. Martinus was about to pass without speaking, but Robert bowed politely and said:

"I'm most sorry, Mr. Martinus, that we did not succeed in capturing your burglar last night, but my Onondaga friend followed him to the river, which he swam, then escaping. 'Tis true that he escaped, but nevertheless Tayoga salvaged a piece of a letter that he destroyed as he ran, and upon the fragment was written a name which we're quite sure was that of the bold robber."

Robert paused, and he saw the face of Martinus whiten.

"You do not ask me the name, Mynheer Martinus," he said. "Do you feel no curiosity at all about it?"

"What was it?" asked Martinus, thickly.

"Achille Garay."

Martinus trembled violently, but by a supreme effort controlled himself.

"I never heard it before," he said. "It sounds like a French name."

"It is a French name. I'm quite confident of it. I merely wanted you to understand that we haven't lost all trace of your robber, that we know his name, and that we may yet take him."

"It does look as if you had a clew," said Martinus. He was as white as death, though naturally rubicund, and without another word he walked on. Robert looked after him and saw the square shoulders drooping a little. He had not the slightest doubt of the man's guilt, and he was filled with indignant wonder that anyone's love of money should be strong enough to create in him the willingness to sell his country. He was sure Mynheer Jacobus was right. Martinus was sending their military secrets into Canada for French gold, and yet they had not a particle of proof. The man must be allowed to go his way until something much more conclusive offered. Both he and Tayoga talked it over with Willet, and the hunter agreed that they could do nothing for the present.

"But," he said, "the time may come when we can do much."

Then Martinus disappeared for a while from Robert's mind, because the next day he met the famous old Indian known in the colonies as King Hendrik of the Mohawks. Hendrik, an ardent and devoted friend of the Americans and English, had come to Albany to see Colonel William Johnson, and to march with him against the French and Indians. There was no hesitation, no doubt about him, and despite his age he would lead the Mohawk warriors in person into battle. Willet, who had known him long, introduced Robert, who paid him the respect and deference due to an aged and great chief.

Hendrik, who was a Mohegan by birth but by adoption a Mohawk, adoption having all the value of birth, was then a full seventy years of age. He spoke English fluently, he had received education in an American school, and a substantial house, in which he had lived for many years, stood near the Canajoharie or upper castle of the Mohawks. He had been twice to England and on each occasion had been received by the king, the head of one nation offering hospitality to the allied head of another. A portrait of him in full uniform had been painted by a celebrated London painter.

He had again put on his fine uniform upon the occasion of his meeting with Colonel Johnson on the Albany flats, and when Robert saw him he was still clothed in it. His coat was of superfine green cloth, heavily ornamented with gold epaulets and gold lace. His trousers were of the same green cloth with gold braid all along the seams, and his feet were in shoes of glossy leather with gold buckles. A splendid cocked hat with a feather in it was upon his head. Beneath the shadow of the hat was a face of reddish bronze, aged but intelligent, and, above all, honest.

Hendrik in an attire so singular for a Mohawk might have looked ridiculous to many a man, but Robert, who knew so much of Indian nature, found him dignified and impressive.

"I have heard of you, my son," said Hendrik, in the precise, scholarly English which Tayoga used. "You are a friend of the brave young chief, Daganoweda, and to you, because of your gift of speech, has been given the name, Dagaeoga. The Onondaga, Tayoga, of the clan of the Bear, is your closest comrade, and you are also the one who made the great speech in the Vale of Onondaga before the fifty sachems against the missionary, Father Drouillard, and the French leader, St. Luc. They say that words flowed like honey from your lips."

"It was the occasion, not any words of mine," said Robert modestly.

"I was ill then, and could not be present," continued the old chief gravely, "and another took my place. I should have been glad could I have heard that test of words in the Vale of Onondaga, because golden speech is pleasant in my ears, but Manitou willed it otherwise, and I cannot complain, as I have had much in my long life. Now the time for words has passed. They have failed and the day of battle is at hand. I go on my last war trail."

"No! No, Hendrik!" exclaimed Willet. "You will emerge again the victor, covered with glory."

"Yes, Great Bear, it is written here," insisted the old Mohawk, tapping his forehead. "It is my last war trail, but it will be a great one. I know it. How I know it I do not know, but I know it. The voice of Manitou has spoken in my ear and I cannot doubt. I shall fall in battle by the shores of Andiatarocte (the Iroquois name of Lake George) and there is no cause to mourn. I have lived the three score years and ten which the Americans and English say is the allotted age of man, and what could be better for a Mohawk chief, when the right end for his days has come, than to fall gloriously at the head of his warriors? I have known you long, Great Bear. You have always been the friend of the Hodenosaunee. You have understood us, you have never lied to us, and tricked us, as the fat traders do. I think that when I draw my last breath you will not be far away and it will be well. I could not wish for any better friend than Great Bear to be near when I leave this earth on my journey to the star on which the mighty Hayowentha, the Mohawk chief of long ago, lives."

Willet was much affected, and he put his hand on the shoulder of his old friend.

"I hope you are wrong, Hendrik," he said, "and that many years of good life await you, but if you do fall it is fitting, as you say, to fall at the head of your warriors."

The old chief smiled. It was evident that he had made his peace with his Manitou, and that he awaited the future without anxiety.

"Remember the shores of Andiatarocte," he said. "They are bold and lofty, covered with green forest, and they enclose the most beautiful of all the lakes. It is a wonderful lake. I have known it more than sixty years. The mountains, heavy with the great forest, rise all around it. Its waters are blue or green or silver as the skies over it change. It is full of islands, each like a gem in a cluster. I have gone there often, merely to sit on a great cliff a half mile above its waters, and look down on the lake, Andiatarocte, the Andiatarocte of the Hodenosaunee that Manitou gave to us because we strive to serve him. It is a great and glorious gift to me that I should be allowed to die in battle there and take my flight from its shores to Hayowentha's star, the star on which Hayowentha sits, and from which he talks across infinite space, which is nothing to them, to the great Onondaga chieftain Tododaho, also on his star to which he went more than four centuries ago."

The face of the old chief was rapt and mystic. The black eyes in the bronzed face looked into futurity and infinity. Robert was more than impressed, he had a feeling of awe. A great Indian chief was a great Indian chief to him, as great as any man, and he did not doubt that the words of Hendrik would come true. And like Hendrik himself he did not see any cause for grief. He, too, had looked upon the beautiful shores of Andiatarocte, and it was a fitting place for a long life to end, preparatory to another and eternal life among the stars.

He gravely saluted King Hendrik with the full respect and deference due him, to which the chief replied, obviously pleased with the good manners of the youth, and then he and the hunter walked to another portion of the camp.

"A great man, a really great man!" said Willet.

"He made a great speech here in Albany more than a year ago to a congress of white men, and he has made many great speeches. He is also a great warrior, and for nearly a half century he has valiantly defended the border against the French and their Indians."

"I wonder if what he says about falling in battle on the shores of Andiatarocte will come true."

"We'll wait and see, Robert, we'll wait and see, but I've an idea that it will. Some of these Indians, especially the old, seem to have the gift of second sight, and we who live so much in the woods know that many strange things happen."

A few days of intense activity followed. The differences between Governor Shirley and the commander, Colonel William Johnson, were composed, and the motley army would soon march forward to the head of Andiatarocte to meet Dieskau and the French. It was evident that the beautiful lake which both English and French claimed, but which really belonged to the Hodenosaunee, had become one of two keys to the North American lock, the other being its larger and scarcely less beautiful sister, Champlain. They and their chains of rivers had been for centuries the great carry between what had become the French and English colonies, and whoever became the ruler of these two lakes would become the ruler of the continent.

It was granted to Robert with his extraordinary imaginative gifts to look far into the future. He had seen the magnificence of the north country, its world of forest and fertile land, its network of rivers and lakes, a region which he believed to be without an equal anywhere on earth, and he knew that an immense and vigorous population was bound to spring up there. He had his visions and dreams, and perhaps his youth made him dream all the more, and more magnificently than older men whose lives had been narrowed by the hard facts of the present. It was in these brilliant, glowing dreams of his that New York might some day be as large as London, with a commerce as large, and that Boston and Philadelphia and other places for which the sites were not yet cleared, would be a match for the great cities of the Old World.

And yet but few men in the colonies were dreaming such dreams, which became facts in a period amazingly short, as the history of the world runs. Perhaps the dream was in the wise and prophetic brain of Franklin or in the great imagination of Jefferson, but there is little to prove that more than a few were dreaming that way. To everybody, almost, the people on the east coast of North America were merely the rival outposts of France and England.

But the army that was starting for the green shores of Andiatarocte bore with it the fate of mighty nations, and its march, hidden and obscure, compared with that of many a great army in Europe, was destined to have a vast influence upon the world.

It was a strange composite force. There were the militiamen from New England, tall, thin, hardy and shrewd, accustomed to lives of absolute independence, full of confidence and eager to go against the enemy. Many of the New Yorkers were of the same type, but the troops of that province also included the Germans and the Dutch, most of the Germans still unable to speak the English language. There was the little Philadelphia troop under Colden, trained now, the wild rangers from the border, and the fierce Mohawks led by King Hendrik and Daganoweda. Colonel Johnson, an Irishman by birth, but more of an American than many of those born on the soil, was the very man to fuse and lead an army of such varying elements.

Robert now saw Waraiyageh at his best. He soothed the vanity of Governor Shirley. He endeared himself to the New England officers and their men. He talked their own languages to the men of German and Dutch blood, and he continued to wield over the Mohawks an influence that no other white man ever had. The Mohawk lad, Joseph Brant, the great Thayendanegea of the future, was nearly always with him, and Tayoga himself was not more eager for the march.

Now came significant arrivals in the camp, Robert Rogers, the ranger, at the head of his men, and with him Black Rifle, dark, saturnine and silent, although Robert noticed that now and then his black eyes flashed under the thick shade of his long lashes. They brought reports of the greatest activity among the French and Indians about the northern end of Andiatarocte, and that Dieskau was advancing in absolute confidence that he would equal the achievement of Dumas, St. Luc, Ligneris and the others against Braddock. All about him were the terrible Indian swarms.

Every settler not slain had fled with his people for their lives. Only the most daring and skilful of the American forest runners could live in the woods, and the price they paid was perpetual vigilance. Foremost among the Indian leaders was Tandakora, the huge Ojibway, and he spared none who fell into his hands. Torture and death were their fate.

The face of Colonel Johnson darkened when Rogers told him the news. "My poor people!" he groaned. "Why were we compelled to wait so long?" And by his "people" he meant the Mohawks no less than the whites. The valiant tribe, and none more valiant ever lived, was threatened with destruction by the victorious and exultant hordes.

Refugees poured into Albany, bringing tales of destruction and terror. Albany itself would soon be attacked by Dieskau, with his regulars, his cannon, his Canadians and his thousands of Indians, and it could not stand before them. Robert, Tayoga and Willet were with

Colonel Johnson, when Rogers and Black Rifle arrived, and they saw his deep grief and anger.

"The army will march in a few more days, David, old friend," he said, "but it must move slowly. One cannot take cannon and wagons through the unbroken forest, and so I am sending forward two thousand men to cut a road. Then our main force will advance, but we should do something earlier, something that will brush back these murderous swarms. David, old friend, what are we to do?"

Willet looked around in thought, and he caught the flashing eyes of Rogers. He glanced at Black Rifle and his dark eyes, too, were sparkling under their dark lashes. He understood what was in their minds, and it appealed to him.

"Colonel Johnson," he said, "one must burn the faces of the French and Indians, and show them a victory is not theirs until they've won it. Let Mr. Rogers here take the rangers he has, other picked ones from the camp, Robert, Tayoga and me, perhaps also a chosen band of Mohawks under Daganoweda, and go forward to strike a blow that will delay Dieskau."

The sombre face of Waraiyageh lightened.

"David Willet," he said, "you are a man. I have always known it, but it seems to me that every time I meet you you have acquired some new virtue of the mind. 'Tis a daring task you undertake, but a noble one that I think will prove fruitful. Perhaps, though, you should leave the lads behind."

Then up spoke Robert indignantly.

"I've been through a thousand dangers with Dave, and I'll not shirk a new one. I have no commission in the army and it cannot hold me. I shall be sorry to go without your permission, Colonel Johnson, but go I surely will."

"For more centuries than man knows, my ancestors have trod the war trail," said Tayoga, "and I should not be worthy to have been born a son of the clan of the Bear, of the nation Onondaga, of the great League of the Hodenosaunee, if I did not go now upon the greatest war trail of them all, when the nations gather to fight for the lordship of half a world. When the Great Bear and the Mountain Wolf and Dagaeoga and the others leave this camp for the shores of Andiatarocte I go with them!"

He stood very erect, his head thrown back a little, his eyes flashing, his face showing unalterable resolve. Colonel Johnson laughed mellowly.

"What a pair of young eagles we have!" he exclaimed in a pleased tone. "And if that fiery child, Joseph Brant, were here he would be wild to go too! And if I let him go on such a venture Molly Brant would never forgive me. Well, it's a good spirit and I have no right to make any further objection. But do you, Dave Willet, and you, Rogers, and you, Black Rifle, see that they take no unnecessary risks."

Grosvenor also was eager to go, but they thought his experience in the woods was yet too small for him to join the rangers, and, to his great disappointment, the band was made up without him. Then they arranged for their departure.

Chapter 7

On the Great Trail

Robert appreciated fully all the dangers they were sure to encounter upon their perilous expedition to the lakes. Having the gift of imagination, he saw them in their most alarming colours, but having a brave heart also, he was more than willing, he was eager to encounter them with his chosen comrades by his side. The necessity of striking some quick and sharp blow became more apparent every hour, or the lakes, so vital in the fortunes of the war, would soon pass into the complete possession of the French and Indians.

The band was chosen and equipped with the utmost care. It included, of course, all of Rogers' rangers, Robert, Tayoga, Willet and Black Rifle, making a total of fifty white men, all of tried courage and inured to the forest. Besides there were fifty Mohawks under Daganoweda, the very pick of the tribe, stalwart warriors, as tough as hickory, experienced in every art of wilderness trail and war, and eager to be at the foe. Every white man was armed with a rifle, a pistol, a hatchet and a knife, carrying also a pouch containing many bullets, a large horn of powder, a blanket folded tightly and a knapsack full of food. The Mohawks were armed to the teeth in a somewhat similar fashion, and, it being midsummer and the weather warm, they were bare to the waist. Rogers, the ranger, was in nominal command of the whole hundred, white and red, but Willet and Daganoweda in reality were on an equality, and since the three knew one another well and esteemed one another highly they were sure to act in perfect coordination. Black Rifle, it was understood, would go and come as he pleased. He was under the orders of no man.

"I give you no instructions," said Colonel William Johnson to the three leaders, "because I know of none to be given under such circumstances. No man can tell what awaits you in the forest and by the lakes. I merely ask you in God's name to be careful! Do not walk into any trap! And yet 'tis foolish of me to warn Robert Rogers, David Willet, Black Rifle and Daganoweda, four foresters who probably haven't their equal in all North America. But we can ill afford to lose you. If you do not see your way to strike a good blow perhaps it would be better to come back and march with the army."

"You don't mean that, William, old friend," said Willet, smiling and addressing him familiarly by his first name. "In your heart you would be ashamed of us if we returned without achieving at least one good deed for our people. And turning from William, my old friend, to Colonel William Johnson, our commander, I think I can promise that a high deed will be achieved. Where could you find a hundred finer men than these, fifty white and fifty red?"

Daganoweda, who understood him perfectly, smiled proudly and glanced at the ranks of Mohawks who stood impassive, save for their eager, burning eyes.

"But be sure to bring back the good lads, Robert and Tayoga," said Mynheer Jacobus Huysman, who stood with Colonel William Johnson. "I would keep them from going, if I could, but I know I cannot and perhaps I am proud of them, because I know they will not listen to me."

King Hendrik of the Mohawks, in his gorgeous coloured clothes, was also present, his bronzed and aged face lighted up with the warlike gleam from his eyes. Evidently his mind was running back over the countless forays and expeditions he had led in the course of fifty years. He longed once more for the forests, the beautiful lakes and the great war trail. His seventy years had not quenched his fiery spirit, but they had taken much of his strength, and so he would abide with the army, going with it on its slow march.

"My son," he said, with the gravity and dignity of an old Indian sachem, to Daganoweda, "upon this perilous chance you carry the honour and fortune of the Ganeagaono, the great warlike nation of the Hodenosaunee. It is not necessary for me to bid you do your duty and show to the Great Bear, the Mountain Wolf, Black Rifle and the other white men that a young Mohawk chief will go where any other will go, and if need be will die with all his men before yielding a foot of ground. I do not bid you do these things because I know that you will do them without any words from me, else you would not be a Mohawk chief, else you would not be Daganoweda, son of fire and battle."

Daganoweda smiled proudly. The wise old sachem had struck upon the most responsive chords in his nature.

"I will try to bear myself as a Mohawk should," he said simply.

Colden and Grosvenor were also there.

"I'm sorry our troop can't go with you," said the young Philadelphian, "but I'm not one to question the wisdom and decision of our commander-in-chief. Doubtless we'd be a drag upon such a band as yours, but I wish we could have gone. At least, we'll be with the army which is going to march soon, and perhaps we'll overtake you at Lake George before many days."

"And I," said Grosvenor to Robert and Tayoga, "am serving on the staff of the commander. I'm perhaps the only Englishman here and I'm an observer more than anything else. So I could be spared most readily, but the colonel will not let me go. He says there is no reason why we should offer a scalp without price to Tandakora, the Ojibway."

"And I abide by what I said," laughed Colonel Johnson, who heard. "You're in conditions new to you, Grosvenor, though you've had one tragic and dreadful proof of what the Indians can do, but there's great stuff in you and I'm not willing to see it thrown away before it's developed. Don't be afraid the French and Indians won't give you all the fighting you want, though I haven't the slightest doubt you'll stand up to it like a man."

"Thank you, sir," said Grosvenor, modestly.

The lad, Peter, was also eager to go, and he was soothed only by the promise of Mynheer Jacobus Huysman that he might join the army on the march to Lake George.

Then the leaders gave the word and the hundred foresters, fifty white and fifty red, plunged into the great northern wilderness which stretched through New York into Canada, one of the most beautiful regions on earth, and at that particular time the most dangerous, swarming with ruthless Indians and daring French partisans.

It was remarkable how soon they reached the wilds after leaving Albany. The Dutch had been along the Hudson for more than a century, and the English had come too, but all of them had clung mostly to the river. Powerful and warlike tribes roamed the great northern forests, and the French colonies in the north and the English colonies in the south had a healthy respect for the fighting powers of one another. The doubtful ground between was wide and difficult, and anyone who ventured into it now had peril always beside him.

The forest received the hundred, the white and the red, and hid them at once in its depths. It was mid-summer, but there was yet no brown on the leaves. A vast green canopy overhung the whole earth, and in every valley flowed brooks and rivers of clean water coming down from the firm hills. The few traces made by the white man had disappeared since the war. The axe was gone, and the scalp-hunters had taken its place.

Robert, vivid of mind, quickly responsive to the externals of nature, felt all the charm and majesty that the wilderness in its mightiest manifestations had for him. He did not think of danger yet, because he was surrounded by men of so much bravery and skill. He did not believe that in all the world there was such another hundred, and he was full of pride to be the comrade of such champions.

Daganoweda and the Mohawks reverted at once to the primitive, from which they had never departed much. The young Mohawk chieftain was in advance with Willet. He had a blanket but it was folded and carried in a small pack on his back. He was bare to the waist and his mighty chest was painted in warlike fashion. All his warriors were in similar attire or lack of it.

Daganoweda was happy. Robert saw his black eyes sparkling, and he continually raised his nose to scent the wind like some hunting animal. Robert knew that in his fierce heart he was eager for the sight of a hostile band. The enemy could not come too soon for Daganoweda and the Mohawks. Tayoga's face showed the same stern resolve, but the Onondaga, more spiritual than the Mohawk, lacked the fierceness of Daganoweda.

When they were well into the wilderness they stopped and held a consultation, in which Rogers, Willet, Black Rifle, Daganoweda, Robert and Tayoga shared. They were to decide a question of vital importance—their line of march. They believed that Dieskau and the main French army had not yet reached Crown Point, the great French fortress on Lake Champlain, but there was terrible evidence that the swarms of his savage allies were not only along Champlain but all around Lake George, and even farther south. Unquestionably the French partisan leaders were with them, and where and when would it be best for the American-Iroquois force to strike?

"I think," said Willet, "that St. Luc himself will be here. The Marquis de Vaudreuil, the new Governor General of Canada, knows his merit and will be sure to send him ahead of Dieskau."

Robert felt the thrill that always stirred him at the mention of St. Luc's name. Would they meet once more in the forest? He knew that if the Chevalier came all their own skill and courage would be needed to meet him on equal terms. However kindly St. Luc might feel toward him he would be none the less resolute and far-seeing in battle against the English and Americans.

"I think we should push for the western shore of Andiatarocte," said Willet. "What is your opinion, Daganoweda?"

"The Great Bear is right. He is nearly always right," replied the Mohawk. "If we go along the eastern shore and bear in toward Champlain we might be trapped by the French and their warriors. West of Andiatarocte the danger to us would not be so great, while we would have an equal chance to strike."

"Well spoken, Daganoweda," said Rogers. "I agree with you that for the present it would be wise for us to keep away from Oneadatote (the Indian name for Lake Champlain) and keep to Andiatarocte. The Indians are armed at Crown Point on Oneadatote, which was once our own Fort Saint Frederick, founded by us, but plenty of them spread to the westward and we'll be sure to have an encounter."

The others were of a like opinion, and the line of march was quickly arranged. Then they settled themselves for the night, knowing there was no haste, as the French and Indians would come to meet them, but knowing also there was always great need of caution, since if their foes were sure to come it was well to know just when they would come. The Mohawks asked for the watch, meaning to keep it with three relays of a dozen warriors each, a request that Rogers and Willet granted readily, and all the white forest runners prepared for sleep, save the strange and terrible man whom they commonly called Black Rifle.

Black Rifle, whose story was known in some form along the whole border, was a figure with a sort of ominous fascination for Robert, who could not keep from watching him whenever he was within eyeshot. He had noticed that the man was restless and troubled at Albany. The presence of so many people and the absence of the wilderness appeared to vex him. But since they had returned to the forest his annoyance and uneasiness were gone. He was confident and assured, he seemed to have grown greatly in size, and he was a formidable and menacing figure.

Black Rifle did not watch with the Mohawk sentinels, but he was continually making little trips into the forest, absences of ten or fifteen minutes, and whenever he returned his face bore a slight look of disappointment. Robert knew it was because he had found no Indian sign, but to the lad himself the proof that the enemy was not yet near gave peace. He was eager to go on the great war trail, but he was not fond of bloodshed, though to him more perhaps than to any other was given the vision of a vast war, and of mighty changes with results yet more mighty flowing from those changes. His heart leaped at the belief that he should have a part in them, no matter how small the part.

He lay on the grass with his blanket beneath him, his head on a pillow of dead leaves. Not far away was Tayoga, already asleep. They had built no fires, and as the night was dark the bronze figures of the Indian sentinels soon grew dim. Rogers and Willet also slept, but Robert still lay there awake, seeing many pictures through his wide-open eyes, Quebec, the lost Stadacona of the Mohawks, the St. Lawrence, Tandakora, the huge Ojibway who had hunted him so fiercely, St. Luc, De Courcelles, and all the others who had passed out of his life for a while, though he felt now, with the prescience of old King Hendrik, that they were coming back again. His path would lie for a long time away from cities and the gay and varied life that appealed to him so much, and would lead once more through the wilderness, which also appealed to him, but in another way. Hence when he slept his wonderfully vivid imagination did not permit him to sleep as soundly as the others.

He awoke about midnight and sat up on his blanket, looking around at the sleeping forms, dim in the darkness. He distinguished Tayoga near him, just beyond him the mighty figure of Willet, then that of Rogers, scarcely less robust, and farther on some of the white men. He did not see Black Rifle, but he felt sure that he was in the forest, looking for the signs of Indians and hoping to find them. Daganoweda also was invisible and it was likely that the fiery young Mohawk chief was outside the camp on an errand similar to that of Black Rifle. He was able to trace on the outskirts the figures of the sentinels, shadowy and almost unreal in the darkness, but he knew that the warriors of the Ganeagaono watched with eyes that saw everything even in the dusk, and listened with ears that heard everything, whether night or day.

He fell again into a doze or a sort of half sleep in which Tarenyawagon, the sender of dreams, made him see more pictures and see them much faster than he ever saw them awake. The time of dreams did not last more than half an hour, but in that period he lived again many years of his life. He passed once more through many scenes of his early boyhood when Willet was teaching him the ways of the forest. He met Tayoga anew for the first time, together they went to the house of Mynheer Jacobus Huysman in Albany, and together they went to the school of Alexander McLean; then he jumped over a long period and with Willet and Tayoga had his first meeting with St. Luc and Tandakora. He was talking to the Frenchman when he came out of that period of years which was yet less than an hour, and sat up.

All the others save the sentinels were asleep, but his delicate senses warned him that something was moving in the forest. It was at first an instinct rather than anything seen or heard, but soon he traced against the misty background of the dusk the shadowy figures of moving Mohawks. He saw the tall form of Daganoweda, who had come back from the forest, and who must have come because he had something to tell. Then he made out behind the Mohawk chief, Black Rifle, and, although he could not see his features, the white man nevertheless looked swart and menacing, an effect of the day carried over into the night.

It was Robert's first impulse to lie down again and pretend not to know, but he remembered that he was in the full confidence of them all, a trusted lieutenant, welcomed at any time, anywhere, and so remembering, he arose and walked on light foot to the place where Daganoweda stood talking with the others. The Mohawk chief gave him one favouring glance, telling him he was glad that he had come. Then he returned his attention to a young Indian warrior who stood alert, eager and listening.

"Haace (Panther), where did you find the sign that someone had passed?" he asked.

"Two miles to the north *Gao* (the wind) brought me a sound," replied Haace. "It was light. It might have been made by the boughs of *Oondote* (a tree) rubbing together, but the ears of Haace told him it was not so. I crept through *Gabada* (the forest) to the place, whence the sound had come, and lo! it and whatever had made it were gone, but I found among the bushes traces to show that moccasins had passed."

Fire leaped up in the black eyes of Daganoweda.

"Did you follow?" he asked.

"For a mile, and I found other traces of moccasins passing. The traces met and fused into one trail. All the owners of the moccasins knelt and drank at a *Dushote* (a spring), and as they were very thirsty they must have come far."

"How do you know, Haace?"

"Because the imprints of their knees were sunk deep in the earth, showing that they drank long and with eagerness. *Oneganosa* (the water) was sweet to their lips, and they would not have drunk so long had they not been walking many miles. I would have followed further, but I felt that I should come back and tell to my chief, Daganoweda, what I had seen."

"You have done well, Haace. Some day the Panther will turn into a chief."

The black eyes of the young warrior flashed with pleasure, but he said nothing, silence becoming him when he was receiving precious words of praise from his leader.

"I saw sign of the savages too," said Black Rifle. "I came upon the coals of a dead fire about two days' old. By the side of it I found these two red beads that had dropped from the leggings or moccasins of some warrior. I've seen beads of this kind before, and they all come from the French in Canada."

"Then," said Robert, speaking for the first time, "you've no doubt the enemy is near?"

"None in the world," replied Black Rifle, "but I think they're going west, away from us. It's not likely they know yet we're here, but so large a band as ours can't escape their notice long."

"If they did not find that we are here," said Daganoweda proudly, "we would soon tell it to them ourselves, and in such manner that they would remember it."

"That we would," said Black Rifle, with equal emphasis. "Now, what do you think, Daganoweda? Should we wake the Great Bear and the Mountain Wolf?"

"No, Black Rifle. Let them sleep on. They will need tomorrow the sleep they get tonight. Man lives by day in the sleep that he has at night, and we wish the eyes of them all to be clear and the arms of them all to be strong, when the hour of battle, which is not far away, comes to us."

"You're right, Daganoweda, right in both things you say, right that they need all their strength, and right that we'll soon meet St. Luc, at the head of the French and Indians, because I'm as sure as I know that I'm standing here that he's now leading 'em. Shall we finish out the night here, and then follow on their trail until we can bring 'em to battle on terms that suit us?"

"Yes, Black Rifle. That is what the Great Bear and the Mountain Wolf would say too, and so I shall not awake them. Instead, I too will go to sleep."

Daganoweda, as much a Viking as any that ever lived in Scandinavia, lay down among his men and went quickly to the home over which Tarenyawagon presided. Haace, filled with exultation that he had received the high approval of his chief, slid away among the trees on another scout, and, in like manner, the forest swallowed up Black Rifle. Once more the camp was absolutely silent, only the thin and shadowy figures of the bronze sentinels showing through the misty gloom. Robert lay down again and Tarenyawagon, the sender of dreams, held him in his spell. His excited brain, even in sleep, was a great sensitive plate, upon which pictures, vivid and highly coloured, were passing in a gorgeous procession.

Now, Tarenyawagon carried him forward and not back. They met St. Luc in battle, and it was dark and bloody. How it ended he did not know, because a veil was dropped over it suddenly, and then he was in the forest with Tayoga, fleeing for his life once more from Tandakora, De Courcelles and their savage band. Nor was it given to him to know how the pursuit ended, because the veil fell again suddenly, and when it was lifted he was in a confused and terrible battle not far from a lake, where French soldiers, American soldiers and English soldiers were mingled in horrible conflict. For some strange reason, one that he wondered at then, he stood among the French, but while he wondered, and while the combat increased in ferocity the veil slipped down and it was all gone like a mist. Then came other pictures, vivid in colour, but vague in detail, that might or might not be scenes in his future life, and he awoke at last to find the dawn had come.

Tayoga was already awake and handed him a piece of venison.

"Eat, Dagaeoga," he said, "and drink at the little spring in the wood on our right. I have learned what Haace and Black Rifle saw in the night, and we march in half an hour."

Robert did more than drink at the spring; he also bathed his face, neck and hands at the little brook that ran away from it, and although Tarenyawagon had been busy shifting his kaleidoscope before him while he slept, he was as much refreshed as if he had slumbered without dreams. The dawn, clear but hot in the great forest, brought with it zeal and confidence. They would follow on the trail of the French and Indian leaders, and he believed, as surely as a battle came, that Willet, Rogers, Daganoweda and their men would be the victors.

As soon as the brief and cold breakfast was finished the hundred departed silently. The white rangers wore forest dress dyed green that blended with the foliage, and the Mohawks still wore scarcely anything at all. It was marvellous the way in which they travelled, and it would not have been possible to say that white man or red man was the better. Robert heard now and then only the light brush of a moccasin. A hundred men flitted through the greenwood and they passed like phantoms.

In a brief hour they struck the trail that Haace had found, and followed it swiftly, but with alert eyes for ambush. Presently other little trails flowed into it, some from the east, and some from the west, and the tributaries included imprints, which obviously were those of white men. Then the whole broad trail, apparently a force of about one hundred, curved back toward the west.

"They go to Andiatarocte," said Daganoweda. "Perhaps they meet another force there."

"It's probably so," said Willet. "Knowing that our army is about to advance they wouldn't come to the southwest shore of the lake unless they were in strength. I still feel that St. Luc is leading them, but other Frenchmen are surely with him. It behoves us to use all the caution of which white men and red together are capable. In truth, there must be no ambush for us. Besides the loss which we should suffer it would be a terrible decrease of prestige for it to be known that the Mountain Wolf and Daganoweda, the most warlike of all the chiefs of the Ganeagaono, were trapped by the French and their savage allies."

Willet spoke artfully and the response was instantaneous. The great chest of Daganoweda swelled, and a spark leaped from his eyes.

"It will never be told of us," he said, "because it cannot happen. There are not enough of the French and their savage allies in the world to trap the Great Bear, the Mountain Wolf, Daganoweda, and the lads Tayoga and Dagaeoga."

Willet smiled. It was the reply that he had expected. Moreover, both his words and those of the chief were heard by many warriors, and he knew that they would respond in every fibre to the battle cry of their leader. His contemptuous allusion to the allies of the French as "savages" met a ready response in their hearts, since the nations of the Hodenosaunee considered themselves civilized and enlightened, which, in truth, they were in many respects.

Robert always remembered the place at which they held their brief council. They stood in a little grove of oaks and elms, clear of underbrush. The trees were heavy with foliage, and the leaves were yet green. The dawn had not yet fully come, and the heavens, save low down in the east, were still silver, casting a silvery veil which gave an extraordinary and delicate tint to the green of foliage. In the distance on the right was the gleam of water, silver like the skies, but it was one of the beautiful lakelets abundant in that region and not yet Andiatarocte, which was still far away. The bronze figures of the Indians, silent and impassive as they listened to their chief, fitted wonderfully into the wilderness scene, and the white men in forest green, their faces tanned and fierce, were scarcely less wild in look and figure. Robert felt once more a great thrill of pride that he had been chosen a member of such a company.

They talked less than five minutes. Then Black Rifle, alone as usual because he preferred invariably to be alone, disappeared in the woods to the right of the great trail. Three young warriors, uncommonly swift of foot, soon followed him, and three more as nimble of heel as the others, sank from sight in the forest to the left. Both right and left soon swallowed up several of the rangers also, who were not inferior as scouts and trailers to the Mohawks.

"The wings of our force are protected amply now," said Tayoga, in his precise school English. "When such eyes as those of our flankers are looking and watching, no ambush against us is possible. Now our main force will advance with certainty."

Twenty men had been sent out as scouts and the remaining eighty, eager for combat, white and red, advanced on the main trail, not fast but steadily. Now and then the cries of bird or beast, signals from the flankers, came from right or left, and the warriors with Daganoweda responded.

"They are telling us," said Tayoga to Robert, "that they have not yet found a hostile presence. The enemy has left behind him no skirmishers or rear guard. It may be that we shall not overtake them until we approach the lake or reach it."

"How do you know that we will overtake them at all, Tayoga? They may go so fast that we can't come up."

"I know it, Dagaeoga, because if they are led by St. Luc, and I think they are, they will not try to get away. If they believe we are not about to overtake them they will wait for us at some place they consider good."

"You're probably right, Tayoga, and it's likely that we'll be in battle before night. One would think there is enough country here on this continent for the whole world without having the nations making war over any part of it. As I have said before, here we are fighting to secure for an English king or a French king mountains and lakes and rivers and forests which neither of them will ever see, and of the existence of which, perhaps, they don't know."

"And as I have told you before, Dagaeoga, the mountains and lakes and rivers and forests for which the English and French kings have their people fight, belong to neither, but to the great League of the Hodenosaunee and other red nations."

"That's true, Tayoga. Sometimes I'm apt to forget it, but you know I'm a friend of the Hodenosaunee. If I had the power I'd see that never an acre of their country was filched from them by the white men."

"I know it well, Dagaeoga."

The pursuit continued all the morning, and the great trail left by the French and Indians broadened steadily. Other trails flowed into and merged with it, and it became apparent that the force pursued was larger than the force pursuing. Yet Willet, Rogers and Daganoweda did not flinch, clinging to the trail, which now led straight toward Andiatarocte.

Chapter 8

Areskoui's Favour

In the dusk of the evening the whole force came to the crest of a hill from which through a cleft they caught a glimpse of the shimmering waters of the lake, called by the Iroquois Andiatarocte, by the French, St. Sacrement, and by the English, George. It was not Robert's first view of it, but he always thrilled at the prospect.

"Both Andiatarocte and Oneadatote must be ours," he said to Tayoga. "They're too fine and beautiful to pass into possession of the French."

"What about the Hodenosaunee? Do you too forget, Dagaeoga?"

"I don't forget, Tayoga. When I said 'ours' I meant American, Hodenosaunee and English combined. You've good eyes, and so tell me if I'm not right when I say I see a moving black dot on the lake."

"You do see it, my friend, and also a second and a third. The segment of the lake that we can see from here is very narrow. At this distance it does not appear to be more than a few inches across, but I know as surely as Tododaho sits on his star watching over us, that those are canoes, or perhaps long boats, and that they belong to our enemies."

"A force on the water cooperating with that on land?"

"It seems so, Dagaeoga."

"And they mean to become the rulers of the lakes! With their army powerfully established at Crown Point, and their boats on both Andiatarocte and Oneadatote, it looks as if they were getting a great start in that direction."

"Aye, Dagaeoga. The French move faster than we. They seize what we both wish, and then it will be for us to put them out, they being in possession and entrenched. Look, Black Rifle comes out of the forest! And Haace is with him! They have something to tell!"

It was the honour and pleasure of young Lennox and the Onondaga to be present at the councils, and though they said nothing to their elders unless asked for an opinion, they always listened with eagerness to everything. Now Willet, Rogers and Daganoweda drew together, and Black Rifle and Haace, their dark eyes gleaming, made report to them.

"A strong force, at least one hundred and fifty men, lies about five miles to the north, on the shore of the lake," said Black Rifle. "About twenty Frenchmen are with it, and it is commanded by St. Luc. I saw him from the bushes. He has with him the Canadian, Dubois. De Courcelles and Jumonville are there also. At least a hundred warriors and Frenchmen are on the lake, in canoes and long boats. I saw Tandakora too."

"A formidable force," said Willet. "Do you wish to turn back, Daganoweda?"

The eyes of the Mohawk chieftain glittered and he seemed to swell both in size and stature.

"We are a hundred," he replied proudly. "What does it matter how many they are? I am astonished that the Great Bear should ask me such a question."

Willet laughed softly.

"I asked it," he said, "because I knew what the answer would be. None other could come from a Mohawk chieftain."

Again the eyes of Daganoweda glittered, but this time with pride.

"Shall we advance and attack St. Luc's force tonight?" said Willet, turning to Rogers.

"I think it would be best," replied the Mountain Wolf. "A surprise is possible tonight only. Tomorrow his scouts are sure to find that we are near. What say you, Daganoweda?"

"Tonight," replied the Mohawk chief, sententiously.

There was no further discussion, and the whole force, throwing out skirmishers, moved cautiously northward through the great, green wilderness. It was a fair night for a march, not enough moonlight to disclose them at a distance, and yet enough to show the way. Robert kept close to Tayoga, who was just behind Willet, and they bore in toward the lake, until they were continually catching glimpses of its waters through the vast curtain of the forest.

Robert's brain once more formed pictures, swift, succeeding one another like changes of light, but in high colours. The great lake set in the mountains and glimmering under the moon had a wonderful effect upon his imagination. It became for the time the core of all the mighty struggle that was destined to rage so long in North America. The belief became a conviction that whoever possessed Andiataroete and Oneadatote was destined to possess the continent.

The woods themselves, like the lake, were mystic and brooding. Their heavy foliage was ruffled by no wind, and no birds sang. The wild animals, knowing that man, fiercer than they, would soon join in mortal combat, had all fled away. Robert heard only the faint crush of moccasins as the hundred, white and red, sped onward.

An hour, and a dim light showed on a slope gentler than the rest, leading down to the lake. It was a spark so faint and vague that it might have passed to the ordinary eye as a firefly, but rangers and Mohawks knew well that it came from some portion of St. Luc's camp and that the enemy was close at hand. Then the band stopped and the three leaders talked together again for a few moments.

"I think," said Willet, "that the force on land is in touch with the one in the boats, though a close union has not been effected. In my opinion we must rush St. Luc."

"There is no other way," said Rogers.

"It is what I like best," said Daganoweda.

They promptly spread out, the entire hundred in a half circle, covering a length of several hundred yards, and the whole force advanced swiftly. Robert and Tayoga were in the centre, and as they rushed forward with the others, their moccasined feet making scarcely any sound, Robert saw the fireflies in the forest increase, multiply and become fixed. If he had felt any doubt that the camp of St. Luc was just ahead it disappeared now. The brilliant French leader too, despite all his craft, and lore of the forest, was about to be surprised.

Then he heard the sharp reports of rifles both to right and left. The horns of the advancing crescent were coming into contact with St. Luc's sentinels. Then Daganoweda, knowing that the full alarm had been given, uttered a fierce and thrilling cry and all the Mohawks took it up. It was a tremendous shout, making the blood leap and inciting to battle.

Robert, by nature kindly and merciful, felt the love of combat rising in him, and when a bullet whistled past his ear a fury against the enemy began to burn in his veins. More bullets came pattering upon the leaves, and one found its target in a ranger who was struck through the heart. Other rangers and Mohawks received wounds, but under the compelling orders of their leaders they held their fire until they were near the camp, when nearly a hundred rifles spoke together in one fierce and tremendous report.

St. Luc's sentinels and skirmishers were driven back in a minute or two, many of them falling, but his main force lay along a low ridge, timbered well, and from its shelter his men, French and Indians, sent in a rapid fire. Although taken by surprise and suffering severely in the first rush, they were able to stem the onset of the rangers and Mohawks, and soon they were uttering fierce and defiant cries, while their bullets came in showers. The rangers and Mohawks also took to cover, and the battle of the night and the wilderness was on.

Robert pulled Tayoga down, and the two lay behind a fallen log, where they listened to the whining of an occasional bullet over their heads.

"We may win," said the Onondaga gravely, "but we will not win so easily. One cannot surprise Sharp Sword (St. Luc) wholly. You may attack when he is not expecting it, but even then he will make ready for you."

"That's true," said Robert, and he felt a curious and contradictory thrill of pleasure as he listened to Tayoga. "It's not possible to take the Chevalier in a trap."

"No, Dagaeoga, it is not. I wish, for the sake of our success, that some other than he was the leader of the enemy, but Manitou has willed that my wish should not come true. Do you not think the dark shadow passing just then on the ridge was Tandakora?"

"The size indicated to me the Ojibway, and I was about to seize my rifle and fire, but it's too far for a shot with any certainty. I think our men on the horns of the crescent are driving them in somewhat."

"The shifting of the firing would prove that it is so, Dagaeoga. Our sharpshooting is much better than theirs, and in time we will push them down to the lake. But look at Black Rifle! See how he craves the battle!"

The swart ranger, lying almost flat on the ground, was creeping forward, inch by inch, and as Robert glanced at him he fired, a savage in the opposing force uttering his death yell. The ranger uttered a shout of triumph, and, shifting his position, sought another shot, his dark body drawn among the leaves and grass like that of some fierce wild animal. He fired a second time, repeated his triumphant shout and then his sliding body passed out of sight among the bushes.

Both Rogers and Willet soon joined Robert and Tayoga behind the logs where they had a good position from which to direct the battle, but Daganoweda on the right, with all of his Mohawks, was pushing forward steadily and would soon be able to pour a flanking fire into St. Luc's little army. The forest resounded now with the sharp reports of the rifles and the shouts and yells of the combatants. Bullets cut leaves and twigs, but the rangers and the Mohawks were advancing.

"Do you know how many men we have lost, Rogers?" asked Willet.

"Three of the white men and four of the Mohawks have been slain, Dave, but we're winning a success, and it's not too high a price to pay in war. If Daganoweda can get far enough around on their left flank we'll drive 'em into the lake, sure. Ah, there go the rifles of the Mohawks and they're farther forward than ever. That Mohawk chief is a bold fighter, crafty and full of fire."

"None better than he. I think they're well around the flank, Rogers. Listen to their shouts. Now, we'll make a fresh rush of our own."

They sprang from the shelter of the log, and, leading their men, rushed in a hundred yards until they dropped down behind another one. Robert and Tayoga went with them, firing as they ran, borne on by the thrill of combat, but Robert felt relief nevertheless when he settled again in the shelter of the second log and for the time being was secure from bullets.

"I think," said Willet to Rogers, "that I'll go around toward the left, where the flanking force is composed mostly of rangers, and press in there with all our might. If the two horns of the crescent are able to enclose St. Luc, and you charge at the centre, we should win the victory soon."

"It's the right idea, Dave," said Rogers. "When we hear your shots and a shout or two we'll drive our hardest."

"I'd like to take Tayoga and Robert with me."

"They're yours. They're good and brave lads, and I'll need 'em, but you'll need 'em too. How many more of the men here will you want?"

"About ten."

"Then take them too."

Willet, with Robert, Tayoga and the ten, began a cautious circuit in the darkness toward the western horn of the crescent, and for a few minutes left the battle in the distance. As they crept through the bushes, Robert heard the shouts and shots of both sides and saw the pink flashes of flame as the rifles were fired. In the darkness it seemed confused and vague, but he knew that it was guided by order and precision. Now and then a spent bullet pattered upon the leaves, and one touched him upon the wrist, stinging for a moment or two, but doing no harm.

But as they passed farther and farther to the west the noise of the battle behind them gradually sank, while that on the left horn of the crescent grew.

In a few more minutes they would be with the rangers who were pressing forward so strenuously at that point, and as Robert saw dusky figures rise from the bushes in front of them he believed they were already in touch. Instead a dozen rifles flashed in their faces. One of the rangers went down, shot through the head, dead before he touched the ground, three more sustained slight wounds, including Robert who was grazed on the shoulder, and all of them gave back in surprise and consternation. But Willet, shrewd veteran of the forest, recovered himself quickly.

"Down, men! Down and give it back to 'em!" he cried. "They've sent out a flanking force of their own! It was clever of St. Luc!"

All the rangers dropped on their faces instantly, but as they went down they gave back the fire of the flanking party. Robert caught a glimpse of De Courcelles, who evidently was leading it, and pulled trigger on him, but the Frenchman turned aside at that instant, and his bullet struck a St. Regis Indian who was just behind him. Now the return volley of the rangers was very deadly. Two Frenchmen were slain here and four warriors, and De Courcelles, who had not expected on his circling movement to meet with a new force, was compelled to give back. He and his warriors quickly disappeared in the forest, leaving their dead behind them, and Willet with his own little force moved on triumphantly, soon joining his strength to that of the rangers on the left.

The combined force hurled itself upon St. Luc's flank and crumpled it up, at the same time uttering triumphant shouts which were answered from the right and centre, rangers and Mohawks on all fronts now pressing forward, and sending in their bullets from every covert. So fierce was their attack that they created the effect of double or triple their numbers, and St. Luc's French and Indians were driven down the slope to the edge of the lake, where the survivors were saved by the second band in the canoes and great boats.

The defeated men embarked quickly, but not so quickly that several more did not fall in the water. At this moment Robert saw St. Luc, and he never admired him more. He, too, was in forest green, but it was of the finest cloth, trimmed with green yet darker. A cap of silky fur was on his head, and his hair was clubbed in a queue behind. March and forest battle had not dimmed the cleanliness and neatness of his attire, and, even in defeat, he looked the gallant chevalier, without fear and without reproach.

St. Luc was in the act of stepping into one of the long boats when a ranger beside Robert raised his rifle and took aim squarely at the Frenchman's heart. It was not a long shot and the ranger would not have missed, but young Lennox at that moment stumbled and fell against him, causing the muzzle of his weapon to be deflected so much that his bullet struck the uncomplaining water. Robert's heart leaped up as he saw the chevalier spring into the boat, which the stalwart Indians paddled swiftly away.

The entire Indian fleet now drew together, and it was obviously making for one of the little islands, so numerous in Andiatarocte, where it would be safe until the English and Americans built or brought boats of their own and disputed the rulership of the lake. But the rangers and the Mohawks, eager to push the victory, rushed down to the water's edge and sent after the flying fleet bullets which merely dropped vainly in the water. Then they ceased, and, standing there, uttered long thrilling shouts of triumph.

Robert had never beheld a more ferocious scene but he felt in it, too, a sort of fierce and shuddering attraction. His veins were still warm with the fire of battle, and his head throbbed wildly. Everything took on strange and fantastic shapes, and colours became glaring and violent. The moonlight, pouring down on the lake, made it a vast sea of crumbling silver, the mountains on the farther shores rose to twice or thrice their height, and the forests on the slopes and crests were an immense and unbroken curtain, black against the sky.

Five or six hundred yards away hovered the Indian fleet, the canoes and boats dark splotches upon the silver surface of the water. The island upon which they intended to land was just beyond them, but knowing that they were out of rifle range they had paused to look at the victorious force, or as much of it as showed itself, and to send back the defiant yells of a defeated, but undaunted band.

Robert clearly saw St. Luc again, standing up in his boat, and apparently giving orders to the fleet, using his small sword, as a conductor wields a baton, though the moonlight seemed to flash in fire along the blade as he pointed it here and there. He beheld something fierce and unconquerable in the man's attitude and manner. He even imagined that he could see his face, and he knew that the eye was calm, despite defeat and loss. St Luc, driven from the field, would be none the less dangerous than if he had been victor upon it.

The whole Indian fleet formed in a half circle and the Chevalier ceased to wave orders with his sword. Then he drew himself up, stood rigidly erect, despite his unstable footing, faced the land, and, using the sword once more, gave a soldier's salute to the foe. The act was so gallant, so redolent of knightly romance that despite themselves the rangers burst into a mighty cheer, and the Mohawks, having the Indian heart that always honoured a brave foe, uttered a long and thrilling whoop of approval.

Robert, carried away by an impulse, sprang upon a rock and whirled his rifle around his head in an answering salute. St. Luc evidently saw, and evidently, too, he recognized Robert, as he lifted his sword in rejoinder. Then the Indians, bent to their paddles, and the fleet, hanging together, swept around the island and out of sight. But they knew that the French and Indian force landed there, as fires soon blazed upon its heavily-wooded crest, and they saw dusky figures passing and repassing before the flames.

"The victory has been given to us tonight," said Tayoga gravely to Robert, "but Manitou has not allowed us to complete it. Few triumph over St. Luc, and, though his manner may have been gay and careless, his heart burns to win back what he has lost."

"I take it you're right, Tayoga," said Robert. "His is a soul that will not rest under defeat, and I fancy St. Luc on the island is a great danger. He can get at us and we can't get at him."

"It is true, Dagaeoga. If we strike we must strike quickly and then be off. This, for the time being, is the enemy's country, yet I think our leaders will not be willing to withdraw. Daganoweda, I know, will want to push the battle and to attack on the island."

The Onondaga's surmise was correct. The triumph of the rangers and the Mohawks, although not complete, was large, as at least one-third of St. Luc's force was slain, and the three leaders alike were eager to make it yet larger, having in mind that in some way they could yet reach the French and Indian force on the island. So they built their own fires on the slope and the Mohawks began to sing songs of triumph, knowing that they would infuriate the foe, and perhaps tempt him to some deed of rashness.

"Did you see anything of Tandakora?" asked Robert of Tayoga. "I know it's no crime to wish that he fell."

"No, it's no crime, Dagaeoga," replied the Onondaga soberly, "and my wish is the same as yours, but this time we cannot have it. I saw him in one of the boats as they passed around the island."

The two then sat by one of the fires and ate venison, thankful that they had escaped with only slight wounds, and as there was no immediate call for their services they wrapped themselves in their blankets, by and by, and went to sleep. When Robert awoke, the morning was about half gone and the day was bright and beautiful beyond compare.

Although the hostile forces still confronted each other there was no other evidence of war, and Robert's first feelings were less for man and more for the magnificence of nature. He had never seen Andiatarocte, the matchless gem of the mountains, more imposing and beautiful. Its waters, rippling gently under the wind, stretched far away, silver or gold, as the sunlight fell. The trees and undergrowth on the islands showed deepest green, and the waving leaves shifted and changed in colour with the changing sky. Far over all was a deep velvet blue arch, tinged along the edges with red or gold.

Keenly sensitive to nature, it was a full minute before young Lennox came back to earth, and the struggles of men. Then he found Tayoga looking at him curiously.

"It is good!" said the Onondaga, flinging out his hand. "In the white man's Bible it is said that Manitou created the world in six days and rested on the seventh, but in the unwritten book of the Hodenosaunee it is said that he created Andiatarocte and Oneadatote, and then reposed a bit, and enjoyed his work before he went on with his task."

"I can well believe you, Tayoga. If I had created a lake like George and another like Champlain I should have stopped work, and gloried quite a while over my achievement. Has the enemy made any movement while we slept?"

"None, so far as our people can tell. They have brought part of their fleet around to the side of the island facing us. I count six large boats and twenty canoes there. I also see five fires, and I have no doubt that many of the warriors are sleeping before them. Despite losses, his force is still larger than ours, but I do not think St. Luc, brave as he is, would come back to the mainland and risk a battle with us."

"Then we must get at him somehow, Tayoga. We must make our blow so heavy that it will check Dieskau for a while and give Colonel Johnson's army time to march."

"Even so, Dagaeoga. Look at the Mountain Wolf. He has a pair of field glasses and he is studying the island."

Rogers stood on a knoll, and he was making diligent use of his glasses, excellent for the time. He took them from his eyes presently, and walked down to Robert and Tayoga.

"Would you care to have a look?" he said to Robert.

"Thank you, I'd like it very much," replied young Lennox eagerly.

The powerful lenses at once brought the island very near, and trees and bushes became detached from the general mass, until he saw between them the French and Indian camp. As Tayoga had asserted, many of the warriors were asleep on the grass. When nothing was to be done, the Indian could do it with a perfection seldom attained by anybody else. Tandakora was sitting on a fallen log, looking at the mainland.

As usual, he was bare to the waist, and painted frightfully. Not far away a Frenchman was sleeping on a cloak, and Robert was quite sure that it was De Courcelles. St. Luc himself was visible toward the centre of the island. He, too, stood upon a knoll, and he, too, had glasses with which he was studying his foe.

"The command of the water," said Rogers, "is heavily against us. If we had only been quick enough to build big boats of our own, the tale to be told would have been very different."

"And if by any means," said Willet, "we contrive to drive them from the island, they can easily retreat in their fleet to another, and they could repeat the process indefinitely. George has many islands."

"Then why not capture their fleet?" said Robert in a moment of inspiration.

Rogers and Willet looked at each other.

"It's queer we didn't think of that before," said the hunter.

"'Twill be an attempt heavy with danger," said Rogers.

"So it will, my friend, but have we shirked dangers? Don't we live and sleep with danger?"

"I was merely stating the price, Dave. I was making no excuse for shirking."

"I know it, old friend. Whoever heard of Robert Rogers shunning danger? We'll have a talk with Daganoweda, and you, Robert, since you suggested the plan, and you, Tayoga, since you've a head full of wisdom, shall be present at the conference."

The Mohawk chieftain came, and, when the scheme was laid before him, he was full of eagerness for it.

"Every one of my warriors will be glad to go," he said, "and I, as becomes my place, will lead them. It will be a rare deed, and the news of it will be heard with wonder and admiration in all our castles."

He spoke in the language of the Ganeagaono, which all the others understood perfectly, and the two white leaders knew they could rely upon the courage and enthusiasm of the Mohawks.

"It depends upon the sun whether we shall succeed tonight or not," said Tayoga, glancing up at the heavens, "and at present he gives no promise of favouring us. The sun, as you know, Dagaeoga, is with us the Sun God, also, whom we call Areskoui, or now and then Aieroski, and who is sometimes almost the same as Manitou."

"I know," said Robert, who had an intimate acquaintance with the complex Pantheon of the Hodenosaunee, which was yet not so complex after all, and which also had in its way the elements of the Christian religion in all their beauty and majesty.

Tayoga gazed out upon Andiatarocte.

Robert's eyes followed the Onondaga's.

"It's true," he said, "that the Sun God, your Areskoui, and mine, too, for that matter, makes no promise to us. The warriors of the Hodenosaunee have looked upon Andiatarocte for many centuries, but doubtless there has never been a day before when any one of them saw it more beautiful and more gleaming than it is now."

"Yes, Dagaeoga, the waters slide and ripple before the wind, and they are blue and green, and silver and gold, and all the shades between, as the sunlight shifts and falls, but it is many hours until night and Areskoui may be of another mind by then."

"I know it, Tayoga. I remember the two storms on Champlain, and I don't forget how quickly they can come on either lake. I'm not praying for any storm, but I do want a dark and cloudy night."

"Dagaeoga should not be too particular," said Tayoga, his eyes twinkling. "He has told Areskoui exactly what kind of a night he wishes, but I think he will have to take just the kind of a night that Areskoui may send."

"I don't dispute it, Tayoga, but when you're praying to the Sun God it's as well to pray for everything you want."

"We'll watch Areskoui with more than common interest today, you and I, Dagaeoga, but the warriors of the Ganeagaono, even as the Hurons, the Abenakis and the Ojibways, will go to sleep. Behold, Daganoweda even now lies down upon his blanket!"

The Mohawk chief, as if sure that nothing more of importance was going to happen that day, spread his fine green blanket upon some leaves, and then settling himself in an easy posture upon it, fell asleep, while many of his warriors, and some of the rangers too, imitated his example. But Robert and Tayoga had slept enough, and, though they moved about but little, they were all eyes and ears.

Scouts had been sent far up and down the shores of the lake, and they reported that no other band was near, chance leaving the issue wholly to the two forces that now faced each other. Yet the morning, while remaining of undimmed beauty, had all the appearance of ease, even of laziness. Several of the rangers went down to the edge of the lake, and, removing their clothing, bathed in the cool waters. Then they lay on the slope until their bodies dried, dressed themselves, and waited patiently for the night.

The French and Indians, seeing them engaged in a pleasant task, found it well to do likewise. The waters close to the island were filled with Frenchmen, Canadians and Indians, wading, swimming and splashing water, the effect in the distance being that of boys on a picnic and enjoying it to the utmost.

Robert took a little swim himself, though he kept close to the shore, and felt much refreshed by it. When he had been dried by the sun and was back in his clothes, he stretched himself luxuriously near the rangers on the slope, taking an occasional glance at the sun from under his sheltering hand.

"There is a little mist in the southwest," he said, after a long time, to Tayoga. "Do you think it possible that Areskoui will change his mind and cease to flood the world with beams?"

"I see the vapour," replied Tayoga, looking keenly. "It is just a wisp, no larger than a feather from the wing of an eagle, but it seems to grow. Areskoui changes his mind as he pleases. Who are we to question the purposes of the Sun God? Yet I take it, Dagaeoga, that the chance of a night favourable to our purpose has increased."

"I begin to think, Tayoga, that Areskoui does, in truth, favour us, through no merit of ours, but perhaps because of a lack of merit in Tandakora and De Courcelles. Yet, as I live, you're right when you say the cloud of mist or vapour is growing. Far in the southwest, so it seems to me, the air becomes dim. I know it, because I can't see the forests there as distinctly as I did a half hour ago, and I hold that the change in Areskoui's heart is propitious to our plan."

"A long speech, but your tongue always moves easily, Dagaeoga, and what you say is true. The mist increases fast, and before he goes down on the other side of the world the Sun God will be veiled in it. Then the night will come full of clouds, and dark. Look at Andiatar-octe, and you will see that it is so."

The far shores of the lake were almost lost in the vapours, only spots of forest green appearing now and then, a veil of silver being over the eastern waters. The island on which St. Luc lay encamped was growing indistinct, and the fires there shone through a white mist.

Tayoga stood up and gazed intently at the sun, before which a veil had been drawn, permitting his eyes to dwell on its splendours, now coming in a softened and subdued light.

"All the omens are favourable," he said. "The heart of Areskoui has softened toward us, knowing that we are about to go on a great and perilous venture. Tonight Tododaho on his star will also look down kindly on us. He will be beyond the curtain of the clouds, and we will not see him, but I know that it will be so, because I feel in my heart that it must be so. You and I, Dagaeoga, are only two, and among the many on this earth two can count for little, but the air is full of spirits, and it may be that they have heard our prayers. With the unseen powers the prayers of the humble and the lowly avail as much as those of the great and mighty."

His eyes bore the rapt and distant expression of the seer, as he continued to gaze steadily at the great silver robe that hung before the face of Areskoui's golden home. Splendid young warrior that he was, always valiant and skilful in battle, there was a spiritual quality in Tayoga that often showed. The Onondagas were the priestly nation of the Hodenosaunee and upon him had descended a mantle that was, in a way, the mantle of a prophet. Robert, so strongly permeated by Indian lore and faith, really believed, for a moment, that his comrade saw into the future.

But not the white youth and the red youth alone bore witness to the great change, the phenomenon even, that Areskoui was creating. Both Rogers and Willet had looked curiously at the sun, and then had looked again. Daganoweda, awaking, stood up and gazed in the intent and reverential manner that Tayoga had shown. The soul of the Mohawk chieftain was fierce. He existed for the chase and war, and had no love beyond them. There was nothing spiritual in his nature, but none the less he was imbued with the religion of his race, and believed that the whole world, the air, the forests, the mountains, and the lakes were peopled with spirits, good or bad. Now he saw one of the greatest of them all, Areskoui, the Sun God himself, in action and working a miracle.

The untamable soul of Daganoweda was filled with wonder and admiration. Not spiritual, he was nevertheless imaginative to a high degree. Through the silver veil which softened the light of the sun more and more, permitting his eyes to remain fixed upon it, he saw a mighty figure in the very centre of that vast globe of light, a figure that grew and grew until he knew it was Areskoui, the Sun God himself.

A shiver swept over the powerful frame of Daganoweda. The Mohawk chieftain, whose nerves never quivered before the enemy, felt as a little child in the presence of the mighty Sun God. But his confidence returned. Although the figure of Areskoui continued to grow, his face became benevolent. He looked down from his hundred million miles in the void, beheld the tiny figure of Daganoweda standing upon the earth, and smiled. Daganoweda knew that it was so, because he saw the smile with his own eyes, and, however perilous the venture might be, he knew then it could not fail, because Areskoui himself had smiled upon it.

The great veil of mist deepened and thickened and was drawn slowly across all the heavens. Robert felt a strange thrill of awe. It was, in very truth, to him a phenomenon, more than an eclipse, not a mere passage of the moon before the sun for which science gave a natural account, but a sudden combination of light and air that had in it a tinge of the supernatural.

All the Mohawks were awake now, everybody was awake and everybody watched the sun, but perhaps it was Daganoweda who saw most. No tincture of the white man's religion had ever entered his mind to question any of his Iroquois beliefs. There was Areskoui, in the very centre of the sun, mighty and shining beyond belief, and still smiling across his hundred million miles at the earth upon which Daganoweda stood. But, all the while he was drawing his silver robe, fold on fold, thicker and tighter about himself, and his figure grew dim.

One after another the distant islands in the lake sank out of sight, and the fires were merely a faint red glow on the one occupied by St. Luc. Over the waters the vapours swept in great billows and columns. Daganoweda drew a great breath. The sun itself was fading. Areskoui had shown his face long enough and now he meant to make the veil between himself and man impenetrable. He became a mere shadow, the mists and vapours rolled up wave on wave, and he was gone entirely. Then night came down over mountains, forest and Andiatarocte. The last fire on St Luc's island had been permitted to die out, and it, too, sank into the mists and vapours with the others, and was invisible to the watchers on the mainland slope.

But little could be seen of Andiatarocte itself, save occasional glimmers of silver under the floating clouds. Not a star was able to come out, and all the lake and country about it were wrapped in a heavy greyish mist which seemed to Robert to be surcharged with some kind of exciting solution. But the three leaders, Rogers, Willet and Daganoweda, gathered in a close council, did not yet give any order save that plenty of food be served to rangers and Mohawks alike.

Thus a long time was permitted to pass and the mists and vapours over Andiatarocte deepened steadily. No sound came from St. Luc's island, nor was any fire lighted there. For all the darkness showed, it had sunk from sight forever. It was an hour till midnight when the three leaders gave their orders and the chosen band began to prepare. Robert had begged to be of the perilous number. He could never endure it if Tayoga went and not he, and Willet, though reluctant, was compelled to consent. Willet himself was going also, and so was Daganoweda, of course, and Black Rifle, but Rogers was to remain behind, in command of the force on the slope.

Thirty rangers and thirty Mohawks, all powerful swimmers, were chosen, and every man stripped to the skin. Firearms, of necessity, were left behind with the clothes, but everyone buckled a belt around his bare body, and put in it his hatchet and hunting knife. The plan was to swim silently for the island and then trust to courage, skill and fortune. Buoyed up by the favour of Areskoui, who had worked a miracle for them, the sixty dropped into the water, and began their night of extreme hazard.

Chapter 9

On Andiatarocte

Robert, as was natural, swam by the side of Tayoga, his comrade in so many hardships and dangers, and, after the long period of tense and anxious waiting, he felt a certain relief that the start was made, even though it was a start into the very thick of peril.

Willet was on the right wing of the swimming column and Daganoweda was on the left, the white leader and the red understanding each other thoroughly, and ready to act in perfect unison. Beneath the hovering mists and above the surface of the water, the bronze faces of the Mohawks and the brown faces of the rangers showed, eager and fierce. There was not one among them whose heart did not leap, because he was chosen for such a task.

Robert felt at first a chill from the water, as Andiatarocte, set among its northern mountains, is usually cold, but after a few vigorous strokes the blood flowed warm in his veins again, and the singular exciting quality with which the mists and vapours seemed to be surcharged entered his mind also. The great pulse in his throat leaped, and the pulses in his temples beat hard. His sensitive and imaginative mind, that always went far ahead of the present, had foreseen all the dangers, and, physically at least, he had felt keen apprehension when he stepped into the lake. But now it was gone. Youth and the strong comrades around him gave imagination another slant, allowing it to paint wonderful deeds achieved, and victory made complete.

His eyes, which in his condition of superheated fancy enlarged or intensified everything manifold, saw a flash of light near him. It was merely Tayoga drawing his knife from his belt and putting the blade between his teeth, where the whitish mist that served for illumination had thrown back a reflection. He glanced farther down the swimming line and saw that many others had drawn their hunting knives and had clasped them between their teeth, where they would be ready for instant use. Mechanically he did likewise, and he felt something flow from the cold steel into his body, heating his blood and inciting him to battle. He knew at the time that it was only imagination, but the knowledge itself took nothing from the power of the sensation. He became every instant more eager for combat.

It seemed that Tayoga caught glimpses of his comrade's face and with his Onondaga insight read his mind.

"Dagaeoga, who wishes harm to nobody, now craves the battle, nevertheless," he said, taking the knife from between his teeth for a moment or two.

"I'm eager to be in it as soon as I can in order to have it over as soon as we can," said Robert, imitating him.

"You may think the answer wholly true, though it is only partly so. There come times when the most peaceful feel the incitement of war."

"I believe it's the strangeness of the night, the quality of the air we breathe and that singular veiling of the sun just when we wished it, and as if in answer to our prayers."

"That is one of the reasons, Dagaeoga. We cannot see Areskoui, because he is on the other side of the world now, but he turned his face toward us and bade us go and win. Nor can we see Tododaho on his star, because of the mighty veil that has been drawn between, but the great Onondaga chief who went away to eternal life more than four hundred centuries ago still watches over his own, and I know that his spirit is with us."

"Can you see the island yet, Tayoga? My eyes make out a shadow in the mist, but whether it's land, or merely a darker stream of vapour, I can't tell."

"I am not sure either, but I do not think it is land. The island is four hundred yards away, and the mist is so thick that neither the earth itself nor the trees and bushes would yet appear through it."

"You must be right, and we're swimming slowly, too, to avoid any splashing of the water that would alarm St. Luc's sentinels. At what point do you think we'll approach the island, Tayoga?"

"From the north, because if they are expecting us at all they will look for us from the west. See, Daganoweda already leads in the curve toward the north."

"It's so, Tayoga. I can barely make out his figure, but he has certainly changed our course. I don't know whether it's my fancy or not, but I seem to feel a change, too, in the quality of the air about us. A stream of new and stronger air is striking upon the right side of my face, that is, the side toward the south."

"It is reality and not your fancy, Dagaeoga. A wind has begun to blow out of the south and west. But it does not blow away the vapours. It merely sends the columns and waves of mist upon one another, fusing them together and then separating them again. It is the work of Areskoui. Though there is now a world between us and him he still watches over us and speeds us on to a great deed. So, Dagaeoga, the miracle of the sky is continued into the night, and for us. Areskoui will clothe us in a mighty blanket of mist and water and fire."

The Onondaga's face was again the rapt face of a seer, and his words were heavy with import like those of a prophet of old.

"Listen!" he said. "It is Areskoui himself who speaks!"

Robert shivered, but it was not from the cold of the water. It was because a mighty belief that Tayoga spoke the truth had entered his soul, and what the Onondaga believed he, too, believed with an equal faith.

"I hear," he replied.

A low sound, deep and full of menace, came out of the south, and rumbled over Andiatarocte and all the mountains about it. It was the voice of thunder, but Tayoga and Robert felt that its menace was not for them.

"One of the sudden storms of the lake comes," said the Onondaga. "The mists will be driven away now, but the clouds in their place will be yet darker, Areskoui still holds his shrouding blanket before us."

"But the lightning which will come soon, Tayoga, and which you meant, when you spoke of fire, will not that unveil us to the sentinels of St. Luc?"

"No, because only our heads are above the water and at a little distance they are blended with it. Yet the same flashes of fire will disclose to us their fleet and show us our way to it. Andiatarocte has already felt the wind in the south and is beginning to heave and surge."

Robert felt the lake lift him up on a wave and then drop him down into a hollow, but he was an expert swimmer, and he easily kept his head on the surface. The thunder rumbled again. There was no crash, it was more like a deep groan coming up out of the far south. The waters of Andiatarocte lifted themselves anew, and wave after wave pursued one another northward. A wind began to blow, straight and strong, but heavy floating clouds came in its train, and the darkness grew so intense that Robert could not see the face of Tayoga beside him.

Daganoweda called from the north end of the swimming line, and the word was passed from Mohawk and ranger until Willet at the south end replied. All were there. Not a man, white or red, had dropped out, and not one would.

"In a minute or two the lightning will show the way," said Tayoga.

As the last word left his lips a flaming sword blazed across the lake, and disclosed the island, wooded and black, not more than two hundred yards distant, and the dim shadows of canoes and boats huddled against the bank. Then it was gone and the blackness, thicker and heavier than ever, settled down over island, lake and mountain. But Robert, Tayoga and all the others had seen the prize they were seeking, and their course lay plain before them now.

Robert's emotion was so intense and his mind was concentrated so powerfully upon the object ahead that he was scarcely conscious of the fact that he was swimming. An expert in the water, he kept afloat without apparent effort, and the fact that he was one of fifty all doing the same thing gave him additional strength and skill. The lightning flashed again, blue now, almost a bar of violet across the sky, tinting the waters of the lake with the same hue, and he caught another glimpse of the Indian fleet drawn up against the shore, and of the Indian sentinels, some sitting in the boats, and others standing on the land.

Then the wind strengthened, and he felt the rain upon his face. It was a curious result, but he sank a little deeper in the water to shelter himself from the storm. Light waves ran upon the surface of the lake, and his body lifted with them. The fleet could not be more than a hundred yards away now, and his heart began to throb hard with the thought of imminent action. Yet he knew that he was in a mystic and unreal world. His singular position, the night, the coming of the storm with its swift alternations of light and blackness, heated his blood and imagination until he saw many things that were not, and did not see some that were. He saw a triumph and the capture of the Indian fleet, and in his eager anticipation he failed to see the dangers just ahead.

The air grew much colder and the rain beat upon his face like hail. The thunder which had rumbled almost incessantly, like a mighty groaning, now ceased entirely, and the last flash of lightning burned across the lake. It showed the fleet of the foe not more than fifty yards away now, and, so far as Robert could tell, the Indian sentinels had yet taken no alarm. Three were crouched in the boats with their blankets drawn about their shoulders to protect them from the cold rain, and the four who had been standing on the land were huddled under the trees with their blankets wrapped about their bodies also.

"Do you think we'll really reach the fleet unobstructed?" whispered Robert to Tayoga.

"It does not seem possible," the Onondaga whispered back. "The favour of Areskoui is great to us, but the miracle he works in our behalf could hardly go so far. Now the word comes from both Daganoweda and the Great Bear, and we swim faster. The rain, too, grows and it drives in sheets, but it is well for us that it does so. Rifles and muskets cannot be used much in the storm, but our knives and tomahawks can. Perhaps this rain is only one more help that Areskoui has sent to us."

The swimming line was approaching fast, and a few more strokes would bring them to the canoes, when one of the warriors on the land suddenly came from the shelter of his tree, leaned forward a little and peered intently from under his shading hand. He had seen at last the dark heads on the dark water, and springing back he uttered a fierce whoop.

"Now we swim for our lives and victory!" said Tayoga.

Willet and Daganoweda, attempting no farther concealment, cried to their men to hurry. In a moment more the boarders were among the boats. Robert shut his eyes as the knives flashed in the dusk, and the dead bodies of the sentinels were thrown into the water. He seized the side of a long canoe, which he gladly found to be empty, pulled himself in, to discover Tayoga sitting just in front of him, paddle in hand also. All around him men, red and white, were laying hold of canoes and boats and at the edge of the water the sentinels were attacking.

On the island a terrific turmoil arose. Despite the rain a great fire flared up as the forces of St. Luc kindled some bonfire anew, and they heard him shouting in French and more than one Indian language to his men. They heard also heavy splashes, as the warriors leaped into the water to defend their fleet. A dark figure rose up by the side of the boat in which young Lennox and his comrade sat. The knife of Tayoga flashed and Robert involuntarily shut his eyes. When he opened them again the dark figure was gone, and the knife was back in the Onondaga's belt.

St. Luc, although surprised again, was rallying his men fast. The French were shouting their battle cries, the Indians were uttering the war whoop, as they poured down to the edge of the island, leaping into the lake to save their fleet. The water was filled with dusky forms, Mohawk and Huron met in the death grasp, and sometimes they found their fate beneath the waters, held tight in the arms of each other. Confused and terrible struggles for the boats ensued, and in the darkness and rain it was knife and hatchet and then paddles, which many snatched up and used as clubs.

Above the tumult Robert heard the trumpet tones of St. Luc cheering his men and directing them. Once he caught a glimpse of him standing up to his knees in the water, waving the small gold-hilted sword that he carried so often, and he might have brought him down with a bullet had he carried a rifle, but he would have had no thought of drawing trigger upon him. Then he was gone in the mist, and the gigantic painted figure of Tandakora appeared in his place for a moment. Then the mists closed in for a second time, and he saw through it only fleeting forms and flashes of fire, when rifles and muskets were fired by the enemy.

His feeling of unreality increased. The elements themselves had conspired to lend to everything a tinge weird and sinister to the last degree. There was a lull for a little in the wind and rain, but Andiatarocte was heaving, and great waves were chasing one another over the surface of the water, after threatening to overturn the canoes and boats for which both sides fought so fiercely. The thunder began to mutter again, furnishing a low and menacing under note like the growling of cannon in battle. Occasional streaks of lightning flashed anew across the lake, revealing the strained faces of the combatants and tingeing the surface of the waters with red. Then both thunder and lightning ceased again, and wind and rain came with a renewed sweep and roar.

Robert and Tayoga still occupied their captured long boat alone, and they hovered near the edge of the battle, not ready to withdraw with the prize until their entire force, whether victor or vanquished, turned back from the island. Now and then Robert struck with his tomahawk at some foe who came swimming to the attack, but, as the violence of the storm grew, both he and Tayoga were compelled to take up their paddles, and use all their skill to keep the boat from being capsized. The shouting and the shots and the crash of the storm made a turmoil from which he could detach little, but he knew that the keen eyes of the Onondaga, dusk or no dusk, confusion or no confusion, would pierce to the heart of things.

"What do you see, Tayoga?" he exclaimed. "How goes the battle?"

"I cannot see as much as I wish, Dagaeoga, but it turns in our favour. I saw the Great Bear just then in a boat, and when the lightning flared last I saw Daganoweda in another. Beware, Dagaeoga! Beware!"

His shout of warning was just in time. A figure rose out of the water beside their boat, and aimed a frightful blow at him with a tomahawk. It was an impulse coming chiefly from the words of Tayoga, but Robert threw himself flat in the boat and the keen weapon whistled through the empty air. He sprang up almost instantly, and, not having time to draw either hatchet or knife, struck with his clenched fist at the dark face glaring over the side of the boat. It was a convulsive effort, and the fist was driven home with more than natural power. The figure disappeared like a stone dropped into the water.

Despite the dusk, Robert had seen the countenance, and he recognized the sinister features of the French spy whom they had tried to catch in Albany, the man whose name he had no doubt was Achille Garay. He had felt a fierce joy when his fist came into contact with his face, but he was quite sure the spy had not perished. Hardy men of the wilderness did not die from a blow with the naked hand. The water would revive him, and he would quickly come up again to fight elsewhere.

Tayoga leaned over suddenly and pulled in a dusky figure dripping with wounds, a Mohawk warrior, hurt badly and sure to have been lost without quick help. There was no time to bind up his hurts, as the combat was growing thicker and fiercer, and they drove their boat into the middle of it, striking out with hatchet and knife whenever an enemy came within reach.

A shrill whistle presently rose over all the noise of battle, and it seemed to have a meaning in it.

"What is it, Tayoga?" shouted Robert.

"It is the whistle of the Great Bear himself, and I have no doubt it is a signal to retire. Reason tells me, too, that it is so. We have captured as much of the enemy's fleet as we may at this time, and we must make off with it lest we be destroyed ourselves."

The whistle still rose shrill, penetrating and insistent, and at the other end of the line Daganoweda began to shout commands to the Ganeagaono. Robert and Tayoga paddled away from the island, and on either side of them they saw canoes and boats going in the same direction. Flashes of fire came from the land, where the French and Indians, raging up and down, sought to destroy those who had captured most of their fleet. But the darkness made their aim uncertain, almost worthless, and only two or three of the invaders were struck, none mortally. Twenty canoes and boats were captured, and the venture was a brilliant success. Areskoui had not worked his miracles in vain, and a triumphant shout, very bitter for the enemy, burst from rangers and Mohawks. Willet, alone in a captured canoe, paddled swiftly up and down the line, seeing like a good commander what the losses and gains might be, and also for personal reasons peering anxiously through the dusk for something that he hoped to see. Suddenly he uttered a low cry of pleasure.

"Ah, it is you, Robert!" he exclaimed. "And you, Tayoga! And both unhurt!"

"Yes, except for scratches," replied Robert. "I think that Tayoga's Areskoui was, in very truth, watching over us, and watching well. In the darkness and confusion all the bullets passed us by, but I was attacked at the boat's edge by a Frenchman, the one whom I saw in Albany, the one who I am quite sure is Achille Garay. Luck saved me."

"Some day we'll deal with that Achille Garay," said the hunter, "but now we must draw off in order, and see to our wounded."

He passed on in his canoe, and met Daganoweda in another. The young Mohawk chieftain was dripping from seven wounds, but they were all in the shoulders and forearms and were slight, and they were a source of pride to him rather than inconvenience.

"'Twas well done, Daganoweda," said Willet.

"It is a deed of which the Ganeagaono in their castles will hear with pride," said the Mohawk. "The fleet of Onontio and his warriors, or most of it, is ours, and we dispute with them the rulership of the lake."

"Great results, worthy of such a risk. I'm sorry we didn't take every boat and canoe, because then we might have cooped up St. Luc on his island, and have destroyed his entire force."

"It is given to no man, Great Bear, to achieve his whole wish. We have done as much as we hoped, and more than we expected."

"True, Daganoweda! True! What are your losses?"

"Nine of my men have been slain, but they fell as warriors of the Ganeagaono would wish to fall. Two more will die and others are hurt, but they need not be counted, since they will be in any other battle that may come. And what have you suffered, Great Bear?"

"Five of the rangers have gone into the hereafter, another will go, and as for the hurt, like your Mohawks they'll be good for the next fight, no matter how soon it comes. We'd better go along the line, Daganoweda, and caution them all to be steady. The wind and rain are driving hard and Andiatarocte is heaving mightily. We don't want to lose a man or a canoe."

"No, Great Bear, after taking the fleet in battle we must not give it up to the waters of the lake. See, the flare of a great fire on the mainland! The Mountain Wolf and the rest of the men await us with joy."

Then Daganoweda achieved a feat which Willet himself would have said a moment before was impossible. He stood suddenly upright in his rocking canoe, whirled his paddle around his head, and uttered a tremendous shout, long and thrilling, that pierced far above the roar of wind and rain. Then Mohawks and rangers took it up in a tremendous chorus, and the force of Rogers on land joined in, too, adding to the mighty volume. When it sank into the crash and thunder of the storm, a shrill whoop of defiance came from the island.

"Are they trying pursuit?" asked Robert.

"They would not dare," replied Tayoga. "They do not know, of course, that we have only the edges of our tomahawks and hunting knives with which to meet them, and even in the darkness they dread our rifles."

Robert glanced back, catching only the dark outline of the island through the rain and fog, and that, too, for but a moment, as then the unbroken dark closed in, and wind and rain roared in his ears. He realized for the first time, since their departure on the great adventure, that he was without clothes, and as the fierce tension of mind and body began to relax he felt cold. The rain was driving upon him in sheets and he began to paddle with renewed vigour in order to keep up his circulation.

"I'll welcome the fire, Tayoga," he said.

"And I, too," said the Onondaga in his precise fashion. "The collapse is coming after our mighty efforts of mind and body. We will not reach shore too soon. The Mountain Wolf and his men build the fire high, so high that it can defy the rain, because they know we will need it."

A shout welcomed them as they drew in to the mainland, and the spectacle of the huge fire, sputtering and blazing in the storm, was grateful to Robert. All the captured boats and canoes were drawn out of the water, well upon the shore, and then, imitating a favourite device of the Indians, they inverted the long boats, resting the ends on logs before the fires, and sat or stood under them, sheltered from the rain, while they warmed white or brown bodies in the heat of the flames.

"'Twas a great achievement, Dave," said Rogers to Willet, "and improves our position wonderfully, but 'twas one of the hardest things I've ever had to do to stand here, just waiting and listening to the roar of the battle."

"Tayoga says we were helped by Areskoui, and we must have been helped by some power greater than our own. We paid a price for our victory, though it wasn't too high, and tomorrow we'll see what St. Luc will do. 'Tis altogether possible that we may have a naval fight."

"It's so, Dave, but this is a fine deed you and Daganoweda and your men have done."

"Nothing more than you would have done, Rogers, if you had been in our place."

They spoke in ordinary tones, being men too much hardened to danger and mighty tasks to show emotion. Robert stood under the same inverted boat that sheltered them, and he heard their words in a kind of daze, his brain still benumbed after the long and terrible test. But it was a pleasant numbing, a provision of nature, a sort of rest that was akin to sleep.

The storm had not abated a particle. Wind and rain roared across Andiatarocte and along the slopes and over the mountains. The waters of the lake whenever they were disclosed were black and seething, and all the islands were invisible.

Robert looked mostly at the great fire that crackled and blazed so near. It was fed continually by Indians and rangers, who did not care for the rain, and it alone defied the storm. The sheets of rain, poured upon it, seemed to have no effect. The coals merely hissed as if it were oil instead of water, and the flames leaped higher, deep red at the heart and often blue at the edges.

Robert had never seen a more beautiful fire, a vast core of warmth and light that challenged alike darkness, wind and rain. There had been a time, so he had heard, in the remote, dim ages when man knew nothing of fire. It might have been true, but he did not see how man could have existed, and certainly no cheer ever came into his life. He turned himself around, as if he were broiling on a spit, and heated first one side and then the other, until the blood in his veins sparkled with new life and vigour. Then he dressed, still pervaded by that enormous feeling of comfort and content, and ate of the food that Rogers ordered to be served to the returned and refreshed men. He also resumed his rifle and pistol, but kept his seat under the inverted boat, where the rain could not reach him.

He would have slept, but the ground was too wet, and he waited with the others for the approach of day and the initiative of St. Luc. The rangers and Mohawks had made the first move, and it was now for the French leader to match it. Robert wondered what St. Luc would attempt, but that he would try something he never doubted for a moment.

A log was rolled beneath the long boat under which the leaders stood, and, spreading their blankets over it, they sat down on it. There was room at the end for Robert and Tayoga, too, and Robert found that his comfort increased greatly. He was in a kind of daze, that was very soothing, and yet he saw everything that went on around him. But he still looked mostly at the great fire which zealous hands fed and which stood up a pillar of light in the darkness and cold. He reflected dimly that it was a beautiful fire, a magnificent, a most magnificent fire. How the first man who saw the first fire must have rejoiced in it!

Toward morning the wind sank, and the sheets of rain grew thinner. Once or twice thunder moaned in the southwest, and there were occasional streaks of lightning, but they were faint, and merely disclosed fleeting strips of a black lake and a black forest.

"Before the sun rises the storm will be gone," said Tayoga. "The miracle that Areskoui worked in our behalf is finished, and the rest must be done by our own courage and skill. Who are we to ask more for ourselves than the Sun God has done?"

"We've been splendidly favoured," said Robert, "and if he does not help us with another miracle he'll at least shine for us before long. After such a night as this, I'll be mighty glad to see the day, the green mountains, and the bright waters of Andiatarocte again."

"I feel the dawn already, Dagaeoga. The rain, as you see, has almost stopped, and the troubled wind will now be still. The storm will pass away, and it will leave not a mark, save a fallen tree here and there."

Tayoga's words came true. In a half hour both wind and rain died utterly, and they breathed an air clean and sweet, as if the world had been washed anew. A touch of silver appeared on the eastern mountains, and then up came the dawn, crisp and cool after the storm, and the world was more splendid and beautiful than ever. The green on slopes and ridges had been deepened and the lake was all silver in the morning light.

The islands stood up, sharp and clear, and there were the forces of St. Luc still on his island, and Rogers, through his powerful glasses, was able to make out the French leader himself walking about, while white men and Indians were lighting the fires on which they expected to cook their breakfasts.

Several boats and canoes were visible drawn upon the shore, showing that St. Luc had saved a portion of his fleet, and it appeared that he and his men did not fear another attack, or perhaps they wanted it. Meanwhile rangers and Mohawks prepared their own breakfasts and awaited with patience the word of their leaders. Apparently there was nothing but peace. It was a camping party on the island and another on the mainland, and the waters of the lake danced in the sunshine, reflecting one brilliant colour after another.

"Reinforcements are coming for St. Luc," said Robert, who saw black specks on the lake to the eastward of the island. "I think that's a fleet of Indian canoes."

"It's what I expected," said Tayoga. "The French and their allies had complete control of Andiatarocte until we appeared, and it is likely, when the storm began to die, Sharp Sword sent for the aid that is now coming."

The canoes soon showed clear outlines in the intense sunlight, and, as well as Rogers could judge through his glasses, they brought about fifty men, ten of whom were Frenchmen. But there were no long boats, a fact at which they all rejoiced, as in a naval battle the canoes would be at a great disadvantage opposed to the heavier craft.

"When do you think it best to make the attack?" Willet asked the leader of the rangers.

"Within an hour," replied Rogers. "If we had been in condition we might have gone at them before their help came, but it was wise to let the men rest a little after last night's struggle."

"And it will be better for our purpose to beat two forces instead of one."

"So it will, and that's the right spirit, Dave. You can always be depended upon to take the cheerful view of things. It's good, old friend, for us to be together again, doing our best."

"So it is, and it's a time that demands one's best. The world's afire, and our part of it is burning with the rest. What do your glasses tell you now?"

"The reinforcements are landing on the island. St. Luc himself has gone forward to meet them. He's a fine leader. He impresses red men and white men alike, and he'll make the new force feel that it's the most important and timely in the world. Have you found anything in the woods, Black Rifle?"

"No," replied the swart forester, who had been circling about the camp. "Nobody is there. It's just ourselves and the fellows out there on the island."

"Do you see any more canoes, Rogers, coming to the help of St. Luc?" asked Willet.

The ranger searched long and carefully over the surface of the lake with his strong glasses and then replied:

"Not a canoe. If they have any more force afloat it's too far in the north to reach here in time. We've all of our immediate enemy before us, and we'll attack at once."

The boats and canoes were lifted into the water and the little force made ready for the naval battle.

Chapter 10

The Naval Combat

Robert and Tayoga went into a long boat with Willet, a boat that held eight men, all carrying paddles, while their rifles were laid on the bottom, ready to be substituted for the paddles when the time came. Daganoweda was in another of the large boats, and Rogers commanded a third, the whole fleet advancing slowly and in almost a straight line toward St. Luc's stronghold.

Doubtless many a combat between Indians had taken place on Andiatarocte in the forgotten ages, but Robert believed the coming encounter would be the first in which white men had a part, and, for the moment, he forgot his danger in the thrilling spectacle that opened before him.

St. Luc, when he saw the enemy approaching, quickly launched his own fleet, and filled it with men, although he kept it well in the lee of the land, and behind it posted a formidable row of marksmen, French, Canadians and Indians. Rogers, who had the general command, paddled his boat a little in front of the others and examined the defence cautiously through his glasses. Tayoga could see well enough with the naked eye.

"St. Luc is leaning on the stump of a wind-blown tree near the water," he said, "and he holds in his hand his small sword with which he will direct the battle. But there is a canoe almost at his feet, and if need be he will go into it. De Courcelles is in a large boat on the right, and Tandakora is in another on the left. On the land, standing behind St. Luc, is the Canadian, Dubois."

"A very good arrangement to meet us," said Willet. "St. Luc will stay on the island, but if he finds we're pressing him too hard, he'll have himself paddled squarely into the centre of his fleet, and do or die. Now, it's a lucky thing for us that our rangers are such fine marksmen, and that they have the good, long-barrelled rifles."

The boats containing the Mohawks were held back under the instructions of Rogers, despite the eagerness of Daganoweda, who, however, was compelled to yield to the knowledge that red men were never equal to the finest white sharpshooters, and it was important to use the advantage given to them by the long rifles. Willet's boat swung in by the side of that of Rogers, and several more boats and canoes, containing rangers, drew level with them. Rogers measured the distance anxiously.

"Do you think you can reach them with your rifle, Dave?" he asked.

"A few yards more and a bullet will count," replied the hunter.

"We'll go ahead, then, and tell me as soon as you think we're near enough. All our best riflemen are in front, and we should singe them a bit."

The boats glided slowly on, and, at the island, the enemy was attentive and waiting, with the advantage wholly on his side, had it not been for the rifles of great range, surpassing anything the French and Indians carried. St. Luc did not move from his position, and he was a heroic figure magnified in the dazzling sunlight.

Willet held up his hand.

"This will do," he said.

At a sign from Rogers the entire fleet stopped, and, at another sign from Willet, twenty rangers, picked marksmen, raised their rifles and fired. Several of the French and Indians fell, and their comrades gave forth a great shout of rage. Those in the canoes and boats fired, but all their bullets fell short, merely pattering in vain on the water. Daganoweda and his warriors, when they saw the result, uttered an exultant war whoop that came back in echoes from the mountains. Rogers himself rejoiced openly.

"That's the way to do it, Dave!" he cried. "Reload and give 'em another volley. Unless they come out and attack us we can decimate 'em."

Although it was hard to restrain the rangers, who wished to crowd closer, Rogers and Willet nevertheless were able to make them keep their distance, and they maintained a deadly fire that picked off warrior after warrior and that threatened the enemy with destruction. St. Luc's Indians uttered shouts of rage and fired many shots, all of which fell short. Then Robert saw St. Luc leave the stump and enter his waiting canoe.

"They'll come to meet us now," he said. "We've smoked 'em out."

"Truly they will," said Tayoga. "They must advance or die at the land's edge."

The portion of his fleet which St. Luc and his men had managed to save was almost as large as that of the Americans and Mohawks, and seeing that they must do it, they put out boldly from the land, St. Luc in the centre in his canoe, paddled by a single Indian. As they approached, the rifles of Daganoweda's men came into action also, and St. Luc's force replied with a heavy fire. The naval battle was on, and it was fought with all the fury of a great encounter by fleets on the high seas. Robert saw St. Luc in his canoe, giving orders both with his voice and the waving of his sword, while the single Indian in the light craft paddled him to and fro as he wished, stoically careless of the bullets.

In the heat and fury of the combat the fleet of Rogers came under the fire of the French and Indians on the island, many being wounded and some slain. These reserves of St. Luc in their eagerness waded waist deep into the water, and pulled trigger as fast as they could load and reload.

A ranger in Willet's boat was killed and two more received hurts, but the hunter kept his little command in the very thick of the battle, and despite the great cloud of smoke that covered the fleets of both sides Robert soon saw that the rangers and Mohawks were winning. One of the larger boats belonging to St. Luc, riddled with bullets, went down, and the warriors who had been in it were forced to swim for their lives. Several canoes were rammed and shattered. Willet and Tayoga meanwhile were calmly picking their targets through the smoke, and when they fired they never missed.

The rangers, too, were showing their superiority as sharpshooters to the French and Indians, and were doing deadly execution with their long rifles. St. Luc, in spite of the great courage shown by his men, was compelled to sound the recall, and, hurriedly taking on board all the French and Indians who were on land, he fled eastward across the lake with the remnant of his force. Rogers pursued, but St. Luc was still able to send back such a deadly fire and his French and Indians worked so desperately with the paddles that they reached the eastern rim, abandoned the fragments of their fleet, climbed the lofty shore and disappeared in the forest, leaving Rogers, Willet, Daganoweda and their men in triumphant command of Andiatarocte, for a little while, at least.

But the victors bore many scars. More men had been lost, and their force suffered a sharp reduction in numbers. The three leaders, still in their boats, conferred. Daganoweda was in favour of landing and of pushing the pursuit to the utmost, even to the walls of Crown Point on Champlain, where the fugitives would probably go.

"There's much in favour of it," said Willet. "There's nothing like following a beaten enemy and destroying him, and there is also much to be said against it. We might run into an ambush and be destroyed ourselves. Although we've paid a price for it, we've a fine victory and we hold command of the lake for the time being. By pushing on we risk all we've won in order to obtain more."

But Daganoweda was still eager to advance, and urged it in a spirited Mohawk speech. Rogers himself favoured it. The famous leader of rangers had a bold and adventurous mind. No risk was too great for him, and dangers, instead of repelling, invited him.

Robert, as became him, listened to them in silence. Prudence told him that they ought to stay on the lake, but his was the soul of youth, and the fiery eloquence of Daganoweda found an answer in his heart. It was decided at last to leave a small guard with the fleet, while rangers and Mohawks to the number of fifty should pursue toward Oneadatote. All three of the leaders, with Black Rifle, Tayoga and Robert, were to share in the pursuit, while a trusty man named White was left in command of the guard over the boats.

The fifty—the force had been so much reduced by the fighting that no more could be mustered—climbed the lofty shore, making their way up a ravine, thick with brush, until they came out on a crest more than a thousand feet above the lake. Nor did they forget, as they climbed, to exercise the utmost caution, looking everywhere for an ambush. They knew that St. Luc, while defeated, would never be dismayed, and it would be like him to turn on the rangers and Mohawks in the very moment of their victory and snatch it from them. But there was no sign of a foe's presence, although Daganoweda's men soon struck the trail of the fleeing enemy.

They paused at the summit a minute or two for breath, and Robert looked back with mixed emotions at Andiatarocte, a vast sheet of blue, then of green under the changing sky, the scene of a naval victory of which he had not dreamed a few days ago. But the lake bore no sign of strife now. The islands were all in peaceful green and the warlike boats were gone, save at the foot of the cliff they had just climbed. There they, too, looked peaceful enough, as if they were the boats of fishermen, and the guards, some of whom were aboard the fleet and some of whom lay at ease near the edge of the water, seemed to be men engaged in pursuits that had nothing to do with violence and war.

Tayoga's eyes followed Robert's.

"Andiatarocte is worth fighting for," he said. "It is well for us to be the rulers of it, even for a day. Where will you find a more splendid lake, a lake set deep in high green mountains, a lake whose waters may take on a dozen colours within a day, and every colour beautiful?"

"I don't believe the world can show its superior, Tayoga," replied Robert, "and I, like you, am full of pride, because we are lords of it for a day. I hope the time will soon come when we shall be permanent rulers of both lakes, Andiatarocte and Oneadatote."

"We shall have to be mighty warriors before that hour arrives," said Tayoga, gravely. "Even if we gain Andiatarocte we have yet to secure a footing on the shores of Oneadatote. The French and their allies are not only in great force at Crown Point, but we hear that they mean to fortify also at the place called Ticonderoga by the Hodenosaunee and Carillon by the French."

The order to resume the march came, and they pressed forward on the trail through the deep woods. Usually at this time of the year it was hot in the forest, but after the great storm and rain of the night before a brisk, cool wind moved in waves among the trees, shaking the leaves and sending lingering raindrops down on the heads of the pursuers.

Black Rifle curved off to the right as a flanker against ambush, and two of Daganoweda's best scouts were sent to the left, while the main force went on directly, feeling now that the danger from a hidden force had been diminished greatly, their zeal increasing as the trail grew warmer. Daganoweda believed that they could overtake St. Luc in three or four hours, and he and his Mohawks, flushed with victory on the lake, were now all for speed, the rangers being scarcely less eager.

The country through which they were passing was wooded heavily, wild, picturesque and full of game. But it was well known to Mohawks and rangers, and the two lads had also been through it. They started up many deer that fled through the forest, and the small streams and ponds were covered with wild fowl.

"I don't wonder that the settlers fail to come in here on this strip of land between George and Champlain," said Robert to Tayoga. "It's a No Man's land, roamed over only by warriors, and even the most daring frontiersman must have some regard for the scalp on his head."

"I could wish it to be kept a No Man's land," said Tayoga earnestly.

"Maybe it will—for a long time, anyway. But, Tayoga, you're as good a trailer as Black Rifle or any Mohawk. Judging from the traces they leave, how many men would you say St. Luc now has with him?"

"As many as we have, or more, perhaps seventy, though their quality is not as good. The great footprint in the centre of the trail is made by Tandakora. He, at least, has not fallen, and the prints that turn out are those of St. Luc, De Courcelles and doubtless of the officer Jumonville. The French leaders walked together, and here they stopped and talked a minute or two. St. Luc was troubled, and it was hard for him to make up his mind what to do."

"How do you know that, Tayoga?"

"Because, as he stood by the side of this bush, he broke three of its little stems between his thumb and forefinger. See, here are the stumps. A man like St. Luc would not have had a nervous hand if he had not been perplexed greatly."

"But how do you know it was St. Luc who stood by the bush, and not De Courcelles or Jumonville?"

"Because I have been trained from infancy, as an Onondaga and Iroquois, to notice everything. We have to see to live, and I observed long ago that the feet of St. Luc were smaller than those of De Courcelles or Jumonville. You will behold the larger imprints that turn out just here, and they face St. Luc, who stood by the bush. Once they not only thought of turning back to meet us, but actually prepared to do so."

"What proof have you?"

"O Dageaoga, you would not have asked me that question if you had used your eyes, and had thought a little. The print is so simple that a little child may read. The toes of their moccasins at a point just beyond the bush turn about, that is, back on the trail. And here the huge moccasins of Tandakora have taken two steps back. Perhaps they intended to meet us in full face or to lay an ambush, but at last they continued in their old course and increased their speed."

"How do you know they went faster, Tayoga?"

"O Dagaeoga, is your mind wandering today that your wits are so dull? See, how the distance between the imprints lengthens! When you run faster you leap farther. Everybody does."

"I apologize, Tayoga. It was a foolish question to be asked by one who has lived in the forest as long as I have. Why do you think they increased their speed, and how does St. Luc know that they are followed?"

"It may be that they know a good place of ambush farther ahead, and St. Luc is sure that he is pursued, because he knows the minds of Willet, Rogers and Daganoweda. He knows they are the kind of minds that always follow and push a victory to the utmost. Here the warriors knelt and drank. They had a right to be thirsty after such a battle and such a retreat."

He pointed to numerous imprints by the bank of a clear brook, and rangers and Mohawks, imitating the example of those whom they pursued, drank thirstily. Then they resumed the advance, and they soon saw that the steps of St. Luc's men were shortening.

"They are thinking again of battle or ambush," said Tayoga, "and when they think of it a second time they are likely to try it. It becomes us now to go most warily."

Daganoweda and Willet also had noticed St. Luc's change of pace, and stopping, they took counsel with themselves. About two miles ahead the country was exceedingly rough, cut by rocky ravines, and covered heavily with forest and thickets.

"If St. Luc elects to make a stand," said Willet, "that is the place he will choose. What say you, Daganoweda?"

"I think as the Great Bear thinks," replied the Mohawk chieftain.

"And you, Rogers?"

"Seems likely to me, too. At any rate, we must reckon on it."

"And so reckoning on it, we'd better stop and throw out more scouts."

Both Rogers and Daganoweda agreed, and flankers were sent off in each direction. Tayoga asked earnestly for this service, and Robert insisted on going with him. As the great skill of the Onondaga was known to the three leaders, he was obviously the proper selection for the errand, and it was fitting that Robert, his comrade in so many dangers and hardships, should accompany him. Daganoweda and Rogers said yes at once, and Willet was not able to say no. They were the best choice for such an errand, and although the hunter was reluctant for the youth, who was almost a son to him, to go on such a perilous duty, he knew that he must yield to the necessity.

The two lads went off to the left or northern flank, and in less than a minute the deep forest hid them completely from the main force. They were buried in the wilderness, and, for all the evidence that came to them, the band of rangers and Mohawks had ceased to exist.

They passed about a half mile to the north of the main force, and then they began to look everywhere for traces of trails, or evidence that an ambush was being prepared.

"Do you think St. Luc will make a new stand at the ridges?" asked Robert.

"All the chances favour it," replied the Onondaga. "We know that Sharp Sword, besides being a great leader, is full of pride. He will not like to go to Crown Point, and report that he has not only lost his fleet and the temporary command of Andiatarocte, but a large part of his force as well. If he can strike a heavy and deadly blow at his pursuers he will feel much better."

"Your reasoning seems good to me, and, therefore, it behoves us to be mighty careful. What do you take this imprint to be, Tayoga? Is it that of a human foot?"

"It is so very faint one can tell little of it. Your eye was keen, Dagaeoga, to have seen it at all, though I think the hoof of a buck and not the foot of a man trod here on the fallen leaves, but the tread was so light that it left only a partial impression."

"I can find no other trace like it farther on."

"No, the ground grows very hard and rocky, and it leaves no impression. We will advance for a little while toward the ridge, and then it will be well for us to lie down in some cover and watch, because I think St. Luc will send out skirmishers."

"And naturally he will send them to both right and left as we do."

"Of course, Dagaeoga."

"And then, if we keep moving on, we're sure to meet them?"

"It would appear so, Dagaeoga."

"And for that reason, Tayoga, I'm in favour of the greatest care. I hope we'll come soon to a covert so deep and thick that when we hide in it we can't be seen five yards away."

"So do I, Dagaeoga. It is no shame to us to wish to save our lives. Lost, they would be of no use either to ourselves or to those whom we are here to serve. I think I see now the place that is waiting for us."

He pointed to a dense clump of scrub cedars growing on hard and rocky ground.

"I see," said Robert. "We can approach it without leaving any trail, and in that mass of green no foe will notice us unless his eyes are almost against us."

"Dagaeoga, at times, shows understanding and wisdom. The day may come when he will be a great scout and trailer—if he lives long enough."

"Go ahead, Tayoga, if it amuses you to make game of me. If humour can be produced at such a time I'm glad to be the occasion of it."

"It's best for us, Dagaeoga, to await all things with a light heart. Our fates are in the hands of Manitou."

"That's good philosophy, Tayoga, though I'm bound to say I can't look upon my life as a thing mapped out for me in every detail, though I live to be a hundred. Manitou knows what's going to happen, but I don't, and so my heart will jump anyhow when the danger comes. Now, you're sure we've left no trail among those rocks?"

"Not a trace, Dagaeoga. If Tododaho himself were to come back to earth he could not find our path."

"And you're sure that we're thoroughly hidden among these little cedars?"

"Quite sure of it. I doubt whether the bird singing over our heads sees us, and Manitou has given to the bird a very good eye that he may see his food, which is so small. It may be that the birds and animals which have given us warning of the enemy's approach before may do it again."

"At any rate, we can hope so. Are we as deserving now as we were then?"

"Yes, we can hope, Dagaeoga. Hope is never forbidden to anybody."

"I see that you're a philosopher, Tayoga."

"I try to be one," said the Onondaga, his eyes twinkling.

"Do you think that bird singing with so much power and beauty overhead sees us at last?"

"No, because he would certainly have stopped long enough to gratify his curiosity. Even a bird would want to know why strange creatures come into his thicket."

"Then as long as he sings I shall know that danger is not near. We have been watched over by birds before."

"Again you talk like a little child, Dagaeoga. I teach you the wisdom of the woods, and you forget. The bird may see a worm or a moth or something else that is good to eat, and then he will stop singing to dart for his food. A bird must eat, and his love of music often gives way to his love of food."

"You speak as if you were talking from a book."

"I learned your language mostly out of books, and so I speak as they are written. Ah, the song of the bird has stopped and he has gone away! But we do not know whether he has been alarmed by the coming of our enemy or has seen food that he pursues."

"It's food, Tayoga; I can hear him, faintly, singing in another tree, some distance to our right. Probably having captured the worm or the moth or whatever it was he was pursuing, and having devoured it, he is now patting his stomach in his pleasure and singing in his joy."

"And as a sentinel he is no longer of any use to us. Then we will watch for the little animals that run on the ground. They cannot fly over the heads of Ojibway and Caughnawaga warriors, and so, if our enemies come, they, too, are likely to come our way."

"Then I'll rest awhile, Tayoga, and it may be that I'll doze. If a rabbit runs in our direction wake me up."

"You may pretend to sleep, Dagaeoga, but you will not. You may close your eyes, but you cannot close your ears, nor can you still your nerves. One waits not with eyes and ears alone, but with all the fibre of the body."

"True, Tayoga. I was but jesting. I couldn't sleep if I tried. But I can rest."

He stretched himself in an easy position, a position, also, that allowed him to go into instant action if hostile warriors came, and he awaited the event with a calmness that surprised himself. Tayoga was crouched by his side, intent and also waiting.

A full half hour passed, and Robert heard nothing stirring in the undergrowth, save the wandering but gentle winds that rustled the leaves and whispered in the grass. Had he been left to himself he would have grown impatient, and he would have continued the scouting curve on which he had been sent. But he had supreme confidence in Tayoga. If the Onondaga said it was best for them to stay there in the bush, then it was best, and he would remain until his comrade gave the word to move on.

So sure was he of Tayoga that he did close his eyes for a while, although his ears and all the nerves of his body watched. But it was very peaceful and restful, and, while he lay in a half-dreamy state, he accumulated new strength for the crisis that might come.

"Any little animals running away yet, Tayoga?" he asked, partly in jest.

"No, Dagaeoga, but I am watching. Two rabbits not twenty feet from us are nibbling the leaves on a tiny weed, that is, they nibble part of the time, and part of the time they play."

"They don't sing like the bird, because they can't, but I take it from what you say they're just as happy."

"Happy and harmless, Dagaeoga. We Iroquois would not disturb them. We kill only to eat."

"Well, I've learned your way. You can't say, Tayoga, that I'm not, in spirit and soul at least, half an Iroquois, and spirit and soul mean more than body and manners or the tint of the skin."

"Dagaeoga has learned much. But then he has had the advantage of associating with one who could teach him much."

"Tayoga, if it were not for that odd little chord in your voice, I'd think you were conceited. But though you jest, it is true I've had a splendid chance to discover that the nations of the Hodenosaunee know some things better than we do, and do some things better than we do. I've found that the wisdom of the world isn't crystallized in any one race. How about the rabbits, Tayoga? Do they still eat and play, as if nobody anywhere near them was thinking of wounds and death?"

"The rabbits neither see nor hear anything strange, and the strange would be to them the dangerous. They nibble at the leaves a little, then play a little, then nibble again."

"I trust they'll keep up their combination of pleasure and sustenance some time, because it's very nice to lie here, rest one's overstrained system, and feel that one is watched over by a faithful friend, one who can do your work as well as his. You're not only a faithful friend, Tayoga, you're a most useful one also."

"Dagaeoga is lazy. He would not have as a friend one who is lazy like himself. He needs a comrade to take care of him. Perhaps it is better so. Dagaeoga is an orator; an orator has privileges, and one of his privileges is a claim to be watched over by others. One cannot speak forever and work, too."

Robert opened his eyes and smiled. The friendship between him and Tayoga, begun in school days, had been tested by countless hardships and dangers, and though each made the other an object of jest, it was as firm as that of Orestes and Pylades or that of Damon and Pythias.

"What are the rabbits doing now?" asked young Lennox, who had closed his eyes again.

"They eat less and play less," replied the Onondaga. "Ah, their attitude is that of suspicion! It may be that the enemy comes! Now they run away, and the enemy surely comes!"

Robert sat up, and laid his rifle across his knee. All appearance of laziness or relaxation disappeared instantly. He was attentive, alert, keyed to immediate action.

"Can you see anything, Tayoga?" he whispered.

"No, but I think I hear the sound of footsteps approaching. I am not yet sure, because the footfall, if footfall it be, is almost as light as the dropping of a feather."

Both remained absolutely still, not moving a leaf in their covert, and presently a huge and sinister figure walked into the open. It seemed to Robert that Tandakora was larger than ever, and that he was more evil-looking. His face was that of the warrior who would show no mercy, and his body, save for a waistcloth, was livid with all the hideous devices of war paint. Behind him came a Frenchman whom Robert promptly recognized as Achille Garay, and a half dozen warriors, all of whom turned questing eyes toward the earth.

"They look for a trail," whispered Tayoga. "It is well, Dagaeoga, that we took the precaution to walk on rocks when we came into this covert, or Tandakora, who is so eager for our blood, would find the traces."

"Tandakora costs me great pain," Robert whispered back. "It's my misfortune always to be seeing him just when I can't shoot at him.

I'm tempted to try it, anyhow. That's a big, broad chest of his, and I couldn't find a finer target."

"No, Dagaeoga, on your life, no! Our scalps would be the price, and some day we shall take the life of Tandakora and yet keep our own. I know it, because Tododaho has whispered it to me in the half world that lies between waking and sleeping."

"You're right, of course, Tayoga, but it's a tremendous temptation."

The Onondaga put his hand on his lips to indicate that even a whisper now was dangerous, and the two sank once more into an utter silence. The chest of Tandakora still presented a great and painted target, and Robert's hand lay on the trigger, but his will kept him from pressing it. Yet he did not watch the Ojibway chief with more eagerness than he bestowed upon the Frenchman, Achille Garay.

Garay's face was far from prepossessing. In its way it was as evil as that of Tandakora. He had sought Robert's life more than once. In the naval battle he had seen the Frenchman pull trigger upon him. Why? Why had he singled him out from the others in the endeavour to make a victim of him? There must be some motive, much more powerful than that of natural hostility, and he believed now if they were discovered that not Tayoga but he would be the first object of Garay's attack.

But Tandakora and his men passed on, bearing to the right and from the main force. Robert and Tayoga saw their figures vanish among the bushes and heard the fall of their moccasins a little longer, and then the question of their own course presented itself to them. Should they go back to Rogers with a warning of the hostile flankers, or should they follow Tandakora and see what he meant? They decided finally in favour of the latter course, and passing quietly from their covert, began to trail those who were seeking to trail a foe. The traces led toward the west, and it was not hard to follow them, as Tandakora and his men had taken but little care, evidently not thinking any scouting rangers or Mohawks might be near.

Robert and Tayoga followed carefully for several hundred yards; then they were surprised to see the trail curve sharply about, and go back toward the main force.

"We must have passed them," said Robert, "although we were too far away to see each other."

"It would seem so," said the Onondaga. "Tandakora may have come to the conclusion that no enemy is on his extreme flank, and so has gone back to see if any has appeared nearer the centre."

"Then we must follow him in his new course."

"If we do what we are sent to do we will follow."

"Lead on, Tayoga."

The Onondaga stooped that the underbrush might hide him, advanced over the trail, and Robert was close behind. The thickets were very still. All the small wild creatures, usually so numerous in them, had disappeared, and there was no wind. Tayoga saw that the imprints of the moccasins were growing firmer and clearer, and he knew that Tandakora and his men were but a short distance ahead. Then he stopped suddenly and he and Robert crouched low in the thicket.

They had heard the faint report of rifles directly in front, and they believed that Tandakora had come into contact with a party of rangers or Mohawks. As they listened, the sound of a second volley came, and then the echo of a faint war whoop. Tayoga rose a little higher, perhaps expecting to see something in the underbrush, and a rifle flashed less than forty yards away. The Onondaga fell without a cry before the horrified eyes of his comrade, and then, as Robert heard a shout of triumph, he saw an Indian, horribly painted, rush forward to seize what he believed to be a Mohawk scalp.

Young Lennox, filled with grief and rage, stood straight up, and a stream of fire fairly poured from the muzzle of his rifle as his bullet met the exultant warrior squarely in the heart. The savage fell like a log, having no time to utter his death cry, and paying no further attention to him, feeling that he must be merely a stray warrior from the main band, Robert turned to his fallen comrade.

Tayoga was unconscious, and was bleeding profusely from a wound in the right shoulder. Robert seized his wrist and felt his pulse. He was not dead, because he detected a faint beat, but it was quite evident that the wound from a big musket bullet had come near to cutting the thread of life.

For a moment or two Lennox was in despair, while his heart continued to swell with grief and rage. It was unthinkable that the noblest young Onondaga of them all, one fit to be in his time the greatest of sachems, the very head and heart of the League, should be cut down by a mere skulker. And yet it had happened. Tayoga lay, still wholly unconscious, and the sounds of firing to the eastward were increasing. A battle had begun there. Perhaps the full forces of both sides were now in conflict.

The combat called to Robert, he knew that he might bear a great part in it, but he never hesitated. Such a thought as deserting his stricken comrade could not enter his mind. He listened a moment longer to the sounds of the conflict now growing more fierce, and then, fastening Tayoga's rifle on his back with his own, he lifted his wounded comrade in his arms and walked westward, away from the battle.

Chapter 11

The Comrades

Robert settled the inert form of the Onondaga against his left shoulder, and, being naturally very strong, with a strength greatly increased by a long life in the woods, he was able to carry the weight easily. He had no plan yet in his mind, merely a vague resolve to carry Tayoga outside the fighting zone and then do what he could to resuscitate him. It was an unfortunate chance that the hostile flankers had cut in between him and the main force of Rogers, but it could not be helped, and the farther he was from his own people the safer would he and Tayoga be.

Two hundred yards more and putting his comrade on the ground he cut away the deerskin, disclosing the wound. The bullet had gone almost through the shoulder, and as he felt of its path he knew with joy that it had touched no bone. Then, unless the loss of blood became great, it could not prove mortal. But the bullet was of heavy type, fired from the old smoothbore musket and the shock had been severe. Although it had not gone quite through the shoulder he could feel it near the surface, and he decided at once upon rude but effective surgery.

Laying Tayoga upon his face, he drew his keen hunting knife and cut boldly into the flesh of the shoulder until he reached the bullet. Then he pried it out with the point of the knife, and threw it away in the bushes. A rush of blood followed and Tayoga groaned, but Robert, rapidly cutting the Onondaga's deerskin tunic into suitable strips, bound tightly and with skill both the entrance and the exit of the wound. The flow of blood was stopped, and he breathed a fervent prayer of thankfulness to the white man's God and the red man's Manitou. Tayoga would live, and he knew that he had saved the life of his comrade, as that comrade had more than once saved his.

Yet both were still surrounded by appalling dangers. At any moment St. Luc's savages might burst through the woods and be upon them. As he finished tying the bandage and stood erect the flare of the fighting came from a point much nearer, though between them and the ranger band, forbidding any possible attempt to rejoin Rogers and Willet. Tayoga opened his eyes, though he saw darkly, through a veil, and said in feeble tones:

"They have closed again with the forces of St. Luc. You would be there, Dagaeoga, to help in the fighting. Go, I am useless. It is not a time to cumber yourself with me."

"If I lay there as you are, and you stood here as I am would you leave me?" asked Robert.

The Onondaga was silent.

"You know you wouldn't," continued Robert, "and you know I won't. Listen, the battle comes nearer. St. Luc must have received a reinforcement."

He leaned forward a little, cupping his ear with his right hand, and he heard distinctly all the sounds of a fierce and terrible conflict, rifle shots, yells of the savages, shouts of the rangers, and once or twice he thought he saw faintly the flashes of rifles as they were fired in the thickets.

"Go," said Tayoga again. "I can see that your spirit turns to the battle. They may not find me, and, perhaps in a day, I shall be able to walk and take care of myself."

Robert made no reply in words, but once more he lifted the Onondaga in his sinewy arms, settled his weight against his left shoulder and resumed his walk away from the battle. Tayoga did not speak, and Robert soon saw that he had relapsed again into unconsciousness. He went at least three hundred yards before resting, and all the while the battle called to him, the shots, the yells and the shouts still coming clearly through the thin mountain air.

He rested perhaps fifteen minutes, and he saw that, while Tayoga was unconscious, the flow of blood was still held in check by the bandages. Resuming his burden, he went on through the forest, a full quarter of a mile now, and the last sound of the battle sank into nothingness behind him. He was consumed with anxiety to know who had won, but there was not a sign to tell.

He came to a brook, and putting Tayoga down once more, he bathed his face freely, until the Onondaga opened his eyes and looked about, not with a veil before his eyes now, but clearly.

"Where are we, Dagaeoga?" he asked.

"I'd tell you if I could, but I can't," replied Robert, cheerfully, rejoiced at the sight of his comrade's returning strength.

"You have left the battle behind you?"

"Yes. I can state in general terms that we're somewhere between Andiatarocte and Oneadatote, which is quite enough for you to know at the present time. I'm the forest doctor, and as this is the first chance I've ever had to exert authority over you, I mean to make the most of it."

Tayoga smiled wanly.

"I see that you have bound up my wound," he said. "That was well. But since I cannot see the wound itself I do not know what kind of a bullet made it."

"It wasn't a bullet at all, Tayoga. It was a cannon ball, though it came out of a wide-mouthed musket, and I'm happy to tell you that it somehow got through your shoulder without touching bone."

"The bullet is out?"

"Yes, I cut it out with this good old hunting knife of mine."

Again Tayoga smiled wanly.

"You have done well, Dagaeoga," he said. "Did I not say to others in your defence that you had intelligence and, in time, might learn? You have saved my life, a poor thing perhaps, but the only life I have, and I thank you."

Robert laughed, and his laugh was full of heartiness. He saw the old Tayoga coming back.

"You'll be a new man tomorrow," he said. "With flesh and blood as healthy as yours a hole through your shoulder that I could put my fist in would soon heal."

"What does Dagaeoga purpose to do next?"

"You'll find out in good time. I'm master now, and I don't intend to tell my plans. If I did you'd be trying to change 'em. While I'm ruler I mean to be ruler."

"It is a haughty spirit you show. You take advantage of my being wounded."

"Of course I do. As I said, it's the only chance I've had. Stop that! Don't try to sit up! You're not strong enough yet. I'll carry you awhile."

Tayoga sank back, and, in a few more minutes, Robert picked him up and went on once more. But he noticed that the Onondaga did not now lie a dead weight upon his shoulder. Instead, there was in him again the vital quality that made him lighter and easier to carry. He knew that Tayoga would revive rapidly, but it would be days before he was fit to take care of himself. He must find not only a place of security, but one of shelter from the fierce midsummer storms that sometimes broke over those mountain slopes. Among the rocks and ravines and dense woods he might discover some such covert. Food was contained in his knapsack and the one still fastened to the back of Tayoga, food enough to last several days, and if the time should be longer his rifle must find more.

The way became rougher, the rocks growing more numerous, the slopes increasing in steepness, and the thickets becoming almost impenetrable.

"Put me down," said Tayoga. "We are safe from the enemy, for a while at least. All the warriors have been drawn by the battle, and, whether it goes on now or not, they have not yet had time to scatter and seek through the wilderness."

"I said I was going to be absolute master, but it looks, Tayoga, as if you meant to give advice anyhow. And as your advice seems good, and I confess I'm a trifle weary, I'll let you see if you can sit up a little on this heap of dead leaves, with your back against this old fallen trunk. Here we go! Gently now! Oh, you'll soon be a warrior again, if you follow my instructions!"

Tayoga heaved a little sigh of relief as he leaned back against the trunk. His eyes were growing clearer and Robert knew that the beat of his pulse was fuller. All the amazing vitality that came from a powerful constitution, hard training and clean living was showing itself. Already, and his wound scarcely two hours old, his strength was coming back.

"You look for a wigwam, Dagaeoga?" he said.

"Well, scarcely that," replied Robert. "I'm not expecting an inn in this wilderness, but I'm seeking some sort of shelter, preferably high up among the rocks, where we might find protection from storms."

"Two or three hundred yards farther on and we'll find it."

"Come, Tayoga, you're just guessing. You can't know such a thing."

"I am not guessing at all, Dagaeoga, and I do know. Your position as absolute ruler was brief. It expired between the first and second hour, and now you have an adviser who may become a director."

"Then proceed with your advice and direction. How do you know there is shelter only two or three hundred yards farther on?"

"I look ahead, and I see a narrow path leading up among the rocks. Such paths are countless in the wilderness, and many of them are untrodden, but the one before my eyes has sustained footsteps many times."

"Come down to earth, Tayoga, and tell me what you see."

"I see on the rocks on either side of this path long, coarse hairs. They were left by a wild animal going back and forth to its den. It was a large wild animal, else it would not have scraped against the rocks on either side. It was probably a bear, and if you will hand me the two or three twisted hairs in the crevice at your elbow I will tell you."

Robert brought them to him and Tayoga nodded assent.

"Aye, it was a bear," he said, "and a big one."

"But how do you know his den is only two or three hundred yards away?"

"That is a matter of looking as far as the eyes can reach. If you will only lift yours and gaze over the tops of those bushes you will see that the path ends against a high stone face or wall, too steep for climbing. So the den must be there, and let us hope, Dagaeoga, that it is large enough for us both. The bear is likely to be away, as this is summer. Now, lift me up. I have talked all the talk that is in me and as much as I have strength to utter."

Robert carried him again, and it was hard travelling up the steep and rocky path, but Tayoga's words were quickly proved to be true. In the crumbling face of the stone cliff they found not only an opening but several, the bear having preferred one of the smaller to the largest, which ran back eight or ten feet and which was roomy enough to house a dozen men. It bore no animal odour, and there was before it an abundance of dead leaves that could be taken in for shelter.

"Now Manitou is kind," said Tayoga, "or it may be that Areskoui and Tododaho are still keeping their personal watch over us. Lay me in the cave, Dagaeoga. Thou hast acquitted thyself as a true friend. No *sachem* of the Onondagas, however great, could have been greater in fidelity and courage."

Robert made two beds of leaves. On one he spread the blanket that was strapped to Tayoga's back. Then he built his own place and felt that they were sheltered and secure for the time, and in truth they were housed as well as millions of cave men for untold centuries had been. It was a good cave, sweet-smelling, with pure, clean air, and Robert saw that if it rained the water would not come in at the door, but would run past it down the slope, which in itself was one of the luckiest strokes of fortune.

Tayoga lay on his blanket on his bed of leaves, and, looking up at the rough and rocky roof, smiled. He had begged Robert to leave him and go to the battle, and he knew that if his comrade had gone, he, wounded as he was, would surely have perished. If a hostile skirmisher did not find him, which was more than likely, he would have been overcome by the fever of his wound, and, lying unconscious while some rainstorm swept over him, his last chance would be gone. He could feel the fever creeping into his veins now, and he knew that they had found the refuge just in time. Yet he was grateful and cheerful, and in his heart he said silent thanks to Tododaho, Areskoui and Manitou. Then he called to Robert.

"See if you can find water," he said. "There should be more than one stream among these rocky hollows. Bring the water here in your cap and wash my wound."

Iroquois therapeutics were very simple, but wonderfully effective, and, as Robert had seen both Onondagas and Mohawks practice their healing art, he understood.

He discovered a good stream not many yards away, and carefully removing Tayoga's bandages, and bringing his cap filled to the brim with water, he cleansed the wound thoroughly. Then the bandages were put on again firmly and securely. This in most cases constituted the whole of the Iroquois treatment, so far as the physical body was concerned. The wound must be kept absolutely clean and away from the air, nature doing the rest. Now and then the juices of powerful herbs were used, but they were not needed for one so young and so wholesome in blood as Tayoga.

When the operation was finished the Onondaga lay back on his bed and smiled once more at the rough and rocky roof.

"Again you show signs of intelligence, Dagaeoga," he said. "As you have learned to be a warrior, perhaps you can learn to be a medicine man also, not the medicine man who deals with spirits, but one who heals. Now, as you have done your part, I shall do mine."

"What do you mean, Tayoga?"

"I will resolve to be well. You know that among my people the healers held in highest honour are those who do not acknowledge the existence of any disease at all. The patient is sick because he has not willed that he should be well. So the medicine man exerts a will for him and by reciting to himself prayers or charms drives away the complaint which the sick man fancies that he has. Now, I do not accept all their belief. A bullet has gone through my shoulder, and I know it. Nothing can alter the fact. Yet I do know that the will has great control over the nerves, which direct the body, and I shall strengthen my will as much as I can, and make it order my body to get well."

Robert knew that what he said was true. Already the Iroquois were, and long had been, practicing what came to be known much later among the white people as Christian Science.

"Try to sleep, Tayoga," he said. "I know the power of your will. If you order yourself to sleep, sleep you will. I have your rifle and mine, and if the enemy should come I think I can hold 'em off."

"They will not come," said Tayoga, "at least, not today nor in the night that will follow. They are so busy with the Great Bear and the

Mountain Wolf and Daganoweda that they will not have time to hunt among the hills for the two who have sought refuge here. What of the skies, Dagaeoga? What do they promise?"

Robert, standing in the entrance, took a long look at the heavens.

"Rain," he replied at last; "I can see clouds gathering in the west, and a storm is likely to come with the night. I think I hear distant thunder, but it is so low I'm not sure."

"Areskoui is good to us once more. The kindness of his heart is never exhausted. Truly, O Dagaeoga, he has been a shield between us and our enemies. Now the rain will come, it will pour hard, it will sweep along the slopes, and wash away any faint trace of a trail that we may have left, thus hiding our flight from the eyes of wandering warriors."

"All that's true, and now that you've explained it to your satisfaction, you obey me, exercise your will and go to sleep. I've recovered my rulership, and I mean to exercise it to the full for the little time that it may last."

Tayoga obeyed, composing himself in the easiest attitude on his blanket and bed of leaves, and he exerted his will to the utmost. He wished sleep, and sleep must come, yet he knew that the fever was still rising in his veins. The shock and loss of blood from the great musket ball could not be dismissed by a mere effort of the mind, but the mind nevertheless could fight against their effects and neutralize them.

As the fever rose steadily he exerted his will with increasing power. He said to himself again and again how fortunate he was to be watched over by such a brave and loyal friend, and to have a safe and dry refuge, when other warriors of his nation, wounded, had lain in the forest to die of exhaustion or to be devoured by wild beasts. He knew from the feel of the air that a storm was coming, and again he was thankful to his patron saint, Tododaho, and also to Areskoui, and to Manitou, greatest of all, because a bed and a roof had been found for him in this, the hour of his greatest need.

The mounting fever in his veins seemed to make his senses more vivid and acute for the time. Although Robert could not yet hear in reality the rumbling thunder far down in the southwest, the menace came very plainly to the ears of Tayoga, but it was no menace to him. Instead, the rumble was the voice of a friend, telling him that the deluge was at hand to wash away all traces of their flight and to force their enemies into shelter, while his fever burned itself out.

Tayoga on his blanket, with the thick couch of dry leaves beneath, could still see the figure of Robert, rifle across his knees, crouched at the doorway, a black silhouette against the fading sky. The Onondaga knew that he would watch until the storm came in full flood, and nothing would escape his keen eyes and ears. Dagaeoga was a worthy pupil of Willet, known to the Hodenosaunee as the Great Bear, a man of surpassing skill.

Tayoga also heard the rushing of the rain, far off, coming, perhaps, from Andiatarocte, and presently he saw the flashes of lightning, every one a vast red blaze to his feverish eyes. It was only by the light of these sabre strokes across the sky that he could now see Robert, as the dark had come, soon to be followed by floods of rain. Then he closed his eyes, and calling incessantly for sleep, refused to open them again. Sleep came by and by, though it was Tarenyawagon, the sender of dreams, who presided over it, because as he slept, and his fever grew higher, visions, many and fantastic, flitted through his disordered brain.

Robert watched until long after the rain had been pouring in sheets, and it was pitchy dark in the cave. Then he felt of Tayoga's forehead and his pulse, and observed the fever, though without alarm. Tayoga's wound was clean and his blood absolutely pure. The fever was due and it would run its course. He could do nothing more for his comrade at present, and lying down on his own spread of leaves, he soon fell asleep.

Robert's slumber was not sound. Although the Onondaga might be watched over by Tododaho, Areskoui and even Manitou himself, he had felt the weight of responsibility. The gods protected those who protected themselves, and, even while he slept, the thought was nestling somewhere in his brain and awoke him now and then. Upon every such occasion he sat up and looked out at the entrance of the cave, to see, as he had hoped, only the darkness and black sheets of driving rain, and also upon every occasion devout thanks rose up in his throat. Tayoga had not prayed to his patron saint and to the great Areskoui and Manitou in vain, else in all that wilderness, given over to night and storm, they would not have found so good a refuge and shelter.

Tayoga's fever increased, and when morning came, with the rain still falling, though not in such a deluge as by night, it seemed to Robert, who had seen many gunshot wounds, that it was about at the zenith. The Onondaga came out of his sleep, but he was delirious for a little while, Robert sitting by him, covering him with his blanket and seeing that his hurt was kept away from the air.

The rain ceased by and by, but heavy fogs and vapours floated over the mountains, so dense that Robert could not see more than fifteen or twenty feet beyond the mouth of the cave, in front of which a stream of water from the rain a foot deep was flowing. He was thankful. He knew that fog and flood together would hide them in absolute security for another day and night at least.

He ate a little venison and regretted that he did not have a small skillet in which he could make soup for Tayoga later on, but since he did not have it he resolved to pound venison into shreds between stones, when the time came. Examining Tayoga again, he found, to his great joy, that the fever was decreasing, and he washed the wound anew. Then he sat by him a long time while the morning passed. Tayoga, who had been muttering in his fever, sank into silence, and about noon, opening his eyes, he said in a weak voice:

"How long have we been here, Dagaeoga?"

"About half of the second day is now gone," replied Robert, "and your fever has gone with it. You're as limp as a towel, but you're started fairly on the road to recovery."

"I know it," said Tayoga gratefully, "and I am thankful to Tododaho, to Areskoui, to Manitou, greatest of all, and to you, Dagaeoga, without whom the great spirits of earth and air would have let me perish."

"You don't owe me anything, Tayoga. It's what one comrade has a right to expect of another. Did you exert your will, as you said, when you were delirious, and help along nature with your cure?"

"I did, Dagaeoga. Before I lapsed into the unconsciousness of which you speak, I resolved that today, when my fever should have passed, my soul should lift me up. I concentrated my mind upon it, I attuned every nerve to that end, and while I could not prevent the fever and the weakness, yet the resolution to get well fast helps me to do so. By so much does my mind rule over my body."

"I've no doubt you're right about it. Courage and optimism can lift us up a lot, as I've seen often for myself, and you're certainly out of danger now, Tayoga. All you have to do is to lie quiet, if the French and Indians will let us. In a week you'll be able to travel and fight, and in a few weeks you'll never know that a musket ball passed through your shoulder. When do you think you can eat? I'll pound some of the venison very fine."

"Not before night, and then but little. That little, though, I should have. Tomorrow I will eat much more, and a few days later it will be all Dagaeoga can do to find enough food for me. Be sure that you wait on me well. It is the first rest that I have had in a long time, and it is my purpose to enjoy it. If I should be fretful, humour me; if I should be hungry, feed me; if I should be sleepy, let me sleep, and see that I am not disturbed while I do sleep; if my bed is hard, make me a better, and through it all, O Dagaeoga, be thou the finest medicine man that ever breathed in these woods."

"Come, now, Tayoga, you lay too great a burden upon me. I'm not all the excellencies melted into one, and I've never pretended to be. But I can see that you're getting well, because the spirit of rulership is upon you as strong as ever, and, since you're so much improved, I may take it into my mind to obey your commands, though only when I feel like it."

The two lads looked at each other and laughed, and there was immense relief in Robert's laugh. Only now did he admit to himself that he had been terribly alarmed about Tayoga, and he recognized the enormous relief he felt when the Onondaga had passed his crisis.

"In truth, you pick up fast, Tayoga," he said whimsically. "Suppose we go forth now and hunt the enemy. We might finish up what Rogers, Willet and Daganoweda have left of St. Luc's force."

"I would go," replied Tayoga in the same tone, "but Tododaho and Areskoui have told me to bide here awhile. Only a fear that my disobedience might cause me to lose their favour keeps me in the cave. But I wish you to bear in mind, Dagaeoga, that I still exert my will as the medicine men of my nation bid the sick and the hurt to do, and that I feel the fevered blood cooling in my veins, strength flowing back into my weak muscles, and my nerves, that were all so loose and unattuned, becoming steady."

"I'll admit that your will may help, Tayoga, but it's chiefly the long sleep you've had, the good home you enjoy, and the superb care of Dr. Robert Lennox of Albany, New York, and the Vale of Onondaga. On the whole, weighing the question carefully, I should say that the ministrations of Dr. Lennox constitute at least eighty per cent of the whole."

"You are still the great talker, Dagaeoga, that you were when you defeated St. Luc in the test of words in the Vale of Onondaga, and it is well. The world needs good talkers, those who can make speech flow in a golden stream, else we should all grow dull and gloomy, though I will say for you, O Lennox, that you act as well as talk. If I did not, I, whose life you have saved and who have seen you great in battle, should have little gratitude and less perception."

"I've always told you, Tayoga, that when you speak English you speak out of a book, because you learned it out of a book and you take delight in long words. Now I think that 'gratitude' and 'perception' are enough for you and you can rest."

"I will rest, but it is not because you think my words are long and I am exhausted, Dagaeoga. It is because you wish to have all the time yourself for talking. You are cunning, but you need not be so now. I give my time to you."

Robert laughed. The old Tayoga with all his keenness and sense of humour was back again, and it was a sure sign that a rapid recovery had set in.

"Maybe you can go to sleep again," he said. "I think it was a stupor rather than sleep that you passed through last night, but now you ought to find sleep sweet, sound and healthy."

"You speak words of truth, O great white medicine man, and it being so my mind will make my body obey your instructions."

He turned a little on his side, away from his wounded shoulder, and either his will was very powerful or his body was willing, as he soon slept again, and now Tarenyawagon sent him no troubled and disordered dreams. Instead his breathing was deep and regular, and when Robert felt his pulse he found it was almost normal. The fever was gone and the bronze of Tayoga's face assumed a healthful tint.

Then Robert took a piece of venison, and pounded it well between two stones. He would have been glad to light a fire of dry leaves and sticks, that he might warm the meat, but he knew that it was yet too dangerous, and so strong was Tayoga's constitution that he might take the food cold, and yet find it nutritious.

It was late in the afternoon when the Onondaga awoke, yawned in human fashion, and raised himself a little on his unwounded shoulder.

"Here is your dinner, Tayoga," said Robert, presenting the shredded venison. "I'm sorry it's not better, but it's the best the lodge affords, and I, as chief medicine man and also as first assistant medicine man and second assistant medicine man, bid you eat and find no fault."

"I obey, O physician, wise and stern, despite your youth," said Tayoga. "I am hungry, which is a most excellent sign, and I will say, too, that I begin to feel like a warrior again."

He ate as much as Robert would let him have, and then, with a great sigh of content, sank back on his bed of leaves.

"I can feel my wound healing," he said. "Already the clean flesh is spreading over the hurt and the million tiny strands are knitting closely together. Some day it shall be said in the Vale of Onondaga that the wound of Tayoga healed more quickly than the wound of any other warrior of our nation."

"Good enough as a prophecy, but for the present we'll bathe and bind it anew. A little good doctoring is a wonderful help to will and prediction."

Robert once more cleansed the hurt very thoroughly, and he was surprised to find its extremely healthy condition. It had already begun to heal, a proof of amazing vitality on the part of

Tayoga, and unless the unforeseen occurred he would set a record in recovery. Robert heaped the leaves under his head to form a pillow, and the young warrior's eyes sparkled as he looked around at their snug abode.

"I can hear the water running by the mouth of the cave," he said. "It comes from last night's rain and flood, but what of tonight, Dagaeoga? The skies and what they have to say mean much to us."

"It will rain again. I've been looking out. All the west is heavy with clouds and the light winds come, soaked with damp. I don't claim to be any prophet like you, Tayoga, because I'm a modest man, I am, but the night will be wet and dark."

"Then we are still under the protection of Tododaho, of Areskoui and of Manitou, greatest of all. Let the dark come quickly and the rain fall heavily, because they will be a veil about us to hide us from Tandakora and his savages."

All that the Onondaga wished came to pass. The clouds, circling about the horizon, soon spread to the zenith, and covered the heavens, hiding the moon and the last star. The rain came, not in a flood, but in a cold and steady pour lasting all night. The night was not only dark and wet outside, but it was very chill also, though in the cave the two young warriors, the white and the red, were warm and dry on their blankets and beds of leaves.

Robert pounded more of the venison the next morning and gave Tayoga twice as much as he had eaten the day before. The Onondaga clamoured for an additional supply, but Robert would not let him have it.

"Epicure! Gourmand! Gorger!" said young Lennox. "Would you do nothing but eat? Do you think it your chief duty in this world to be a glutton?"

"No, Dagaeoga," replied Tayoga, "I am not a glutton, but I am yet hungry, and I warn thee, O grudging medicine man, that I am growing strong fast. I feel upon my arm muscles that were not there yesterday and tomorrow or the next day my strength will be so great that I shall take from you all the food of us both and eat it."

"By that time we won't have any left, and I shall have to take measures to secure a new supply. I must go forth in search of game."

"Not today, nor yet tomorrow. It is too dangerous. You must wait until the last moment. It is barely possible that the Great Bear or Black Rifle may find us."

"I don't think so. We'll have to rely on ourselves. But at any rate, I'll stay in the cave today, though I think the rain is about over. Don't you see the sun shining in at the entrance? It's going to be a fine day in the woods, Tayoga, but it won't be a fine day for us."

"That is true, Dagaeoga. It is hard to stay here in a hole in the rocks, when the sun is shining and the earth is drying. The sun has brought back the green to the leaves and the light now must be wonderful on Andiatarocte and Oneadatote. Their waters shift and change with all the colours of the rainbow. It fills me with longing when I think of these things. Go now, Dagaeoga, and find the Great Bear, the Mountain Wolf and Daganoweda. I am well past all danger from my wound, and I can take care of myself."

"Tayoga, you talk like a foolish child. If I hear any more such words I shall have to gag you, for two reasons, because they make a weariness in my ear, and because if anyone else were to hear you he would think you were weak of mind. It's your reputation for sanity that I'm thinking about most. You and I stay here together, and when we leave we leave together."

Tayoga said no more on the subject. He had known all the while that Robert would not leave him, but he had wished to give him the chance. He lay very quiet now for many hours, and Robert sitting at the door of the cave, with his rifle across his knees, was also quiet. While a great talker upon occasion, he had learned from the Iroquois the habit of silence, when silence was needed, and it required no effort from him.

Though he did not speak he saw much. The stream, caused by the flood, still flowed before the mouth of the cave, but it was diminishing steadily. By the time night came it would sink to a thin thread and vanish. The world itself, bathed and cleansed anew, was wonderfully sweet and fresh. The light wind brought the pleasant odours of flower and leaf and grass. Birds began to sing on the overhanging boughs, and a rabbit or two appeared in the valley. These unconscious sentinels made him feel quite sure that no savages were near.

Curiosity about the battle between the forces of St. Luc and those of the rangers and Mohawks, smothered hitherto by his anxiety and care for Tayoga, was now strong in his breast. It was barely possible that St. Luc had spread a successful ambush and that all of his friends had fallen. He shuddered at the thought, and then dismissed it as too unlikely. Tayoga fell asleep again, and when he awoke he was not only able to sit up, but to walk across the cave.

"Tomorrow," he said, "I shall be able to sit near the entrance and load and fire a rifle as well as ever. If an enemy should come I think I could hold the refuge alone."

"That being the case," said Robert, "and you being full of pride and haughtiness, I may let you have the chance. Not many shreds of our venison are left, and as I shall have in you a raging wolf to feed, I'll go forth and seek game. It seems to me I ought to find it soon. You don't think it's all been driven away by marching rangers and warriors, do you, Tayoga?"

"No, the rangers and warriors have been seeking one another, not the game, and perhaps the deer and the moose know it. Why does man think that Manitou watches over him alone? Perhaps He has told the big animals that they are safer when the men fight. On our way here I twice saw the tracks of a moose, and it may be your fortune to find one tomorrow, Dagaeoga."

"Not fortune, at all, Tayoga. If I bring down one it will be due to my surpassing skill in trailing and to my deadly sharpshooting, for which I am renowned the world over. Anyhow, I think we can sleep another night without a guard and then we'll see what tomorrow will bring forth."

Chapter 12

The Sinister Siege

Dawn came, very clear and beautiful, with the air crisp and cool. Robert divided the last of the venison between Tayoga and himself, and when he had eaten his portion he was still hungry. He was quite certain that the Onondaga also craved more, but a stoic like Tayoga would never admit it. His belief the day before that this was the time for him to go forth and hunt was confirmed. The game would be out, and so might be the savages, but he must take the chance.

Tayoga had kept his bow and quiver of arrows strapped to his back during their retreat, and now they lay on a shelf in the cave. Robert looked at them doubtfully and the eyes of the Onondaga followed him.

"Perhaps it would be best," he said.

"I can't bend the bow of Ulysses," said Robert, "but I may be able to send in a useful arrow or two nevertheless."

"You can try."

"But I don't want any shot to go amiss."

"Strap your rifle on your back, and take the bow and arrows also. If the arrows fail you, or rather if you should fail the arrows, which always go where they are sent, you can take the rifle, with which you are almost as good as the Great Bear himself. And if you should encounter hostile warriors prowling through the woods the rifle will be your best defence."

"I'll do as you advise, Tayoga, and do you keep a good watch at the entrance. You're feeling a lot stronger today, are you not?"

"So much so that I am almost tempted to take the bow and arrows myself, while I leave you on guard."

"Don't be too proud and boastful. Let's see you walk across the cave."

Tayoga rose from the bed of leaves, on which he had been sitting, and strode firmly back and forth two or three times. He was much thinner than he had been a week before, but his eyes were sparkling now and the bronze of his skin was clear and beautiful. All his nerves and muscles were under complete control.

"You're a great warrior again, Tayoga, thanks to my protecting care," said Robert, "but I don't think you're yet quite the equal of Tododaho and Hayowentha when they walked the earth, and, for that reason, I shall not let you go out hunting. Now, take your rifle, which I saved along with you, and sit on that ledge of stone, where you can see everything approaching the cave and not be seen yourself."

"I obey, O Dagaeoga. I obey you always when the words you speak are worth being obeyed. See, I take the seat you direct, and I hold my rifle ready."

"Very good. Be prepared to fire on an instant's notice, but be sure you don't fire at me when I come striding down the valley bearing on my shoulders a fat young deer that I have just killed."

"Have no fear, Dagaeoga. I shall be too glad to see you and the deer to fire."

With the rifle so adjusted across his back that, if need be, he could disengage it at once, the quiver fastened also and Tayoga's bow in his hand, Robert made ready.

"Now, Tayoga," he said, "exert that famous will of yours like a true medicine man of the Hodenosaunee. While I am absent, so direct me with the concentrated power of your mind that I shall soon find a fat young deer, and that my arrow shall not miss. I'll gratefully receive all the help you can give me in this way, though I won't neglect, if I see the deer, to take the best aim I can with bow and arrow."

"Do not scoff, O Dagaeoga. The lore and belief of my nation and of the whole Hodenosaunee are based upon the experience of many centuries. And do you not say in your religion that the prayer of the righteous availeth? Do you think your God, who is the same as my Manitou, intended that only the prayers of the white men should have weight, and that those of the red men should vanish into nothingness like a snowflake melting in the air? I may not be righteous,—who knows whether he is righteous or not?—but, at least, I shall pray in a righteous cause."

"I don't mock, Tayoga, and maybe the power of your wish, poured in a flood upon me, will help. Yes, I know it will, and I go now, sure that I will soon find what I seek."

He left the cave and passed up the valley, full of confidence. The earnestness of Tayoga had made a great impression upon him, clothing him about with an atmosphere that was surcharged with belief, and, as he breathed in this air, it made his veins fairly sparkle, not alone with hope, but with certainty.

He walked up a deep defile which gradually grew shallower, and then ascended rapidly. Finally he came out on a crest, crowned with splendid trees, and he drew a great breath of pleasure as he looked upon a vast green wilderness, deepened in colour by the long and recent rains, and upon the far western horizon a dim but splendid band of silver which he knew was Andiatarocte. A lover of beauty, and with the soul of a poet, he could have stood, gazing a long time, but there was a sterner task forward than the contemplation of nature in the wild.

He must sink the poet in the hunter, and he began to look for tracks of game, which he felt sure would be plentiful in the forest, since men had long been hunting one another instead of the deer. He had an abundance of will of his own, but he felt also, despite a certain incredulity of the reason, that the concentrated will of his distant comrade was driving him on.

He walked about a mile, remaining well under cover, having a double object, to keep himself hidden from foes and also to find traces of game. His confidence that he would find it, and very quickly, was not abated, and, at the end of a mile, he saw a broad footprint on the turf that made him utter a low exclamation of delight. It was larger than that of a cow, and more pointed. He knew at once that it had been made by a moose, the great animal which was then still to be found in the forests of Northern New York.

The tracks led northward and he studied them with care. The wind had risen and was blowing toward him, which was favourable for his pursuit, as the sound of his own footsteps rustling the grass or breaking a little stick would not be likely to reach the ear of the moose. He was convinced, too, that the tracks were not much more than two hours old, and since the big animal was likely to be rambling along, nibbling at the twigs, the chance was in favour of the hunter overtaking him very soon.

It was easy to follow the trail, the hoof prints were so large, and he soon saw, too, the broken ends of twigs that had been nibbled by the moose, and also exposed places on the trunks of trees where the bark had been peeled off by the animal's teeth. He was sure that the game could not be much more than a mile ahead, and his soul was filled with the ardour of the chase. He was confident that he was pursuing a big bull, as the fact was indicated by the size of the prints, the length of the stride, and the height at which the moose had browsed on the twigs. There were other facts he had learned among the Iroquois, indicating to him it was a bull. While the tracks were pointed, they were less pointed than those the cow generally makes, and the twigs that had been nibbled were those of the fir, while the cow usually prefers the birch.

The tracks now seemed to Robert to grow much fresher. Tayoga, with his infallible eye and his wonderful gifts, both inherited and improved, would have known just how fresh they were, but Robert was compelled to confine his surmise to the region of the comparative. Nevertheless, he knew that he was gaining upon the moose and that was enough. But as it was evident by his frequent browsing that the animal was going slowly, he controlled his eagerness sufficiently to exercise great wariness on his own part. It might be that while he was hunting he could also become the hunted. It was not at all impossible that the warriors of Tandakora would fall upon his own track and follow.

He looked back apprehensively, and once he returned and retraced his steps for a little distance, but he could discern no evidence of an enemy and he resumed his pursuit of the moose, going faster now, and seeing twigs which apparently had been broken off only a few minutes before. Then, as he topped a little rise, he saw the animal itself, browsing lazily on the succulent bushes. It was a large moose, but to Robert, although an experienced hunter, it loomed up at the moment like an elephant. He had staked so much upon securing the game, and the issue was so important that his heart beat hard with excitement.

The wind was still in his favour, and, creeping as near as he dared, he fitted an arrow to Tayoga's bow and pulled the string. The arrow struck well in behind the shoulder and the moose leaped high. Another arrow sang from the bow and found its heart, after which it ran a few steps and fell. Robert's laborious task began, to remove at least a part of the skin, and then great portions of the meat, as much as he could carry, wrapped in the folds of the skin, portions from which he intended to make steaks.

He secured at least fifty pounds, and then he looked with regret at the great body. He was not one to slay animals for sport's sake, and he wished that the rangers and Mohawks might have the hundreds of pounds of good moose meat, but he knew it was not destined for them. As he drew away with his own burden his heirs to the rest were already showing signs of their presence. From the thick bushes about came the rustling of light feet, and now and then an eager and impatient snarl. Red eyes showed, and as he turned away the wolves of the hills made a wild rush for the fallen monarch. Robert, for some distance, heard them yapping and snarling over the feast, and, despite his own success in securing what he needed so badly, he felt remorse because he had been compelled to give so fine an animal over to the wolves.

His heart grew light again as he made his way back to the defile and the cave. He carried enough food to last Tayoga and himself many days, if necessity compelled them to remain long in the cave, but he did not forget in his triumph to take every precaution for the hiding of his trail, devoutly glad that it was hard ground, thick with stones, on which he could step from one to another.

Thus he returned, bearing his burden, and Tayoga, sitting near the entrance, rifle on knee, greeted him with becoming words as one whom Tododaho and Areskoui had guided to victory.

"It is well, Dagaeoga," he said. "I was wishing for you to find a moose and you found one. You were not compelled to use the rifle!"

"No, the bow served, but I had to shoot two arrows where you would have shot only one."

"It is no disgrace to you. The bow is not the white man's weapon, at least not on this continent. You withdrew the arrows, cleaned them and returned them to the quiver?"

"Yes. I didn't forget that. I know how precious arrows are, and now, Tayoga, since it's important for you to get back your strength faster than a wounded man ever got it back before, I think we'd better risk a fire, and broil some of these fat, juicy steaks."

"It is a danger, but we will do it. You gather the dead wood and we will build the fire beside the mouth of the cave. Both of us can cook."

It was an easy task for two such foresters to light a fire with flint and steel, and they soon had a big bed of coals. Then they broiled the steaks on the ends of sharpened sticks, passing them back and forth quickly, in order to retain the juices.

"Now, Tayoga," announced Robert, "I have a word or two to say to you."

"Then say them quickly and do not let your eloquence become a stream, because I am hungry and would eat, and where the moose steaks are plenty talk is needed but little."

"I merely wished to tell you that besides being our hunter, I'm also the family doctor. Hence I give you my instructions."

"What are they, O youth of many words?"

"You can eat just as much of the moose steak as you like, and the quicker you begin the better you will please me, because my manners won't allow me to start first. Fall on, Tayoga! Fall on!"

They ate hungrily and long. They would have been glad had they bread also, but they did not waste time in vain regrets. When they had finished and the measure of their happiness was full, they extinguished the coals carefully, hid their store of moose meat on a high ledge in the cave, and withdrew also to its shelter.

"How much stronger do you feel now, Tayoga?" asked Robert.

"In the language of your schools, my strength has increased at least fifty per cent in the last hour."

"I've the strength of two men myself now, and thinking it over, Tayoga, I've come to the conclusion that was the best moose I ever tasted. He was a big bull, and he may not have been young, but he furnished good steaks. I'm sorry he had to die, but he died in a good cause."

"Even so, Dagaeoga, and since we have eaten tremendously and have cooked much of the meat for further use, it would be best for us to put out the fire, and hide all trace of it, a task in which I am strong enough to help you."

They extinguished carefully every brand and coal, and even went so far as to take dead leaves from the cave and throw them over the remains of the fire in careless fashion as if they had been swept there by the wind.

"And now," said Robert, "if I had the power I would summon from the sky another mighty rain to hide all signs of our banquet and of the preparations for it. Suppose, Tayoga, you pray to Tododaho and Areskoui for it and also project your mind so forcibly in the direction of your wish that the wish will come true."

"It is well not to push one's favour too far," replied Tayoga gravely. "The heavens are too bright and shining now for rain. Moreover, if one should pray every day for help, Tododaho and Areskoui would grow tired of giving it. I think, however, that we have covered our traces well, and the chance of discovery here by our enemies is remote."

They put away the moose meat on a high ledge in the cave, and sat down again to wait. Tayoga's wound was healing rapidly. The miracle for which he had hoped was happening. His recovery was faster than that of any other injured warrior whom he had ever known. He could fairly feel the clean flesh knitting itself together in innumerable little fibres, and already he could move his left arm, and use the fingers of his left hand. Being a stoic, and hiding his feelings as he usually did, he said:

"I shall recover, I shall be wholly myself again in time for the great battle between the army of Waraiyageh and that of Dieskau."

"I think, too, that we'll be in it," said Robert confidently. "Armies move slowly and they won't come together for quite a while yet. Meantime, I'm wondering what became of the rangers and the Mohawks."

"We shall have to keep on wondering, but I am thinking it likely that they prevailed over the forces of St. Luc and have passed on toward Crown Point and Oneadatote. It may be that the present area of conflict has passed north and east of us and we have little to fear of our enemies."

"It sounds as if you were talking out of a book again, Tayoga, but I believe you're right."

"I think the only foes whom we may dread in the next night and day are four-footed."

"You mean the wolves?"

"Yes, Dagaeoga. When you left the body of the moose did they not appear?"

"They were fighting over it before I was out of sight. But they wouldn't dare to attack you and me."

"It is a strange thing, Dagaeoga, but whenever there is war in the woods among men the wolves grow numerous, powerful and bold. They know that when men turn their arms upon one another they are turned aside from the wolves. They hang upon the fringes of the bands and armies, and where the wounded are they learn to attack. I have noticed, too, since the great war began that we have here bigger and fiercer wolves than any we've ever known before, coming out of the vast wilderness of the far north."

"You mean the timber wolves, those monsters, five or six feet long, and almost as powerful and dangerous as a tiger or a lion?"

"So I do, Dagaeoga, and they will be abroad tonight, led by the body of your moose and the portion we have here. Tododaho, sitting on his star, has whispered to me that we are about to incur a great danger, one that we did not expect."

"You give me a creepy feeling, Tayoga. All this is weird and uncanny. We've nothing to fear from wolves."

"A thousand times we might have nothing to fear from them, but one time we will, and this is the time. In a voice that I did not hear, but which I felt, Tododaho told me so, and I know."

"Then all we have to do is to build a fire in front of the cave mouth and shut them off as thoroughly, as if we had raised a steel wall before us."

"The danger from a fire burning all night would be too great. While I do not think any warriors of the enemy are wandering in this immediate region, yet it is possible, and our bonfire would be a beacon to draw them."

"Then we'll have to meet 'em with bullets, but the reports of our rifles might also draw Tandakora's warriors."

"We will not use the rifles. We will sit at the entrance of the cave, and you shall fight them with my bow and arrows. If we are pressed too hard, we may resort to the rifles."

Tayoga's words were so earnest and sententious, his manner so much that of a prophet, that Robert, in spite of himself, believed in the great impending danger that would come in the dark, and the hair on the back of his neck lifted a little. Yet the day was still great and shining, the forest tinted gold with the flowing sunlight, and the pure fresh air blowing into the cave. There the two youths, the white and the red, took their seats at either side of the entrance. Tayoga held his rifle across his knees, but Robert put his and the quiver at his feet, while he held the bow and one arrow in his hands.

They talked a little from time to time and then relapsed into a long silence. Robert noticed that nothing living stirred in the defile. No more rabbits came out to play and no birds sang in the trees. He considered it a sign, nay more, an omen that Tayoga's prediction was coming true. The peril threatening them was great and imminent. His sense of the sinister and uncanny increased. A chill ran through his veins. The great shining day was going, and, although it was midsummer, a cold wind was herald of the coming twilight. He shivered again, and looked at the long shadows falling in the defile.

"Tayoga," he said, "that uncanny talk of yours has affected me, but I believe you've just made it all up. No wolves are coming to attack us."

"Dagaeoga does not believe anything of the kind. He believes, instead, what I have told him. His voice and his manner show it. He is sure the wolves are coming."

"You're right, Tayoga, I do believe it. There's every reason why I shouldn't, but, in very truth and fact, I do. Our fine day is going fast. Look how the twilight is growing on the mountains. From our nook here I can just see the rim of the sun, who is your God, Areskoui. Soon he will be gone entirely and then all the ridges will be lost in the dusk. I hope—and I'm not jesting either—that you've said your prayer to him."

"As I told you, Dagaeoga, one must not ask too many favours. But now the sun is wholly gone and the night will be dark. The wind rises and it moans like the soul of an evil warrior condemned to wander between heaven and earth. The night will be dark, and in two hours the wolves will be here."

Robert looked at him, but the face of the Onondaga was that of a seer, and once more the blood of the white youth ran chill in his veins. He was silent again, and now the minutes were leaden-footed, so slow, in truth, that it seemed an hour would never pass and the two hours Tayoga had predicted were an eternity. The afterglow disappeared and the darkness was deep in the defile. The trees above were fused into a black mass, and then, after an infinity of waiting, a faint note, sinister and full of menace, came out of the wilderness. Tayoga and Robert glanced at each other.

"It is as you predicted," said Robert.

"It is the howl of the great timber wolf from the far north who has made himself the leader of the band," said the Onondaga. "When he howls again he will be much nearer."

Robert waited for an almost breathless minute or two, and then came the malignant note, much nearer, as Tayoga had predicted, and directly after came other howls, faint but equally sinister.

"The great leader gives tongue a second time," said Tayoga, "and his pack imitate him, but their voices are not so loud, because their lungs are not so strong. They come straight toward us. Do you see, Dagaeoga, that your nerves are steady, your muscles strong and your eyes bright. I would that I could use the bow myself tonight, for the chance will be glorious, but Manitou has willed otherwise. It is for you, Dagaeoga, to handle my weapon as if you had been familiar with it all your life."

"I will do my best, Tayoga. No man can do more."

"Dagaeoga's best is very good indeed. Remember that if they undertake to rush us we will use our rifles, but they are to be held in reserve. Hark, the giant leader howls for the third time!"

The long, piercing note came now from a point not very distant. Heard in all the loneliness of the black forest it was inexpressively threatening and evil. Not until his own note died did the howl of his pack follow. All doubts that Robert may have felt fled at once. He believed everything that Tayoga had said, and he knew that the wolf-pack, reinforced by mighty timber wolves from the far north, was coming straight toward the cave for what was left of the moose meat and Tayoga and himself. His nerves shook for an instant, but the next moment he put them under command, and carefully tested the bowstring.

"It is good and strong," he said to Tayoga. "It will not be any fault of the bow and arrow if the work is not done well. The fault will be mine instead."

"You will not fail, Dagaeoga," said the Onondaga. "Your great imagination always excites you somewhat before the event, but when it comes you are calm and steady."

"I'll try to prove that you estimate me correctly."

As their eyes were used to the dusk they could see each other well, sitting on opposite sides of the cave mouth and sheltered by the projection of the rocks. The great wolf howled once more and the pack howled after him, but there followed an interval of silence that caused Robert to think they had, perhaps, turned aside. But Tayoga whispered presently:

"I see the leader on the opposite side of the defile among the short bushes. The pack is farther back. They know, of course, that we are here. The leader is, as we surmised, a huge timber wolf, come down from the far north. Do not shoot, Dagaeoga, until you get a good chance."

"Do you think I should wait for the leader himself?"

"No. Often the soul of a wicked warrior goes into the body of a wolf, and the wolf becomes wicked, and also full of craft. The leader may not come forward at first himself, but will send others to receive our blows."

There was no yapping and snarling from the wolves such as was usual, and such as Robert had often heard, but they had become a phantom pack, silent and ghost-like, creeping among the bushes, sinister and threatening beyond all reckoning. Robert began to feel that, in very truth, it was a phantom pack, and he wondered if his arrows, even if they struck full and true, would slay. Nature, in her chance moments, touches one among the millions with genius, and she had so tipped him with living fire. His vivid and powerful imagination often made him see things others could not see and caused him to clothe objects in colours invisible to common eyes.

Now the wolves, with their demon leader, were moving in silence among the bushes, and he felt that in truth he would soon be fighting with what Tayoga called evil spirits. For the moment, not the demon leader alone, but every wolf represented the soul of a wicked warrior, and they would approach with all the cunning that the warriors had known and practiced in their lives.

"Do you see the great beast now, Tayoga?" he whispered.

"No, he is behind a rock, but there is another slinking forward, drawing himself without noise over the ground. He must have been in life a savage from the far region, west of the Great Lakes, perhaps an eater of his own kind, as the wolf eats his."

"I see him, Tayoga, just there on the right where the darkness lies like a shroud. I see his jaws slavering too. He comes forward as a stalker, and I've no doubt the soul of a most utter savage is hidden in his body. He shall meet my arrow."

"Wait a little, Dagaeoga, until you can be sure of your shot. There is another creeping forward on the left in the same manner, and you'll want to send a second arrow quickly at him."

"I never saw a wolf-pack attack in this way before. They come like a band of warriors with scouts and skirmishers, and I can see that they have a force massed in the centre for the main rush."

"In a few more seconds you can take the wolf on the right. Bury your arrow in his throat. It is as I said, Dagaeoga. Now that the moment has come your hand is steady, your nerves are firm, and even in the dusk I can see that your eyes are bright."

It was true. Robert's imagination had painted the danger in the most vivid colours, but now, that it was here, the beat of his pulse was as regular as the ticking of a clock. Yet the unreal and sinister atmosphere that clothed him about was not dispelled in the least, and he could not rid himself of the feeling that in fighting them he was fighting dead and gone warriors.

Nearer and nearer came the great wolf on his right, dragging his body over the ground for all the world like a creeping Indian. Robert's eyes, become uncommonly keen in the dusk, saw the long fangs, the slavering jaws and the red eyes, and he also saw the spot in the pulsing throat where he intended that the sharp point of his arrow should strike.

"Now!" whispered Tayoga.

Robert fitted the shaft to the string, and deftly throwing his weight into it bent the great bow. Then he loosed the arrow, and, singing through the air, it buried itself almost to the feather in the big beast's throat, just at the spot that he had chosen. The strangled howl of despair and death that followed was almost like that of a human being, but Robert did not stop to listen, as with all speed he fitted another arrow to the string and fired at the beast on the left, with equal success, piercing him in the heart.

"Well done, Dagaeoga," whispered Tayoga. "Two shots and two wolves slain. The skirmisher on the right and the skirmisher on the left both are gone. There will be a wait now while the living devour their dead comrades. Listen, you can hear them dragging the bodies into the bushes."

"After they have finished their cannibalism perhaps they will go away."

"No, it is a great pack, and they are very hungry. In ten or fifteen minutes they will be stalking us again. You must seek a shot at the giant leader, but it will be hard for you to get it because he will keep himself under cover, while he sends forth his warriors to meet your arrows. Ah, he is great and cunning! Now, I am more sure than ever that his body contains the soul of one of the most wicked of all warriors, perhaps that of a brother of Tandakora. Yes, it must be a brother, the blood of Tandakora."

"Then Tandakora's brother would better beware. My desire to slay him has increased, and if he's incautious and I get good aim I think I can place an arrow so deep in him that the Ojibway's wicked soul will have to seek another home."

"Hear them growling and snarling in the bushes. It is over their cannibalistic feast. Soon they will have finished and then they will come back to us."

The deadly stalking, more hideous than that carried on by men, because it was more unnatural, was resumed. Robert discharged a third arrow, but the fierce yelp following told him that he had inflicted only a wound. He glanced instinctively at the Onondaga, fearing a reproof, but Tayoga merely said:

"If one shoots many times one must miss sometimes."

A fourth shot touched nothing, but the Onondaga had no rebuke, a fifth shot killed a wolf, a sixth did likewise, and Robert's pride returned. The wolves drew off, to indulge in cannibalism again, and to consult with their leader, who carried the soul of a savage in his body.

Robert had sought in vain for a fair shot at the giant wolf. He had caught one or two glimpses of him, but they were too fleeting for the flight of an arrow, and, despite all reason and logic, he found himself accepting Tayoga's theory that he was, in reality, a lost brother of Tandakora, marshalling forward his forces, but keeping himself secure. After the snarling and yelping over the horrible repast, another silence followed in the bushes.

"Perhaps they've had enough and have gone away," said Robert, hazarding the hopeful guess a second time.

"No. They will make a new attack. They care nothing for those that have fallen. Watch well, Dagaeoga, and keep your arrows ready."

"I think I'll become a good bowman in time," said Robert lightly, to ease his feelings, "because I'm getting a lot of practice, and it seems that I'll have a lot more. Perhaps I need this rest, but, so far as my feelings are concerned, I wish the wolves would come on and make a final rush. Their silence and invisibility are pretty hard on the nerves."

He examined the bow carefully again, and put six arrows on the floor of the cave beside him, with the quiver just beyond them. Tayoga sat immovable, his rifle across his knees, ready in the last emergency to use the bullet. Thus more time passed in silence and without action.

It often seemed to Robert afterward that there was something unnatural about both time and place. The darkness came down thicker and heavier, and to his imaginative ear it had a faint sliding sound like the dropping of many veils. So highly charged had become his faculties that they were able to clothe the intangible and the invisible with bodily reality. He glanced across at his comrade, whom his accustomed eyes could see despite the blackness of the night. Tayoga was quite still. So far as Robert could tell he had not stirred by a hair's breadth in the last hour.

"Do you hear anything?" whispered the white youth.

"Nothing," replied the Onondaga. "Not even a dead leaf stirs before the wind. There is no wind to stir it. But I think the pack will be coming again very soon. They will not leave us until you shoot their demon leader."

"You mean Tandakora's brother! If I get a fair chance I'll certainly send my best arrow at him, and I'm only sorry that it's not Tandakora himself. You persist in your belief that the soul of a wicked warrior is in the body of the wolf?"

"Of course! As I have said, it is surely a brother of Tandakora, because Tandakora himself is alive, and, as it cannot be his own, it must be that of a monstrous one so much like his that it can be only a brother's. That is why the wolf leader is so large, so fierce and so cunning. I persist, too, in saying that all the wolves of this pack contain the souls of wicked warriors. It is natural that they should draw together and hunt together, and hunt men as they hunted them in life."

"I'm not disputing you, Tayoga. Both day and night have more things than I can ever hope to understand, but it seems to me that night has the more. I've been listening so hard, Tayoga, that I can't tell now where imagination ends and reality begins, but I think I hear a footfall, as soft as that of a leaf dropping to the ground, but a footfall just the same."

"I hear it too, Dagaeoga, and it is not the dropping of a leaf. It is a wolf creeping forward, seeking to stalk us. He is on the right, and there are others on both right and left. Now I know they are warriors, or have been, since they use the arts of warriors rather than those of wolves."

"But if they should get in here they would use the teeth and claws of wolves."

"Teeth and claws are no worse than the torch, the faggot and the stake, perhaps better. I hear two sliding wolves now, Dagaeoga, but I know that neither is the giant leader. As before, he keeps under cover, while he sends forward others to the attack."

"Which proves that Tandakora's brother is a real general. I think I can make out a dim outline now. It is that of the first wolf on the right, and he does slide forward as if he were a warrior and not a wolf. I think I'll give him an arrow."

"Wait until he comes a dozen feet nearer, Dagaeoga, and you can be quite sure. But when you do shoot snatch up another arrow quicker than you ever did before in your life, because the leader, thinking you are not ready, may jump from the shelter of the rocks to drive the rest of the pack in a rush upon us."

"You speak as if they were human beings, Tayoga."

"Such is my thought, Dagaeoga."

"Very well. I'll bear in mind what you say, and I'll pick an arrow for Tandakora's brother."

He chose a second arrow carefully and put it on the ledge beside him, where it required but one sweep of his hand to seize it and fit it to the string, when the first had been sent. He now distinctly saw the creeping wolf, and again fancy laid hold of him and played strange tricks with his eyes. The creeping figure changed. It was not that of a wolf, but a warrior, intent upon his life. A strange terror, the terror of the weird and unknown, seized him, but in an instant it passed, and he drew the bowstring. When he loosed it the arrow stood deep in the wolf's throat, but Robert did not see it. His eyes passed on like a flash of lightning to a gigantic form that up-reared itself from the rocks, an enormous wolf with red eyes, glistening fangs and slavering jaws.

"Now!" shot forth Tayoga.

Robert had already fitted a second arrow to the string and the immense throat presented a target full and fair. Now, as always in the moment of imminent crisis, his nerves were steady, never had they been more steady, and his eyes pierced the darkness. Never before and never again did he bend so well the bow of Ulysses. The arrow, feathered and barbed, hummed through the air, going as straight and swift as a bullet to its mark, and then it pierced the throat of the wolf so deep that the barb stood out on one side and the feathers on the other.

The wolf uttered a horrible growling shriek that was almost human to Robert, leaped convulsively back and out of sight, but for a minute or two they heard him threshing among the rocks and bushes. The whole pack uttered a dismal howl. Their sliding sounds ceased, and the last dim figure vanished.

"I think it is all over with Tandakora's brother," said Robert.

Tayoga said nothing, and Robert glanced at him. Beads of perspiration stood on the brow of the Onondago, but his eyes glittered.

"You have shot well tonight, O Dagaeoga," he said. "Never did a man shoot better. Tonight you have been the greatest bowman in all the world. You have slain the demon wolf, the leader of the pack. Perhaps the wicked soul that inhabited his body has gone to inhabit the body of another evil brute, but we are delivered. They will not attack again."

"How do you know that, Tayoga?"

"Because Tododaho, Tododaho who protects us, is whispering it to me. I do not see him, but he is leaning down from his star, and his voice enters my ear. Our fight with the wolf pack and its terrible leader is finished. Steady, Dagaeoga! Steady! Make no excuses! The greatest of warriors, the hero of a hundred battles, might well sink for a few moments after such a combat!"

Robert had collapsed suddenly. The great imagination driving forward his will, and attuning him for such swift and tremendous action, failed, now that the crisis had passed, and he dropped back against the ledge, though his fingers still instinctively clutched the bow. Darkness was before his eyes, and he was weak and trembling, but he projected his will anew, and a little later sat upright, collected and firm. Nevertheless, it was Tayoga who now took supreme command.

"You have surely done enough for one night, Dagaeoga," he said. "Tododaho himself, after doing so much, would have rested. Lie down now on your blanket and I will watch for the remainder of the darkness. It is true my left arm is lame and of no use for the present, but nothing will come."

"I'll do as you tell me, Tayoga," said Robert, "but first I give you back your bow and arrows. They've served us well, though I little thought I'd ever have to do work as a bowman."

He was glad enough to stretch himself on the blanket and leaves, as he realized that despite his will he had become weak. Presently he sank into a deep slumber. When he awoke the sun was shining in the mouth of the cave and Tayoga was offering him some of the tenderest of the moose steak.

"Eat, Dagaeoga," he said. "Though a warrior of the clan of the Bear, of the nation Onondaga of the great League of the Hodenosaunee, I am proud to serve the king of bowmen."

"Cease your jesting at my expense, Tayoga."

"It is not wholly a jest, but eat."

"I will. Have you seen what is outside?"

"Not yet. We will take our breakfast together, and then we will go forth to see what we may see."

They ate heartily, and then with rifles cocked passed into the defile, where they found only the bones of wolves, picked clean by the others. But the skeleton of the huge leader was gone, although the arrow that had slain him was lying among the rocks.

"The living must have dragged away his bones. A curious thing to do," said Robert.

Tayoga was silent.

Chapter 13

Tandakora's Grasp

They spent two more days in the cave, and Tayoga's marvellous cure proceeded with the same marvellous rapidity. Robert repeatedly bathed the wound for him, and then redressed it, so the air could not get to it. The Onondaga was soon able to flex the fingers well and then to use the arm a little.

"It is sure now," he said joyfully, "that Waraiyageh and Dieskau cannot meet before I am able to do battle."

"Anyhow, they wouldn't think of fighting until you came, Tayoga," said Robert.

Their spirits were very high. They felt that they had been released from great danger, some of which they could not fathom, and they would soon leave the hollow. Action would bring relief, and they anticipated eagerly what the world outside might disclose to them. Robert collected all the arrows he had shot in the fight with the wolf pack, cleaned them and restored them to the quiver. They also put a plentiful supply of the moose meat in their packs, and then he said:

"Which way, Tayoga?"

"There is but one way."

"You mean we should press on toward Crown Point, and find out what has become of our comrades?"

"That is it. We must know how ended their battle with St. Luc."

"Which entails a search through the forest. That's just what I wanted, but I didn't know how you felt about it with your lame shoulder."

"Tomorrow or next day I shall be able to use the shoulder if we have to fight, but we may not meet any of the French or their allied warriors. I have no wish at all to turn back."

"Then forward it is, Tayoga, and I propose that we go toward the spot where we left them in conflict. Such eyes as yours may yet find there signs that you can read. Then we'll know how to proceed."

"Well spoken, Dagaeoga. Come, we'll go through the forest as fast as we may."

The cave had been a most welcome place. It had served in turn as a home, a hospital and a fort, and, in every capacity, it had served well, but both Robert and Tayoga were intensely glad to be out again in the open world, where the winds were blowing, where vast masses of green rested and pleased the eye, and where the rustling of leaves and the singing of birds soothed the ear.

"It's a wonderful, a noble wilderness!" said Robert. "I'm glad I'm here, even if there are Frenchmen and Indians in it, seeking our lives. Why, Tayoga, I can feel myself growing in such an atmosphere! Tell me, am I not an inch taller than I was when I left that hollow in the rocks?"

"You do look taller," said the Onondaga, "but maybe it's because you stand erect now. Dagaeoga, since the wolves have been defeated, has become proud and haughty again."

"At any rate, your wonderful cure is still going on at wonderful speed. You use your left arm pretty freely and you seem to have back nearly all your old strength."

"Yes, Tododaho still watches over me. He is far better to me than I deserve."

They pushed on at good speed, returning on the path they had taken, when Tayoga received his wound, and though they slept one night on the way, to give Tayoga's wound a further chance, they came in time to the place where the rangers and the Mohawks had met St. Luc's force in combat. The heavy rains long since had wiped out all traces of footsteps there, but Robert hoped that the keen eyes of the Onondaga would find other signs to indicate which way the battle had gone. Tayoga looked a long time before he said anything.

"The battle was very fierce," he said at last. "Our main force lay along here among these bushes."

"How do you know, Tayoga?" asked Robert.

"It is very simple. For a long distance the bushes are shattered and broken. It was rifle balls and musket balls that did it. Indians are not usually good marksmen, and they shot high, cutting off twigs above the heads of the Mohawks and rangers."

"Suppose we look at the opposing ridge and line of bushes where St. Luc's warriors must have stationed themselves."

They crossed the intervening space of sixty or seventy yards and found that the bushes there had not been cut up so much.

"The rangers and Mohawks are the better marksmen," said Tayoga. "They aimed lower and probably hit the target much oftener. At least they did not cut off so many twigs."

He walked back into the open space between the two positions, his eye having been caught by something dark lying in a slight depression of the earth. It was part of the brushy tail of a raccoon, such as the borderers wore in their caps.

"Our men charged," said the Onondaga.

"Why do you say so?" asked Robert.

"Because of the raccoon tail. It was shot from the cap of one of the charging men. The French and the Indians do not wear such a decoration. See where the bullet severed it. I think St. Luc's men must have broken and run before the charge, and we will look for evidence of it."

They advanced in the direction of Champlain, and, two or three hundred yards farther on, Tayoga picked up a portion of an Indian headdress, much bedraggled.

"Their flight was headlong," he said, "or the warrior would not have lost the frame and feathers that he valued so much. It fell then, before the storm, as the muddy and broken condition of the feathers shows that it was lying on the ground when the great rain came."

"And here," said Robert, "is where a bullet went into the trunk of this big oak."

"Which shows that the rangers and Mohawks were still pursuing closely. It is possible that the French and Indians tried to make a brief stand at this place. Let us see if we can find the track of other bullets."

They discovered the paths of two more in tree trunks and saw the boughs of several shattered bushes, all leading in a line toward Crown Point.

"They were not able to stand long," said Tayoga. "Our men rushed them again. Ah, this shows that they must have been in a panic for a few moments."

He picked an Indian blanket, soiled and worn, from a gulley.

"See the mud upon it," he said. "It, too, fell before the rain, because when the flood came a stream ran in the gulley, a stream that has left the blanket in this state. The warrior must have been in tremendous haste to have lost his blanket. We know now that they were routed, and that the victory was ours. But it is likely that our leaders continued the pursuit toward Oneadatote and up to the walls of Crown Point itself. And if your wish be the same as mine, Dagaeoga, we will follow on."

"You know, Tayoga, that I wouldn't think of anything else."

"But the dangers grow thick as we approach Crown Point."

"Not any thicker for me than for you."

"To that I can make no reply. Dagaeoga is always ready with words."

"But while I want to go on, I'm not in favour of taking any needless risks. I like to keep my scalp on top of my head, the place where it belongs, and so I bid you, Tayoga, use those keen eyes and ears of yours to the utmost."

Tayoga laughed.

"Dagaeoga is learning wisdom," he said. "A great warrior does not throw his life away. He will not walk blind through the forest. I will do all I can with my ears and so will you."

"I mean to do so. Do you see that silver flash through the tangle of foliage? Don't you think it comes from the waters of Champlain?"

"It cannot be doubted. Once more we see the great lake, and Crown Point itself is not so many miles away. It is in my mind that Black Rifle, Great Bear, Mountain Wolf, Daganoweda and our men have been scouting about it."

"And we might meet 'em coming back. I've had that thought too."

They walked on toward Champlain, through a forest apparently without sign of danger, and Tayoga, hearing a slight noise in a thicket, turned off to the right to see if a deer were browsing there. He found nothing, but as the sound came again from a point farther on, he continued his search, leaving his comrade out of sight behind him. The thickets were very dense and suddenly the warning of Tododaho came.

He sprang back as quick as lightning, and doubtless he would have escaped had it not been for his wounded shoulder. He hurled off the first warrior who threw himself upon him, slipped from the grasp of a second, but was unable to move when the mighty Tandakora and another seized him by the shoulders.

But in the moment of dire peril he remembered his comrade and uttered a long and thrilling cry of warning, which the huge hand of Tandakora could not shut off in time. Then, knowing he was trapped and would only injure his shoulder by further struggles, he ceased to resist, submitting passively to the binding of his arms behind him.

He saw that Tandakora had seven or eight warriors with him, and a half dozen more were bounding out on the trail after Robert. He heard a shot and then another, but he did not hear any yell of triumph, and he drew a long breath of relief. His warning cry had been uttered in time. Dagaeoga would know that it was folly, for him also to fall into the hands of Tandakora, and he would flee at his greatest speed.

So he stood erect with his wrists bound behind him, his face calm and immovable. It did not become an Onondaga taken prisoner to show emotion, or, in fact, feeling of any kind before his captors, but his heart was full of anxiety as he waited with those who held him. A quarter of an hour they stood thus, and then the pursuing warriors, recognizing the vain nature of their quest, began to return. Tandakora did not upbraid them, because he was in high good humour.

"Though the white youth, Lennox, has escaped," he said in Iroquois, "we have done well. We have here Tayoga, of the clan of the Bear, of the nation Onondaga, of the League of the Hodenosaunee, one of our deadliest enemies. It is more than I had hoped, because, though so young, he is a great warrior, skilful and brave, and we shall soon see how he can bear the live coals upon his breast."

Still Tayoga did not move, nor did he visibly shudder at the threat, which he knew Tandakora meant to keep. The Ojibway had never appeared more repellent, as he exulted over his prisoner. He seemed larger than ever, and his naked body was covered with painted and hideous devices.

"And so I have you at last, Tayoga," he said. "Your life shall be short, but your death shall be long, and you shall have full chance to prove how much an Onondaga can bear."

"Whether it be much or little," said Tayoga, "it will be more than any Ojibway can endure."

The black eyes of Tandakora flashed angrily, and he struck Tayoga heavily in the face with his open palm. The Onondaga staggered, but recovered himself, and gazed steadily into the eyes of the Ojibway.

"You have struck a bound captive, O Tandakora," he said. "It is contrary to the customs of your nation and of mine, and for it I shall have your life. It is now written that you shall fall by my hand."

His calm tones, and the fearless gaze with which he met that of Tandakora, gave him all the aspect of a prophet. The huge Ojibway flinched for a moment, and then he laughed.

"If it is written that I am to die by your hand it is written falsely," he said, "because before another sun has set all chance for it will be gone."

"I have said that you will die by my hand, and I say it again. It is written," repeated Tayoga firmly.

Though he showed no emotion there was much mortification in the soul of the young Onondaga. He had practically walked into the hands of Tandakora, and he felt that, for the present, at least, there was a stain upon his skill as a forest runner. The blow of Tandakora had left its mark, too, upon his mind. He had imbibed a part of the Christian doctrine of forgiveness, but it could not apply to so deadly and evil an enemy as the Ojibway. To such an insult offered to a helpless prisoner the reply could be made only with weapons.

Although Tododaho from his star, invisible by day, whispered to him to be of good heart, Tayoga was torn by conflicting beliefs. He was going to escape, and yet escape seemed impossible. The last of the warriors who had gone on the trail of young Lennox had come in, and he was surrounded now by more than a dozen stalwart men. The promise of Tododaho grew weak. Although his figure remained firm and upright and his look was calm and brave he saw no possibility of escape. He thought of Daganoweda, of the Mohawks and the rangers, but the presence of Tandakora and his men indicated that they had gone back toward the army of Waraiyageh, and were perhaps with him now.

He thought of St. Luc, but he did not know whether the gallant Chevalier was alive or dead. But if he should come he would certainly keep Tandakora from burning him at the stake. Tayoga did not fear death, and he knew that he could withstand torture. No torture could last forever, and when his soul passed he would merely go to the great shining star on which Tododaho lived, and do to perfection, forever and without satiety, the things that he loved in life here.

But Tayoga did not want to die. As far as life here was concerned he was merely at the beginning of the chapter. So many things were begun and nothing was finished. Nor did he want to die at the hands of Tandakora, and allow his enemy to have a triumph that would always be sweet to the soul of the fierce Ojibway. He saw many reasons why he did not wish yet to go to Tododaho's great and shining star, despite the perfection of an eternal existence there, and, casting away the doubts that had assailed him, he hoped resolutely.

Tandakora had been regarding him with grim satisfaction. It may be that he read some of the thoughts passing in the mind of the Onondaga, as he said:

"You look for your white friends, Tayoga, but you do not see them. Nor will they come. Do you want to know why?"

"Why, Tandakora?"

"Because they are dead. In the battle back there, toward Andiatarocte, Daganoweda, the Mohawk, was slain. His scalp is hanging in the belt of a Pottawattomie who is now with Dieskau. Black Rifle will roam the forest no more. He was killed by my own men, and the wolves have eaten his body. The hunter Willet was taken alive, but he perished at the stake. He was a very strong man, and he burned nearly a whole day before the spirit left him. The ranger, Rogers, whom you called the Mountain Wolf, was killed in the combat, and the wolves have eaten his body, too."

"Now, I know, O Tandakora," said the Onondaga, "that you are a liar, as well as a savage and a murderer. Great Bear lives, Daganoweda lives, and the Mountain Wolf and Black Rifle live, too. St. Luc was defeated in the battle, and he has gone to join Dieskau at Crown Point, else he would be here. I see into your black heart, Tandakora, and I see there nothing but lies."

The eyes of the huge savage once more shot dark fire, and he lifted his hand, but once again he controlled himself, though the taunts of Tayoga had gone in deep and they stung like barbs. Then, feeling that the talk was not in his favour, but that the situation was all to his liking, he turned away and gave orders to his warriors. They formed instantly in single file, Tayoga near the centre, Tandakora just behind him, and marched swiftly toward the north.

The Onondaga knew that their course would not bring them to Crown Point, which now lay more toward the east. Nor was it likely that they would go there. Dieskau and the French officers would scarcely allow him to be burned in their camp, and Tandakora would keep away from it until his hideous work was done.

Now Tayoga, despite his cynicism and apparent indifference, was all watchfulness. He knew that, for the present, any attempt to escape was hopeless, but he wished to observe the country through which he was passing, and see everything pertaining to it as far as the eye could reach. It was always well to know where one was, and he had been taught from infancy to observe everything, the practice being one of the important conditions of life in the wilderness.

The soul of Tandakora, who walked just behind him, was full of savage joy. It was true that Lennox had escaped, but Tayoga was an important capture. He was of a powerful family of the Onondagas, whom the Ojibway hated. Despite his youth, his fame as a warrior was already great, and in destroying him Tandakora would strike both at the Hodenosaunee and the white people who were his friends. Truly, it had been the Ojibway's lucky day.

As they went on, Tandakora's belief that it was his day of days became a conviction. Perhaps they would yet find Lennox, who had taken to such swift flight, and before the sun set they could burn the two friends together. His black heart was full of joy as he laughed in silence and to himself. In the forest to his right a bird sang, a sweet, piercing note, and he thought the shoulders of the captive in front of him quivered for a single instant. And well they might quiver! It was a splendid world to leave amid fire and pain, and the sweet, piercing note of the bird would remind Tayoga of all that he was going to lose.

There was no pity in the heart of Tandakora. He was a savage and he could never be anything but a savage. He might admire the fortitude with which Tayoga would endure the torture, but he would have no thought of remitting it on that account. The bird sang again, or another like it, because it was exactly the same sweet, piercing note, but now Tandakora did not see the shoulders of the Onondaga quiver. Doubtless after the first stab of pain that the bird had brought him he had steeled himself to its renewal.

Tandakora would soon see how the Onondaga could stand the fire. The test should be thorough and complete The Ojibway chieftain was a master artist upon such occasions, and, as he continued the march, he thought of many pleasant little ways in which he could try the steel of Tayoga's nature. The captive certainly had shown no signs of shrinking so far, and Tandakora was glad of it. The stronger the resistance the longer and the more interesting would be the test.

The Ojibway had in mind a certain little valley a few miles farther to the north, a secluded place where a leader of men like himself could do as he pleased without fear of interruption. Already he was exulting over the details, and to him, breathing the essence of triumph, the wilderness was as beautiful as it had ever been to Robert and Tayoga, though perhaps in a way that was peculiarly his own. Unlike Tayoga, he had heard little of the outside world, and he cared nothing at all for it. His thoughts never went beyond the forest, and the customs of savage ancestors were his. What he intended to do they had often done, and the tribes thought it right and proper.

"In half an hour, Tayoga, we will be at the place appointed," he said.

No answer.

"You said I would die at your hand, but there is only a half hour left in which to make good the prophecy."

Still no answer.

"Tododaho, the patron saint of the Onondagas, is hidden on his star, which is now on the other side of the world, and he cannot help you."

And still no answer.

"Does not fear strike into your heart, Tayoga? The flames that will burn you are soon to be lighted. You are young, but a boy, you are not a seasoned warrior, and you will not be able to bear it."

Tayoga laughed aloud, a laugh full and hearty. "I have heard frogs croak in the muddy edge of a pond," he said. "I could not tell what they meant, but there was as much sense in their voices as in yours, Tandakora."

"At last you have found your tongue, youth of the Onondagas. You have heard the frogs croak, but your voice at the stake will sound like theirs."

"The flames shall not be lighted around me, Tandakora."

"How do you know?"

"Tododaho has whispered in my ear the promise that he will save me. Twice has he whispered it to me as we marched."

"Tododaho in life was no warrior of the Ojibways," said Tandakora, "and since he has passed away he is no god of ours. His whispers, if he has whispered at all to you, are false. There is less than half an hour in which you can be saved, and Manitou himself would need all that time."

Tayoga gave him a scornful look. Tandakora was talking sacrilege, but he had no right to expect anything else from a savage Ojibway. He refused to reply. They came presently to the little valley that Tandakora had in mind, an open place, with a tree in the centre, and much dead wood scattered about. Tayoga knew instinctively that this was their destination, and his heart would have sunk within him had it not been for the whispers of Tododaho that he had heard on the march. The Ojibway gave the word and the file of warriors stopped. The hills enclosing the valley were much higher on the right than elsewhere, and touching Tayoga on the arm, he said:

"Walk with me to the crest there."

Tayoga, without a word, walked with him, while the other warriors stood watching, musket or rifle in hand.

The Onondaga, wrists bound behind him, knew that he did not have the slightest chance of escape, even if he made a sudden dash into the woods. He would be shot down before he went a dozen steps, and his pride and will restrained the body that was eager for the trial.

They reached the crest, and Tayoga saw then that the hill itself rose from a high plateau. When he gazed toward the east he saw a vast expanse of green wilderness, beyond it a ribbon of silver, and beyond the silver high green mountains, outlined sharply against a sky of clear blue.

"Oneadatote," said Tandakora.

"Yes, it is the great lake," said Tayoga.

"And if you will turn and look in the other direction you will see where Andiatarocte lies," said Tandakora. "There are greater lakes to the west, some so vast that they are as big as the white man's ocean, but there is none more beautiful than these. Think, Tayoga, that when you stand here upon this hill you have Oneadatote on one side of you and Andiatarocte on the other, and all the country between is splendid, every inch of it. Look! Look your fill, Tayoga! I have brought you here that you might see, that this might be your last sight before you go to your Tododaho on his star."

The Onondaga knew that the Ojibway was taunting him, that the torture had begun, that Tandakora intended to contrast the magnificent world from which he intended to send him with the black death that awaited him so soon. But the dauntless youth appeared not to know.

"The lakes I have seen many times," he said. "They are, as you truly call them, grand and beautiful, and they are the rightful property of the Hodenosaunee, the great League to which my nation belongs. I shall come to see them many more times all through my life, and when I am an old, old man of ninety summers and winters I shall lay myself down on a high shore of Andiatarocte, and close my eyes while Tododaho bears my spirit away to his star."

It is possible that Tandakora's eyes expressed a fleeting admiration. Savage and treacherous as he was, he respected courage, and the Onondaga had not shown the slightest trace of fear. Instead, he spoke calmly of a long life to come, as if the shadow of death were not hovering near at that moment.

"Look again," he said. "Look around all the circle of the world as far as your eyes can reach. It may help you a half hour from now, when you are in the flames, to remember the cool, green forest. And I tell you, too, Tayoga, that your white friend Lennox, the one whom you call Dagaeoga, shall soon follow you into the other world and by the same flaming path. When you are but ashes, which will be by the setting of the sun, my warriors will take up his trail, and he cannot escape us."

"Dagaeoga will live long, even as I do," said Tayoga calmly. "His summers and winters will be ninety each, even as mine. Tododaho has whispered that to me also, and the whispers of Tododaho are never false."

Tandakora turned back toward the valley, motioning to his captive to descend, and Tayoga obeyed without resistance. The glen was secluded, just suited to his purpose, which required time, and he did not wish the Frenchman, St. Luc, to come upon him suddenly, and interfere with the pleasure that he anticipated.

He was quite sure that the forest was empty of everything save themselves, though he heard again and for the third time the note of the bird, piercing and sweet, trilling among the bushes.

The warriors, knowing what was to be done, were doing it already, having piled many pieces of dead wood around the trunk of the lone tree in the centre of the opening. Two had cut shavings with their hunting knives, and one stood ready with flint and steel.

"Do you not tremble, Tayoga?" asked the Ojibway. "Many an old and seasoned warrior has not been able to endure the fire without a groan."

"You shall not hear any groan from me," replied Tayoga, "because I shall not stand among the flames."

"There is no way to escape them. Even now the pile is built, and the warrior is ready with flint and steel to make the sparks."

High, thrillingly sweet, came the voice of the bird in the bushes, and Tayoga suddenly leaped with all his might against the great chest of Tandakora. Vast as was the strength of the Ojibway he was thrown from his feet by the violent and unexpected impact, and as he fell Tayoga, leaping lightly away, ran like a deer through the bushes.

The warriors in the valley uttered a shout, but the reply was a shattering volley, before which half of them fell. Tandakora understood at once. If he had the mind and heart of a savage he had also all the craft and cunning of one whose life was incessantly in danger. Instead of springing up, he rolled from the crest of the hill, then, rising to a stooping position, darted away at incredible speed through the forest.

Rangers and Mohawks, Robert, Daganoweda, Willet, Black Rifle and Rogers at their head, burst into the glen and the Mohawks began the pursuit of Tandakora's surviving warriors, who had followed their leader in his flight. But Robert turned back to meet Tayoga and cut the thongs from his wrists.

"I thank you, Dagaeoga," said the Onondaga. "You came in time."

"Yes, they were making ready. A half hour more and we should have been too late. But you knew that we were coming, Tayoga?"

"Yes. I heard the bird sing thrice, but I knew the bird was in the throat of the Great Bear. I will say this, though, to you, Dagaeoga, that I have heard many birds sing and sing sweetly, but never any so sweetly as the one that sang thrice in the throat of the Great Bear."

"It is not hard for me to believe you," said Robert, smiling, "and I can tell you in turn, Tayoga, that your patron saint, Tododaho, must in very truth have watched over you, because when I heard your warning cry and took to flight, hoping for a chance later on to rescue you, I ran within two hours straight into the camp of the rangers and the Mohawks. You can easily surmise how glad I was to see them, and how quickly we followed Tandakora."

"And we'd have attacked sooner," said Willet, "but we could not get up all our force in time. We've annihilated this band, but I'm sure we did not get Tandakora. He fled like the wind, and we'll have to settle accounts with him some other day."

"It was not possible for Tandakora to fall before your arms today," said Tayoga.

"Why not?" asked Willet, curiously.

"It is reserved for him to die by my hand, though the time is yet far off. I know it, because Tododaho whispered it to me more than once today. Let him go now, but his hour will surely come."

"You may be right, Tayoga. I'm not one to question your prophecies, but it's not wise for us to continue the pursuit of him, as we've other things to do. We destroyed the forces of St. Luc in the battle, but he escaped with some of his men to Crown Point, and there are still Indian warriors in the forest, though we mean to continue skirmishing and scouting up to the walls of Crown Point, or until we meet Dieskau's army on the march."

Words of approval came from the fierce Daganoweda, who stood by, listening. The young Mohawk chieftain, in the midst of a great and terrible war, was living the life he loved. The Keepers of the Eastern Gate were taking revenge for Quebec, their lost Stadacona, and he and his warriors could boast already of more than one victory. Around him, too, stood the white allies whom he respected and admired most, Black Rifle, Willet, Rogers and Dagaeoga, the youth of golden speech. Willet, looking at him, read his mind.

"What do you say, Daganoweda?" he asked. "Now that Tayoga and Dagaeoga have been recovered, shall we go back and join the army of Waraiyageh, or shall we knock on the walls of Crown Point?"

"The time to turn back has not yet come," replied the Mohawk. "We must know all about the army of Dieskau before we return to Waraiyageh."

Willet laughed.

"I knew that would be your reply," he said. "I merely asked in order to hear you speak the words. As I've said already, it's in my mind to go on toward Crown Point, and I know Rogers feels that way too. But I think we'd first better rest and refresh ourselves a bit. Although Tayoga won't admit it, food and an hour or two of ease here in the very valley where they meant to burn him alive, will do him a power of good."

After throwing out competent sentinels, they lighted a fire by the very tree to which Tandakora meant to bind Tayoga for the flames, and broiled venison over the coals. They also had bread and *samp*, which were most welcome, and the whole force ate with great zest. The warriors, in their flight, had dropped Tayoga's bow and quiver of arrows, and their recovery gave him keen delight, though he said little as he strapped them over his shoulder.

They spent two hours in the valley, and for the Onondaga the air was full of the good spirits that watched over him. The dramatic and extraordinary change, occurring in a few minutes, made an ineffaceable impression upon a mind that saw meaning in everything. Here was the glen in which he had been held by Tandakora and his most deadly enemies, and there was the lone tree against which they had already heaped the fuel for burning him alive. Such a sudden and marvellous change could not have come if he were not in the special favour of both Tododaho and Areskoui. Secure in his belief that he was protected by the mighty on their stars, he awaited the future with supreme confidence.

Chapter 14

Sharp Sword

The rangers and Mohawks had suffered a further thinning in the last conflict with St. Luc, but they were still a formidable body, not so much through numbers as through skill, experience, courage and quality of leadership. There was not one among them who was not eager to advance toward Crown Point and hazard every peril. But they were too wise in wilderness ways not to have a long and anxious council before they started, as there was nothing to be gained and much to be lost by throwing away lives in reckless attempts.

They decided at last on a wide curve to the west, in order that they might approach Crown Point from the north, where they would be least suspected, and they decided also that they would make most of the journey by night, when they would be better hidden from wandering warriors. So concluding, they remained in the glen much longer than they had intended, and the delay was welcome to Robert, whose nervous system needed much restoration, after the tremendous exertions, the hopes and fears of recent days. But he was able to imitate the Onondaga calm. He spread his blanket on the turf, lay down upon it, and lowered his eyelids. He had no intention of going to sleep, but he put himself into that drowsy state of calm akin to the Hindu's Nirvana. By an effort of the will he calmed every nerve and refused to think of the future. He merely breathed, and saw in a dim way the things about him, compelling his soul to stay a while in peace.

Most of the rangers and Mohawks were lying in the same stillness. Stern experience had taught them to take rest, and make the most of it when they could find it. Only the watchful sentinels at the rim of the valley and beyond stirred, and their moccasins made no sound as they slid among the bushes, looking and listening with all their eyes and ears for whatever might come.

The sun was sunk far in the western heavens, tinting with gold the surface of both lakes, for the rulership of which the nations fought, and outlining the mountains, crests and ridges, sharp and clear against a sky of amazing blue. Yet so vast was the wilderness and so little had it been touched by man, that the armies were completely hidden in it, and neither Dieskau nor Johnson yet knew what movement the other intended.

The east was already dim with the coming twilight when the three leaders stood up, and, as if by preconcerted signal, beckoned to their men. Scarcely a word was spoken, but everyone looked to his arms, the sentinels came in, and the whole force, now in double file, marched swiftly toward the north, but inclining also to the east. Robert and Tayoga were side by side.

"I owe thee many thanks, Dagaeoga," said the Onondaga.

"You owe me nothing," said Robert. "I but paid an instalment on a debt."

Then they spoke no more for a long time, because there was nothing to say, and because the band was now moving so fast that all their breath was needed for muscular effort. The sun went down in a sea of golden clouds, then red fire burned for a little while at the rim of the world, and, when it was gone, a luminous twilight, which by and by faded into darkness, came in its place.

But the band in double file sped on through the dusk. Daganoweda, who knew the way, was at the head, and so skilful were they that no stick crackled and no leaf rustled as they passed. Mile after mile they flitted on, over hill and valley and through the deep woods. Far in the night they stopped to drink at a clear little brook that ran down to Lake Champlain, but no other halt was made until the dawn broke over a vast silver sheet of water, and high green mountains beyond.

"Oneadatote," said Tayoga.

"And a great lake it is," said Robert. "We had a naval encounter on it once, and now we've had a battle, too, on George."

"But the French and their allies hold all of Oneadatote, while we only dispute the possession of Andiatarocte. They will march against us from Crown Point on the shores of this lake."

"We'll take George from 'em, all of it, and then we'll come and drive 'em from Champlain, too."

The eyes of the Onondaga sparkled.

"Dagaeoga has a brave heart," he said, "and we will do all that he predicts, but, as I have said before, it will be a long and terrible war."

They descended to a point nearer the lake, but, still remaining hidden in the dense forest, ate their breakfast of venison, bread and *samp*, and drank again from a clear brook. They were now several miles north of Crown Point, and the leaders talked together again about the best manner of approach. They not only wished to see what the army of Dieskau was doing, but they thought it possible to strike some blow that would inflict severe loss, and delay his advance. Rogers used his glasses again, and was able to discern many Indian canoes on the lake, both north and south of the point where they lay, although they were mostly scattered, indicating no certain movement.

"Those canoes ought to be ours," he said. "'Tis a great pity that we've let the French take control of Champlain. It's easier to hold a thing in the beginning than it is, having let your enemy seize it without a fight, to win it back again."

"It's better to do that than to be rash," said Willet. "I was with Braddock when we marched headlong into the wilderness. If we had been slower then we'd have now a good army that we've lost. Still, it's hard to see the French take the lead from us. We dance to their tune."

"Dave," said Rogers, "I see a whole fleet of Indian canoes far down the lake below Crown Point. One can see many miles in such a clear air as this, and I'm sure they're canoes, though they look like black dots crawling on the water. Take the glasses and have a look."

Willet held the glasses to his eyes a long time, and when he took them down he said with confidence:

"They're canoes, a hundred of 'em at least, and while they hold complete command of the lake, it don't seem natural that so many of 'em should be in a fleet away down there below the French fort. It means something unusual. What do you think, Tayoga?"

"Perhaps Dieskau is already on the march," said the Onondaga. "The glories that St. Luc, Dumas, Ligneris and the others won at Duquesne will not let him sleep. He would surpass them. He would repeat on the shores of Andiatarocte what they did so triumphantly by the ford of the Monongahela."

"Thunderation!" exclaimed Rogers. "The boy may be right! They may be even now stealing a march on us! If our army down below should be wiped out as Braddock's was, then we might never recover!"

Robert, who could not keep from hearing all the talk, listened to it with dismay. He had visions of Johnson's army of untrained militia attacked suddenly by French veterans and a huge force of Indians. It would be like the spring of a monstrous beast out of the dark, and defeat, perhaps complete destruction for his own, would be the result. But his courage came back in an instant. The surprise could not be carried out so long as the band to which he belonged was in existence.

"I think," said Willet, "that we'd better go south along the shore of the lake, and approach as near to the fort as we dare. Then Daganoweda and a half dozen of his best warriors will scout under its very walls. Do you care for the task, Daganoweda?"

The eyes of the young Mohawk chieftain glittered. Willet had judged him aright. It would be no task for him, it would be instead a labour of pleasure. In fifteen minutes he was off with his warriors, disappearing like shadows in the undergrowth, and Robert knew that whatever report Daganoweda might bring back it would not only be true but full.

The main band followed, though far more slowly, keeping well back from the lake, that no Indian eye might catch their presence in the woods, but able, nevertheless, to observe for immense distances everything that passed on the vast silver sheet of water. Rogers observed once more the fleet of Indian canoes rowing southward, and he and Willet were firmer than ever in their belief that it indicated some measure of importance.

Their own march through the woods was peaceful. They frightened no game from their path, indicating that the entire region had been hunted over thoroughly by the great force that had lain at Crown Point, and, after a while, they passed a point parallel to the fort, though several miles to the westward. Willet, Tayoga and Robert looked for trails or traces of bands or hunters, but found none. Apparently the forest had been deserted by the enemy for some days, and their alarming belief was strengthened anew.

Four miles farther on they were to meet Daganoweda and his warriors, at a tiny silver pond among the hills, and now they hurried their march.

"I'm thinking," said Robert, "that Daganoweda will be there first, waiting with a tale to tell."

"All signs point to it," said Tayoga. "It is well that we came north on this scouting expedition, because we, too, may have something to say when we return to Waraiyageh."

"You know this pond at which we are to meet?"

"Yes, it is in the hills, and the forest is thick all about it. Often Onondaga and Mohawk have met there to take council, the one with the other."

In another hour they were at the pond, and they found the Mohawk chieftain and his men sitting at its edge.

"Well, Daganoweda," said Willet, "is it as we thought?" Daganoweda rose and waved his hand significantly toward the south.

"Dieskau with his army has gone to fall upon Waraiyageh," he said. "We went close up to the walls, and we even heard talk. The French and the warriors were eager to advance, and so were their leaders. It was said that St. Luc, whom we call Sharp Sword, urged them most, and the larger part of his great force soon started in canoes. A portion of it he left at Ticonderoga, and the rest is going on. They intend to take the fort called Lyman, that the English and Americans have built, and then to fall upon Waraiyageh."

"It is for us to reach Waraiyageh first," said Willet, quietly, "and we will. God knows there is great need of our doing it. If Johnson's army is swept away, then Albany will fall, the Hodenosaunee, under terrific pressure, might be induced to turn against us, and the Province of New York would be ravaged with fire and the scalping knife."

"But we will reach Waraiyageh and tell him," said Tayoga, firmly. "He will not be swept away. Albany will not fall, and nothing can induce the Hodenosaunee to join the French."

The eyes of the Great Bear glistened as he looked at the tall young warrior.

"That's brave talk, and it's true, too!" he exclaimed. "You shame us, Tayoga! If it's for us to save our army by carrying the news of Dieskau's sudden march, then we'll save it."

Daganoweda had told the exact truth. Dieskau had reached Crown Point with a force mighty then for the wilderness, and, after a short rest, he issued orders to his troops to be prepared for advance at a moment's notice. He especially directed the officers to keep themselves in light marching order, every one of them to take only a bearskin, a blanket, one extra pair of shoes, one extra shirt, and no luxuries at all.

His orders to the Indians showed a savagery which, unfortunately, was not peculiar then to him. In the heat of battle they were not to scalp those they slew, because time then was so valuable. While they were taking a scalp they could kill ten men. But when the enemy was routed completely they could go back on the field and scalp as they wished.

The Indian horde was commanded by Legardeur de St. Pierre, who had with him De Courcelles and Jumonville, and St. Luc with his faithful Dubois immediately organized a daring band of French Canadians and warriors to take the place of the one he had lost. So great was his reputation as a forest fighter, and so well deserved was it, that his fame suffered no diminution, because of his defeat by the rangers and Mohawks, and the young French officers were eager to serve under him.

It was this powerful army, ably led and flushed with the general triumph of the French arms, that Daganoweda and his warriors had seen advancing, though perhaps no one in all the force dreamed that he was advancing to a battle that in reality would prove one of the most decisive in the world's history, heavy with consequences to which time set scarcely any limit. Nor did Robert himself, vivid as was his imagination, foresee it. His thoughts and energies were bounded for the time, at least, by the present, and, with the others, he was eager to save Johnson's army, which now lay somewhere near Lake George, and which he was sure had been occupied in building forts, as Waraiyageh, having spent most of his life in the wilderness, knew that it was well when he had finished a march forward to make it secure before he undertook another.

The rangers and Mohawks now picked up the trail of Dieskau's army, which was moving forward with the utmost speed. Yet the obstinacy of his Indian allies compelled the German baron to abandon the first step in his plan. They would not attack Fort Lyman, as it was defended by artillery, of which the savages had a great dread, but they were willing to go on, and fall suddenly upon Johnson, who, they heard, though falsely, had no cannon. Dieskau and his French aides, compelled to hide any chagrin they may have felt, pushed on for Lake George with the pick of their army, consisting of the battalions of Languedoc, and La Reine, a strong Canadian force, and a much larger body of Indian warriors, among whom the redoubtable Tandakora, escaped from rangers and Mohawks, was predominant.

Willet, Rogers, Black Rifle, Daganoweda and their small but formidable band read the trail plainly, and they knew the greatness of the danger. Dieskau was not young, and he was a soldier of fortune, not belonging to the race that he led, but he was full of ardour, and the daring French partisans were urging him on. Robert felt certain that St. Luc himself was in the very van and that he would probably strike the first blow.

After they had made sure that Dieskau would not attack Fort Lyman, but was marching straight against Johnson, the little force turned aside, and prepared to make a circuit with all the speed it could command.

As Willet put it tersely:

"It's not enough for us to know what Dieskau means to do, but to keep him from doing it. It's muscle and lungs now that count."

So they deserved to the full the name of forest runners, speeding on their great curve, using the long, running walk with which both

Indians and frontiersmen devoured space, and apparently never grew weary. In the night they passed Dieskau's army, and, from the crest of a lofty hill, saw his fires burning in a valley below. Tayoga and some of the Mohawks slipped down through the undergrowth and reported that the camp had been made with all due precaution—the French partisan leaders saw to that—with plenty of scouts about, and the whole force in swift, marching order. It would probably be up and away again before dawn, and if they were to pass it and reach Johnson in good time not a single moment could be wasted.

"Now I wonder," said Willet, "if they suspect the advance of this warning force. St. Luc, of course, knows that we were back there by Champlain, as we gave him the most complete proofs of it that human beings could give. So does Tandakora, and they may prevail upon Dieskau to throw out a swift band for the purpose of cutting us off. If so, St. Luc is sure to lead it. What do you say, Tayoga?"

"I think St. Luc will surely come," replied the Onondaga youth gravely. "We have been trailing the army of Dieskau, and tomorrow, after we have passed it, we shall be trailed in our turn. It does not need the whisper of Tododaho to tell me that St. Luc and Tandakora will lead the trailers, because, as we all know, they are most fitting to lead them."

"Then there's no sleep for us tonight," said Rogers; "we'll push on and not close our eyes again until we reach Colonel Johnson."

They travelled many miles before dawn, but with the rising of the sun they knew that they were followed, and perhaps flanked. The Mohawk scouts brought word of it. Daganoweda himself found hostile signs in the bushes, a bead or two and a strand of deerskin fringe caught on a bush.

"It's likely," said Willet, "that they were even more cautious than we reckoned. It may be that before Dieskau left his force at Ticonderoga he sent forward St. Luc with a swift band to intercept us and any others who might take a warning to Colonel Johnson."

"I agree with you," said Rogers. "St. Luc started before we did, and, all the time, has been ahead of us. So we have him in front, Dieskau behind, and it looks as if we'd have to fight our way through to our army. Oh, the Frenchmen are clever! Nobody can deny it, and they're always awake. What's your opinion, Daganoweda?"

"We shall have to fight," replied the Mohawk chieftain, although the prospect caused him no grief. "The traces that we have found prove Sharp Sword to be already across our path. We have yet no way to know the strength of his force, but, if a part of us get through, it will be enough."

Robert heard them talking, and while he was able once more to preserve outward calm, his heart, nevertheless, throbbed hard. More than any other present, with the possible exception of Tayoga, his imagination pictured what was to come, and before it was fought he saw the battle. They were to march, too, into an ambush, knowing it was there, but impossible to be avoided, because they must get through in some fashion or other. They were now approaching Andiatarocte again, and although the need of haste was still great they dropped perforce into a slow walk, and sent ahead more scouts and skirmishers.

Robert and Tayoga went forward on the right, and they caught through the bushes the gleam from the waters of a small stream that ran down to the lake. Going a little nearer, they saw that the farther bank was high and densely wooded, and then they drew back, knowing that it was a splendid place for an ambush, and believing that St. Luc was probably there. Tayoga lay almost flat, face downward, and stared intently at the high bank.

"I think, Dagaeoga," he said, "that so long as we keep close to the earth we may creep a little nearer, and perhaps our eyes, which are good, may be able to pick out the figures of our foes from the leaves and bushes in which they probably lie hidden."

They dragged themselves forward about fifty yards, taking particular care to make nothing in the thickets bend or wave in a manner for which the wind could not account. Robert stared a long time, but his eyes separated nothing from the mass of foliage.

"What do you see, Tayoga?" he whispered at last.

"No proof of the enemy yet, Dagaeoga. At least, no proof of which I am sure. Ah, but I do now! There was a flash in the bushes. It was a ray of sunlight penetrating the leaves and striking upon the polished metal of a gun barrel."

"It means that at least one Indian or Frenchman is there. Keep on looking and see if you don't see something more."

"I see a red feather. At this distance you might at first take it for a feather in the wing of a bird, but I know it is a feather in the scalplock of a warrior."

"And that makes two, at least. Look harder than ever, Tayoga, and tell me what more you see."

"Now I catch a glimpse of white cloth with a gleam of silver. The cloth is on the upper arm, and the silver is on the shoulder of an officer."

"A uniform and an epaulet. A French officer, of course."

"Of course, and I think it is Sharp Sword himself."

"Look once more, Tayoga, and maybe your eyes can pick out something else from the foliage."

"I see the back and painted shoulder of a warrior. It may be those of Tandakora, but I cannot be sure."

"You needn't be. You've seen quite enough to prove that the whole force of St. Luc is there in the bushes, awaiting us, and we must tell our leaders at once."

They crept back to the centre, where Willet and Rogers lay, Daganoweda being on the flank, and told them what they had seen.

"It's good enough proof," said Rogers. "St. Luc with his whole force in the bushes means to hold the stream against us and keep us from taking a warning to Johnson, but the hardest way to do a thing isn't always the one you have to choose."

"I take it that you mean to flank him out of his position."

"It was what I had in mind. What do you think, Dave?"

"The only possible method. Those Mohawks are wonders at such operations, and we'd better detail as many of the rangers as we can spare to join 'em, while a force here in the centre makes a demonstration that will hold 'em to their place in the bushes. I'll take the picked men and join Daganoweda."

Rogers laughed. "It's like you, Dave," he said, "to choose the most dangerous part, and leave me here just to make a noise."

"But the commander usually stays in the centre, while his lieutenants lead on the wings."

"That's true. You have precedent with you, but it wouldn't have made any difference, anyhow."

"But when we fall on 'em you'll lead the centre forward, and with such a man as St. Luc I fancy you'll have all the danger you crave."

Rogers laughed again.

"Go ahead, old fire-eater," he said. "It was always your way. I suppose you'll want to take Tayoga and Lennox with you."

"Oh, yes, I need 'em, and besides, I have to watch over 'em, in a way."

"And you watch over 'em by leading 'em into the very thickest of the battle. But danger has always been a lure for you, and I know you're the best man for the job."

Willet quickly picked twenty men, including Black Rifle and the two lads, and bore away with speed toward the flank where Daganoweda and the Mohawks already lay. As Robert left he heard the rifle shots with which the little force of Rogers was opening the battle, and he heard, too, the rifles and muskets of the French and Indians on the other side of the stream replying.

Fortunately, as the forest was very dense, and it was not possible for any of St. Luc's men to see the flanking movement, Willet and his rangers joined Daganoweda quickly and without hindrance, the eyes of the chieftain glittering when he saw the new force, and heard the plan to cross the stream far down and fall on St. Luc's flank.

"It is good," he said with satisfaction. "Sharp Sword has eyes to see much, but he cannot see everything."

"But one thing must be understood," said Willet, gravely. "If we see that we are getting the worst of the fight and our men are falling fast, the good runners must leave the conflict at once and make all speed for Waraiyageh. Tayoga, you are the fastest and surest of all, and you must leave first, and, Daganoweda, do you pick three of your swift young warriors for the same task."

"I have one request to make," said Tayoga.

"What is it?"

"When I leave let me take Dagaeoga with me. We are comrades who have shared many dangers, and he, too, is swift of foot and hardy. It may be that there will be danger also in the flight to Waraiyageh's camp. Then, if one should fall the other will go on."

"Well put, Tayoga. Robert, do you hear? If the tide seems to be turning against us join Tayoga in his flight toward Johnson."

Robert nodded, and the young warriors chosen by Daganoweda also indicated that they understood. Then the entire force began its silent march through the woods on their perilous encircling movement. They waded the river at a ford where the water did not rise above their knees, and entered the deep woods, gradually drawing back toward the point where St. Luc's force lay.

As they approached they began to hear the sounds of the little battle Rogers was waging with the French leader, a combat which was intended to keep the faculties and energies of the French and Indians busy, while the more powerful detachment under Willet and Daganoweda moved up for the main blow. Faint reports of rifle and musket shots came to them, and also the long whining yell of the Indians, so like, in the distance, to the cry of a wolf. Then, as they drew a little nearer they heard the shouts of the rangers, shouts of defiance or of triumph rattling continuously like a volley.

"That's a part of their duty," said Willet. "Rogers has only twenty men, but he means to make 'em appear a hundred."

"Sounds more like two hundred," said Robert. "It's the first time I ever heard one man shout as ten."

As they drew nearer the volume of the firing seemed to increase. Rogers was certainly carrying out his part of the work in the most admirable manner, his men firing with great rapidity and never ceasing their battle shouts. Even so shrewd a leader as St. Luc might well believe the entire force of rangers and Mohawks, instead of only twenty men, was in front of him. But Robert was quite sure from the amount of firing coming from the Frenchman's position that he was in formidable force, perhaps outnumbering his opponents two to one, and the fight, though with the advantage of a flank attack by Willet and Daganoweda, was sure to be doubtful. It seemed that Tayoga read his thought as he whispered:

"Once more, Dagaeoga, we may leave the combat together, when it is at its height. Remember the duty that has been laid upon us. If the battle appears doubtful we are to flee."

"A hard thing to do at such a time."

"But we have our orders from the Great Bear."

"I had no thought of disobeying. I know the importance of our getting through, if our force is defeated, or even held. Why couldn't our whole detachment have gone around St. Luc just as we've done, and have left him behind without a fight?"

"Because if the Mountain Wolf had not been left in his front, Sharp Sword would have discovered immediately the absence of us all and would have followed so fast that he would have forced us to battle on his terms, instead of our being able to force him on ours."

"I see, Tayoga. Look out!"

He seized the Onondaga suddenly and pulled him down. A rifle cracked in the bushes sixty or seventy yards in front of them, and a bullet whistled where the red youth's head had been. The shot came from an outlying sentinel of St. Luc's band, and knowing now that the time for a hidden advance had passed, Willet and all of his men charged with a mighty shout.

Their cheering also was a signal to the twenty men of Rogers on the other side of the river, and they, too, rushed forward. St. Luc was taken by surprise, but, as Robert had feared, his French and Indians outnumbered them two to one. They fell back a little, thus giving Rogers and his twenty a chance to cross the river, but they took up a new and strong position upon a well-wooded hill, and the battle at close range became fierce, sanguinary and doubtful.

Robert caught two glimpses of St. Luc directing his men with movements of his small sword, and once he saw another white man, who, he was sure was Dubois, although generally the enemy was invisible, keeping well under the shelter of tree and bush. But while human forms were hidden, the evidences of ferocious battle were numerous. The warriors on each side uttered fierce shouts, rifles and muskets crackled rapidly, now and then a stricken man uttered his death cry, and the depths of the forest were illuminated by the rapid jets of the firing.

The sudden and heavy attack upon his flank compelled St. Luc to take the defensive, and put him at a certain disadvantage, but he marshalled his superior numbers so well that the battle became doubtful, with every evidence that it would be drawn out to great length. Moreover, the chevalier had manoeuvred so artfully that his whole force was now drawn directly across the path of the rangers and Mohawks, and the way to Johnson was closed, for the time, at least.

An hour, two hours, the battle swayed to and fro among the trees and bushes. Had their opponent been any other than St. Luc the three leaders, Willet, Rogers and Daganoweda, would have triumphed by that time, but French, Canadians and Indians alike drew courage from the dauntless Chevalier. More than once they would have abandoned the field, but he marshalled them anew, and always he did it in a manner so skilful that the loss was kept at the lowest possible figure.

The forest was filled with smoke, though the high sun shot it through with luminous rays. But no one looking upon the battle could have told which was the loser and which the winner. The losses on the two sides were about equal, and St. Luc, holding the hill, still lay across the path of rangers and Mohawks. Robert, who was crouched behind the trunk of a great oak, felt a light touch upon his arm, and, looking back, saw Tayoga.

"The time has come, Dagaeoga," said the Onondaga.

"What time?"

"The time for us to leave the battle and run as fast as we may to Waraiyageh."

"I had forgotten. The conflict here had gotten so much into my blood that I couldn't think of anything else. But, as I said it would be, it's hard to go."

"Go, Robert!" called Willet from a tree twenty feet away. "Curve around St. Luc. Do what Tayoga says—he can scent danger like an animal of the forest—and make all speed to Johnson. Maybe we'll join you in his camp later on."

"Good-by, Dave," said Robert, swallowing hard. He crept away with the Onondaga, not rising to his full height for a long time. Then the two stood for a few moments, listening to the sounds of the battle, which seemed to be increasing in violence. Far through the forest they faintly saw the drifting smoke and the sparks of fire from the rifles and muskets.

"Once more I say it's hard to leave our friends there," exclaimed Robert.

"But our path leads that way," said Tayoga, pointing southward.

They struck, without another word, into the long, loping run that the forest runners use with such effect, and sped southward. The sounds of the conflict soon died behind them, and they were in the stillness of the woods, where no enemy seemed near. But they did not decrease their pace, leaping the little brooks, wading the wider streams, and flitting like shades through forest and thicket. Twice they crossed Indian trails, but paid no heed to them. Once a warrior, perhaps a hunter, fired a long shot at them, but as his bullet missed they paid no attention to him, but, increasing their speed, fled southward at a pace no ordinary man could overtake.

"Now that we have left," said Robert, after a while, "I'm glad we did so. It will be a personal pleasure for us two to warn Johnson."

"We may carry the fate of a war with us, Dagaeoga. Think of that!"

"I've thought of it. But our friends behind us, engaged in the battle with St. Luc! What of them? Does Tododaho whisper to you anything about their fate?"

"They are great and skilful men, cunning and crafty in all the ways of the forest. They have escaped great dangers a thousand times before and Tododaho tells me they will escape the thousand and first. Be of good heart, Dagaeoga, and do not worry about them."

They dropped almost to a walk for a while, permitting their muscles to rest. Tayoga's wound had healed so fast, the miracle was so nearly complete, that it did not trouble him, and, after walking two hours, they struck into the long, easy run again. The miles dropped fast behind them, and now Johnson's camp was not far away. It was well for Tayoga and Robert that they were naturally so strong and that they had lived such healthy lives, as now they were able to go on all through the day, and the setting sun found them still travelling, the Onondaga leading with an eye as infallible for the way as that of a bird in the heavens. Some time after dark they stopped for a half hour and sat on fallen logs while they took fresh breath. Robert was apprehensive about Tayoga's wound and expressed his solicitude.

"There is no pain," replied the young warrior, "and there will be none. Tododaho and Areskoui gave me the miraculous cure for a purpose. It was that I might have the strength to be a messenger to Waraiyageh, because if he is crushed then the French and the Indians will strike at the Hodenosaunee, and they will ravage the Vale of Onondaga itself with fire and the tomahawk. Tododaho watches over his people."

"The stars have come out, Tayoga. Can you see the one on which Tododaho lives? And if so, what is he saying to you now?"

Tayoga looked up a long time. He had received the white man's culture, but the Indian soul was strong within him, nevertheless, and he was steeped, too, in Indian lore. All the legends of his race, all the Iroquois religion, came crowding upon him. A faint silvery vapour overspread the sky, the stars in myriads quivered and danced, and there in a remote corner of space was the great star on which Tododaho lived. It hung in the heavens a silver shield, small in the distance, but vast, Tayoga knew, beyond all conception. There were fine lines across its face, but they were only the snakes in Tododaho's hair.

Gradually the features and countenance of the great Onondaga emerged upon the star, and the blood of Tayoga ran in a chill torrent through his veins, though the chill was not the chill of fear. He was, in effect, meeting the mighty Onondaga of four hundred years ago, face to face. The forest around him glided away, Robert vanished, the solid earth melted from under his feet, and he was like a being who hung in the air suspended from nothing. He leaned his head forward a little in the attitude of one who listens, and he distinctly heard Tododaho say:

"Go on, Tayoga. As I have protected you so far on the way I shall protect you to the end. Four hundred years ago I left my people, but my watch over them is as vigilant now as it was when I was on earth. The nations of the Hodenosaunee shall not perish, and they shall remain great and mighty."

The voice ceased, the face of the mighty Onondaga disappeared, Tayoga was no longer suspended without a support in the air, the forest came back, and his good comrade, Robert Lennox, stood by his side, staring at him curiously.

"Have you been in a trance, Tayoga?" asked Robert.

"No, Dagaeoga, I have not, but I can answer your question. I not only heard Tododaho, but I saw him face to face. He spoke to me in a voice like the wind among the pines, and he said that he would watch over me the rest of the way, and that the Hodenosaunee should remain great and powerful. Come, Dagaeoga, all danger for us on this march has passed."

They rose, continued their flight without hindrance, and the next morning entered the camp of Johnson.

CHAPTER 15

The Lake Battle

Robert and Tayoga approached the American camp in the early dawn of a waning summer, and the air was crisp and cool. The Onondaga's shoulder, at last, had begun to feel the effects of his long flight, and he, as well as Robert, was growing weary. Hence it was with great delight that they caught the gleam of a uniform through a thicket, and knew they had come upon one of Johnson's patrols. It was with still greater delight as they advanced that they recognized young William Wilton of the Philadelphia troop, and a dozen men. Wilton looked wan and hollow-eyed, as if he had been watching all night, but his countenance was alert, and his figure erect nevertheless.

Hearing the steps of Tayoga and Robert in the bushes, he called sharply:

"Who's there?"

His men presented their arms, and he stepped forward, sword in hand. Robert threw up his own hands, and, emerging from the thicket, said in tones which he made purposely calm and even.

"Good morning, Will. It's happy I am to see you keeping such a good watch."

Then he dropped his hands and walked into the open, Tayoga following him. Wilton stared as if he had seen someone come back from another star.

"Lennox, is it really you?" he asked.

"Nobody else."

"You in the flesh and not a ghost?"

"In the flesh and no ghost."

"And is that Tayoga following you?"

"The Onondaga himself."

"And he is not any ghost, either?"

"No ghost, though Tandakora's men tried hard to make him one, and took a good start at it. But he's wholly in the flesh, too."

"Then shake. I was afraid, at first, to touch hands with a ghost, but, God bless you, Robert, it fills me with delight to see you again, and you, too, Tayoga, no less. We thought you both were dead, and Colden and Carson and Grosvenor and I and a lot of others have wasted a lot of good mourning on you."

Robert laughed, and it was probably a nervous laugh of relief at having arrived, through countless dangers, upon an errand of such huge importance.

"Both of you look worn out," said Wilton. "I dare say you've been up all night, walking through the interminable forest. Come, have a good, fat breakfast, then roll between the blankets and sleep all day long."

Robert laughed again. How little the young Quaker knew or suspected!

"We neither eat nor sleep yet, Will," he said. "Where is Colonel Johnson? You must take us to him at once!"

"The colonel himself, doubtless, has not had his breakfast. But why this feverish haste? You talk as if you and Tayoga carried the fate of a nation on your shoulders."

"That's just what we do carry. And, in truth, the fate of more than one, perhaps. Lead on, Will! Every second is precious!"

Wilton looked at him again, and, seeing the intense earnestness in the blue eyes of young Lennox, gave a command to his little troop, starting without another word across the clearing, Robert and Tayoga following close behind. The two lads were ragged, unkempt, and bore all the signs of war, but they were unconscious of their dilapidated appearance, although many of the young soldiers stared at them as they went by. They passed New England and New York troops cooking their breakfast, and on a low hill a number of Mohawks were still sleeping.

They approached the tent of Colonel Johnson and were fortunate enough to find him standing in the doorway, talking with Colonel Ephraim Williams and Colonel Whiting. But he was so engrossed in the conversation that he did not see them until Wilton saluted and spoke.

"Messengers, sir!" he said.

Colonel Johnson looked up, and then he started.

"Robert and Tayoga!" he exclaimed. "I see by your faces that you have word of importance! What is it?"

"Dieskau's whole army is advancing," said Robert. "It long since left Crown Point, put a garrison in Ticonderoga, and is coming along Lake George to fall on you by surprise, and destroy you."

Waraiyageh's face paled a little, and then a spark leaped up in his eye. "How do you know this?" he asked.

"I have seen it with my own eyes. I looked upon Dieskau's marching army, and so did Tayoga. St. Luc was thrown across our path to stop us, and we left Willet, Rogers and Daganoweda in battle with him, while we fled, according to instructions, to you."

"Then you have done well. Go now and seek rest and refreshment. You are good and brave lads. Our army will be made ready at once. We'll not wait for Dieskau. We'll go to meet him. What say you, Williams, and you, Whiting?".

"Forward, sir! The troops would welcome the order!" replied Colonel Williams, and Whiting nodded assent.

Johnson was now all activity and energy and so were his officers. He seemed not at all daunted by the news of Dieskau's rapid advance. Rather he welcomed it as an end to his army's doubts and delays, and as a strong incentive to the spirits of the men.

"Go, lads, and rest!" he repeated to Robert and Tayoga, and now that their supreme task was achieved they felt the need of obeying him. Both were sagging with weariness, and it was well for the Onondaga to look to his shoulder, which was still a little lame. As they saluted and left the tent a young Indian lad sprang toward them and greeted them eagerly. It was young Joseph Brant, the famous Thayendanega of later days, the brother of Molly Brant, Colonel William Johnson's Mohawk wife.

"Hail, Tayoga! Hail, Dagaeoga!" he exclaimed in the Mohawk tongue. "I knew that you were inside with Waraiyageh! You have brought great news, it is rumoured already! It is no secret, is it?"

"We do have news, mighty news, and it is no secret," replied Robert. "It's news that will give you your opportunity of starting on the long path that leads to the making of a great chief. Dieskau has marched suddenly and is near. We're going to meet him."

The fierce young Mohawk uttered a shout of joy and rushed for his arms. Robert and Tayoga, after a brief breakfast, lay down on their blankets and, despite all the turmoil and bustle of preparation, fell asleep.

While the two successful but exhausted messengers slumbered, Colonel Johnson called a council of war, at which the chief militia officers and old Hendrik, the Mohawk *sachem*, were present. The white men favoured the swift advance of a picked force to save Edward, one of the new forts erected to protect the frontier, from the hordes, and the dispatch of a second chosen force to guard Lyman, another fort, in the same manner. The wise old Mohawk alone opposed the plan, and his action was significant.

Hendrik picked up three sticks from the ground and held them before the eyes of the white men.

"Put these together," he said, "and you cannot break them. Take them one by one and you break them with ease."

But he could not convince the white leaders, and then, a man of great soul, he said that if his white comrades must go in the way they had chosen he would go with them. Calling about him the Mohawk warriors, two hundred in number, he stood upon a gun carriage and addressed them with all the spirit and eloquence of his race. Few of the Americans understood a word he said, but they knew from his voice that he was urging his men to deeds of valour.

Hendrik told the warriors that the French and their allies were at hand, and the forces of Waraiyageh were going out to meet them. Waraiyageh had always been their friend, and it became them now to fight by his side with all the courage the Ganeagaono had shown through unnumbered generations. A fierce shout came from the Mohawks, and, snatching their tomahawks from their belts, they waved them about their heads.

To the young Philadelphians and to Grosvenor, the Englishman, who stood by, it was a sight wild and picturesque beyond description. The Mohawks were in full war paint and wore little clothing. Their dark eyes flashed, as the eloquence of Hendrik made the intoxication of battle rise in their veins, and when two hundred tomahawks were swung aloft and whirled about the heads of their owners the sun flashed back from them in glittering rays. Now and then fierce shouts of approval burst forth, and when Hendrik finished and stepped down from the gun carriage, they were ready to start on a march, of which the wise old sachem had not approved.

The militia also were rapidly making ready, and Robert and Tayoga, awakened and refreshed, took their places with the little Philadelphia troop and the young Englishman, Grosvenor. Hendrik was too old and stout to march on foot, and he rode at the head of his warriors on a horse, lent him by Colonel Johnson, an unusual spectacle among the Iroquois, who knew little of horses, and cared less about them.

This was the main force, and the Philadelphia troop, with Robert, Tayoga and Grosvenor, was close behind the Iroquois as they plunged into the deep woods bordering the lake, a mass of tangled wilderness that might well house a thousand ambushes. Grosvenor glanced about him apprehensively.

"I don't like the looks of it," he said. "It reminds me too much of the forest into which we marched with Braddock, God rest his soul!"

"I wasn't there," said young Captain Colden, "but Heaven knows I've heard enough horrible tales about it, and I've seen enough of the French and Indians to know they're expert at deadly snares."

"But we fight cunning with cunning," said Robert, cheerfully. "Look at the Mohawks ahead. There are two hundred of 'em, and every one of 'em has a hundred eyes."

"And look at old Hendrik, trotting along in the very lead on his horse," said Wilton. "I'm a man of peace, a Quaker, as you know, but my Quakerish soul leaps to see that gallant Indian, old enough to be the grandfather of us all, showing the way."

"Bravery and self-sacrifice are quite common among Indians. You'll learn that," said Robert. "Now, watch with all your eyes, every man of you, and notice anything that stirs in the brush."

Despite himself, Robert's own mind turned back to Braddock also, and all the incidents of the forest march that had so terrible an ending. Johnson's army knew more of the wilderness than Braddock's, but the hostile force was also far superior to the one that had fought at Duquesne. The French were many times more numerous here than there, and, although he had spoken brave words, his heart sank. Like the old Mohawk chief, he knew the army should not have been divided.

The region was majestic and beautiful. Not far away lay the lake, Andiatarocte, glittering in the sun. Around them stretched the primeval forest, in which the green was touched with the brown of late summer. Above them towered the mountains. The wilderness, picturesque and grand, gave forth no sound, save that of their own marching. The regiments of Williams and Whiting followed the Mohawks, and the New England and New York men were confident.

Robert heard behind him the deep hum and murmur that an advancing army makes, the sound of men talking that no commands could suppress, the heavy tread of the regiments and the clank of metal. That wild region had seen many a battle, but never before had it been invaded by armies so great as those of Dieskau and Johnson, which were about to meet in deadly combat.

His apprehensions grew. The absence of sounds save those made by themselves, the lack of hostile presence, not even a single warrior or Frenchman being visible, filled him with foreboding. It was just this way, when he marched with Braddock, only the empty forest, and no sign of deadly danger.

"Tayoga! Tayoga!" he whispered anxiously. "I don't like it."

"Nor do I, Dagaeoga."

"Think you we are likely to march into an ambush again?"

"Tododaho on his star is silent. He whispers nothing to me, yet I believe the trap is set, just ahead, and we march straight into it."

"And it's to be another Duquesne?"

"I did not say so, Dagaeoga. The trap will shut upon us, but we may burst it. Behold the Mohawks, the valiant Ganeagaono! Behold all the brave white men who are used to the forest and its ways! It is a strong trap that can hold them, one stronger, I think, than any the sons of Onontio and their savage allies can build."

Robert's heart leaped up at the brave words of Tayoga.

"I think so, too," he said. "It may be an ambush, but if so we will break from it. Old Hendrik tried to stop 'em, to keep all our force together, but since he couldn't do it, he's riding at the very head of this column, a shining target for hidden rifles."

"Hendrik is a great sachem, and as he is now old and grown feeble of the body, though not of the mind, this may well be his last and most glorious day."

"I hope he won't fall."

"Perhaps he may wish it thus. There could be no more fitting death for a great *sachem*."

They ceased talking, but both continued to watch the forest on either side with trained eyes. There was no wind, though now and then Robert thought he saw a bough or a bush move, indicating the presence of a hidden foe. But he invariably knew the next instant that it was merely the product of an uncommonly vivid imagination, always kindling into a burning fire in moments of extreme danger. No, there was nothing in the woods, at least, nothing that he could see.

Ahead of him the band of Mohawks, old Hendrik on horseback at their head, marched steadily on, warily watching the woods and thickets for their enemies. They, at least, were in thorough keeping with the wildness of the scene, with their painted bodies, their fierce eyes and their glittering tomahawks. But around Robert and Tayoga were the young Philadelphians, trained, alert men now, and following them was the stream of New York and New England troops, strong, vigorous and alive with enthusiasm.

The wilderness grew wilder and more dense, the Mohawks entering a great gorge, forested heavily, down the centre of which flowed a brook of black water. Thickets spread everywhere, and there were extensive outcroppings of rock. At one point rose precipices, with the stony slopes of French Mountain towering beyond. At another point rose West Mountain, though it was not so high, but at all points nature was wild and menacing.

The air seemed to Robert to grow darker, though he was not sure whether it was due to his imagination or to the closing in of the forests and mountains. At the same time a chill ran through his blood, a chill of alarm, and he knew instinctively that it was with good cause.

"Look at the great *sachem*!" suddenly exclaimed Tayoga.

Hendrik, loyal friend of the Americans and English, had reined in his horse, and his old eyes were peering into the thicket on his left, the mass of Mohawks behind him also stopping, because they knew their venerable leader would give no alarm in vain. Tayoga, Robert, Grosvenor and the Philadelphians stopped also, their eyes riveted on Hendrik. Robert's heart beat hard, and millions of motes danced in the air before his eyes.

The *sachem* suddenly threw up one hand in warning, and with the other pulled back his horse. The next instant a single rifle cracked in the thicket, but in a few seconds it was followed by the crashing fire of hundreds. Many of the Mohawks fell, a terrible lane was cut through the ranks of the Colonials, and the bullets whistled about the heads of the Philadelphia troop.

"The ambush!" cried Robert.

"The ambush!" echoed the Philadelphians.

Tayoga uttered a groan. His eyes had seen a sight they did not wish to see, however much he may have spoken of a glorious death for the old on the battlefield. Hendrik's horse had fallen beneath the leader, but the old chief leaped to his feet. Before he could turn a French soldier rushed up and killed him with a bayonet. Thus died a great and wise *sachem*, a devoted friend of the Americans, who had warned them in vain against marching into a trap, but who, nevertheless, in the very moment of his death, had saved them from going so completely into the trap that its last bar could close down.

A mighty wail arose from the Mohawks when they saw their venerated leader fall, but the wail merged into a fierce cry for vengeance, to which the ambushed French and Indians replied with shouts of exultation and increased their fire, every tree and bush and rock and log hiding a marksman.

"Give back!" shouted Tayoga to those around him. "Give back for your lives!"

The Mohawks and the frontiersmen alike saw they must slip from the trap, which they had half entered, if they were not to perish as Braddock's army had perished, and like good foresters they fell back without hesitation, pouring volley after volley into the woods and thickets where French and Indians still lay hidden. Yet the mortality among them was terrible. Colonel Williams noted a rising ground on their right, and led his men up the slope, but as they reached the summit he fell dead, shot through the brain. A new and terrible fire was poured upon his troops there from the bordering forest, and, unable to withstand it, they broke and began to retreat in confusion.

The young Philadelphians, with Robert, Tayoga and Grosvenor, rushed to their aid, and they were followed swiftly by the other regiment under Whiting. Yet it seemed that they would be cut to pieces when Robert suddenly heard a tremendous war cry from a voice he thought he knew, and looking back, he saw Daganoweda, the Mohawk, rushing into the battle.

The young chieftain looked a very god of war, his eyes glittering, the feathers in his headdress waving defiantly, the blade of his tomahawk flashing with light, when he swung it aloft. Now and then his lips opened as he let loose the tremendous war cry of the Ganeagaono. Close behind him crowded the warriors who had survived the combat with St. Luc, and there were Black Rifle, Willet, Rogers and the rangers, too, come just in time, with their stout hearts and strong arms to help stay the battle.

Robert himself uttered a shout of joy and the dark eyes of Tayoga glowed. But from the Mohawks of Hendrik came a mighty, thrilling cry when they saw the rush of their brethren under Daganoweda to their aid. Hendrik had fallen, and he had been a great and a wise sachem who would be missed long by his nation, but Daganoweda was left, a young chief, a very thunderbolt in battle, and the fire from his own ardent spirit was communicated to theirs. Willet, Black Rifle and the rangers were also pillars of strength, and the whole force, rallying, turned to meet the foe.

The French and Indians, sure now of a huge triumph, were rushing from their coverts to complete it, to drive the fugitives in panic and turmoil upon the main camp, where Johnson had remained for the present, and then to annihilate him and his force too. Above the almost continuous and appalling yells of the savages the French trumpets sang the song of victory, and the German baron who led them felt that he already clutched laurels as great as those belonging to the men who had defeated Braddock.

But the triumphant sweep of the Northern allies was suddenly met by a deadly fire from Mohawks, rangers and Colonials. Daganoweda and his men, tomahawk in hand, leaped upon the van of the French Indians and drove them back. The rangers and the frontiersmen, sheltering themselves behind logs and tree trunks, picked off the French regulars and the Canadians as they advanced. A bullet from the deadly barrel of Black Rifle slew Legardeur de St. Pierre, who led Dieskau's Indians, and whom they always trusted. The savage mass, wholly triumphant a minute ago, gave back, and the panic among the Mohawks and Colonials was stopped.

When St. Pierre fell Robert saw a gallant figure appear in his place, a figure taller and younger, none other than St. Luc himself, the Chevalier, arriving in time to help his own, just as Daganoweda, Willet and the others had come in time to aid theirs. The Chevalier was unhurt, and while one dauntless leader had fallen, another as brave and perhaps more skilful had taken his place. Robert saw him raise a whistle to his lips, and at its clear, piercing call, heard clearly above the crash of the battle, the Indians, turning, attacked anew and with yet greater impetuosity.

The smoke from so much firing was growing very thick, but through it the regulars of the regiments, Languedoc and La Reine, in their white uniforms, could be seen advancing, with the dark mass of the Canadians on one flank and the naked and painted Indians on the other, confident now that their check had been but momentary, and that the victory would yet be utter and complete.

Nevertheless, the Colonials and the Mohawks had rallied, order was restored, and while they were giving ground they were retreating in good formation, and with the rapid fire of their rifles were making the foe pay dearly for his advance.

Grosvenor had snatched up a rifle and ammunition from a fallen man, and was pulling trigger as fast as he could reload. His face was covered with smoke, perspiration and the stains of burned gunpowder, the whole forming a kind of brown mask, through which his eyes, nevertheless, gleamed with a dauntless light.

"It won't be Duquesne over again! It won't be! It won't be!" he repeated to all the world.

"But if you're not more careful you'll never know anything about it!" exclaimed Robert, as he grasped him suddenly by the coat and pulled him down behind a log, a half dozen musket balls whistling the next moment where his body had been. Grosvenor, in the moment of turmoil and excitement, did not forget to be grateful.

"Thanks, my dear fellow," he said to Robert. "I'll do as much for you some time."

Robert was about to reply, but a joyous shout from the rear stopped him. Over a hill behind them a strong body of provincials appeared coming to help. Waraiyageh in his camp had received news of ambush and battle, and knowing that his men must be in desperate case had hurried forward relief. Never was a force more welcome. Along the retreating line ran a welcoming shout, and all facing about as if by a single order, they gave the pursuing French and Indians a tremendous volley.

Robert saw regulars, Canadians and Indians drop as if smitten by a thunderbolt, and the whole pursuing army, reeling back, stopped. Then he heard the French trumpets again, and waiting behind the log, he saw that the hostile array was no longer advancing. The trumpets of Dieskau were sounding the recall, for the time, at least. Robert did not know until afterward that the Indian allies of the French had suffered so much that they were wavering, and not even the eloquence and example of St. Luc could persuade them, for the time being, to continue such a dangerous pursuit.

A few minutes of precious rest were allowed to the harried vanguard of Johnson, and now, holding their fire for a time when it would be needed more, the men continued to fall back toward the main camp, from which they had so recently come. The crash of rifles and muskets sank, but both sides were merely preparing for a new battle. Robert examined himself carefully, but found no trace of a wound.

"How is it with you, Tayoga?" he asked.

"Tododaho and Areskoui have protected me once more," replied the Onondaga. "The exertion has made my shoulder stiff and sore a little, but I have taken no fresh hurt."

"And you, Grosvenor?"

"My head is thumping at a terrible rate, but I feel that it will soon become quieter."

"Its ability to thump shows that you're full of life. How about your men, Captain Colden?"

"Four of my brave lads are sped. God rest their souls! They died in a good cause. Some of the others are wounded, but we won't count wounds now."

Robert was still able to see the indistinct figures of the French and Indians, through the clouds of smoke that hung between the two armies, but he saw also that they were not pursuing. At the distance he heard no sounds from them, and he presumed they were gathering up their dead and wounded, preparing for the new attack that would surely come.

"I was not in the first battle, but I will be in the second," a youthful voice said beside him, and he saw the Mohawk boy, Joseph Brant, his face glowing.

"We heard the firing," continued the boy, "and Colonel Johnson hurried forward a force, as you know. We are almost back at the camp now."

Robert had taken no notice of distance, but facing about, he saw the main camp not far away. Lucky it was for them that Waraiyageh and his officers were men of experience. They had sent enough men to help the vanguard break from the trap, but they had retained the majority, and had made them fortify with prodigious energy. A barricade of wagons, inverted boats, and trees hastily cut down had been built across the front. Three cannon were planted in the centre, where it was expected the main Indian and French force would appear, and another was dragged to the crest of a hill to rake their flank.

The retreating force uttered a tremendous shout as they saw how their comrades had prepared for them, and then, in good order, sought the shelter of the barricade, where they were welcomed by those who had not yet been in battle.

"Get fresh breath while you may!" exclaimed Tayoga, as he threw himself down on the ground. "The delay will not be long. Sharp Sword will drive the warriors forward, and the regulars and Canadians will charge. It will be a great battle, and a desperate one, nor does Tododaho yet whisper to me which side will win."

Robert and his comrades breathed heavily for a while, until they felt new strength pouring back into their veins. Then they rose, looked to their arms and took their place in the line of battle. The trumpets of Dieskau were sounding again in the forest in front of them, and the new attack was at hand.

"Keep close, Grosvenor," said Robert. "They'll fire the first volley and we'll let it pass over our heads."

"I know the wisdom of what you say," replied the Englishman, "but it's hard to refrain from looking when you know a French army and a mass of howling savages are about to rush down upon you."

"But one must, if he intends to live and fight."

Clear and full sang the trumpets of Dieskau once more. Despite his advice to Grosvenor, Robert peeped over the log and saw the enemy gathering in the forest. The French regulars were in front, behind them the Canadians, and on the flanks hovered great masses of savages. Smoke floated over trees and bushes, and the forest was full of acrid odours. Far to the right he caught another glimpse of St. Luc in his splendid white and silver uniform, marshalling the Indians, a shining mark, but apparently untouched.

"The attack will be fierce," whispered Tayoga, who lay on his left. "They consider their check a matter of but a moment, and they think to sweep over us."

"But we have hundreds and hundreds of good rifles that say them nay. Is Tododaho still silent, Tayoga?"

The Onondaga looked up at the heavens, where the deep blue, beyond the smoke, was unstained. There was the corner, where the star, on which his patron saint lived, came out at night, but no light shone from the silky void and no whisper reached his ear. So he said in reply:

"The great Onondaga chieftain who went away four hundred years ago is silent today, and we must await the event."

"We won't have to wait long, because I hear a single trumpet now, and to me it sounds wonderfully like the call to charge."

The silver note thrilled through the woods, the French regulars and Canadians uttered a shout, which was followed instantly by the terrible yell of the Indians, and then the thickets crashed beneath the tread of the attacking army.

"Here they come!" shouted Grosvenor, and, laying his rifle across the log, he fired almost at random into the charging mass. Robert and Tayoga picked their targets, and their bullets sped true. All along the American line ran the fierce fire, the crest of the whole barricade blazing with red, while the artillery, which the savages always dreaded, opened on them with showers of grape.

The Indians, despite all the bravery and example of St. Luc, wavered, and, as their dead fell around them, they began to give forth laments, instead of triumphant yells. But the regulars in the centre, led by Dieskau, came on as steadily as ever, and the little group behind the log, of which Tayoga and Robert were the leading spirits, turned their rifles upon them. Robert presently heard a youthful shout of exultation at the far end of the log, and he saw the boy, Joseph Brant, reloading the rifle which he had fired in his first battle. The French regulars suddenly stopped, and Grosvenor cried:

"It will be no Duquesne! No Duquesne again!"

The French were not withdrawing. Upon that field, as well as every other in North America, they showed that they were the bravest of the brave. Wheeling his regulars and Canadians to the right, Dieskau sought to crush there the three American regiments of Titcomb, Ruggles and Williams, and for an hour the battle at that point swayed to and fro, often almost hand to hand. Titcomb was slain and many of his officers fell, but when Dieskau himself came into view an

American rifleman shot him through the leg. His adjutant, a gallant young officer named Montreuil, although wounded himself, rushed from cover, seized his wounded chief in his arms and bore him to the shelter of a tree.

But he was not safe long even there. While they were washing his wounds he was struck again by two bullets, in the knee and in the thigh. Two Canadians attempted to carry him to the rear. One was killed instantly, and Montreuil took his place, but Dieskau made them put him down and directed the adjutant to lead the French again in a desperate charge to regain a day that had started so brilliantly, and that now seemed to be wavering in the balance.

Colonel Johnson himself had been wounded severely, and had been compelled to retire to his tent, but the American colonels, at least those who survived, conducted the battle with skill and valour. The cannon, protected by the riflemen, still sent showers of grape shot among the French and Indians. The huge Tandakora with St. Luc tried to lead the savages anew upon the American lines, but the hearts of the red men failed them.

The French regulars, urged on by Montreuil, charged once more, and once more were driven back, and the Americans, rising from their logs and coverts, rushed forward in their turn. The regulars and Canadians were driven back in a rout, and Dieskau himself lying among the bushes was taken, being carried to the tent of Johnson, where the two wounded commanders, captor and captive, talked politely of many things.

The victory became more complete than the Americans had hoped. The Indians who had stayed far in the rear to scalp those fallen in the morning were attacked suddenly by a band of frontiersmen, coming to join Johnson's army, and, although they fought desperately and were superior in numbers, they were routed as Dieskau had been, the survivors fleeing into the forest.

Thus, late in the afternoon, closed the momentous battle of Lake George. The French and Indian power had received a terrible blow, the whole course of the war, which before had been only a triumphant march for the enemy, was changed, and men took heart anew as the news spread through all the British colonies.

When Dieskau's regulars, the Canadians and the Indians, broke in the great defeat, Robert, Tayoga, Willet, Grosvenor, the Philadelphia troop, Black Rifle and Daganoweda, all fierce with exultation, followed in pursuit. But the enemy melted away before them, and then, from the crest of a hill, Robert heard the distant note of a French song he knew:

Hier, sur le pont d'Avignon
J'ai oui chanter la belle Lon, la,
J'ai oui chanter la belle,
Elle chantait d'un ton si doux
Comme une demoiselle Lon, la,
Comme une demoiselle.

"At least he has escaped," said Robert.

"The bullet that kills him is not moulded and never will be," said Tayoga.

"How do you know?" asked Willet, startled.

"Because Tododaho has whispered it to me. I heard his voice in the breath of the wind as we pursued through the forest."

Robert caught a glimpse of St. Luc, in his uniform of white and silver, still apparently unstained, erect and defiant. Then he disappeared and they heard only the singing of the wind among the leaves.

THE FRENCH & INDIAN WAR NOVELS

The Masters of the Peaks

A Story of the
Great North Woods

Foreword

The Masters of the Peaks, while presenting a complete story in itself is the fourth volume of the French and Indian War Series, of which the predecessors were *The Hunters of the Hills*, *The Shadow of the North*, and *The Rulers of the Lakes*. Robert Lennox, Tayoga, Willet, and all the other important characters of the earlier romances reappear in the present book.

Characters in the French and Indian War Series

Robert Lennox	A lad of unknown origin
Tayoga	A young Onondaga warrior
David Willet	A hunter
Raymond Louis De St. Luc	A brilliant French officer
Aguste De Courcelles	A French officer
François De Jumonville	A French officer
Louis De Galisonnière	A young French officer
Jean De Mézy	A corrupt Frenchman
Armand Glandelet	A young Frenchman
Pierre Boucher	A bully and bravo
Philibert Drouillard	A French priest
The Marquis Duquesne	Governor-General of Canada
Marquis De Vaudreuil	Governor-General of Canada
François Bigot	Intendant of Canada
Marquis De Montcalm	French commander-in-chief
De Levis	A French general
Bourlamaque	A French general
Bougainville	A French general
Armand Dubois	A follower of St. Luc
M. De Chatillard	An old French Seigneur
Charles Langlade	A French partisan
The Dove	The Indian wife of Langlade
Tandakora	An Ojibway chief
Daganoweda	A young Mohawk chief

Hendrick	An old Mohawk chief
Braddock.	A British General
Abercrombie	A British general
Wolfe	A British general
Col. William Johnson	Anglo-American leader
Molly Brant	Col. Wm. Johnson's Indian wife
Joseph Brant	Young brother of Molly Brant; afterward the great Mohawk Chief Thayendanegea
Robert Dinwiddie	Lieutenant-Governor of Virginia
William Shirley	Governor of Massachusetts
Benjamin Franklin	Famous American patriot
James Colden	A young Philadelphia captain
William Wilton	A young Philadelphia lieutenant
Hugh Carson	A young Philadelphia lieutenant
Jacobus Huysman	An Albany burgher
Caterina	Jacobus Huysman's cook
Alexander Mclean	An Albany schoolmaster
Benjamin Hardy	A New York merchant
Johnathan Pillsbury	Clerk to Benjamin Hardy
Adrian Van Zoon	A New York merchant
The Slaver	A nameless rover
Achille Garay	A French spy
Alfred Grosvenor	A young English officer
James Cabell	A young Virginian
Walter Stuart	A young Virginian
Black Rifle	A famous "Indian fighter"
Elihu Strong	A Massachusetts colonel
Alan Hervey	A New York financier
Stuart Whyte	Captain of the British sloop Hawk
John Latham	Lieutenant of the British sloop Hawk
Edward Charteris	A young officer of the Royal Americans
Zebedee Crane	A young scout and forest runner
Robert Rogers	Famous Captain of American Rangers

Chapter 1

In the Deep Woods

A light wind sang through the foliage, turned to varying and vivid hues now by the touch of autumn, and it had an edge of cold that made Robert Lennox shiver a little, despite a hardy life in wilderness and open. But it was only a passing feeling. A moment or two later he forgot it, and, turning his eyes to the west, watched the vast terraces of blazing colour piled one above another by the sinking sun.

Often as he had seen it the wonderful late glow over the mighty forest never failed to stir him, and to make his pulse beat a little faster. His sensitive mind, akin in quality to that of a poet, responded with eagerness and joy to the beauty and majesty of nature. Forgetting danger and the great task they had set for themselves, he watched the banks of colour, red and pink, salmon and blue, purple and yellow, shift and change, while in the very heart of the vast panorama the huge, red orb, too strong for human sight, glittered and flamed.

The air, instinct with life, intoxicated him and he became rapt as in a vision. People whom he had met in his few but eventful years passed before him again in all the seeming of reality, and then his spirit leaped into the future, dreaming of the great things he would see, and in which perhaps he would have a share.

Tayoga, the young Onondaga, looked at his comrade and he understood. The same imaginative thread had been woven into the warp of which he was made, and his nostrils and lips quivered as he drank in the splendour of a world that appealed with such peculiar force to him, a son of the woods.

"The spirit of Areskoui (the Sun God) is upon Dagaeoga, and he has left us to dwell for a little while upon the seas of colour heaped against the western horizon," he said.

Willet, the hunter, smiled. The two lads were very dear to him. He knew that they were uncommon types, raised by the gift of God far above the normal. "Let him rest there, Tayoga," he said, "while those brilliant banks last, which won't be long. All things change, and the glorious hues will soon give way to the dark."

"True, Great Bear, but if the night comes it, in turn, must yield to the dawn. All things change, as you say, but nothing perishes. The sun tomorrow will be the same sun that we see today. Black night will not take a single ray from its glory."

"It's so, Tayoga, but you talk like a book or a prophet. I'm wondering if our lives are not like the going and coming of the sun. Maybe we pass on from one to another, forever and forever, without ending."

"Great Bear himself feels the spell of Areskoui also."

"I do, but we'd better stop rhapsodizing and think about our needs. Here, Robert, wake up and come back to earth! It's no time to sing a song to the sun with the forest full of our red enemies and the white too, perhaps."

Robert awoke with a start.

"You dragged me out of a beautiful world," he said.

"A world in which you were the central star," rejoined the hunter.

"So I was, but isn't that the case with all the imaginary worlds a man creates? He's their sun or he wouldn't create 'em."

"We're getting too deep into the unknown. Plant your feet on the solid earth, Robert, and let's think about the problems a dark night is going to bring us in the Indian country, not far south of the St. Lawrence."

Young Lennox shivered again. The terraces in the west suddenly began to fade and the wind took on a fresh and sharper edge.

"I know one thing," he said. "I know the night's going to be cold. It always is in the late autumn, up here among the high hills, and I'd like to see a fire, before which we could bask and upon which we could warm our food."

The hunter glanced at the Onondaga.

"That tells the state of my mind, too," he said, "but I doubt whether it would be safe. If we're to be good scouts, fit to discover the plans of the French and Indians, we won't get ourselves cut off by some rash act in the very beginning."

"It may not be a great danger or any at all," said Tayoga. "There is much rough and rocky ground to our right, cut by deep chasms, and we might find in there a protected recess in which we could build a smothered fire."

"You're a friend at the right time, Tayoga," said Robert. "I feel that I must have warmth. Lead on and find the stony hollow for us."

The Onondaga turned without a word, and started into the maze of lofty hills and narrow valleys, where the shadows of the night that was coming so swiftly already lay thick and heavy.

The three had gone north after the great victory at Lake George, a triumph that was not followed up as they had hoped. They had waited to see Johnson's host pursue the enemy and strike him hard again, but there were bickerings among the provinces which were jealous of one another, and the army remained in camp until the lateness of the season indicated a delay of all operations, save those of the scouts and roving bands that never rested. But Robert, Willet and Tayoga hoped, nevertheless, that they could achieve some deed of importance during the coming cold weather, and they were willing to undergo great risks in the effort.

They were soon in the heavy forest that clothed all the hills, and passed up a narrow ravine leading into the depths of the maze. The wind followed them into the cleft and steadily grew colder. The glowing terraces in the west broke up, faded quite away, and night, as yet without stars, spread over the earth.

Tayoga was in front, the other two following him in single file, stepping where he stepped, and leaving to him without question the selection of a place where they could stay. The Onondaga, guided by long practice and the inheritance from countless ancestors who had lived all their lives in the forest, moved forward with confidence. His instinct told him they would soon come to such a refuge as they desired, the rocky uplift about him indicating the proximity of many hollows.

The darkness increased, and the wind swept through the chasms with alternate moan and whistle, but the red youth held on his course for a full two miles, and his comrades followed without a word. When the cliffs about them rose to a height of two or three hundred feet, he stopped, and, pointing with a long forefinger, said he had found what they wished.

Robert at first could see nothing but a pit of blackness, but gradually as he gazed the shadows passed away, and he traced a deep recess in the stone of the cliff, not much of a shelter to those unused to the woods, but sufficient for hardy forest runners.

"I think we may build a little fire in there," said Tayoga, "and no one can see it unless he is here in the ravine within ten feet of us."

Willet nodded and Robert joyfully began to prepare for the blaze. The night was turning even colder than he had expected, and the chill was creeping into his frame. The fire would be most welcome for its warmth, and also because of the good cheer it would bring. He swept dry leaves into a heap within the recess, put upon them dead wood, which was abundant everywhere, and then Tayoga with artful use of flint and steel lighted the spark.

"It is good," admitted the hunter as he sat Turkish fashion on the leaves, and spread out his hands before the growing flames. "The nights grow cold mighty soon here in the high hills of the north, and the heat not only loosens up your muscles, but gives you new courage."

"I intend to make myself as comfortable as possible," said Robert. "You and Tayoga are always telling me to do so and I know the advice is good."

He gathered great quantities of the dry leaves, making of them what was in reality a couch, upon which he could recline in halfway fashion like a Roman at a feast, and warm at the fire before him the food he carried in a deerskin knapsack. An appetizing odour soon arose, and, as he ate, a pleasant warmth pervaded all his body, giving him a feeling of great content. They had venison, the tender meat of the young bear which, like the Indians, they loved, and they also allowed themselves a slice apiece of precious bread. Water was never distant in the northern wilderness, and Tayoga found a brook not a hundred yards away, flowing down a ravine that cut across their own. They drank at it in turn, and, then, the three lay down on the leaves in the recess, grateful to the Supreme Power which provided so well for them, even in the wild forest.

They let the flames die, but a comfortable little bed of coals remained, glowing within the shelter of the rocks. Young Lennox heaped up the leaves until they formed a pillow under his head, and then half dreaming, gazed into the heart of the fire, while his comrades reclined near him, each silent but with his mind turned to that which concerned him most.

Robert's thoughts were of St. Luc, of the romantic figure he had seen in the wilderness after the battle of Lake George, the knightly chevalier, singing his gay little song of mingled sentiment and defiance. An unconscious smile passed over his face. He and St. Luc could never be enemies. In very truth, the French leader, though an official enemy, had proved more than once the best of friends, ready even to risk his life in the service of the American lad. What was the reason? What could be the tie between them? There must be some connection. What was the mystery of his origin? The events of the last year indicated to him very clearly that there was such a mystery. Adrian Van Zoon and Master Benjamin Hardy surely knew something about it, and Willet too. Was it possible that a thread lay in the hand of St. Luc also?

He turned his eyes from the coals and gazed at the impassive face of the hunter. Once the question trembled on his lips, but he was sure the Great Bear would evade the answer, and the lad thought too much of the man who had long stood to him in the place of father to cause him annoyance. Beyond a doubt Willet had his interests at heart, and, when the time came for him to speak, speak he would, but not before.

His mind passed from the subject to dwell upon the task they had set for themselves, a thought which did not exclude St. Luc, though the chevalier now appeared in the guise of a bold and skilful foe, with whom they must match their wisdom and courage. Doubtless he had formed a new band, and, at the head of it, was already roaming the country south of the St. Lawrence. Well, if that were the case perhaps they would meet once more, and he would have given much to penetrate the future.

"Why don't you go to sleep, Robert?" asked the hunter.

"For the best of reasons. Because I can't," replied the lad.

"Perhaps it's well to stay awake," said the Onondaga gravely.

"Why, Tayoga?"

"Someone comes."

"Here in the ravine?"

"No, not in the ravine but on the cliff opposite us."

Robert strained both eye and ear, but he could neither see nor hear any human being. The wall on the far side of the ravine rose to a considerable height, its edge making a black line against the sky, but nothing there moved.

"Your fancy is too much for you, Tayoga," he said. "Thinking that someone might come, it creates a man out of air and mist."

"No, Dagaeoga, my fancy sleeps. Instead, my ear, which speaks only the truth, tells me a man is walking along the crest of the cliff, and coming on a course parallel with our ravine. My eye does not yet see him, but soon it will confirm what my ear has already told me. This deep cleft acts as a trumpet and brings the sound to me."

"How far away, then, would you say is this being, who, I fear, is mythical?"

"He is not mythical. He is reality. He is yet about three hundred yards distant. I might not have heard him, even with the aid of the cleft, but tonight Areskoui has given uncommon power to my ear, perhaps to aid us, and I know he is walking among thick bushes. I can hear the branches swish as they fly back into place, after his body has passed. Ah, a small stick popped as it broke under his foot!"

"I heard nothing."

"That is not my fault, O Dagaeoga. It is a heavy man, because I now hear his footsteps, even when they do not break anything. He walks with some uncertainty. Perhaps he fears lest he should make a false step, and tumble into the ravine."

"Since you can tell so much through hearing, at such a great distance, perhaps you know what kind of a man the stranger is. A warrior, I suppose?"

"No, he is not of our race. He would not walk so heavily. It is a white man."

"One of Rogers' rangers, then? Or maybe it is Rogers himself, or perhaps Black Rifle."

"It is none of those. They would advance with less noise. It is one not so much used to the forest, but who knows the way, nevertheless, and who doubtless has gone by this trail before."

"Then it must be a Frenchman!"

"I think so too."

"It won't be St. Luc?"

"No, Dagaeoga, though your tone showed that for a moment you hoped it was. Sharp Sword is too skilful in the forest to walk with so heavy a step. Nor can it be either of the leaders, De Courcelles or Jumonville. They also are too much at home in the woods. The right name of the man forms itself on my lips, but I will wait to be sure. In another minute he will enter the bare space almost opposite us and then we can see."

The three waited in silence. Although Robert had expressed doubt he felt none. He had a supreme belief in the Onondaga's uncanny powers, and he was quite sure that a man was moving upon the bluff. A stranger at such a time was to be watched, because white men came but little into this dangerous wilderness.

A dark figure appeared within the prescribed minute upon the crest and stopped there, as if the man, whoever he might be, wished to rest and draw fresh breath. The sky had lightened and he was outlined clearly against it. Robert gazed intently and then he uttered a little cry.

"I know him!" he said. "I can't be mistaken. It's Achille Garay, the one whose name we found written on a fragment of a letter in Albany."

"It's the man who tried to kill you, none other," said Tayoga gravely, "and Areskoui whispered in my ear that it would be he."

"What on earth can he be doing here in this lone wilderness at such a time?" asked Robert.

"Likely he's on his way to a French camp with information about our forces," said Willet. "We frightened Mynheer Hendrik Martinus, when we were in Albany, but I suppose that once a spy and traitor always a spy and traitor. Since the immediate danger has moved from Albany, Martinus and Garay may have begun work again."

"Then we'd better stop him," said Robert.

"No, let him go on," said Willet. "He can't carry any information about us that the French leaders won't find out for themselves. The fact that he's travelling in the night indicates a French camp somewhere near. We'll put him to use. Suppose we follow him and discover what we can about our enemies."

Robert looked at the cheerful bed of coals and sighed. They were seeking the French and Indians, and Garay was almost sure to lead straight to them. It was their duty to stalk him.

"I wish he had passed in the daytime," he said ruefully.

Tayoga laughed softly.

"You have lived long enough in the wilderness, O Dagaeoga," he said, "to know that you cannot choose when and where you will do your work."

"That's true, Tayoga, but while my feet are unwilling to go my will moves me on. So I'm entitled to more credit than you who take an actual physical delight in trailing anybody at any time."

The Onondaga smiled, but did not reply. Then the three took up their arms, returned their packs to their backs and without noise left the alcove. Robert cast one more reluctant glance at the bed of coals, but it was a farewell, not any weakening of the will to go.

Garay, after his brief rest on the summit, had passed the open space and was out of sight in the bushes, but Robert knew that both Tayoga and Willet could easily pick up his trail, and now he was all eagerness to pursue him and see what the chase might disclose. A little farther down, the cliff sloped back to such an extent that they could climb it without trouble, and, when they surmounted the crest, they entered the bushes at the point where Garay had disappeared.

"Can you hear him now, Tayoga?" asked Robert.

"My ears are as good as they were when I was in the ravine," replied the Onondaga, "but they do not catch any sounds from the Frenchman. It is, as we wish, because we do not care to come so near him that he will hear."

"Give him a half mile start," said Willet. "The ground is soft here, and it won't be any sort of work to follow him. See, here are the traces of his footsteps now, and there is where he has pushed his way among the little boughs. Notice the two broken twigs, Robert."

They followed at ease, the trail being a clear one, and the light of moon and stars now ample. Robert began to feel the ardour of the chase. He did not see Garay, but he believed that Tayoga at times heard him with those wonderful ears of his. He rejoiced too that chance had caused them to find the French spy in the wilderness. He remembered that foul attempt upon his life in Albany, and, burning with resentment, he was eager to thwart Garay in whatever he was now attempting to do. Tayoga saw his face and said softly:

"You hate this man Garay?"

"I don't like him."

"Do you wish me to go forward and kill him?"

"No! No, Tayoga! Why do you ask me such a cold-blooded question?"

The Onondaga laughed gently.

"I was merely testing you, Dagaeoga," he said. "We of the Hodenosaunee perhaps do not regard the taking of life as you do, but I would not shoot Garay from ambush, although I might slay him in open battle. Ah, there he is again on the crest of the ridge ahead!"

Robert once more saw the thick, strong figure of the spy outlined against the sky which was now luminous with a brilliant moon and countless clear stars, and the feeling of resentment was very powerful within him. Garay, without provocation, had attempted his life, and he could not forget it, and, for a moment or two, he felt that if the necessity should come in battle he was willing for a bullet from Tayoga to settle him. Then he rebuked himself for harbouring rancour.

Garay paused, as if he needed another rest, and looked back, though it was only a casual glance, perhaps to measure the distance he had come, and the three, standing among the dense bushes, had no fear that he saw them or even suspected that anyone was on his traces. After a delay of a minute or so he passed over the crest and Robert, Willet and Tayoga moved on in pursuit. The Frenchman evidently knew his path, as the chase led for a long time over hills, down valleys and across small streams. Toward morning he put his fingers to his lips and blew a shrill whistle between them. Then the three drew swiftly near until they could see him, standing under the boughs of a great oak, obviously in an attitude of waiting.

"It is a signal to someone," said Robert.

"So it is," said Willet, "and it means that he and we have come to the end of our journey. I take it that we have arrived almost at the French and Indian camp, and that he whistles because he fears lest he should be shot by a sentinel through mistake. The reply should come soon."

As the hunter spoke they heard a whistle, a faint, clear note far ahead, and then Garay without hesitation resumed his journey. The three followed, but when they reached the crest of the next ridge they saw a light shining through the forest, a light that grew and finally divided into many lights, disclosing to them with certainty the presence of a camp. The figure of Garay appeared for a little while outlined against a fire, another figure came forward to meet him, and the two disappeared together.

From the direction of the fires came sounds subdued by the distance, and the aroma of food.

"It is a large camp," said Tayoga. "I have counted twelve fires which proves it, and the white men and the red men in it do not go hungry. They have deer, bear, fish and birds also. The pleasant odours of them all come to my nostrils, and make me hungry."

"That's too much for me," said Robert. "I can detect the blended savour, but I know not of what it consists. Now we go on, I suppose, and find out what this camp holds."

"We wouldn't dream of turning back," said the hunter. "Did you notice anything familiar, Robert, about the figure that came forward to meet Garay?"

"Now that you speak of it, I did, but I can't recall the identity of the man."

"Think again!"

"Ah, now I have him! It was the French officer, Colonel Auguste de Courcelles, who gave us so much trouble in Canada and elsewhere."

"That's the man," said Willet. "I knew him at once. Now, wherever De Courcelles is mischief is likely to be afoot, but he's not the only Frenchman here. We'll spy out this camp to the full. There's time yet before the sunrise comes."

Now the three used all the skill in stalking with which they were endowed so plentifully, creeping forward without noise through the bushes, making so little stir among them that if a wary warrior had been looking he would have taken the slight movement of twig or leaf for the influence of a wandering breeze. Gradually the whole camp came into view, and Tayoga's prediction that it would be a large one proved true.

Robert lay on a little knoll among small bushes growing thick, where the keenest eye could not see him, but where his own vision swept the whole wide shallow dip, in which the French and Indian force was encamped. Twelve fires, all good and large, burned gaily, throwing out ruddy flames from great beds of glowing coals, while the aroma of food was now much stronger and very appetizing.

The force numbered at least three hundred men, of whom about one third were Frenchmen or Canadians, all in uniform. Robert recognized De Courcelles and near him Jumonville, his invariable comrade, and a little farther on a handsome and gallant young face.

"It's De Galissonnière of the Battalion Languedoc, whom we met in Québec," he whispered to Tayoga. "Now I wonder what he's doing here."

"He's come with the others on a projected foray," Tayoga whispered back. "But look beyond him, Dagaeoga, and you will see one more to be dreaded than De Courcelles or Jumonville."

Robert's gaze followed that of the young Onondaga and was intercepted by the huge figure of Tandakora, the Ojibway, who stood erect by one of the fires, bare save for a breech cloth and moccasins, his body painted in the most hideous designs, of which war paint was possible, his brow lowering.

"Tandakora is not happy," said Tayoga.

"No," said Robert. "He is thinking of the battle at Lake George that he did not win, and of all the scalps he did not take. He is thinking of his lost warriors, and the rout of his people and the French."

"Even so, Dagaeoga. Now Tandakora and De Courcelles talk with the spy, Garay. They want his news. They rejoice when he tells them Waraiyageh and his soldiers still make no preparations to advance after their victory by the lake. The long delay, the postponement of a big campaign until next spring will give the French and Indians time to breathe anew and renew their strength. Tandakora and De Courcelles consider themselves fortunate, and they are pleased with the spy, Garay. But look, Dagaeoga! Behold who comes now!"

Robert's heart began to throb as the handsomest and most gallant figure of them all walked into the red glow of the firelight, a tall man, young, lithe, athletic, fair of hair and countenance, his manner at once graceful and proud, a man to whom the others turned with deference, and perhaps in the case of De Courcelles and Jumonville with a little fear. He wore a white uniform with gold facings, and a small gold hilted sword swung upon his thigh. Even in the forest, dress impresses, and Robert was quite sure that St. Luc was in his finest attire, not from vanity, but because he wished to create an effect. It would be like him, when his fortunes were lowest, to assume his highest manner before both friend and foe.

"You'd think from his looks that he had nothing but a string of victories and never knew defeat," whispered Willet. "Anyway, his is the finest spirit in all that crowd, and he's the greatest leader and soldier, too. Notice how they give way to him, and how they stop asking questions of Garay, leaving it to him. And now Garay himself bows low before him, while De Courcelles, Jumonville and Tandakora stand aside. I wish we could hear what they say; then we might learn something worth all our risk in coming here."

But their voices did not reach so great a distance, though the three, eager to use eye even if ear was of no use, still lay in the bushes and watched the flow of life in the great camp. Many of the French and Indians who had been asleep awoke, sat up and began to cook breakfast for themselves, holding strips of game on sharp sticks over the coals. St. Luc talked a long while with Garay, afterward with the French officers and Tandakora, and then withdrew to a little knoll, where he leaned against a tree, his face expressing intense thought. A dark, powerfully built man, the Canadian, Dubois, brought him food which he ate mechanically.

The dusk floated away, and the sun came up, great and brilliant. The three stirred in their covert, and Willet whispered that it was time for them to be going.

"Only the most marvellous luck could save us from detection in the daylight," he said, "because presently the Indians, growing restless, will wander about the camp."

"I'm willing to go," Robert whispered back. "I know the danger is too great. Besides I'm starving to death, and the odours of all their good food will hasten my death, if I don't take an antidote."

They retreated with the utmost care and Robert drew an immense breath of relief when they were a full mile away. It was well to look upon the French and Indian camp, but it was better to be beyond the reach of those who made it.

"And now we make a camp of our own, don't we?" he said. "All my bones are stiff from so much bending and creeping. Moreover, my hunger has grown to such violent pitch that it is tearing at me, so to speak, with red hot pincers."

"Dagaeoga always has plenty of words," said Tayoga in a whimsical tone, "but he will have to endure his hunger a while longer. Let the pincers tear and burn. It is good for him. It will give him a chance to show how strong he is, and how a mighty warrior despises such little things as food and drink."

"I'm not anxious to show myself a mighty warrior just now," retorted young Lennox. "I'd be willing to sacrifice my pride in that respect if I could have carried off some of their bear steaks and venison."

"Come on," said Willet, "and I'll see that you're satisfied. I'm beginning to feel as you do, Robert."

Nevertheless he marshalled them forward pretty sternly and they pursued a westward course for many miles before he allowed a halt. Even then they hunted about among the rocks until they found a secluded place, no fire being permitted, at which it pleased Robert to grumble, although he did not mean it.

"We were better off last night when we had our little fire in the hollow," he said.

"So we were, as far as the body is concerned," rejoined Willet, "but we didn't know then where the Indian camp lay. We've at least increased our knowledge. Now, I'm thinking that you two lads, who have been awake nearly all night and also the half of the morning that has passed, ought to sleep. Time we have to spare, but you know we should practice all the economy we can with our strength. This place is pretty well hidden, and I'll do the watching. Spread your blankets on the leaves, Robert. It's not well even for foresters to sleep on the bare ground. Now draw the other half of it over you. Tayoga has done so already. I'm wondering which of you will get to sleep first. Whoever does will be the better man, a question I've long wanted to decide."

But the problem was still left for the future. They fell asleep so nearly at the same time that Willet could tell no difference. He noticed with pleasure their long, regular breathing, and he said to himself, as he had said so often before, that they were two good and brave lads.

Then he made a very comfortable cushion of fallen leaves to sit upon, and remained there a long time, his rifle across his knees.

His eyes were wide open, but no part of his body stirred. He had acquired the gift of infinite patience, and with it the difficult physical art of remaining absolutely motionless for a long time. So thorough was his mastery over himself that the small wild game began to believe by and by that he was not alive. Birds sang freely over his head and the hare hopped through the undergrowth. Yet the hunter saw everything and his very stillness enabled him to listen with all the more acuteness.

The sun which had arisen great and brilliant, remained so, flooding the world with golden lights and making it wonderfully alluring to Willet, whose eyes never grew weary of the forest's varying shades and aspects. They were all peaceful now, but he had no illusions. He knew that the hostile force would send out many hunters. So many men must have much game and presently they would be prowling through the woods, seeking deer and bear. The chief danger came from them.

The hours passed and noon arrived. Willet had not stirred. He did not sleep, but he rested nevertheless. His great body was relaxed thoroughly, and strength, after weariness, flowed back into his veins.

Presently his head moved forward a little and his attitude grew more intent. A slight sound that was not a part of the wilderness had come to him. It was very faint, few would have noticed it, but he knew it was the report of a rifle. He knew also that it was not a shot fired in battle. The hunters, as he had surmised, were abroad, and they had started up a deer or a bear.

But Willet did not stir nor did his eyelids flicker. He was used to the proximity of foes, and the distant report did not cause his heart to miss a single beat. Instead, he felt a sort of dry amusement that they should be so near and yet know it not. How Tandakora would have rejoiced if there had been a whisper in his ear that Willet, Robert and Tayoga whom he hated so much were within sound of his rifle! And how he would have spread his nets to catch such precious game!

He heard a second shot presently from the other side, and then the hunter began to laugh softly to himself. His faint amusement was turning into actual and intense enjoyment. The Indian hunters were obviously on every side of them but did not dream that the finest game of all was at hand. They would continue to waste their time on deer and bear while the three formidable rangers were within hearing of their guns.

But the hunter was still silent. His laughter was wholly internal, and his lips did not even move. It showed only in his eye and the general expression of his countenance. A third shot and a fourth came, but no anxiety marred his sense of the humorous.

Then he heard the distant shouts of warriors in pursuit of a wounded bear and still he was motionless.

Willet knew that the French and Tandakora suspected no pursuit. They believed that no American rangers would come among the lofty peaks and ridges south of the border, and he and his comrades could lie in safe hiding while the hunt went on with unabated zeal. But he was sure one day would be sufficient for the task. That portion of the wilderness was full of game, and, since the coming of the war, deer and bear were increasing rapidly. Willet often noted how quickly game returned to regions abandoned by man, as if the wild animals promptly told one another the danger had passed.

Joyous shouts came now and then and he knew that they marked the taking of game, but about the middle of the afternoon the hunt drifted entirely away. A little later Tayoga awoke and sat up. Then Willet moved slightly and spoke.

"Tandakora's hunters have been all about us while you slept," he said, "but I knew they wouldn't find us."

"Dagaeoga and I were safe in the care of the Great Bear," said the Onondaga confidently. "Tandakora will rage if we tell him some day that we were here, to be taken if he had only seen us. Now Lennox awakes also! O Dagaeoga, you have slept and missed all the great jest."

"What do you mean, Tayoga?"

"Tandakora built his fire just beyond the big bush that grows ten feet away, and sat there two hours without suspecting our presence here."

"Now I know you are romancing, Tayoga, because I can see the twinkle in your eyes. But I suspect that what you say bears some remote relation to the truth."

"The hostile hunters passed while you slept, and while I slept also, but the Great Bear was all eyes and ears and he did not think it needful to awaken us."

"What are we going to do now, Dave?"

"Eat more venison. We must never fail to keep the body strong."

"And then?"

"I'm not sure. I thought once that we'd better go south to our army at Lake George with news of this big band, but it's a long distance down there, and it may be wiser to stay here and watch St. Luc. What do you say, Robert?"

"Stay here."

"And you, Tayoga?"

"Watch St. Luc."

"I was inclining to that view myself, and it's settled now. But we mustn't move from this place until dark; it would be too dangerous in the day."

The lads nodded and the three settled into another long period of waiting.

Chapter 2

On the Ridges

Late in the afternoon Willet went to sleep and Robert and Tayoga watched, although, as the hunter had done, they depended more upon ear than eye. They too heard now and then the faint report of distant shots from the hunt, and Robert's heart beat very fast, but, if the young Onondaga felt emotion, he did not show it. At twilight, they ate a frugal supper, and when the night had fully come they rose and walked about a little to make their stiffened muscles elastic again.

"The hunters have all gone back to the camp now," said Tayoga, "since it is not easy to pursue the game by dusk, and we need not keep so close, like a bear in its den."

"And the danger of our being seen is reduced to almost nothing," said Robert.

"It is so, Dagaeoga, but we will have another fight to make. We must strive to keep ourselves from freezing. It turns very cold on the mountains! The wind is now blowing from the north, and do you not feel a keener edge to it?"

"I do," replied Robert, sensitive of body as well as mind, and he shivered as he spoke. "It's a most unfortunate change for us. But now that I think of it we've got to expect it up among the high mountains toward Canada. Shall we light another fire?"

"We'll talk of that later with the Great Bear when he comes out of his sleep. But it fast grows colder and colder, Dagaeoga!"

Weather was an enormous factor in the lives of the borderers. Wilderness storms and bitter cold often defeated their best plans, and shelterless men, they were in a continual struggle against them. And here in the far north, among the high peaks and ridges, there was much to be feared, even with official winter yet several weeks away.

Robert began to rub his cold hands, and, unfolding his blanket, he wrapped it about his body, drawing it well up over his neck and ears. Tayoga imitated him and Willet, who was soon awakened by the cold blast, protected himself in a similar manner.

"What does the Great Bear think?" asked the Onondaga.

The hunter, with his face to the wind, meditated a few moments before replying.

"I was testing that current of air on my face and eyes," he said, "and, speaking the truth, Tayoga, I don't like it. The wind seemed to grow colder as I waited to answer you. Listen to the leaves falling before it! Their rustle tells of a bitter night."

"And while we freeze in it," said Robert, whose imagination was already in full play, "the French and Indians build as many and big fires as they please, and cook before them the juicy game they killed today."

The hunter was again very thoughtful.

"It looks as if we would have to kindle a fire," he said, "and tomorrow we shall have to hunt bear or deer for ourselves, because we have food enough left for only one more meal."

"The face of Areskoui is turned from us," said Tayoga. "We have done something to anger him, or we have failed to do what he wished, and now he sends upon us a hard trial to test us and purify us! A great storm with fierce cold comes!"

The wind rose suddenly, and it began to make a sinister hissing among all the passes and gorges. Robert felt something damp upon his face, and he brushed away a melting flake of snow. But another and another took its place and the air was soon filled with white. And the flakes were most aggressive. Driven by the storm they whipped the cheeks and eyes of the three, and sought to insert themselves, often with success, under their collars, even under the edges of the protecting blankets, and down their backs. Robert, despite himself, shivered violently and even the hunter was forced to walk vigorously back and forth in the effort to keep warm. It was evident that the Onondaga had told the truth, and that the face of Areskoui was in very fact turned from them.

Robert awaited the word, looking now and then at Willet, but the hunter hung on for a long time. The leaves fell in showers before the storm, making a faint rustling like the last sigh of the departing, and the snow, driven with so much force, stung his face like hail when it struck. He was anxious for a fire, and its vital heat, but he was too proud to speak. He would endure without complaint as much as his comrades, and he knew that Tayoga, like himself, would wait for the older man to speak.

But he could not keep, meanwhile, from thinking of the French and Indians beside their vast heaps of glowing coals, fed and warmed to their hearts' content, while the three lay in the dark and bitter cold of the wilderness. An hour dragged by, then two, then three, but the storm showed no sign of abating. The sinister screaming of the wind did not cease and the snow accumulated upon their bodies. At last Willet said:

"We must do it."

"We have no other choice," said Tayoga. "We have waited as long as we could to see if Areskoui would turn a favouring face upon us, but his anger holds. It will not avail, if in our endeavour to escape the tomahawk of Tandakora, we freeze to death."

The fire decided upon, they took all risks and went about the task with eagerness. Ordinary men could not have lighted it under such circumstances, but the three had uncommon skill upon which to draw. They took the bark from dead wood, and shaved off many splinters, building up a little heap in the lee of a cliff, which they sheltered on the windward side with their bodies. Then Willet, working a long time with his flint and steel, set to it the sparks that grew into a blaze.

Robert did not stop with the fire. Noticing the vast amount of dead wood lying about, as was often the case in the wilderness, he dragged up many boughs and began to build a wall on the exposed side of the flames. Willet and Tayoga approving of the idea soon helped him, and three pairs of willing hands quickly raised the barrier of trunks and brush to a height of at least a yard.

"A happy idea of yours, Robert," said the hunter. "Now we achieve two ends at once. Our wall hides the glow of the fire and at the same time protects us in large measure from the snow and wind."

"I have bright thoughts now and then," said Robert, whose spirits had returned in full tide. "You needn't believe you and Tayoga have all of 'em. I don't believe either of you would have ever thought of this fine wooden wall. In truth, Dave, I don't know what would become of you and Tayoga if you didn't have me along with you most all the time! How good the fire feels! The warmth touches my fingers and goes stealing up my arms and into my body! It reaches my face too and goes stealing down to meet the fine heat that makes a channel of my fingers! A glorious fire, Tayoga! I tell you, a glorious fire, Dave! The finest fire that's burning anywhere in the world!"

"The quality of a fire depends on the service it gives," said the hunter.

"Dagaeoga has many words when he is happy," said the Onondaga. "His tongue runs on like the pleasant murmur of a brook, but he does it because Manitou made him that way. The world must have talkers as well as doers, and it can be said for Lennox that he acts as well as talks."

"Thanks, I'm glad you put in the saving clause," laughed Robert. "But it's a mighty good thing we built our wooden wall. That wind would cut to the bone if it could get at you."

"The wind at least will keep the warriors away," said Tayoga. "They will all stay close in the camp on such a night."

"And no blame to them," murmured the hunter. "If we weren't in the Indian country I'd build our own fire five times as big. Now, Robert, suppose you go to sleep."

"I can't, Dave. You know I slept all the morning, but I'm not suffering from dullness. I'm imagining things. I'm imagining how much worse off we'd be if we didn't have flint and steel. I can always find pleasure in making such contrasts."

But he crouched down lower against the cliff, drew his blanket closer and spread both hands over the fire, which had now died down into a glowing mass of coals. He was wondering what they would do on the morrow, when their food was exhausted. They had not only the storm to fight, but possible starvation in the days to come. He foresaw that instead of discovering all the plans of the enemy they would have a struggle merely to live.

"Areskoui must truly be against us, Tayoga," he said. "Who would have predicted such a storm so early in the season?"

"We are several thousand feet above the sea level," said Willet, "and that will account for the violent change. I think the wind and snow will last all tonight, and probably all tomorrow."

"Then," said Robert, "we'd better gather more wood, build our wall higher and save ample fuel for the fire."

The other two found the suggestion good, and all three acted upon it promptly, ranging through the forest about them in search of brushwood, which they brought back in great quantities. Robert's blood began to tingle with the activity, and his spirits rose. Now the snow, as it drove against his face, instead of making him shiver, whipped his blood. He was the most energetic of the three, and went the farthest, in the hunt for fallen timber. One of his trips took him into the mouth of a little gorge, and, as he bent down to seize the end of a big stick, he heard just ahead a rustling that caused him with instinctive caution to straighten up and spring back, his hand, at the same time, flying to the butt of the pistol in his belt. A figure, tall and menacing, emerged from the darkness, and he retreated two or three steps.

It was his first thought that a warrior stood before him, but reason told him quickly no Indian was likely to be there, and, then, through the thick dusk and falling snow, he saw a huge black bear, erect on his hind legs, and looking at him with little red eyes. The animal was so near that the lad could see his expression, and it was not anger but surprise and inquiry. He divined at once that this particular bear had never seen a human being before, and, having been roused from some warm den by Robert's advance, he was asking what manner of creature the stranger and intruder might be.

Robert's first impulse was one of friendliness. It did not occur to him to shoot the bear, although the big fellow, fine and fat, would furnish all the meat they needed for a long time. Instead his large blue eyes gave back the curious gaze of the little red ones, and, for a little space, the two stood there, face to face, with no thought of danger or attack on the part of either.

"If you'll let me alone I'll let you alone," said the lad.

The bear growled, but it was a kindly, reassuring growl.

"I didn't mean to disturb you. I was looking for wood, not for bear."

Another growl, but of a thoroughly placid nature.

"Go wherever you please and I'll return to the camp with this fallen sapling."

A third growl, now ingratiating.

"It's a cold night, with fire and shelter the chief needs, and you and I wouldn't think of fighting."

A fourth growl which clearly disclosed the note of friendship and understanding.

"We're in agreement, I see. Good night, I wish you well."

A fifth growl, which had the tone of benevolent farewell, and the bear, dropping on all fours, disappeared in the brush. Robert, whose fancy had been alive and leaping, returned to the camp rather pleased with himself, despite the fact that about three hundred pounds of excellent food had walked away undisturbed.

"I ran upon a big bear," he said to the hunter and the Onondaga.

"I heard no shot," said Willet.

"No, I didn't fire. Neither my impulse nor my will told me to do so. The bear looked at me in such brotherly fashion that I could never have sent a bullet into him. I'd rather go hungry."

Neither Willet nor Tayoga had any rebuke for him.

"Doubtless the soul of a good warrior had gone into the bear and looked out at you," said the Onondaga with perfect sincerity. "It is sometimes so. It is well that you did not fire upon him or the face of Areskoui would have remained turned from us too long."

"That's just the way I felt about it," said Robert, who had great tolerance for Iroquois beliefs. "His eyes seemed fully human to me, and, although I had my pistol in my belt and my hand when I first saw him flew to its butt, I made no attempt to draw it. I have no regrets because I let him go."

"Nor have we," said Willet. "Now I think we can afford to rest again. We can build our wall six feet high if we want to and have wood enough left over to feed a fire for several days."

The two lads, the white and the red, crouched once more in the lee of the cliff, while the hunter put two fresh sticks on the coals. But little of the snow reached them where they lay, wrapped well in their blankets, and all care disappeared from Robert's mind. Inured to the wilderness he ignored what would have been discomfort to others. The trails they had left in the snow when they hunted wood would soon be covered up by the continued fall, and for the night, at least, there would be no danger from the warriors. He felt an immense comfort and security, and by-and-by fell asleep again. Tayoga soon followed him to slumberland, and Willet once more watched alone.

Tayoga relieved Willet about two o'clock in the morning, but they did not awaken Robert at all in the course of the night. They knew that he would upbraid them for not summoning him to do his share, but there would be abundant chance for him to serve later on as a sentinel.

The Onondaga did not arouse his comrades until long past daylight, and then they opened their eyes to a white world, clear and cold. The snow had ceased falling, but it lay several inches deep on the ground, and all the leaves had been stripped from the trees, on the high point where they lay. The coals still glowed, and they heated over them the last of their venison and bear meat, which they ate with keen appetite, and then considered what they must do, concluding at last to descend into the lower country and hunt game.

"We can do nothing at present so far as the war is concerned," said Willet. "An army must eat before it can fight, but it's likely that the snow and cold will stop the operations of the French and Indians also. While we're saving our own lives other operations will be delayed, and later on we may find Garay going back."

"It is best to go down the mountain and to the south," said Tayoga, in his precise school English. "It may be that the snow has fallen only on the high peaks and ridges. Then we'll be sure to find game, and perhaps other food which we can procure without bullets."

"Do you think we'd better move now?" asked Robert.

"We must send out a scout first," said Willet.

It was agreed that Tayoga should go, and in about two hours he returned with grave news. The warriors were out again, hunting in the snow, and although unconscious of it themselves they formed an almost complete ring about the three, a ring which they must undertake to break through now in full daylight, and with the snow ready to leave a broad trail of all who passed.

"They would be sure to see our path," said Tayoga. "Even the short trail I made when I went forth exposes us to danger, and we must trust to luck that they will not see it. There is nothing for us to do, but to remain hidden here, until the next night comes. It is quite certain that the face of Areskoui is still turned from us. What have we done that is displeasing to the Sun God?"

"I can't recall anything," said Robert.

"Perhaps it is not what we have done but what we have failed to do, though whatever it is Areskoui has willed that we lie close another day."

"And starve," said Robert ruefully.

"And starve," repeated the Onondaga.

The three crouched once more under the lee of the cliff, but toward noon they built their wooden wall another foot higher, driven to the work by the threatening aspect of the sky, which turned to a sombre brown. The wind sprang up again, and it had an edge of damp.

"Soon it will rain," said Tayoga, "and it will be a bitter cold rain. Much of the snow will melt and then freeze again, coating the earth with ice. It will make it more difficult for us to travel and the hunting that we need so much must be delayed. Then we'll grow hungrier and hungrier."

"Stop it, Tayoga," exclaimed Robert. "I believe you're torturing me on purpose. I'm hungry now."

"But that is nothing to what Dagaeoga will be tonight, after he has gone many hours without food. Then he will think of the juicy venison, and of the tender steak of the young bear, and of the fine fish from the mountain streams, and he will remember how he has enjoyed them in the past, but it will be only a memory. The fish that he craves will be swimming in the clear waters, and the deer and the bear will be far away, safe from his bullet."

"I didn't know you had so much malice in your composition, Tayoga, but there's one consolation; if I suffer you suffer also."

The Onondaga laughed.

"It will give Dagaeoga a chance to test himself," he said. "We know already that he is brave in battle and skilful on the trail, and now we will see how he can sit for days and nights without anything to eat, and not complain. He will be a hero, he will draw in his belt notch by notch, and never say a word."

"That will do, Tayoga," interrupted the hunter. "While you play upon Robert's nerves you play upon mine also, and they tell me you've said enough. Actually I'm beginning to feel famished."

Tayoga laughed once more.

"While I jest with you I jest also with myself," he said. "Now we'll sleep, since there is nothing else to do."

He drew his blanket up to his eyes, leaned against the stony wall and slept. Robert could not imitate him. As the long afternoon, one of the longest he had ever known, trailed its slow length away, he studied the forest in front of them, where the cold and mournful rain was still falling, a rain that had at least one advantage, as it had long since obliterated all traces of a trail left by Tayoga on his scouting expedition, although search as he would he could find no other profit in it.

Night came, the rain ceased, and, as Tayoga had predicted, the intense cold that arrived with the dark, froze it quickly, covering the earth with a hard and polished glaze, smoother and more treacherous than glass. It was impossible for the present to undertake flight over such a surface, with a foe naturally vigilant at hand, and they made themselves as comfortable as they could, while they awaited another day. Now Robert began to draw in his belt, while a hunger that was almost too fierce to be endured assailed him. His was a strong body, demanding much nourishment, and it cried out to him for relief. He tried to forget in sleep that he was famished, but he only dozed a while to awaken to a hunger more poignant than ever.

Yet he said never a word, but, as the night with its illimitable hours passed, he grew defiant of difficulties and dangers, all of which became but little things in presence of his hunger. It was his impulse to storm the Indian camp itself and seize what he wanted of the supplies there, but his reason told him the thought was folly. Then he tried to forget about the steaks of bear and deer, and the delicate little fish from the mountain stream that Tayoga had mentioned, but they would return before his eyes with so much vividness that he almost believed he saw them in reality.

Dawn came again, and they had now been twenty-four hours without food. The pangs of hunger were assailing all three fiercely, but they did not yet dare go forth, as the morning was dark and gloomy, with a resumption of the fierce, driving rain, mingled with hail, which rattled now and then like bullets on their wooden wall.

Robert shivered in his blanket, not so much from actual cold as from the sinister aspect of the world, and his sensitive imagination, which always pictured both good and bad in vivid colours, foresaw the enormous difficulties that would confront them. Hunger tore at him, as with the talons of a dragon, and he felt himself growing weak, although his constitution was so strong that the time for a decline in vitality had not yet really come. He was all for going forth in the storm and seeking game in the slush and cold, ignoring the French and Indian danger. But he knew the hunter and the Onondaga would not hear to it, and so he waited in silence, hot anger swelling in his heart against the foes who kept him there. Unable to do anything else, he finally closed his eyes that he might shut from his view the gray and chilly world that was so hostile.

"Is Areskoui turning his face toward us, Tayoga?" he asked after a long wait.

"No, Dagaeoga. Our unknown sin is not yet expiated. The day grows blacker, colder and wetter."

"And I grow hungrier and hungrier. If we kill deer or bear we must kill three of each at the same time, because I intend to eat one all by myself, and I demand that he be large and fat, too. I suppose we'll go out of this place some time or other."

"Yes, Dagaeoga."

"Then we'd better make up our minds to do it before it's too late. I feel my nerves and tissues decaying already."

"It's only your fancy, Dagaeoga. You can exist a week without food."

"A week, Tayoga! I don't want to exist a week without food! I absolutely refuse to do so!"

"The choice is not yours, now, O Dagaeoga. The greatest gift you can have is patience. The warrior, Daatgadose, of the clan of the Bear, of the nation Onondaga, of the great League of the Hodenosaunee, even as I am, hemmed in by enemies in the forest, and with his powder and bullets gone, lay in hiding ten days without food once passing his lips, and took no lasting hurt from it. You, O Dagaeoga, will surely do as well, and I can give you many other examples for your emulation."

"Stop, Tayoga. Sometimes I'm sorry you speak such precise English. If you didn't you couldn't have so much sport with a bad situation."

The Onondaga laughed deeply and with unction. He knew that Robert was not complaining, that he merely talked to fill in the time, and he went on with stories of illustrious warriors and chiefs among his people who had literally defied hunger and thirst and who had lived incredible periods without either food or water. Willet listened in silence, but with approval. He knew that any kind of talk would cheer them and strengthen them for the coming test which was bound to be severe.

Feeling that no warriors would be within sight at such a time they built their fire anew and hovered over the flame and the coals, drawing a sort of sustenance from the warmth. But when the day was nearly gone and there was no change in the sodden skies Robert detected in himself signs of weakness that he knew were not the product of fancy. Every inch of his healthy young body cried out for food, and, not receiving it, began to rebel and lose vigour.

Again he was all for going forth and risking everything, and he noticed with pleasure that the hunter began to shift about and to peer into the forest as if some plan for action was turning in his mind. But he said nothing, resolved to leave it all to Tayoga and Willet, and by-and-by, in the dark, to which his eyes had grown accustomed, he saw the two exchanging glances. He was able to read these looks. The hunter said: "We must try it. The time has come." The Onondaga replied: "Yes, it is not wise to wait longer, lest we grow too feeble for a great effort." The hunter rejoined: "Then it is agreed," and the Onondaga said: "If our comrade thinks so too." Both turned their eyes to young Lennox who said aloud: "It's what I've been waiting for a long time. The sooner we leave the better pleased I'll be."

"Then," said Willet, "in an hour we'll start south, going down the trail between the high cliffs, and we'll trust that either we've expiated our sin, whatever it was, or that Areskoui has forgiven us. It will be terrible travelling, but we can't wait any longer."

They wrapped their blankets about their bodies as additional covering, and, at the time appointed, left their rude shelter. Yet when they were away from its protection it did not seem so rude. When their moccasins sank in the slush and the snow and rain beat upon their faces, it was remembered as the finest little shelter in the world. The bodies of all three regretted it, but their wills and dire necessity sent them on.

The hunter led, young Lennox followed and Tayoga came last, their feet making a slight sighing sound as they sank in the half-melted snow and ice now several inches deep. Robert wore fine high moccasins of tanned moose skin, much stronger and better than ordinary deerskin, but before long he felt the water entering them and chilling him to the bone. Nevertheless, keeping his resolution in mind, and, knowing that the others were in the same plight, he made no complaint but trudged steadily on, three or four feet behind Willet, who chose the way that now led sharply downward. Once more he realized what an enormous factor changes in temperature were in the lives of borderers and how they could defeat supreme forethought and the greatest skill. Winter with its snow and sleet was now the silent but none the less potent ally of the French and Indians in preventing their escape.

They toiled on two or three miles, not one of the three speaking. The sleet and hail thickened. In spite of the blanket and the deerskin tunic it made its way along his neck and then down his shoulders and chest, the chill that went downward meeting the chill that came upward from his feet, now almost frozen. He could not recall ever before having been so miserable of both mind and body. He did not know it just then, but the lack of nourishment made him peculiarly susceptible to mental and physical depression. The fires of youth were not burning in his veins, and his vitality had been reduced at least one half.

Now, that terrible hunger, although he had striven to fight it, assailed him once more, and his will weakened slowly. What were those tales Tayoga had been telling about men going a week or ten days without food? They were clearly incredible. He had been less than two days without it, and his tortures were those of a man at the stake.

Willet's eyes, from natural keenness and long training, were able to pierce the dusk and he showed the way, steep and slippery though it was, with infallible certainty. They were on a lower slope, where by some freak of the weather there was snow instead of slush, when he bent down and examined the path with critical and anxious eyes. Robert and Tayoga waited in silence, until the hunter straightened up again. Then he said:

"A war party has gone down the pass ahead of us. There were about twenty men in it, and it's not more than two hours beyond us. Whether it's there to cut us off, or has moved by mere chance, I don't know, but the effect is just the same. If we keep on we'll run into it."

"Suppose we try the ascent and get out over the ridges," said Robert.

Willet looked up at the steep and lofty slopes on either side.

"It's tremendously bad footing," he replied, "and will take heavy toll of our strength, but I see no other way. It would be foolish for us to go on and walk straight into the hands of our enemies. What say you, Tayoga?"

"There is but a single choice and that a desperate one. We must try the summits."

They delayed no longer, and, Willet still leading, began the frightful climb, choosing the westward cliff which towered above them a full four hundred feet, and, like the one that faced it, almost precipitous. Luckily many evergreens grew along the slope and using them as supports they toiled slowly upward. Now and then, in spite of every precaution, they sent down heaps of snow that rumbled as it fell into the pass. Every time one of these miniature avalanches fell Robert shivered. His fancy, so vitally alive, pictured savages in the pass, attracted by the noise, and soon to fire at his helpless figure, outlined against the slope.

"Can't you go a little faster?" he said to Willet, who was just ahead.

"It wouldn't be wise," replied the hunter. "We mustn't risk a fall. But I know why you want to hurry on, Robert. It's the fear of being shot in the back as you climb. I feel it too, but it's only fancy with both of us."

Robert said no more, but, calling upon his will, bent his mind to their task. Above him was the dusky sky and the summit seemed to tower a mile away, but he knew that it was only sixty or seventy yards now, and he took his luxurious imagination severely in hand. At such a time he must deal only in realities and he subjected all that he saw to mathematical calculation. Sixty or seventy yards must be sixty or seventy yards only and not a mile.

After a time that seemed interminable Willet's figure disappeared over the cliff, and, with a gasp, Robert followed, Tayoga coming swiftly after. The three were so tired, their vitality was so reduced that they lay down in the snow, and drew long, painful breaths. When some measure of strength was restored they stood up and surveyed the place where they stood, a bleak summit over which the wind blew sharply. Nothing grew there but low bushes, and they felt that, while they may have escaped the war band, their own physical case was worse instead of better. Both cold and wind were more severe and a bitter hail beat upon them. It was obvious that Areskoui did not yet forgive, although it must surely be a sin of ignorance, of omission and not of commission, with the equal certainty that a sin of such type could not be unforgivable for all time.

"We seem to be on a ridge that runs for a great distance," said Tayoga. "Suppose we continue along the comb of it. At least we cannot make ourselves any worse off than we are now."

They toiled on, now and then falling on the slippery trail, their vitality sinking lower and lower. Occasionally they had glimpses of a vast desolate region under a sombre sky, peaks and ridges and slopes over which clouds hovered, the whole seeming to resent the entry of man and to offer to him every kind of resistance.

Robert was now wet through and through. No part of his body

had escaped and he knew that his vitality was at such a low ebb that at least seventy-five per cent, of it was gone. He wanted to stop, his cold and aching limbs cried out for rest, and he craved heat at the cost of every risk, but his will was still firm, and he would not be the first to speak. It was Willet who suggested when they came to a slight dip that they make an effort to build a fire.

"The human body, no matter how strong it may be naturally, and how much it may be toughened by experience, will stand only so much," he said.

They were constantly building fires in the wilderness, but the fire they built that morning was the hardest of them all to start. They selected, as usual, the lee of a rocky uplift, and, then by the patient use of flint and steel, and, after many failures, they kindled a blaze that would last. But in their reduced state the labour exhausted them, and it was some time before they drew any life from the warmth. When the circulation had been restored somewhat they piled on more wood, taking the chance of being seen. They even went so far as to build a second fire, that they might sit between the two and dry themselves more rapidly. Then they waited in silence the coming of the dawn.

CHAPTER 3

The Brave Defence

Robert hoped for a fair morning. Surely Areskoui would relent now! But the sun that crept languidly up the horizon was invisible to them, hidden by a dark curtain of clouds that might shed, at any moment, torrents of rain or hail or snow. The whole earth swam in chilly damp. Banks of cold fog filled the valleys and gorges, and shreds and patches of it floated along the peaks and ridges. The double fires had dried his clothing and had sent warmth into his veins, increasing his vitality somewhat, but it was far below normal nevertheless. He had an immense aversion to further movement. He wanted to stay there between the coals, awaiting passively whatever fate might have for him. Somehow, his will to make an effort and live seemed to have gone.

While weakness grew upon him and he drooped by the fire, he did not feel hunger, but it was only a passing phase. Presently the desire for food that had gnawed at him with sharp teeth came back, and with it his wish to do, like one stirred into action by pain. Hunger itself was a stimulus and his sinking vitality was arrested in its decline. He looked around eagerly at the sodden scene, but it certainly held out little promise of game. Deer and bear would avoid those steeps, and range in the valleys. But the will to action, stimulated back to life, remained. However comfortable it was between the fires they must not stay there to perish.

"Why don't we go on?" he said to Willet.

"I'm glad to hear you ask that question," replied the hunter.

"Why, Dave?"

"Because it shows that you haven't given up. If you've got the courage to leave such a warm and dry place you've got the courage also to make another fight for life. And you were the first to speak, too, Robert."

"We must go on," said Tayoga. "But it is best to throw slush over the fire and hide our traces."

The task finished they took up their vague journey, going they knew not where, but knowing that they must go somewhere, their uncertain way still leading along the crests of narrow ridges, across shallow dips and through drooping forests, where the wind moaned miserably. At intervals, it rained or snowed or hailed and once more they were wet through and through. The recrudescence of Robert's strength was a mere flare-up. His vitality ebbed again, and not even the fierce gnawing hunger that refused to depart could stimulate it. By-and-by he began to stumble, but Tayoga and Willet, who noticed it, said nothing—they staggered at times themselves. They toiled on for hours in silence, but, late in the afternoon, Robert turned suddenly to the Onondaga.

"Do you remember, Tayoga," he said, "something you said to me a couple of days since, or was it a week, or maybe a month ago? I seem to remember time very uncertainly, but you were talking about repasts, banquets, Lucullan banquets, more gorgeous banquets than old Nero had, and they say he was king of epicures. I think you spoke of tender venison, and juicy bear steaks, and perhaps of a delicate broiled trout from one of these clear mountain streams. Am I not right, Tayoga? Didn't you mention viands? And perhaps you may still be thinking of them?"

"I *am*, Dagaeoga. I am thinking of them all the time. I confess to you that I am so hungry I could gnaw the inside of the fresh bark upon a tree, and if I were turned loose upon a deer, slain and cooked, I could eat him all from the tip of his nose to the tip of his tail."

"Stop, you boys," said Willet sternly. "You only aggravate your sufferings. Isn't that a valley to the right, Tayoga, and don't you catch the gleam of a little lake among its trees?"

"It is a valley, Great Bear, and there *is* a small lake in the centre. We will go there. Perhaps we can catch fish."

Hope sprang up in Robert's heart. Fish? Why, of course there were fish in all the mountain lakes! and they never failed to carry hooks and lines in their packs. Bait could be found easily under the rocks. He did not conceal his eagerness to descend into the valley and the others were not less forward than he.

The valley was about half a square mile in area, of which the lake in the centre occupied one-fourth, the rest being in dense forest. The three soon had their lines in water, and they waited full of anticipation, but they waited in vain until long after night had come. Not one of the three received a bite. The lines floated idly.

"Every lake in the mountains except one is full of fish—except one!" exclaimed Robert bitterly, "and this is the one!"

"No, it is not that," said Tayoga gravely. "It means that the face of Areskoui is still turned from us, that the good Sun God does not relent for our unknown sin. We must have offended him deeply that he should remain angry with us so long. This lake is swarming with fish, like the others of the mountains, but he has willed that not one should hang upon our hooks. Why waste time?"

He drew his line from the water, wound it up carefully and replaced it in his pack. The others, after a fruitless wait, imitated him, convinced that he was right. Then, after infinite pains, as before, they built two fires again, and slept between them. But the next morning all three were weak. Their vitality had declined fast in the night, and the situation became critical in the extreme.

"We must find food or we die," said Willet. "We might linger a long time, but soon we won't have the strength to hunt, and then it would only be a question of when the wolves took us."

"I can hear them howling now on the slopes," said Tayoga. "They know we are here, and that our strength is declining. They will not face our rifles, but will wait until we are too weak to use them."

"What is your plan, Dave?" asked Robert.

"There must be game on the slopes. What say you, Tayoga?"

"If Areskoui has willed for game to be there it will be there. He will even send it to us. And perhaps he has decided that he has now punished us enough."

"It certainly won't hurt for us to try, and perhaps we'd better separate. Robert, you go west; Tayoga, you take the eastern slopes, and I'll hunt toward the north. By night we'll all be back at this spot, full-handed or empty-handed, as it may be, but full-handed, I hope."

He spoke cheerfully, and the others responded in like fashion. Action gave them a mental and physical tonic, and bracing their weak bodies they started in the direction allotted to each. Robert forgot, for a little while, the terrible hunger that seemed to be preying upon his very fibre, and, as he started away, showed an elasticity and buoyancy of which he could not have dreamed himself capable five minutes before.

Westward stretched forest, lofty in the valley, high on the slopes and everywhere dense. He plunged into it, and then looked back. Tayoga and Willet were already gone from his sight, seeking what he sought. Their experience in the wilderness was greater than his, and they were superior to him in trailing, but he was very hopeful that it would be his good fortune to find the game they needed so badly, the game they must have soon, in truth, or perish.

The valley was deep in slush and mire, and the water soaked through his leggings and moccasins again, but he paid no attention to it now. His new courage and strength lasted. Glancing up at the heavens he beheld a little rift in the western clouds. A bar of light was let through, and his mind, so imaginative, so susceptible to the influences of earth and air, at once saw it as an omen. It was a pillar of fire to him, and his faith was confirmed.

"Areskoui is turning back his face, and he smiles upon us," he said to himself. Then looking carefully to his rifle, he held it ready for an instant shot.

He came to the westward edge of the valley, and found the slope before him gentle but rocky. He paused there a while in indecision, and, then glancing up again at the bar of light that had grown broader, he murmured, so much had he imbibed the religion and philosophy of the Iroquois:

"O Areskoui, direct me which way to go."

The reply came, almost like a whisper in his ear:

"Try the rocks."

It always seemed to him that it was a real whisper, not his own mind prompting him, and he walked boldly among the rocks which stretched for a long distance along the slopes. Then, or for the time, at least, he felt sure that a powerful hand was directing him. He saw tracks in the soft soil between the strong uplifts and he believed that they were fresh. Hollows were numerous there, and game of a certain kind would seek them in bitter weather.

His heart began to pound hard, too heavily, in fact, for his weakened frame, and he was compelled to stop and steady himself. Then he resumed the hunt once more, looking here and there between the rocky uplifts and in the deep depressions. He lost the tracks and then he found them, apparently fresher than ever. Would he take what he sought? Was the face of Areskoui still inclining toward him? He looked up and the bar of light was steadily growing broader and longer. The smile of the Sun God was deeper, and his doubts went away, one by one.

He turned toward a tall rock and a black figure sprang up, stared at him a moment or two, and then undertook to run away. Robert's rifle leaped to his shoulder, and, at a range so short that he could not miss, he pulled the trigger. The animal went down, shot through the heart, and then, silently exulting, young Lennox stood over him.

Areskoui had, in truth, been most kind. It was a young bear, nearly grown, very fat, and, as Robert well knew, very tender also. Here was food, splendid food, enough to last them many days, and he rejoiced. Then he was in a quandary. He could not carry the bear away, and while he could cut him up, he was loath to leave any part of him there. The wolves would soon be coming, insisting upon their share, but he was resolved they should have none.

He put his fingers over his mouth and blew between them a whistle, long, shrill and piercing, a sound that penetrated farther than the rifle shot. It was answered presently in a faint note from the opposite slope, and, then sitting down, he waited patiently. He knew that Tayoga and Willet would come, and, after a while, they appeared, striding eagerly through the forest. Then Robert rose, his heart full of gratitude and pride, and, in a grand manner, he did the honours.

"Come, good comrades," he said. "Come to the banquet. Have a steak of a bear, the finest, juiciest, tenderest bear that was ever killed. Have two steaks, three steaks, four steaks, any number of them. Here is abundant food that Areskoui has sent us."

Then he reeled and would have fallen to the ground had not Willet caught him in his arms. His great effort, made in his weakened condition, had exhausted him and a sudden collapse came, but he revived almost instantly, and the three together dragged the body of the bear into the valley. Then they proceeded dextrously, but without undue haste, to clean it, to light a fire, and to cook strips. Nor did they eat rapidly, knowing it was not wise to do so, but took little pieces, masticating them long and well, and allowing a decent interval between. Their satisfaction was intense and enormous. Life, fresh and vigorous, poured back into their veins.

"I'm sorry our bear had to die," said Robert, "but he perished in a good cause. I think he was reserved for the especial purpose of saving our lives."

"It is so," said Tayoga with deep conviction. "The face of Areskoui is now turned toward us. Our unknown sin is expiated. We must cook all the bear, and hang the flesh in the trees."

"So we must," said the hunter. "It's not right that we three, who are engaged in the great service of our country, should be hindered by the danger of starvation. We ought now to be somewhere near the French and Indians, watching them."

"Tomorrow we will seek them, Great Bear," said Tayoga, "but do you not think that tonight we should rest?"

"So we should, Tayoga. You're right. We'll take all chances on being seen, keep a good fire going and enjoy our comfort."

"And eat a big black bear steak every hour or so," said Robert.

"If we feel like it that's just what we'll do," laughed Willet. "It's our night, now. Surely, Robert, you're the greatest hunter in the world! Neither Tayoga nor I saw a sign of game, but you walked straight to your bear."

"No irony," said Robert, who, nevertheless, was pleased. "It merely proves that Areskoui had forgiven me, while he had not forgiven you two. But don't you notice a tremendous change?"

"Change! Change in what?"

"Why, everything! The whole world is transformed! Around us a little while ago stretched a scrubby, gloomy forest, but it is now magnificent and cheerful. I never saw finer oaks and beeches. That sky which was black and sinister has all the gorgeous golds and reds and purples of a benevolent sunset. The wind, lately cold and wet, is actually growing soft, dry and warm. It's a grand world, a kind world, a friendly world!"

"Thus, O Dagaeoga," said Tayoga, "does the stomach rule man and the universe. It is empty and all is black, it is filled and all that was black turns to rose. But the rose will soon be gone, because the sunlight is fading and night is at hand."

"But it's a fine night," said Robert sincerely. "I think it about the finest night I ever saw coming."

"Have another of these beautiful broiled steaks," said Willet, "and you'll be sure it's the finest night that ever was or ever will be."

"I think I will," said Robert, as he held the steak on the end of a sharpened stick over the coals and listened to the pleasant sizzling sound, "and after this is finished and a respectable time has elapsed, I may take another."

The revulsion in all three was tremendous. Although they had hidden it from one another, the great decrease in physical vitality had made their minds sink into black despair, but now that strength was returning so fast they saw the world through different eyes. They lay back luxuriously and their satisfaction was so intense that they thought little of danger. Tandakora might be somewhere near, but it did not disturb men who were as happy as they. The night came down, heavy and dark, as had been predicted, and they smothered their fire, but they remained before the coals, sunk in content.

They talked for a while in low tones, but, at length, they became silent. The big hunter considered. He knew that, despite the revulsion in feeling, they were not yet strong enough to undertake a great campaign against their enemies, and it would be better to remain a while in the valley until they were restored fully.

Beside their fire was a good enough place for the time, and Robert kept the first watch. The night, in reality, had turned much warmer and the sky was luminous with stars. The immense sense of comfort remained with him, and he was not disturbed by the howling of the wolves, which he knew had been drawn by the odour of game, but which he knew also would be afraid to invade the camp and attack three men.

His spirits, high as they were already, rose steadily as he watched. Surely after the Supreme Power had cast them down into the depths, a miracle had been worked in their behalf to take them out again. It was no skill of his that had led him to the bear, but strength far greater than that of man was now acting in their behalf. As they had triumphed over starvation they would triumph over everything. His sanguine mind predicted it.

The next morning was crisp and cold, but not wet, and Robert ate the most savoury breakfast he could recall. That bear must have been fed on the choicest of wild nuts, topped off with wild honey, to have been so juicy and tender, and the thought of nuts caused him to look under the big hickory trees, where he found many of them, large and ripe. They made a most welcome addition to their bill of fare, taking the place of bread. Then, they were so well pleased with themselves that they concluded to spend another day and night in the valley.

Tayoga about noon climbed the enclosing ridge to the north, and, when he returned, Willet noticed a sparkle in his eyes. But the hunter said nothing, knowing that the Onondaga would speak in his own good time.

"There is another valley beyond the ridge," said Tayoga, "and a war party is encamped in it. They sit by their fire and eat prodigiously of deer they have killed."

Robert was startled, but he kept silent, he, too, knowing that Tayoga would tell all he intended to tell without urging.

"They do not know we are here, I do not think they dream of our presence," continued the Onondaga, "Areskoui smiles on us now, and Tododaho on his star, which we cannot see by day, is watching over us. Their feet will not bring them this way."

"Then you wouldn't suggest our taking to flight?" said Willet. "You would favour hiding here in peace?"

"Even so. It will please us some day to remember that we rested and slept almost within hearing of our enemies, and yet they did not take us."

"That's grim humour, Tayoga, but if it's the way you feel, Robert and I are with you."

Later in the afternoon they saw smoke rising beyond the ridge and they knew the warriors had built a great fire before which they were probably lying and gorging themselves, after their fashion when they had plenty of food, and little else to do. Yet the three remained defiantly all that day and all through the following night. The next morning, with ample supplies in their packs, they turned their faces southward, and cautiously climbed the ridge in that direction, once more passing into the region of the peaks. To their surprise they struck several comparatively fresh trails in the passes, and they were soon forced to the conclusion that the hostile forces were still all about them. Near midday they stopped in a narrow gorge between high peaks and listened to calls of the inhabitants of the forest, the faint howls of wolves, and once or twice the yapping of a fox.

"The warriors signalling to one another!" said Willet.

"It is so," said Tayoga. "I think they have noticed our tracks in the earth, too slight, perhaps, to tell who we are, but they will undertake to see."

"I hear the call of a moose directly ahead," said Robert, "although I know it is no moose that makes it. Our way there is cut off."

"And there is the howl of the wolf behind us," said Tayoga. "We cannot go back."

"Then," said Robert, "I suppose we must climb the mountain. It's lucky we've got our strength again."

They scaled a lofty summit once more, fortunately being able to climb among rocks, where they left no trail, and, crouched at the crest in dense bushes, they saw two bands meet in the valley below, evidently searching for the fugitives. There was no white man among them, but Robert knew a gigantic figure to be that of Tandakora, seeking them with the most intense and bitter hatred. The muzzle of his rifle began to slide forward, but Willet put out a detaining hand.

"No, Robert, lad," he said. "He deserves it, but his time hasn't come yet. Besides your shot would bring the whole crowd up after us."

"And he belongs to me," added Tayoga. "When he falls it is to be by my hand."

"Yes, he belongs to you, Tayoga," said Willet "Now they've concluded that we continued toward the south, and they're going on that way."

As they felt the need of the utmost caution they spent the remainder of the day and the next night on the crest. Robert kept the late watch, and he saw the dawn come, red and misty, a huge sun shining over the eastern mountains, but shedding little warmth. He was hopeful that Tandakora and his warriors had passed on far into the south, but he heard a distant cry rising in the clear air east of the peak and then a reply to the west. His heart stood still for a moment. He knew that they were the whoops of the savages and he felt that they signified a discovery. Perhaps chance had disclosed their trail. He listened with great intentness, but the shouts did not come again. Nevertheless the omen was bad.

He awoke Willet and the Onondaga, who had been sleeping soundly, and told them what had happened, both agreeing that the shouts were charged with import.

"I think it likely that we will be attacked," said the hunter. "Now we must take another look at our position."

The peak, luckily for them, was precipitous, and its crest did not cover an area of more than twenty or thirty square yards. On the three sides the ascent was so steep that a man could not climb up except with extreme difficulty, but on the fourth, by which they had come, the slope was more gradual. The gentle climb faced the east, and it was here that the hunter and Robert watched, while Tayoga, for the sake of utmost precaution, kept an eye on the steep sides.

Knowing that it was wise to economize and even to increase their strength, they ate abundantly of the bear steaks, afterward craving water, which they were forced to do without—the one great flaw in their position, since the warriors might hold them there to perish of thirst.

Robert soon forgot the desire for water in the tenseness of watching and waiting. But even the anxiety and the peril to his life did not keep him from noticing the singularity of his situation, upon the slender peak of a high mountain far in the wilderness. The sun, full of splendour but still cold, touched with gold all the surrounding crests and ridges and filled with a yellow but luxurious haze every gorge and ravine. He was compelled to admire its wintry beauty, a beauty, though, that he knew to be treacherous, surcharged as it was with savage wile and stratagem, and a burning desire for their lives.

A time that seemed incredible passed without demonstration from the enemy. But he realized that it was only about two hours. He did not expect to see any of the warriors creeping up the slopes toward them, but too wise to watch for their faces he did expect to notice the bushes move ever so slightly under their advance. He and Willet remained crouched in the same positions in the shelter of high rocks. Tayoga, who had been moving about the far side, came to them and whispered:

"I am going down the northern face of the cliff!"

"Why, it's sheer insanity, Tayoga!" said the astonished hunter.

"But I'm going."

"What'll you achieve after you've gone? You'll merely walk into Tandakora's hands!"

"I go, Great Bear, and I will return in a half hour, alive and well."

"Is your mind upset, Tayoga?"

"I am quite sane. Remember, Great Bear, I will be back in a half hour unhurt."

Then he was gone, gliding away through the low vegetation that covered the crest, and Robert and the hunter looked at each other.

"There is more in this than the eye sees," said young Lennox. "I never knew Tayoga to speak with more confidence. I think he will be back just as he says, in half an hour."

"Maybe, though I don't understand it. But there are lots of things one doesn't understand. We must keep our eyes on the slope, and let Tayoga solve his own problem, whatever it is."

There was no wind at all, but once Robert thought he saw the shrubs halfway down the steep move, though he was not sure and nothing followed. But, intently watching the place where the motion had occurred, he caught a gleam of metal which he was quite sure came from a rifle barrel.

"Did you see it?" he whispered to the hunter.

"Aye, lad," replied Willet. "They're there in that dense clump, hoping we've relaxed the watch and that they can surprise us. But it may be two or three hours before they come any farther. Always remember in your dealings with Indians that they have more time than anything else, and so they know how to be patient. Now, I wonder what Tayoga is doing! That boy certainly had something unusual on his mind!"

"Here he is, ready to speak for himself, and back inside his promised half hour."

Tayoga parted the bushes without noise, and sat down between them behind the big rocks. He offered no explanation, but seemed very content with himself.

"Well, Tayoga," said Willet, "did you go down the side of the mountain?"

"As far as I wished."

"What do you mean by that?"

"I have been engaged in a very pleasant task, Great Bear."

"What pleasure can you find in scaling a steep and rocky slope?"

"I have been drinking, Great Bear, drinking the fresh, pure water of the mountains, and it was wonderfully cool and good to my dry throat."

The two gazed at him in astonishment, and he laughed low, but with deep enjoyment.

"I took one drink, two drinks, three drinks," he said, "and when the time comes I shall take more. The fountain also awaits the lips of the Great Bear and of Dagaeoga."

"Tell it all," said Robert.

"When I looked down the steep side a long time I thought I caught a gleam as of falling water in the bushes. It was only twenty or thirty yards below us, and, when I descended to it, I found a little fountain bursting from a crevice in the rock. It was but a thread, making a tiny pool a few inches across, before it dropped away among the bushes, but it is very cool, very clear, and there is always plenty of it for many men."

"Is the descent hard?" asked Willet.

"Not for one who is strong and cautious. There are thick vines and bushes to which to hold, and remember that the splendid water is at the end of the journey."

"Then, Robert, you go," said the hunter, "and mind, too, that you get back soon, because my throat is parching. I'd like to have one deep drink before the warriors attack."

Robert followed Tayoga, and, obeying his instructions, was soon at the fountain, where he drank once, twice, thrice, and then once more of the finest water he could recall. Then, deeply grateful for the Onondaga's observation, he climbed back, and the hunter took his turn.

"It was certainly good, Tayoga," he said, when he was back in position. "Some men don't think much of water, but none of us can live without it. You've saved our lives."

"Perhaps, O Great Bear," responded the Onondaga, "but if the bushes below continue to shake as they are doing we shall have to save them again. Ah!"

The exclamation, long drawn but low, was followed by the leap of his rifle to the shoulder, and the pressing of his finger on the trigger. A stream of fire sprang from the muzzle of the long barrel to be followed by a yell in one of the thickets clustering on the slope. A savage rose to his feet, threw up his arms and fell headlong, his body crashing far below on the rocks. Robert shut his eyes and shivered.

"He was dead before he touched earth, lad," said the hunter. "Now the others are ready to scramble back. Look how the bushes are shaking again!"

Robert had shut his eyes only for a moment, and now he saw the scrub shaking more violently than ever. Then he had a fleeting glimpse of brown bodies as all the warriors descended rapidly. Anyone of the three might have fired with good aim, but they did not raise their rifles. Since their enemies were retreating they would let them retreat.

"They're all back in the valley now," said the hunter after a little while, "and they'll think a lot before they try the steep ascent a second time. Now it's a question of patience, and they hope we'll become so weak from thirst that we'll fall into their hands."

"Tandakora and his warriors would be consumed with anger if they knew of our spring," said Tayoga.

"They'll find out about it soon," said Robert.

"I think not," said Tayoga. "I noticed when I was at the fountain that the rivulet ran back into the cliff about a hundred feet below, and one can see the water only from the crest. If Areskoui has allowed us to be besieged here, he at least has created much in our favour."

He looked toward the east, where the great red sun was shining, and worshiped silently. It seemed to Robert that his young comrade stared unwinking for a long time into the eye of the Sun God, though perhaps it was only a few seconds. But his form expanded and his face was illumined. Robert knew that the Onondaga's confidence had become supreme, and he shared in it.

The hunter and Tayoga kept the watch after a while, and young Lennox was free to wander about the crest as he wished. He examined carefully the three sides they had left unguarded, but was convinced that no warrior, no matter how skilful and tenacious, could climb up there. Then he wandered back toward the sentinels, and, sitting down under a tree, began to study the distant slopes across the gorge.

He saw the warriors gather by-and-by in a deep recess out of rifle shot, light a fire and begin to cook great quantities of game, as if they meant to stay there and keep the siege until doomsday, if necessary. He saw the gigantic figure of Tandakora approach the fire, eat voraciously for a while and then go away. After him came a white man in French uniform. He thought at first it was St. Luc and his heart beat hard, but he was able to discern presently that it was an officer not much older than himself, in a uniform of white faced with violet and a black, three-cornered hat. Finally he recognized young De Galissonnière, whom he had met in Québec, and whom he had seen a few days since in the French camp.

As he looked De Galissonnière left the recess, descended into the valley and then began to climb their slope, a white handkerchief held aloft on the point of his small sword. Young Lennox immediately joined the two watchers at the brink.

"A flag of truce! Now what can he want!" he exclaimed.

"We'll soon see," replied Willet. "He's within good hearing now, and I'll hail him."

He shouted in powerful tones that echoed in the gorge:

"Below there! What is it?"

"I have something to say that will be of great importance to you," replied De Galissonnière.

"Then come forward, while we remain here. We don't trust your allies."

Robert saw the face of the young Frenchman flush, but De Galissonnière, as if knowing the truth, and resolved not to quibble over it, climbed steadily. When he was within twenty feet of the crest the hunter called to him to halt, and he did so, leaning easily against a strong bush, while the three waited eagerly to hear what he had to say.

Chapter 4

The Gods at Play

De Galissonnière gazed at the three faces, peering at him over the brink, and then drew himself together jauntily. His position, perched on the face of the cliff, was picturesque, and he made the most of it.

"I am glad to see you again Mr. Willet, Mr. Lennox and Tayoga, the brave Onondaga," he said. "It's been a long time since we met in Québec and much water has flowed under that bridge of Avignon, of which we French sing, but I can't see that any one of you has changed much."

"Nor you," said Robert, catching his tone and acting as spokesman for the three. "The circumstances are unusual, Captain Louis de Galissonnière, and I'm sorry I can't invite you to come up on our crest, but it wouldn't be military to let you have a look at our fortifications."

"I understand, and I do very well where I am. I wish to say first that I am sorry to see you in such a plight."

"And we, Captain, regret to find you allied with such a savage as Tandakora."

A quick flush passed over the young Frenchman's face, but he made no other sign.

"In war one cannot always choose," he replied. "I have come to receive your surrender, and I warn you very earnestly that it will be wise for you to tender it. The Indians have lost one man already and they are inflamed. If they lose more I might not be able to control them."

"And if we yield ourselves you pledge us our lives, a transfer in safety to Canada where we are to remain as prisoners of war, until such time as we may be exchanged?"

"All that I promise, and gladly."

"You're sure, Captain de Galissonnière, that you can carry out the conditions?"

"Absolutely sure. You are surrounded here on the peak, and you cannot get away. All we have to do is to keep the siege."

"That is true, but while you can wait so can we."

"But we have plenty of water, and you have none."

"You would urge us again to surrender on the ground that it would be the utmost wisdom for us to do so?"

"It goes without saying, Mr. Lennox."

"Then, that being the case, we decline."

De Galissonnière looked up in astonishment at the young face that gazed down at him. The answer he had expected was quite the reverse.

"You mean that you refuse?" he exclaimed.

"It is just what I meant."

"May I ask why, when you are in such a hopeless position?"

"Tayoga, Mr. Willet and I wish to see how long we can endure the pangs of thirst without total collapse. We've had quite a difference on the subject. Tayoga says ten days, Mr. Willet twelve days, but I think we can stand it a full two weeks."

De Galissonnière frowned.

"You are frivolous, Mr. Lennox," he said, "and this is not a time for light talk. I don't know what you mean, but it seems to me you don't appreciate the dire nature of your peril. I liked you and your comrades when I met you in Québec and I do not wish to see you perish at the hands of the savages. That is why I have climbed up here to make you this offer, which I have wrung from the reluctant Tandakora. It was he who assured me that the besieged were you. It pains me that you see fit to reject it."

"I know it was made out of a good heart," said Robert, seriously, "and we thank you for the impulse that brought you here. Some day we may be able to repay it, but we decline because there are always chances. You know, Captain, that while we have life we always have hope. We may yet escape."

"I do not see wherein it is possible," said the young Frenchman, with actual reluctance in his tone. "But it is for you to decide what you wish to do. Farewell."

"Farewell, Captain de Galissonnière," said Robert, with the utmost sincerity. "I hope no bullet of ours will touch you."

The captain made a courteous gesture of good-by and slowly descended the slope, disappearing among the bushes in the gorge, whence came a fierce and joyous shout.

"That was the cry of the savages when he told them our answer," said Willet. "They don't want us to surrender. They think that by-and-by we'll fall into their hands through exhaustion, and then they can work their will upon us."

"They don't know about that fountain, that pure, blessed fountain," said Robert, "the finest fountain that gushes out anywhere in this northern wilderness, the fountain that Tayoga's Areskoui has put here for our especial benefit."

His heart had become very light and, as usual when his optimism was at its height, words gushed forth. Water, and their ability to get it whenever they wanted it, was the key to everything, and he painted their situation in such bright colours that his two comrades could not keep from sharing his enthusiasm.

"Truly, Dagaeoga did not receive the gift of words in vain," said Tayoga. "Golden speech flows from him, and it lifts up the minds of those who hear. Manitou finds a use for everybody, even for the orator."

"Though it was a hard task, even for Manitou," laughed Robert.

They watched the whole afternoon without any demonstration from the enemy—they expected none—and toward evening the Onondaga, who was gazing into the north, announced a dark shadow on the horizon.

"What is it?" asked Robert. "A cloud? I hope we won't have another storm."

"It is no cloud," replied Tayoga. "It is something else that moves very fast, and it comes in our direction. A little longer and I can tell what it is. Now I see; it is a flight of wild pigeons, a great flock, hundreds of thousands, and millions, going south to escape the winter."

"We've seen such flights often."

"So we have, but this is coming straight toward us, and I have a great thought, Dagaeoga. Areskoui has not only forgiven us for our unknown sin—perhaps of omission—but he has also decided to put help in our way, if we will use it. You see many dwarf trees at the southern edge of the crest, and I believe that by dark they will be covered with pigeons, stopping for the night."

"And some of them will stop for our benefit, though we have bear meat too! I see, Tayoga."

Robert watched the flying cloud, which had grown larger and blacker, and then he saw that Tayoga was right. It was an immense flock of wild pigeons, and, as the twilight fell, they covered the trees upon their crest so thickly that the boughs bent beneath them. Young Lennox and the Onondaga killed as many as they wished with sticks, and soon, fat and juicy, they were broiling over the coals.

"Tandakora will guess that the pigeons have fed us," said Robert, "and he will not like it, but he will yet know nothing about the water."

They climbed down in turn in the darkness and took a drink, and Robert, who explored a little, found many vines loaded with wild grapes, ripe and rich, which made a splendid dessert. Then he took a number of the smaller but very tough stems, and knotting them together, with the assistance of Tayoga ran a strong rope from the crest down to the fountain, thus greatly easing the descent for water and the return.

"Now we can take two drinks where we took one before," he said triumphantly when the task was finished. "If you have your water there is nothing like making it easy to be reached. Moreover, while it was safe for an agile fellow like me, you and Dave, Tayoga, being stiff and clumsy, might have tumbled down the mountain and then I should have been lonesome."

Willet, who had been keeping the watch alone, was inclined to the belief that they might expect an attack in the night, if it should prove to be very dark. He felt able, however, should such an attempt come, to detect the advance of the savages, either by sight or hearing, especially the latter, ear in such cases generally informing him earlier than eye. But as neither Robert nor Tayoga was busy they joined him, and all three sat near the brink with their rifles across their knees, and their pistols loosened in their belts, ready for their foes should they come in numbers.

They talked a while in low tones, and then fell silent. The night had come, starless and moonless, favourable to the designs of Tandakora, but they felt intense satisfaction, nevertheless. It was partly physical. Robert's making of an easy road to the water, the coming of the pigeons, to be eaten, apparently sent by Areskoui, and the ease with which they believed they could hold their lofty fortress, combined to produce a victorious state of mind. Robert looked over the brink once or twice at the steep slope, and he felt that the warriors would, in truth, be taking a mighty risk, if they came up that steep path against the three.

He and Tayoga, in the heavy darkness, depended, like Willet, chiefly on ear. It was impossible to see to the bottom of the valley, where the dusk had rolled up like a sea, but, as the night was still, they felt sure they could hear anyone climbing up the peak. In order to make themselves more comfortable they spread their blankets at the very brink, and lay down upon them, thus being able to repose, and at the same time watch without the risk of inviting a shot.

Young Lennox knew that the attack, if it came at all, would not come until late, and restraining his naturally eager and impatient temper, he used all the patience that his strong will could summon, never ceasing meanwhile to lend an attentive ear to every sound of the night. He heard the wind rise, moan a little while in the gorge and then die; he heard a fitful breeze rustle the boughs on the slopes and then grow still, and he heard his comrades move once or twice to ease their positions, but no other sound came to him until nearly midnight, and then he heard the fall of a pebble on the slope, absolute proof to one experienced as he that it had been displaced by the incautious foot of a climbing enemy.

The rattling of the pebble was succeeded by a long interval of silence, and the lad understood that too. The warriors, to whom time was nothing, fearing that suspicion had been aroused by the fall of the pebble, would wait until it had been lulled before resuming their advance. They would flatten themselves like lizards against the slope, not stirring an inch. But the three were as patient as they, and while a full hour passed after the slip of the stone before the slightest sound came from the slope, they did not relax their vigilance a particle. Then all three heard a slight rustle among the bushes and they peered cautiously over.

They were able to discern the dim outline of figures among the bushes about twenty feet below, and Wilier, who directed the defence, whispered that Tayoga and he would take aim, while Robert held his fire in reserve. Then the Onondaga and he picked their targets in the darkness and pulled trigger. Shouts, the fall of bodies and the crackling of rifles came back. A half dozen bullets, fired almost at random, whistled over their heads and then Robert sent his own lead at a shadow which appeared very clearly among the bushes, a crashing fall following at once.

Then the three, not waiting to reload, snatched out their pistols and held themselves ready for a further attack, if it should come. But it did not come. Even the rage of Tandakora had had enough. His second repulse had been bloodier than the first, and it had been proved with the lives of his warriors that they could not storm that terrible steep, in the face of three such redoubtable marksmen.

Robert heard a number of pebbles rolling now, but they were made by men descending, and the three, certain of abundant leisure, reloaded their rifles. Their eyes told them nothing, but they were as sure as if they had seen them that the warriors had disappeared in the sea of darkness with which the gulf was filled. The lad breathed a long sigh of relief.

"You're justified in your satisfaction," said Willet. "I think it's the last direct attack they'll make upon us. Now they'll try the slow methods of siege and our exhaustion by thirst, and how it would make their venom rise if they knew anything about that glorious fountain of ours! Since it's to be a test of patience, we'd better make things easy for ourselves. I'll sit here and watch the slope, and, as the night is turning cold, you and Tayoga, Robert, can build a fire."

There was a dip in the centre of the crest, and in this they heaped the fallen wood, which here as elsewhere in the wilderness was abundant. Wood and water, two great requisites of primitive man, they had in plenty, and had it not been for their eagerness to go forward with their work they would have been content to stay indefinitely on the peak.

The fire was soon blazing cheerfully. Warriors on the opposing peaks or crest might see it, but they did not care. No bullets from rival heights could reach them and the light would appear to their enemies as a beacon of defiance, a sort of challenge that was very pleasing to Robert's soul. He basked in the glow and heat of the coals, ate bear meat and wild pigeon for a late supper, and discoursed on the strength of their natural fortress.

"The peak was reared here by Areskoui for our especial benefit," he said. "It is in every sense a tower of strength, water even being placed in its side that we might not die of thirst."

"And yet we cannot stay here always," said the Onondaga. "Tomorrow we must think of a way of escape."

"Let tomorrow take care of itself. Tayoga, you're too serious! You're missing the pleasure of the night."

"Dagaeoga loves to talk and he talks well. His voice is pleasant in my ear like to the murmur of a silver brook. Perhaps he is right. Lo! the clouds have gone, and I can see Tododaho on his star. Areskoui watches over us by day and Tododaho by night. We are once more the favourites of the Sun God and of the great Onondaga who went away to his everlasting star more than four centuries ago. Again I say Dagaeoga is right; I will enjoy the night, and let the morrow care for itself."

He drew the folds of his blanket to his chin and stretched his length before the fire. Having made up his mind to be satisfied, Tayoga would let nothing interfere with such a laudable purpose. Soon he slept peacefully.

"You might follow him," said Willet.

"I don't think I can do it now," said Robert. "I've a restless spirit."

"Then wander about the peak, and I'll take up my old place at the edge of the slope."

Robert went back to the far side, where he had stretched his rope of grape vines down to the spring, and, craving their cool, fresh taste, he ate more of the grapes. He noticed then that they were uncommonly plentiful. All along the cliff they trailed in great, rich clusters, black and glossy, fairly asking to be eaten. In places the vines hung in perfect mazes, and he looked at them questioningly. Then the thought came to him and he wondered why it had been so slow of arrival. He returned to Willet and said:

"I don't think you need watch any longer here, Dave."

"Why?" was the hunter's astonished reply.

"Because we're going to leave the mountain."

"Leave the mountain! It's more likely, Robert, that your prudence has left you. If we went down the slope we'd go squarely into the horde, and then it would be a painful and lingering end for us."

"I don't mean the slope. We're to go down the other side of the cliff."

"Except here and near the bottom the mountain is as steep everywhere as the side of a house. The only way for us to get down is to fall down and then we'd stop too quick."

"We don't have to fall down, we'll climb down."

"Can't be done, Robert, my boy. There's not enough bushes."

"We don't need bushes, there are miles of grape vines as strong as leather. All we have to do is to knot them together securely and our rope is ready. If we eased our way to the spring with vines then we can finish the journey to the bottom of the cliff with them."

The hunter's gaze met that of the lad, and it was full of approval.

"I believe you've found the way, Robert," said Willet. "Wake Tayoga and see what he thinks."

The Onondaga received the proposal with enthusiasm, and he made the further suggestion that they build high the fire for the sake of deceiving the besiegers.

"And suppose we prop up two or three pieces of fallen tree trunk before it," added Robert. "Warriors watching on the opposite slopes will take them for our figures and will not dream that we're attempting to escape."

That idea, too, was adopted, and in a few minutes the fire was blazing and roaring, while a stream of sparks drifted up merrily from it to be lost in the dusk. Near it the fragments of tree trunks set erect would pass easily, at a great distance and in the dark, for human beings. Then, while Willet watched, Robert and Tayoga knotted the vines with quick and dextrous hands, throwing the cable over a bough, and trying every knot with their double weight. A full two hours they toiled and then they exulted.

"It will reach from the clump of bushes about the fountain to the next clump below, which is low down," said Robert, "and from there we can descend without help."

They called Willet, and the three, leaving the crest which had been such a refuge for them and which they had defended so well, descended to the fountain. At that point they secured their cable with infinite care to the largest of the dwarf trees and let it drop over across a bare space to the next clump of bushes below, a distance that seemed very great, it was so steep. Robert claimed the honour of the first descent, but it was finally conceded to Tayoga, who was a trifle lighter.

The Onondaga fastened securely upon his back his rifle and his pack containing food, and then, grasping the cable firmly with both hands, he began to go down, while his friends watched with great anxiety. He was not obliged to swing clear his whole weight, but was able to brace his feet against the cliff. Thus he steadied the vines, but Robert and Willet nevertheless breathed great sighs of relief, when he reached the bushes below, and detached himself from the cable.

"It is safe," he called back.

Robert went next and Willet followed. When the three were in the bushes, clinging to their tough and wiry strength, they found that the difficulties, as they invariably do, had decreased. Below them the slope was not so steep by any means, and, by holding to the rocky outcrops and scant bushes, they could make the full descent of the mountain. While they rested for a little space where they were, Robert suddenly began to laugh.

"Is Dagaeoga rejoicing so soon?" asked Tayoga

"Why shouldn't I laugh," replied Robert, "when we have such a good jest?"

"What jest? I see none."

"Why, to think of Tandakora sitting at the foot of our peak and watching there three or four days, waiting all the time for us to die of hunger and thirst, and we far to the south. At least he'll see that the mountain doesn't get away, and Tandakora, I take it, has small sense of humour. When he penetrates the full measure of the joke he'll love us none the less. Perhaps, though, De Galissonnière will not mourn, because he knows that if we were taken after a siege he could not save us from the cruelty of the savages."

The hunter and the Onondaga were forced to laugh a little with him, and then, rested thoroughly, they resumed the descent, leaving their cable to tell its own tale, later on. The rest of the slope, although possible, was slow and painful, testing their strength and skill to the utmost, but they triumphed over everything and before day were in a gorge, with the entire height of the peak towering above them and directly between them and their enemies. Here they flung themselves on the ground and rested until day, when they began a rapid flight southward, curving about among the peaks, as the easiest way led them.

The air rapidly grew warmer, showing that the sudden winter had come only on the high mountains, and that autumn yet lingered on the lower levels. The gorgeous reds and yellows and browns and vivid shades between returned, but there was a haze in the air and the west was dusky.

"Storm will come again before night," said Tayoga.

"I think so too," said Willet, "and as I've no mind to be beaten about by it, suppose we build a spruce shelter in the gorge here and wait until it passes."

The two lads were more than willing, feeling that the chance of pursuit had passed for a long time at least, and they set to work with their sharp hatchets, rapidly making a crude but secure *wickiup*, as usual against the rocky side of a hill. Before the task was done the sky darkened much more, and far in the west thunder muttered.

"It's rolling down a gorge," said Robert, "and hark! you can hear it also in the south."

From a point, far distant from the first, came a like rumble, and, after a few moments of silence, a third rumble was heard to the east. Silence again and then the far rumble came from the south.

"That's odd," said Robert. "It isn't often that you hear thunder on all sides of you."

"Listen!" exclaimed Tayoga, whose face bore a rapt and extraordinary look. The four rumbles again went around the horizon, coming from one point after the other in turn.

"It is no ordinary thunder," said the Onondaga in a tone of deep conviction.

"What is it, then?" asked Robert.

"It is Manitou, Areskoui, Tododaho and Hayowentha talking together. That is why we have the thunder north, east, south and west. Hear their voices carrying all through the heavens!"

"Which is Manitou?"

"That I cannot tell. But the great gods talk, one with another, though what they say is not for us to know. It is not right that mere mortals like ourselves should understand them, when they speak across infinite space."

"It may be that you're right, Tayoga," said Willet.

The three did not yet go into the spruce shelter, because, contrary to the signs, there was no rain. The wind moaned heavily and thick black clouds swept up in an almost continuous procession from the western horizon, but they did not let a drop fall. The thunder at the four points of the horizon went on, the reports moving from north to east, and thence to south and west, and then around and around, always in the same direction. After every crash there was a long rumble in the gorges until the next crash came again. Now and then lightning flared.

"It is not a storm after all," said the Onondaga, "or, at least, if a storm should come it will not be until after night is at hand, when the great gods are through talking. Listen to the heavy booming, always like the sound of a thousand big guns at one time. Now the lightning grows and burns until it is at a white heat. The great gods not only talk, but they are at play. They hurl thunderbolts through infinite space, and watch them fall. Then they send thunder rumbling through our mountains, and the sound is as soft to them as a whisper to us."

"Your idea is pretty sound, Tayoga," said Willet, who had imbibed more than a little of the Iroquois philosophy, "and it does look as if the gods were at play because there is so much thunder and lightning and no rain. Look at that flash on the mountain toward the east! I think it struck. Yes, there goes a tree! When the gods play among the peaks it's just as well for us to stay down here in the gorge."

"But the crashes still run regularly from north to east and on around," said Robert. "I suppose that when they finish talking, the rain will come, and we'll have plenty of need for our spruce shelter."

The deep rumbling continued all through the rest of the afternoon. A dusk as of twilight arrived long before sunset, but it was of an unusually dull, greyish hue, and it affected Robert as if he were breathing an air surcharged with gunpowder. It coloured and intensified everything. The peaks and ridges rose to greater heights, the gorges and valleys were deeper, the reports of the thunder, extremely heavy, in fact, were doubled and tripled in fancy; all that Tayoga had said about the play of the gods was true. Tododaho, the great Onondaga, spoke across the void to Hayowentha, the great Mohawk, and Areskoui, the Sun God, conversed with Manitou, the All Powerful, Himself.

The imaginative lad felt awe but no fear. The gods at play in the heavens would not condescend to harm a humble mortal like himself and it was an actual pleasure because he was there to hear them. Just before the invisible sun went over the rim of the horizon, a brilliant red light shot for a minute or two from the west through the gray haze, and fell on the faces of the three, sitting in silence before their spruce shelter.

"It is Areskoui throwing off his most brilliant beams before he goes," said Tayoga. "Now I think the play will soon be over, and we may look for the rain."

The crashes of thunder increased swiftly and greatly in violence, and then, as the Onondaga had predicted, ceased abruptly. The silence that followed was so heavy that it was oppressive. No current of air was moving anywhere. Not a leaf stirred. The greyish haze became thicker and every ridge and peak was hidden. Presently a sound like a sigh came down the gorge, but it soon grew.

"We'll go inside," said Tayoga, "because the deluge is at hand."

They crowded themselves into their crude little hut, and in five minutes the flood was upon them, pouring with such violence that some of it forced its way through the hasty thatch, but they were able to protect themselves with their blankets, and they slept the night through in a fair degree of comfort.

In the morning they saw a world washed clean, bright and shining, and they breathed an autumnal air wonderful in its purity. Feeling safe now from pursuit, they were no longer eager to flee. A brief council of three decided that they would hang once more on the French and Indian flank. It had been their purpose to discover what was intended by the formidable array they had seen, and it was their purpose yet.

They did not go back on their path, but they turned eastward into a land of little and beautiful lakes, through which one of the great Indian trails from the northwest passed, and made a hidden camp near the shore of a sheet of water about a mile square, set in the mountains like a gem. They had method in locating here, as the trail ran through a gorge less than half a mile to the east of their camp, and they had an idea that the spy, Garay, might pass that way, two of them always abiding by the trail, while the third remained in their secluded camp or hunted game. Willet shot a deer and Tayoga brought down a rare wild turkey, while Robert caught some wonderful lake trout. So they had plenty of food, and they were content to wait.

They were sure that Garay had not yet gone, as the storms that had threatened them would certainly have delayed his departure, and neither the hunter nor the Onondaga could discover any traces of footsteps. Fortunately the air continued to turn warmer and the lower country in which they now were had all the aspects of Indian summer. Robert, shaken a little perhaps by the great hardships and dangers through which he had passed, though he may not have realized at the time the weight upon his nerves, recovered quickly, and, as usual, passed, with the rebound, to the heights of optimism.

"What do you expect to get from Garay?" he asked Willet as he changed places with him on the trail.

"I'm not sure," replied the hunter, "but if we catch him we'll find something. We've got to take our bird first, and then we'll see. He went north and west with a message, and that being the case he's bound to take one back. I don't think Garay is a first-class woodsman and we may be able to seize him."

Robert was pleased with the idea of the hunted turning into the hunters, and he and Tayoga now did most of the watching along the trail, a watch that was not relaxed either by day or by night. On the sixth night the two youths were together, and Tayoga thought he discerned a faint light to the north.

"It may be a low star shining over a hill," said Robert.

"I think it is the glow from a small camp fire," said the Onondaga.

"It's a question that's decided easily."

"You mean we'll stalk it, star or fire, whichever it may be?"

"That is what we're here for, Tayoga."

They began an exceedingly cautious advance toward the light, and it soon became evident that it was a fire, though, as Tayoga had said, a small one, set in a little valley and almost hidden by the surrounding foliage. Now they redoubled their caution, using every forest art to make a silent approach, as they might find a band of warriors around the blaze, and they did not wish to walk with open eyes into any such deadly trap. Their delight was great when they saw only one man crouched over the coals in a sitting posture, his head bent over his knees; so that, in effect, only his back was visible, but they knew him at once. It was Garay.

The heart of young Lennox flamed with anger and triumph. Here was the fellow who had tried to take his life in Albany, and, if he wished revenge, the moment was full of opportunity. Yet he could never fire at a man's back, and it was their cue, moreover, to take him alive. Garay's rifle was leaning against a log, six or eight feet from him, and his attitude indicated that he might be asleep. His clothing was stained and torn, and he bore all the signs of a long journey and extreme weariness.

"See what it is to come into the forest and not be master of all its secrets," whispered Tayoga. "Garay is the messenger of Onontio (the Governor General of Canada) and Tandakora, and yet he sleeps, when those who oppose him are abroad."

"A man has to sleep some time or other," said Robert, "or at least a white man must. We're not all like an Iroquois; we can't stay awake forever if need be."

"If one goes to the land of Tarenyawagon when his enemies are at hand he must pay the price, Dagaeoga, and now the price that Garay is going to pay will be a high one. Surely Manitou has delivered him, helpless, into our hands. Come, we will go closer."

They crept through the bushes until they could have reached out and touched the spy with the muzzles of their rifles, and still he did not stir. Into that heavy and weary brain, plunged into dulled slumbers, entered no thought of a stalking foe. The fire sank and the bent back sagged a little lower. Garay had travelled hard and long. He was anxious to get back to Albany with what he knew, and he felt sure that the northern forests contained only friends. He had built his fire without apprehension, and sleep had overtaken him quickly.

A fox stirred in the thicket beyond the fire and looked suspiciously at the coals and the still figure beyond them. He did not see the other two figures in the bushes but his animosity as well as his suspicion was aroused. He edged a little nearer, and then a slight sound in the thicket caused him to creep back. But he was an inquiring fox, and, although he buried himself under a bush, he still looked, staring with sharp, intent eyes.

He saw a shadow glide from the thicket, pick up the rifle of Garay which leaned against the fallen log, and then glide back, soundless. The curiosity of the fox now prevailed over his suspicion. The shadow had not menaced him, and his vulpine intelligence told him that he was not concerned in the drama now about to unfold itself. He was merely a spectator, and, as he looked, he saw the shadow glide back and crouch beside the sleeping man. Then a second shadow came and crouched on the other side.

What the fox saw was the approach of Robert and Tayoga, whom some whimsical humour had seized. They intended to make the surprise complete and Robert, with a memory of the treacherous shot in Albany, was willing also to fill the soul of the spy with terror. Tayoga adroitly removed the pistol and knife from the belt of Garay, and Robert touched him lightly on the shoulder. Still he did not stir, and then the youth brought his hand down heavily.

Garay uttered the sigh of one who comes reluctantly from the land of sleep and who would have gone back through the portals which were only half opened, but Robert brought his hand down again, good and hard. Then his eyes flew open and he saw the calm face beside him, and the calm eyes less than a foot away, staring straight into his own. It must be an evil dream, he thought at first, but it had all the semblance of reality, and, when he turned his head in fear, he saw another face on the other side of him, carved in red bronze, it too only a foot away and staring at him in stern accusation.

Then all the faculties of Garay, spy and attempted assassin, leaped into life, and he uttered a yell of terror, springing to his feet, as if he had been propelled by a galvanic battery. Strong hands, seizing him on either side, pulled him down again and the voice of Tayoga, of the clan of the Bear, of the nation Onondaga, of the great League of the Hodenosaunee said insinuatingly in his ear:

"Sit down, Achille Garay! Here are two who wish to talk with you!"

He fell back heavily and his soul froze within him, as he recognized the faces. His figure sagged, his eyes puffed out, and he waited in silent terror.

"I see that you recognize us, Achille Garay," said Robert, whose whimsical humour was still upon him. "You'll recall that shot in Albany. Perhaps you did not expect to meet my friend and me here in the heart of the northern forests, but here we are. What have you to say for yourself?"

Garay strove to speak, but the half formed words died on his lips.

"We wish explanations about that little affair in Albany," continued his merciless interlocutor, "and perhaps there is no better time than the present. Again I repeat, what have you to say? And you have also been in the French and Indian camp. You bore a message to St. Luc and Tandakora and beyond a doubt you bear another back to somebody. We want to know about that too. Oh, we want to know about many things!"

"I have no message," stammered Garay.

"Your word is not good. We shall find methods of making you talk. You have been among the Indians and you ought to know something about these methods. But first I must lecture you on your lack of woodcraft. It is exceedingly unwise to build a fire in the wilderness and go to sleep beside it, unless there is someone with you to watch. I'm ashamed of you, Monsieur Garay, to have neglected such an elementary lesson. It made your capture easy, so ridiculously easy that it lacked piquancy and interest. Tayoga and I were not able to give our faculties and strength the healthy exercise they need. Come now, are you ready to walk?"

"What are you going to do with me?" asked Garay in French, which both of his captors understood and spoke.

"We haven't decided upon that," replied Robert maliciously, "but whatever it is we'll make it varied and lively. It may please you to know that we've been waiting several days for you, but we scarce thought you'd go to sleep squarely in the trail, just where we'd be sure to see you. Stand up now and march like a man, ready to meet any fate. Fortune has turned against you, but you still have the chance to show your Spartan courage and endurance."

"The warrior taken by his enemies meets torture and death with a heroic soul," said Tayoga solemnly.

Garay shivered.

"You'll save me from torture?" he said to Robert.

Young Lennox shook his head.

"I'd do so if it were left to me," he said, "but my friend, Tayoga, has a hard heart. In such matters as these he will not let me have my way. He insists upon the ancient practices of his nation. Also, David Willet, the hunter, is waiting for us, and he too is strong for extreme measures. You'll soon face him. Now, march straight to the right!"

Garay with a groan raised himself to his feet and walked unsteadily in the direction indicated. Close behind him came the avenging two.

Chapter 5

Taming a Spy

Young Lennox undeniably felt exultation. It fairly permeated his system. The taking of Garay had been so easy that it seemed as if the greater powers had put him squarely in their path, and had deprived him of all vigilance, in order that he might fall like a ripe plum into their hands. Surely the face of Areskoui was still turned toward them, and the gods, having had their play, were benevolent of mood—that is, so far as Robert and Tayoga were concerned, although the spy might take a different view of the matter. The triumph, and the whimsical humour that yet possessed him, moved him to flowery speech.

"Monsieur Garay, Achille, my friend," he said. "You are surprised that we know you so well, but remember that you left a visiting card with us in Albany, the time you sent an evil bullet past my head, and then proved too swift for Tayoga. That's a little matter we must look into some time soon. I don't understand why you wished me to leave the world prematurely.

It must surely have been in the interest of someone else, because I had never heard of you before in my life. But we'll pass over the incident now as something of greater importance is to the fore. It was really kind of you, Achille, to sit down there in the middle of the trail, beside a fire that was sure to serve as a beacon, and wait for us to come. It reflects little credit, however, on your skill as a woodsman, and, from sheer kindness of heart, we're not going to let you stay out in the forest after dark."

Garay turned a frightened look upon him. It was mention of the bullet in Albany that struck renewed terror to his soul. But Robert, ordinarily gentle and sympathetic, was not inclined to spare him.

"As I told you," he continued, "Tayoga and I are disposed to be easy with you, but Willet has a heart as cold as a stone. We saw you going to the French and Indian camp, and we laid an ambush for you on your way back. We were expecting to take you, and Willet has talked of you in merciless fashion. What he intends to do with you is more than I've been able to determine. Ah, he comes now!"

The parting bushes disclosed a tall figure, rifle ready, and Robert called cheerily:

"Here we are, Dave, back again, and we bring with us a welcome guest. Monsieur Achille Garay was lost in the forest, and, taking pity on him, we've brought him in to share our hospitality. Mr. David Willet, Monsieur Achille Garay of everywhere."

Willet smiled grimly and led the way back to the spruce shelter. To Garay's frightened eyes he bore out fully Robert's description.

"You lads seem to have taken him without trouble," he said. "You've done well. Sit down, Garay, on that log; we've business with you."

Garay obeyed.

"Now," said the hunter, "what message did you take to St. Luc and the French and Indian force?"

The man was silent. Evidently he was gathering together the shreds of his courage, as his back stiffened. Willet observed him shrewdly.

"You don't choose to answer," he said. "Well, we'll find a way to make you later on. But the message you carried was not so important as the message you're taking back. It's about you, somewhere. Hand over the dispatch."

"I've no dispatch," said Garay sullenly.

"Oh, yes, you have! A man like you wouldn't be making such a long and dangerous journey into the high mountains and back again for nothing. Come, Garay, your letter!"

The spy was silent.

"Search him, lads!" said Willet.

Garay recoiled, but when the hunter threatened him with his pistol he submitted to the dextrous hands of Robert and Tayoga. They went through all his pockets, and then they made him remove his clothing piece by piece, while they thrust the points of their knives through the lining for concealed documents. But the steel touched nothing. Then they searched his heavy moccasins, and even pulled the soles loose, but no papers were disclosed. There was nowhere else to look and the capture had brought no reward.

"He doesn't seem to have anything," said Robert.

"He must have! He is bound to have!" said the hunter.

"You have had your look," said Garay, a note of triumph showing in his voice, "and you have failed. I bear no message because I am no messenger. I am a Frenchman, it is true, but I have no part in this war. I am not a soldier or a scout. You should let me go."

"But that bullet in Albany."

"I did not fire it. It was someone else. You have made a mistake."

"We've made no mistake," said the hunter. "We know what you are. We know, too, that a dispatch of great importance is about you somewhere. It is foolish to think otherwise, and we mean to have it."

"I carry no dispatch," repeated Garay in his sullen, obstinate tones.

"We mean that you shall give it to us," said the hunter, "and soon you will be glad to do so."

Robert glanced at him, but Willet did not reveal his meaning. It was impossible to tell what course he meant to take, and the two lads were willing to let the event disclose itself. The same sardonic humour that had taken possession of Robert seemed to lay hold of the older man also.

"Since you're to be our guest for a while, Monsieur Garay," he said, "we'll give you our finest room. You'll sleep in the spruce shelter, while we spread our blankets outside. But lest you do harm to yourself, lest you take into your head some foolish notion to commit suicide, we'll have to bind you. Tayoga can do it in such a manner that the thongs will cause you no pain. You'll really admire his wonderful skill."

The Onondaga bound Garay securely with strips, cut from the prisoner's own clothing, and they left him lying within the spruce shelter. At dawn the next day Willet awoke the captive, who had fallen into a troubled slumber.

"Your letter," he said. "We want it."

"I have no letter," replied Garay stubbornly.

"We shall ask you for it once every two hours, and the time will come when you'll be glad to give it to us."

Then he turned to the lads and said they would have the finest breakfast in months to celebrate the good progress of their work.

Robert built up a splendid fire, and, taking their time about it, they broiled bear meat, strips of the deer they had killed and portions of wild pigeon and the rare wild turkey. Varied odours, all appetizing, and the keen, autumnal air gave them an appetite equal to anything. Yet Willet lingered long, seeing that everything was exactly right before he gave the word to partake, and then they remained yet another good while over the feast, getting the utmost relish out of everything. When they finally rose from their seats on the logs, two hours had passed since Willet had awakened Garay and he went back to him.

"Your letter?" he said.

"I have no letter," replied Garay, "but I'm very hungry. Let me have my breakfast."

"Your letter?"

"I've told you again and again that I've no letter."

"It's now about 8:30 o'clock; at half past ten I'll ask you for it again."

He went back to the two lads and helped them to put out the fire. Garay set up a cry for food, and then began to threaten them with the vengeance of the Indians, but they paid no attention to him. At half past ten as indicated by the sun, Willet returned to him.

"The letter?" he said.

"How many times am I to tell you that I have no letter?"

"Very well. At half past twelve I shall ask for it again."

At half past twelve Garay returned the same answer, and then the three ate their noonday meal, which, like the breakfast, was rich and luscious. Once more the savoury odours of bear, deer, wild turkey and wild pigeon filled the forest, and Garay, lying in the doorway of the hut, where he could see, and where the splendid aroma reached his nostrils, writhed in his bonds, but still held fast to his resolution.

Robert said nothing, but the sardonic humour of both the Onondaga and the hunter was well to the fore. Holding a juicy bear steak in his hand, Tayoga walked over to the helpless spy and examined him critically.

"Too fat," he said judicially, "much too fat for those who would roam the forest. Woodsmen, scouts and runners should be lean. It burdens them to carry weight. And you, Achille Garay, will be much better off, if you drop twenty pounds."

"Twenty pounds, Tayoga!" exclaimed Willet, who had joined him, a whole roasted pigeon in his hands. "How can you make such an underestimate! Our rotund Monsieur would be far more graceful and far more healthy if he dropped forty pounds! And it behoves us, his trainers and physicians, to see that he drops 'em. Then he will go back to Albany and to his good friend, Mynheer Hendrik Martinus, a far handsomer man than he was when he left. It may be that he'll be so much improved that Mynheer Hendrik will not know him. Truly, Tayoga, this wild pigeon has a most savoury taste! When wild pigeon is well cooked and the air of the forest has sharpened your appetite to a knife edge nothing is finer."

"But it is no better than the tender steak of young bear," said Tayoga, with all the inflections of a gourmand. "The people of my nation and of all the Indian nations have always loved bear. It is tenderer even than venison and it contains more juices. For the hungry man nothing is superior to the taste or for the building up of sinews and muscles than the steak of fat young bear."

Garay writhed again in his bonds, and closed his eyes that he might shut away the vision of the two. Robert was forced to smile. At half past two, as he judged it to be by the sun, Willet said to Garay once more:

"The papers, Monsieur Achille."

But Garay, sullen and obstinate, refused to reply. The hunter did not repeat the question then, but went back to the fire, whistling gaily a light tune. The three were spending the day in homely toil, polishing their weapons, cleaning their clothing, and making the numerous little repairs, necessary after a prolonged and arduous campaign. They were very cheerful about it, too. Why shouldn't they be? Both Tayoga and the hunter had scouted in wide circles about the camp, and had seen that there was no danger. For a vast distance they and their prisoner were alone in the forest. So, they luxuriated and with abundance of appetizing food made up for their long period of short commons.

At half past four Willet repeated his question, but the lips of the spy remained tightly closed.

"Remember that I'm not urging you," said the hunter, politely. "I'm a believer in personal independence and I like people to do what they want to do, as long as it doesn't interfere with anybody else. So I tell you to think it over. We've plenty of time. We can stay here a week, two weeks, if need be. We'd rather you felt sure you were right before you made up your mind. Then you wouldn't be remorseful about any mistake."

"A wise man meditates long before he speaks," said Tayoga, "and it follows then that our Achille Garay is very wise. He knows, too, that his figure is improving already. He has lost at least five pounds."

"Nearer eight I sum it up, Tayoga," said Willet. "The improvement is very marked."

"I think you are right, Great Bear. Eight it is and you also speak truly about the improvement. If our Monsieur Garay were able to stand up and walk he would be much more graceful than he was, when he so kindly marched into our guiding hands."

"Don't pay him too many compliments, Tayoga. They'll prove trying to a modest man. Come away, now. Monsieur Garay wishes to spend the next two hours with his own wise thoughts and who are we to break in upon such a communion?"

"The words of wisdom fall like precious beads from your lips, Great Bear. For two hours we will leave our guest to his great thoughts."

At half past six came the question, "Your papers?" once more, and Garay burst forth with an angry refusal, though his voice trembled. Willet shrugged his shoulders, turned away, and helped the lads prepare a most luxurious and abundant evening meal, Tayoga adding wild grapes and Robert nuts to their varied course of meats, the grapes being served on blazing red autumn leaves, the whole very pleasing to the eye as well as to the taste.

"I think," said Willet, in tones heard easily by Garay, "that I have in me just a trace of the epicure. I find, despite my years in the wilderness, that I enjoy a well spread board, and that bits of decoration appeal to me; in truth, give an added savour to the viands."

"In the vale of Onondaga when the fifty old and wise *sachems* make a banquet," said Tayoga, "the maidens bring fruit and wild flowers to it that the eye also may have its feast. It is not a weakness, but an excellence in Great Bear to like the decorations."

They lingered long over the board, protracting the feast far after the fall of night and interspersing it with pleasant conversation. The ruddy flames shone on their contented faces, and their light laughter came frequently to the ears of Garay. At half past eight the question, grown deadly by repetition, was asked, and, when only a curse came, Willet said:

"As it is night I'll ask you, Achille Garay, for your papers only once every four hours. That is the interval at which we'll change our guard, and we don't wish, either, to disturb you many times in your pleasant slumbers. It would not be right to call a man back too often from the land of Tarenyawagon, who, you may know, is the Iroquois sender of dreams."

Garay, whom they had now laid tenderly upon the floor of the hut, turned his face away, and Willet went back to the fire, humming in a pleased fashion to himself. At half past twelve he awoke Garay from his uneasy sleep and propounded to him his dreadful query, grown terrifying by its continual iteration. At half past four Tayoga asked it, and it was not necessary then to awake Garay. He had not slept since half past twelve. He snarled at the Iroquois, and then sank back on the blanket that they had kindly placed for him. Tayoga, his bronze face expressing nothing, went back to his watch by the fire.

Breakfast was cooked by Robert and Willet, and again it was luscious and varied. Robert had risen early and he caught several of the fine lake trout that he broiled delicately over the coals. He had also gathered grapes fresh with the morning dew, and wonderfully appetizing, and some of the best of the nuts were left over. Bear, deer, venison and turkey they still had in abundance.

The morning itself was the finest they had encountered so far. Much snow had fallen in the high mountains, but winter had not touched the earth here. The deep colours of the leaves, moved by the light wind, shifted and changed like a prism. The glorious haze of Indian summer hung over everything like a veil of finest gauze. The air was surcharged with vitality and life. It was pleasant merely to sit and breathe at such a time.

"I've always claimed," said Robert, as he passed a beautifully broiled trout to Tayoga and another to the hunter, "that I can cook fish better than either of you. Dave, I freely admit, can surpass me in the matter of venison and Tayoga is a finer hand with bear than I am, but I'm a specialist with fish, be it salmon, or trout, or salmon trout, or perch or pickerel or what not."

"Your boast is justified, in very truth, Robert," said Willet. "I've known none other who can prepare a fish with as much tenderness and perfection as you. I suppose 'tis born in you, but you have a way of preserving the juices and savours which defies description and which is beyond praise. 'Tis worth going hungry a long while to put one's tooth into so delicate a morsel as this salmon trout, and 'tis a great pity, too, that our guest, Monsieur Achille Garay, will not join us, when we've an abundance so great and a variety so rich."

The wretched spy and intermediary could hear every word they said, and Robert fell silent, but the hunter and the Onondaga talked freely and with abounding zest.

"'Tis a painful thing," said Willet, "to offer hospitality and to have it refused. Monsieur Garay knows that he would be welcome at our board, and yet he will not come. I fear, Robert, that you have cooked too many of these superlative fish, and that they must even go to waste, which is a sin. They would make an admirable beginning for our guest's breakfast, if he would but consent to join us."

"It is told by the wise old *sachems* of the great League," said Tayoga, "that warriors have gone many days without food, when plenty of it was ready for their taking, merely to test their strength of body and will. Their sufferings were acute and terrible. Their flesh wasted away, their muscles became limp and weak, their sight failed, pain stabbed them with a thousand needles, but they would not yield and touch sustenance before the time appointed."

"I've heard of many such cases, Tayoga, and I've seen some, but it was always warriors who were doing the fasting. I doubt whether white men could stand it so long, and 'tis quite sure they would suffer more. About the third day 'twould be as bad as being tied to the stake in the middle of the flames."

"Great Bear speaks the truth, as he always does. No white man can stand it. If he tried it his sufferings would be beyond anything of which he might dream."

A groan burst suddenly from the wretched Garay. The hunter and the Onondaga looked at each other and their eyes expressed astonishment.

"Did you hear a sound in the thicket?" asked Willet.

"I think it came from the boughs overhead," said Tayoga.

"I could have sworn 'twas the growl of a bear."

"To me it sounded like the croak of a crow."

"After all, we may have heard nothing. Imagination plays strange tricks with us."

"It is true, Great Bear. We hear queer sounds when there are no sounds at all. The air is full of spirits, and now and then they have sport with us."

A second groan burst from Garay, now more wretched than ever.

"I heard it again!" exclaimed the hunter. "'Tis surely the growl of a bear in the bush! The sound was like that of an angry wild animal! But, we'll let it go. The sun tells meet's half past eight o'clock and I go to ask our guest the usual question."

"Enough!" exclaimed Garay. "I yield! I cannot bear this any longer!"

"Your papers, please!"

"Unbind me and give me food!"

"Your papers first, our fish next."

As he spoke the hunter leaned over, and with his keen hunting knife severed Garay's bonds. The man sat up, rubbed his wrists and ankles and breathed deeply.

"Your papers!" repeated Willet.

"Bring me my pistol, the one that the Indian filched from me while I slept," said Garay.

"Your pistol!" exclaimed the hunter, in surprise. "Now I'd certainly be foolish to hand you a deadly and loaded weapon!"

But Robert's quick intellect comprehended at once. He snatched the heavy pistol from the Onondaga's belt, drew forth the bullet and then drew the charge behind it, not powder at all, but a small, tightly folded paper of tough tissue, which he held aloft triumphantly.

"Very clever! very clever!" said Willet in admiration. "The pistol was loaded, but 'twould never be fired, and nobody would have thought of searching its barrel. Tayoga, give Monsieur Garay the two spare fish and anything else he wants, but see that he eats sparingly because a gorge will go ill with a famished man, and then we'll have a look at his precious document."

The Onondaga treated Garay as the honoured guest they had been calling him, giving him the whole variety of their breakfast, but, at guarded intervals, which allowed him to relish to the full all the savours and juices that had been taunting him so long. Willet opened the letter, smoothed it out carefully on his knee, and holding it up to the light until the words stood out clearly, read:

"To Hendrik Martinus At Albany.

"The intermediary of whom you know, the bearer of this letter, has brought me word from you that the English Colonial troops, after the unfortunate battle at Lake George, have not pushed their victory. He also informs us that the governors of the English colonies do not agree, and that there is much ill feeling among the different Colonial forces. He says that Johnson still suffering from his wound, does not move, and that the spirit has gone out of our enemies. All of which is welcome news to us at this juncture, since it has given to us the time that we need.

"Our defeat but incites us to greater efforts. The Indian tribes who have cast their lot with us are loyal to our arms. All the forces of France and New France are being assembled to crush our foes. We have lost Dieskau, but a great soldier, Louis Joseph de Saint Véran, the Marquis de Montcalm-Gozon, is coming from France to lead our armies. He will be assisted by the incomparable chieftains, the Chevalier de Levis, the Chevalier Bourlamaque and others who understand the warfare of the wilderness. Even now we are preparing to move with a great power on Albany and we may surprise the town.

"Tell those of whom you know in Albany and New York to be ready with rifles and ammunition and other presents for the Indian warriors. Much depends upon their skill and promptness in delivering these valuable goods to the tribes. It seals them to our standard. They can be landed at the places of which we know, and then be carried swiftly across the wilderness. But I bid you once more to exercise exceeding caution. Let no name of those associated with us ever be entrusted to writing, as a single slip might bring our whole fabric crashing to the ground, and send to death those who serve us. After you have perused this letter destroy it. Do not tear it in pieces and throw them away but burn it to the last and least little fragment. In conclusion I say yet again, caution, caution, caution.

Raymond Louis de St. Luc."

The three looked at one another. Garay was in the third course of his breakfast, and no longer took notice of anything else.

"Those associated with us in Albany and New York," quoted Willet. "Now I wonder who they are. I might make a shrewd guess at one, but no names are given and as we have no proof we must keep silent about him for the present. Yet this paper is of vast importance and it must be put in hands that know how to value it."

"Then the hands must be those of Colonel William Johnson," said Robert.

"I fancy you're right, lad. Yet 'tis hard just now to decide upon the wisest policy."

"The colonel is the real leader of our forces," persisted the lad. "It's to him that we must go."

"It looks so, Robert, but for a few days we've got to consider ourselves. Now that we have his letter I wish we didn't have Garay."

"You wouldn't really have starved him, would you, Dave? Somehow it seemed pretty hard."

The hunter laughed heartily.

"Bless your heart, lad," he replied. "Don't you be troubled about the way we dealt with Garay. I knew all the while that he would never get to the starving point, or I wouldn't have tried it with him. I knew by looking at him that his isn't the fibre of which martyrs are made. I calculated that he would give up last night or this morning."

"Are we going to take him back with us a prisoner?"

"That's the trouble. As a spy, which he undoubtedly is, his life is forfeit, but we are not executioners. For scouts and messengers such as we are he'd be a tremendous burden to take along with us. Moreover, I think that after his long fast he'd eat all the game we could kill, and we don't propose to spend our whole time feeding one of our enemies."

"Call Tayoga," said Robert.

The Onondaga came and then young Lennox said to his two comrades:

"Are you willing to trust me in the matter of Garay, our prisoner?"

"Yes," they replied together.

Robert went to the man, who was still immersed in his gross feeding, and tapped him on the shoulder.

"Listen, Garay," he said. "You're the bearer of secret and treacherous dispatches, and you're a spy. You must know that under all the rules of war your life is forfeit to your captors."

Garay's face became gray and ghastly.

"You—you wouldn't murder me?" he said.

"There could be no such thing as murder in your case, and we won't take your life, either."

The face of the intermediary recovered its lost colour.

"You will spare me, then?" he exclaimed joyfully.

"In a way, yes, but we're not going to carry you back in luxury to Albany, nor are we thinking of making you an honoured member of our band. You've quite a time before you."

"I don't understand you."

"You will soon. You're going back to the Chevalier de St. Luc who has little patience with failure, and you'll find that the road to him abounds in hard travelling. It may be, too, that the savage Tandakora will ask you some difficult questions, but if so, Monsieur Achille Garay, it will be your task to answer them, and I take it that you have a fertile mind. In any event, you will be equipped to meet him by your journey, which will be full of variety and effort and which will strengthen and harden your mind."

The face of Garay paled again, and he gazed at Robert in a sort of dazed fashion. The imagination of young Lennox was alive and leaping. He had found what seemed to him a happy solution of a knotty problem, and, as usual in such cases, his speech became fluent and golden.

"Oh, you'll enjoy it, Monsieur Achille Garay," he said in his mellow, persuasive voice. "The forest is beautiful at this time of the year and the mountains are so magnificent always that they must appeal to anyone who has in his soul the strain of poetry that I know you have. The snow, too, I think has gone from the higher peaks and ridges and you will not be troubled by extreme cold. If you should wander from the path back to St. Luc you will have abundant leisure in which to find it again, because for quite a while to come time will be of no importance to you. And as you'll go unarmed, you'll be in no danger of shooting your friends by mistake."

"You're not going to turn me into the wilderness to starve?"

"Not at all. We'll give you plenty of food. Tayoga and I will see you well on your way. Now, since you've eaten enough, you start at once."

Tayoga and the hunter fell in readily with Robert's plan. The captive received enough food to last four days, which he carried in a pack fastened on his back, and then Robert and Tayoga accompanied him northward and back on the trail.

Much of Garay's courage returned as they marched steadily on through the forest. When he summed it up he found that he had fared well. His captors had really been soft-hearted. It was not usual for one serving as an intermediary and spy like himself to escape, when taken, with his life and even with freedom. Life! How precious it was! Young Lennox had said that the forest was beautiful, and it was! It was splendid, grand, glorious to one who had just come out of the jaws of death, and the air of late autumn was instinct with vitality. He drew himself up jauntily, and his step became strong and springy.

They walked on many miles and Robert, whose speech had been so fluent before, was silent now. Nor did the Onondaga speak either.

Garay himself hazarded a few words, but meeting with no response his spirits fell a little. The trail led over a low ridge, and at its crest his two guards stopped.

"Here we bid you farewell, Monsieur Achille Garay," said Robert. "Doubtless you will wish to commune with your own thoughts and our presence will no longer disturb you. Our parting advice to you is to give up the trade in which you have been engaged. It is full perilous, and it may be cut short at any time by sudden death. Moreover, it is somewhat bare of honour, and even if it should be crowned by continued success 'tis success of a kind that's of little value. Farewell."

"Farewell," said Garay, and almost before he could realize it, the two figures had melted into the forest behind him. A weight was lifted from him with their going, and once more his spirits bounded upward. He was Achille Garay, bold and venturesome, and although he was without weapons he did not fear two lads.

Three miles farther on he turned. He did not care to face St. Luc, his letter lost, and the curious, dogged obstinacy that lay at the back of his character prevailed. He would go back. He would reach those for whom his letter had been intended, Martinus and the others, and he would win the rich rewards that had been promised to him. He had plenty of food, he would make a wide curve, advance at high speed and get to Albany ahead of the foolish three.

He turned his face southward and walked swiftly through the thickets. A rifle cracked and a twig overhead severed by a bullet fell upon his face. Garay shivered and stood still for a long time. Courage trickled back, and he resumed his advance, though it was slow. A second rifle cracked, and a bullet passed so close to his cheek that he felt its wind. He could not restrain a cry of terror, and turning again he fled northward to St. Luc.

Chapter 6

Pupils of the Bear

When Robert and Tayoga returned to the camp and told Willet what they had done the hunter laughed a little.

"Garay doesn't want to face St. Luc," he said, "but he will do it anyhow. He won't dare to come back on the trail in face of bullets, and now we're sure to deliver his letter in ample time."

"Should we go direct to Albany?" asked Robert.

The hunter cupped his chin in his hand and meditated.

"I'm all for Colonel Johnson," he replied at last. "He understands the French and Indians and has more vigour than the authorities at Albany. It seems likely to me that he will still be at the head of Lake George where we left him, perhaps building the fort of which they were talking before we left there."

"His wound did not give promise of getting well so very early," said Robert, "and he would not move while he was in a weakened condition."

"Then it's almost sure that he's at the head of the lake and we'll turn our course toward that point. What do you say, Tayoga?"

"Waraiyageh is the man to have the letter, Great Bear. If it becomes necessary for him to march to the defence of Albany he will do it."

"Then the three of us are in unanimity and Lake George it is instead of Albany."

They started in an hour, and changing their course somewhat, began a journey across the maze of mountains toward Andiatarocte, the lake that men now call George, and Robert's heart throbbed at the thought that he would soon see it again in all its splendour and beauty. He had passed so much of his life near them that his fortunes seemed to him to be interwoven inseparably with George and Champlain.

They thought they would reach the lake in a few days, but in a wilderness and in war the plans of men often come to naught. Before the close of the day they came upon traces of a numerous band travelling on the great trail between east and west, and they also found among them footprints that turned out. These Willet and Tayoga examined with the greatest care and interest and they lingered longest over a pair uncommonly long and slender.

"I think they're his," the hunter finally said.

"So do I," said the Onondaga.

"Those long, slim feet could belong to nobody but the Owl."

"It can be only the Owl."

"Now, who under the sun is the Owl?" asked Robert, mystified.

"The Owl is, in truth, a most dangerous man," replied the hunter. "His name, which the Indians have given him, indicates he works by night, though he's no sloth in the day, either. But he has another name, also, the one by which he was christened. It's Charles Langlade, a young Frenchman who was a trader before the war. I've seen him more than once. He's mighty shrewd and alert, uncommon popular among the western Indians, who consider him as one of them because he married a good looking young Indian woman at Green Bay, and a great forester and wilderness fighter. It's wonderful how the French adapt themselves to the ways of the Indians and how they take wives among them. I suppose the marriage tie is one of their greatest sources of strength with the tribes. Now, Tayoga, why do you think the Owl is here so far to the eastward of his usual range?"

"He and his warriors are looking for scalps, Great Bear, and it may be that they have seen St. Luc. They were travelling fast and they are now between us and Andiatarocte. I like it but little."

"Not any less than I do. It upsets our plans. We must leave the trail, or like as not we'll run squarely into a big band. What a pity our troops didn't press on after the victory at the lake. Instead of driving the French and Indians out of the whole northern wilderness we've left it entirely to them."

They turned from the trail with reluctance, because, strong and enduring as they were, incessant hardships, long travelling and battle were beginning to tell upon all three, and they were unwilling to be climbing again among the high mountains. But there was no choice and night found them on a lofty ridge in a dense thicket. The hunter and the Onondaga were disturbed visibly over the advent of Langlade, and their uneasiness was soon communicated to the sympathetic mind of Robert.

The night being very clear, sown with shining stars, they saw rings of smoke rising toward the east, and outlined sharply against the dusky blue.

"That's Langlade sending up signals," said the hunter, anxiously, "and he wouldn't do it unless he had something to talk about."

"When one man speaks another man answers," said Tayoga. "Now from what point will come the reply?"

Robert felt excitement. These rings of smoke in the blue were full of significance for them, and the reply to the first signal would be vital. "Ah!" he exclaimed suddenly. The answer came from the west, directly behind them.

"I think they've discovered our trail," said Willet. "They didn't learn it from Garay, because Langlade passed before we sent him back, but they might have heard from St. Luc or Tandakora that we were somewhere in the forest. It's bad. If it weren't for the letter we could turn sharply to the north and stay in the woods till Christmas, if need be."

"We may have to do so, whether we wish it or not," said Tayoga. "The shortest way is not always the best."

Before morning they saw other smoke signals in the south, and it became quite evident then that the passage could not be tried, except at a risk perhaps too great to take.

"There's nothing for it but the north," said Willet, "and we'll trust to luck to get the letter to Waraiyageh in time. Perhaps we can find Rogers. He must be roaming with his rangers somewhere near Champlain."

At dawn they were up and away, but all through the forenoon they saw rings of smoke rising from the peaks and ridges, and the last lingering hope that they were not followed disappeared. It became quite evident to their trained observation and the powers of inference from circumstances which had become almost a sixth sense with them that there was a vigorous pursuit, closing in from three points of the compass, south, east and west. They slept again the next night in the forest without fire and arose the following morning cold, stiff and out of temper. While they eased their muscles and prepared for the day's flight they resolved upon a desperate expedient.

It was vital now to carry the letter to Johnson and then to Albany, which they considered more important than their own escape, and they could not afford to be driven farther and farther into the recesses of the north, while St. Luc might be marching with a formidable force on Albany itself.

"With us it's unite to fight and divide for flight," said Robert, divining what was in the mind of the others.

"The decision is forced upon us," said Willet, regretfully.

Tayoga nodded.

"We'll read the letter again several times, until all of us know it by heart," said the hunter.

The precious document was produced, and they went over it until each could repeat it from memory. Then Willet said:

"I'm the oldest and I'll take the letter and go south past their bands. One can slip through where three can't."

He spoke with such decision that the others, although Tayoga wanted the task of risk and honour, said nothing.

"And do you, Robert and Tayoga," resumed the hunter, "continue your flight to the northward. You can keep ahead of these bands, and, when you discover the chase has stopped, curve back for Lake George. If by any chance I should fall by the way, though it's not likely, you can repeat the letter to Colonel Johnson, and let's hope you'll be in time. Now good-by, and God bless you both."

Willet never displayed emotion, but his feeling was very deep as he wrung the outstretched hand of each. Then he turned at an angle to the east and south and disappeared in the undergrowth.

"He has been more than a father to me," said Robert.

"The Great Bear is a man, a man who is pleasing to Areskoui himself," said Tayoga with emphasis.

"Do you think he will get safely through?"

"There is no warrior, not even of the Clan of the Bear, of the Nation Onondaga, of the great League of the Hodenosaunee, who can surpass the Great Bear in forest skill and cunning. In the night he will creep by Tandakora himself, with such stealth, that not a leaf will stir, and there will be not the slightest whisper in the grass. His step, too, will be so light that his trail will be no more than a bird's in the air."

Robert laughed and felt better.

"You don't stint the praise of a friend, Tayoga," he said, "but I know that at least three-fourths of what you say is true. Now, I take it that you and I are to play the hare to Langlade's hounds, and that in doing so we'll be of great help to Dave."

"Aye," agreed the Onondaga, and they swung into their gait. Robert had received Garay's pistol which, being of the same bore as his own, was now loaded with bullet and powder, instead of bullet and paper, and it swung at his belt, while Tayoga carried the intermediary's rifle, a fine piece. It made an extra burden, but they had been unwilling to throw it away—a rifle was far too valuable on the border to be abandoned.

They maintained a good pace until noon, and, as they heard no sound behind them, less experienced foresters than they might have thought the pursuit had ceased, but they knew better. It had merely settled into that tenacious kind which was a characteristic of the Indian mind, and unless they could hide their trail it would continue in the same determined manner for days. At noon, they paused a half hour in a dense grove and ate bear and deer meat, sauced with some fine, black wild grapes, the vines hanging thick on one of the trees.

"Think of those splendid banquets we enjoyed when Garay was sitting looking at us, though not sharing with us," said Robert.

Tayoga smiled at the memory and said:

"If he had been able to hold out a little longer he would have had plenty of food, and we would not have had the letter. The Great Bear would never have starved him."

"I know that now, Tayoga, and I learn from it that we're to hold out too, long after we think we're lost, if we're to be the victors."

They came in the afternoon to a creek, flowing in their chosen course, and despite the coldness of its waters, which rose almost to their knees, they waded a long time in its bed. When they went out on the bank they took off their leggings and moccasins, wrung or beat out of them as much of the water as they could, and then let them dry for a space in the sun, while they rubbed vigorously their ankles and feet to create warmth. They knew that Langlade's men would follow on either side of the creek until they picked up the trail again, but their manoeuvre would create a long delay, and give them a rest needed badly.

"Have you anything in mind, Tayoga?" asked Robert. "You know that the farther north and higher we go the colder it will become, and our flight may take us again into the very heart of a great snow storm."

"It is so, Dagaeoga, but it is also so that I do have a plan. I think I know the country into which we are coming, and that tells me what to do. The people of my race, living from the beginning of the world in the great forest, have not been too proud to learn from the animals, and of all the animals we know perhaps the wisest is the bear."

"The bear is scarcely an animal, Tayoga. He is almost a human being. He has as good a sense of humour as we have, and he is more careful about minding his own business, and letting alone that of other people."

"Dagaeoga is not without wisdom. We will even learn from the bear. A hundred miles to the north of us there is a vast rocky region containing many caves, where the bears go in great numbers to sleep the long winters through. It is not much disturbed, because it is a dangerous country, lying between the Hodenosaunee and the Indian nations to the north, with which we have been at war for centuries. There we will go."

"And hole up until our peril passes! Your plan appeals to me, Tayoga! I will imitate the bear! I will even be a bear!"

"We will take the home of one of them before he comes for it himself, and we will do him no injustice, because the wise bear can always find another somewhere else."

"They're fine caves, of course!" exclaimed Robert, buoyantly, his imagination, which was such a powerful asset with him, flaming up as usual. "Dry and clean, with plenty of leaves for beds, and with nice little natural shelves for food, and a pleasant little brook just outside the door. It will be pleasant to lie in our own cave, the best one of course, and hear the snow and sleet storms whistle by, while we're warm and comfortable. If we only had complete assurance that Dave was through with the letter I'd be willing to stay there until spring."

Tayoga smiled indulgently.

"Dagaeoga is always dreaming," he said, "but bright dreams hurt nobody."

When night came, they were many more miles on their way, but it was a very cold darkness that fell upon them and they shivered in their blankets. Robert made no complaint, but he longed for the caves, of which he was making such splendid pictures. Shortly before morning, a light snow fell and the dawn was chill and discouraging, so much so that Tayoga risked a fire for the sake of brightness and warmth.

"Langlade's men will come upon the coals we leave," he said, "but since we have not shaken them off it will make no difference. How much food have we left, Dagaeoga?"

"Not more than enough for three days."

"Then it is for us to find more soon. It is another risk that we must take. I wish I had with me now my bow and arrows which I left at the lake, instead of Garay's rifle. But Areskoui will provide."

The day turned much colder, and the streams to which they came were frozen over. By night, the ice was thick enough to sustain their weight and they travelled on it for a long time, their thick moose hide moccasins keeping their feet warm, and saving them from falling. Before they returned to the land it began to snow again, and Tayoga rejoiced openly.

"Now a white blanket will lie over the trail we have left on the ice," he said, "hiding it from the keenest eyes that ever were in a man's head."

Then they crossed a ridge and came upon a lake, by the side of which they saw through the snow and darkness a large fire burning.

Creeping nearer, they discerned dusky forms before the flames and made out a band of at least twenty warriors, many of them sound asleep, wrapped to the eyes in their blankets.

"Have they passed ahead of us and are they here meaning to guard the way against us?" whispered Robert.

"No, it is not one of the bands that has been following us," replied the Onondaga. "This is a war party going south, and not much stained as yet by time and travel. They are Montagnais, come from Montreal. They seek scalps, but not ours, because they do not know of us."

Robert shuddered. These savages, like as not, would fall at midnight upon some lone settlement, and his intense imagination depicted the hideous scenes to follow.

"Come away," he whispered. "Since they don't know anything about us we'll keep them in ignorance. I'm longing more than ever for my warm bear cave."

They disappeared in the falling snow, which would soon hide their trail here, as it had hidden it elsewhere, and left the lake behind them, not stopping until they came to a deep and narrow gorge in the mountains, so well sheltered by overhanging bushes that no snow fell there. They raked up great quantities of dry leaves, after the usual fashion, and spread their blankets upon them, poor enough quarters save for the hardiest, but made endurable for them by custom and intense weariness. Both fell asleep almost at once, and both awoke about the same time far after dawn.

Robert moved his stiff fingers in his blanket and sat up, feeling cold and dismal. Tayoga was sitting up also, and the two looked at each other.

"In very truth those bear caves never seemed more inviting to me," said young Lennox, solemnly, "and yet I only see them from afar."

"Dagaeoga has fallen in love with bear caves," said the Onondaga, in a whimsical tone. "The time is not so far back when he never talked about them at all, and now words in their praise fall from his lips in a stream."

"It's because I've experienced enlightenment, Tayoga. It is only in the last two or three days that I've learned the vast superiority of a cave to any other form of human habitation. Our remote ancestors lived in them two or three hundred thousand years, and we've been living in houses of wood or brick or stone only six or seven thousand years, I suppose, and so the cave, if you judge by the length of time, is our true home. Hence I'm filled with a just enthusiasm at the thought of going back speedily to the good old ways and the good old days. It's possible, Tayoga, that our remote grandfathers knew best."

"When Dagaeoga comes to his death bed, seventy or eighty years from now, and the medicine man tells him but little more breath is left in his body, what then do you think he will do?"

"What will I do, Tayoga?"

"You will say to the medicine man, 'Tell me exactly how long I have to live,' and the medicine man will reply: 'Ten minutes, O Dagaeoga, venerable chief and great orator.' Then you will say: 'Let all the people be summoned and let them crowd into the wigwam in which I lie,' and when they have all come and stand thick about your bed, you will say, 'Now raise me into a sitting position and put the pillows thick behind my back and head that I may lean against them.' Then you will speak to the people. The words will flow from your lips in a continuous and golden stream. It will be the finest speech of your life. It will be filled with magnificent words, many of them, eight or ten syllables long. It will be mellow like the call of a trumpet. It will be armed with force, and it will be beautiful with imagery; it will be suffused and charged with colour, it will be the very essence of poetry and power, and as the aged Dagaeoga draws his very last breath so he will speak his very last word, and thus, in a golden cloud, his soul will go away into infinite space, to dwell forever in the bosom of Manitou, with the immortal sachems, Tododaho and Hayowentha!"

"Do you know, Tayoga, I think that would be a happy death," said Robert earnestly.

The Onondaga laughed heartily.

"Thus does Dagaeoga show his true nature," he said. "He was born with the spirit and soul of the orator, and the fact is disclosed often. It is well. The orator, be he white or red, will lose himself sometimes in his own words, but he is a gift from the gods, sent to lift up the souls, and cheer the rest of us. He is the bugle that calls us to the chase and we must not forget that his value is great."

"And having said a whole cargo of words yourself Tayoga, now what do you propose that we do?"

"Push on with all our strength for the caves. I know now we are on the right path, because I recall the country through which we are passing. At noon we will reach a small lake, in which the fish are so numerous that there is not room for them all at the same time in the water. They have to take turns in getting the air above the surface on top of the others. For that reason the fish of this lake are different from all other fish. They will live a full hour on the bank after they are caught."

"Tayoga, in very truth, you've learned our ways well. You've become a prince of romancers yourself."

At the appointed time they reached the lake. There were no fish above its surface, but the Onondaga claimed it was due to the fact that the lake was covered with ice which of course kept them down, and which crowded them excessively, and very uncomfortably. They broke two big holes in the ice, let down the lines which they always carried, the hooks baited with fragments of meat, and were soon rewarded with splendid fish, as much as they needed.

Tayoga with his usual skill lighted a fire, despite the driving snow, and they had a banquet, taking with them afterward a supply of the cooked fish, though they knew they could not rely upon fish alone in the winter days that were coming. But fortune was with them. Before dark, Robert shot a deer, a great buck, fine and fat. They had so little fear of pursuit now that they cut up the body, saving the skin whole for tanning, and hung the pieces in the trees, there to freeze. Although it would make quite a burden they intended to carry practically all of it with them.

Many mountain wolves were drawn that night by the odour of the spoils, but they lay between twin fires and had no fear of an attack. Yet the time might come when they would be assailed by fierce wild animals, and now they were glad that Tayoga had kept Garay's rifle, and also his ammunition, a good supply of powder and bullets. It was possible that the question of ammunition might become vital with them, but they did not yet talk of it.

On the second day thereafter, bearing their burdens of what had been the deer, they reached the stony valley Tayoga had in mind, and Robert saw at once that its formation indicated many caves.

"Now, I wonder if the bears have come," he said, putting down his pack and resting. "The cold has been premature and perhaps they're still roaming through the forest. I shouldn't want to put an interloper out of my own particular cave, but, if I have to do it, I will."

"The bears haven't arrived yet," said Tayoga, "and we can choose. I do not know, but I do not think a bear always occupies the same winter home, so we will not have to fight over our place."

It was a really wonderful valley, where the decaying stone had made a rich assortment of small caves, many of them showing signs of former occupancy by large wild animals, and, after long searching, they found one that they could make habitable for themselves. Its entrance was several feet above the floor of the valley, so that neither storm nor winter flood could send water into it, and its own floor was fairly smooth, with a roof eight or ten feet high. It could be easily defended with their three rifles, the aperture being narrow, and they expected, with skins and pelts, to make it warm.

It was but a cold and bleak refuge for all save the hardiest, and for a little while Robert had to use his last ounce of will to save himself from discouragement. But vigorous exertion and keen interest in the future brought back his optimism. The hide of the deer they had slain was spread at once upon the cave floor and made a serviceable rug. They spoke hopefully of soon adding to it.

A brook flowed less than a hundred yards away, and they would have no trouble about their water supply, while the country about seemed highly favourable for game. But on their first day there they did not do any hunting. They rolled several large stones before the door of their new home, making it secure against any prying wild animals, and then, after a hearty meal, they wrapped themselves in their blankets and slept prodigiously.

Tayoga went into the forest the next day and set traps and snares, while Robert worked in the valley, breaking up fallen wood to be used for fires, and doing other chores. The Onondaga in the next three or four days shot a large panther, a little bear, and caught in the traps and snares a quantity of small game. The big pelts and the little pelts, after proper treatment, were spread upon the floor or hung against the walls of the cave, which now began to assume a much more inviting aspect, and the flesh of the animals that were eatable, cured after the primitive but effective processes, was stored there also.

Providence granted them a period of good weather, days and nights alike being clear and cold. The game, evidently not molested for a long time, fairly walked into their traps, and they were compelled to draw but little upon their precious supply of ammunition. Food for the future accumulated rapidly, and the floor and walls of the cave were soon covered entirely with furs.

Not one of the numerous caves and hollows about them contained an occupant and Robert wondered if their presence would frighten away the wild animals, so many of which had hibernated there so often. Yet he had a belief that the bears would come. His present mode of life and his isolation from the world gave him a feeling almost of kinship with them, and in some strange way, and through some medium unknown to him, they might reciprocate. He and Tayoga had killed several bears, it was true, but far from the cave, and they made up their minds to molest nothing in the valley or just about it.

It was a land of many waters and they caught with ease numerous fish, drying all the surplus and storing it with the other food in the cave. They also made soft beds for themselves of the little branches of the evergreen, over which they spread their blankets, and when they rolled the stone before the doorway at night they never failed to sleep soundly.

They did their cooking in front of the cave door, but it was always a smothered fire. While they felt safe from wandering bands in that lofty and remote region, they took no unnecessary risks. The valley itself, though deep, was much broken up into separate little valleys, and most of the caves were hidden from their own. It was this fact that made Robert still think the bears would come, despite coals and flame. In the evenings they would talk of Willet, and both were firm in the opinion that the hunter had got through to Lake George and that Johnson and Albany had been warned in time. Each was confirmed in his opinion by the other and in a few days it became certainty.

"I think Tododaho on his star whispered in my ear while I slept that Great Bear has passed the hostile lines," said Tayoga with conviction, "because I know it, just as if the Great Bear himself had told it to me, though I do not know how I know it."

"It's some sort of mysterious information," said Robert in the same tone of absolute belief, "and I don't worry any more about Dave and the letter. The men of the Hodenosaunee seem to have a special gift. You know the old chief, Hendrik, foretold that he would die on the shores of Andiatarocte, and it came to pass just as he had said."

"It was a glorious death, Dagaeoga, and it was, perhaps, he who saved our army, and made the victory possible."

"So it was. There's not a doubt of it, but, here, I don't feel much like taking part in a war. The great struggle seems to have passed around us for a while, at least. I appear to myself as a man of peace, occupied wholly with the struggle for existence and with preparations for a hard winter. I don't want to harm anything."

"Perhaps it's because nothing we know of wants to harm us. But, Dagaeoga, if the bears come at all they will come quickly, because in a few days winter will be roaring down upon us."

"Then, Tayoga, we must hurry our labours, and since the mysterious message brought in some manner through the air has told us that Dave has reached the lake, I'm rather anxious for it to rush down. While it keeps us here it will also hold back the forces of St. Luc."

"That's true, Dagaeoga. It's a poor snow that doesn't help somebody. Now, I will make a bow and arrow to take the place of my great bow and quiver, which await me elsewhere, because we must draw but little upon our powder and bullets."

The Onondaga had hatchet and knife and he worked with great rapidity and skill, cutting and bending a bow in two or three days, and making a string of strong sinews, after which he fashioned many arrows and tipped them with sharp bone. Then he contemplated his handiwork with pride.

"Hasty work is never the best of work," he said, "and these are not as good as those I left behind me, but I know they will serve. The game here, hunted but little, is not very wary and I can approach near."

His skill both in construction and use was soon proved, as he slew with his new weapons a great moose, two ordinary deer, and much smaller game, while the traps caught beaver, otter, fox, wolf and other animals, with fine pelts. Many splendid furs were soon drying in the air and were taken later into the cave, while they accumulated dried and jerked game enough to last them until the next spring.

Both worked night and day with such application and intensity that their hands became stiff and sore, and every bone in them ached. Nevertheless Robert took time now and then to examine the little caves in the other sections of the valley, only to find them still empty. He thought, for a while, that the presence of Tayoga and himself and their operations with the game might have frightened the bears away, but the feeling that they would come returned and was strong upon him. As for Tayoga he never doubted. It had been decreed by Tododaho.

"The animals have souls," he said. "Often when great warriors die or fall in battle their souls go into the bodies of bear, or deer, or wolf, but oftenest into that of bear. For that reason the bear, saving only the dog which lives with us, is nearest to man, and now and then, because of the warrior soul in him, he is a man himself, although he walks on four legs—and he does not always walk on four legs, sometimes he stands on two. Doubt not, Dagaeoga, that when the stormy winter sweeps down the bears will come to their ancient homes, whether or not we be here."

The winds grew increasingly chill, coming from the vast lakes beyond the Great Lakes, those that lay in the far Canadian north, and the skies were invariably leaden in hue and gloomy. But in the cave it was cosy and warm. Furs and skins were so numerous that there was no longer room on the floor and walls for them all, many being stored in glossy heaps in the corners.

"Some day these will bring a good price from the Dutch traders at Albany," said Robert, "and it may be, Tayoga, that you and I will need the money. I've been a scout and warrior for a long time, and now I've suddenly turned fur hunter. Well, that spirit of peace and of a friendly feeling toward all mankind grows upon me. Why shouldn't I be full of brotherly love when your patron saint, Tododaho, has been so kind to us?"

He swept the cave once more with a glance of approval. It furnished shelter, warmth, food in abundance, and with its furs even a certain velvety richness for the eye, and Tayoga nodded assent. Meanwhile they waited for the fierce blasts of the mountain winter.

CHAPTER 7

The Sleeping Sentinels

A singular day came when it seemed to Robert that the wind alternately blew hot and cold, at least by contrast, and the deep, leaden skies were suffused with a peculiar mist that made him see all objects in a distorted fashion. Everything was out of proportion. Some were too large and some too small. Either the world was awry or his own faculties had become discoloured and disjointed. While his interest in his daily toil decreased and his thoughts were vague and distant, his curiosity, nevertheless, was keen and concentrated. He knew that something unusual was going to happen and nature was preparing him for it.

The occult quality in the air did not depart with the coming of night, though the winds no longer alternated, the warm blasts ceasing to blow, while the cold came steadily and with increasing fierceness. Yet it was warm and close in the cave, and the two went outside for air, wandering up the face of the ridge that enclosed the northern side of their particular valley in the chain of little valleys. Upon the summit they stood erect, and the face of Tayoga became rapt like that of a seer. When Robert looked at him his own blood tingled. The Onondaga shut his eyes, and he spoke not so much to Robert as to the air itself:

"O Tododaho," he said, "when mine eyes are open I do not see you because of the vast clouds that Manitou has heaped between, but when I close them the inner light makes me behold you sitting upon your star and looking down with kindness upon this, the humblest and least of your servants. O Tododaho, you have given my valiant comrade and myself a safe home in the wilderness in our great need, and I beseech you that you will always hold your protecting shield between us and our enemies."

He paused, his eyes still closed, and stood tense and erect, the north wind blowing on his face. A shiver ran through Robert, not a shiver of fear, but a shiver caused by the mysterious and the unknown. His own eyes were open, and he gazed steadily into the northern heavens. The occult quality in the air deepened, and now his nerves began to tingle. His soul thrilled with a coming event. Suddenly the deep, leaden clouds parted for a few moments, and in the clear space between he could have sworn that he saw a great dancing star, from which a mighty, benevolent face looked down upon them.

"I saw him! I saw him!" he exclaimed in excitement. "It was Tododaho himself!"

"I did not see him with my eyes, but I saw him with my soul," said the Onondaga, opening his eyes, "and he whispered to me that his favour was with us. We cannot fail in what we wish to do."

"Look in the next valley, Tayoga. What do you behold now?"

"It is the bears, Dagaeoga. They come to their long winter sleep."

Rolling figures, enlarged and fantastic, emerged from the mist. Robert saw great, red eyes, sharp teeth and claws, and yet he felt neither fear nor hostility. Tayoga's statement that they were bears, into which the souls of great warriors had gone, was strong in his mind, and he believed. They looked up at him, but they did not pause, moving on to the little caves.

"They see us," he said.

"So they do," said Tayoga, "but they do not fear us. The spirits of mighty warriors look out of their eyes at us, and knowing that they were once as we are they know also that we will not harm them."

"Have you ever seen the like of this before, Tayoga?"

"No! But a few of the old men of the Hodenosaunee have told of their grandfathers who have seen it. I think it is a mark of favour to us that we are permitted to behold such a sight. Now I am sure Tododaho has looked upon us with great approval. Lo, Dagaeoga, more of them come out of the mist! Before morning every cave, save those in our own little corner of the valley, will be filled. All of them gaze up at us, recognize us as friends and pass on. It is a wonderful sight, Dagaeoga, and we shall never look upon its like again."

"No," said Robert, as the extraordinary thrill ran through him once more. "Now they have gone into their caves, and I believe with you, Tayoga, that the souls of great warriors truly inhabit the bodies of the bears."

"And since they are snugly in their homes, ready for the long winter sleep, lo! the great snow comes, Dagaeoga!"

A heavy flake fell on Robert's upturned face, and then another and another. The circling clouds, thick and leaden, were beginning to pour down their burden, and the two retreated swiftly to their own dry and well furnished cave. Then they rolled the great stones before the door, and Tayoga said:

"Now, we will imitate our friends, the bears, and take a long winter sleep."

Both were soon slumbering soundly in their blankets and furs, and all that night and all the next day the snow fell on the high mountains in the heart of which they lay. There was no wind, and it came straight down, making an even depth on ridge, slope and valley. It blotted out the mouths of the caves, and it clothed all the forest in deep white. Robert and Tayoga were but two motes, lost in the vast wilderness, which had returned to its primeval state, and the Indians themselves, whether hostile or friendly, sought their villages and lodges and were willing to leave the war trail untrodden until the months of storm and bitter cold had passed.

Robert slept heavily. His labours in preparation for the winter had been severe and unremitting, and his nerves had been keyed very high by the arrival of the bears and the singular quality in the air. Now, nature claimed her toll, and he did not awake until nearly noon, Tayoga having preceded him a half hour. The Onondaga stood at the door of the cave, looking over the stones that closed its lower half. Fresh air poured in at the upper half, but Robert saw there only a whitish veil like a foaming waterfall.

"The time o' day, Sir Tayoga, Knight of the Great Forest," he said lightly and cheerfully.

"There is no sun to tell me," replied the Onondaga. "The face of Areskoui will be hidden long, but I know that at least half the day is gone. The flakes make a thick and heavy white veil, through which I cannot see, and great as are the snows every winter on the high mountains, this will be the greatest of them all."

"And we've come into our lair. And a mighty fine lair it is, too. I seem to adapt myself to such a place, Tayoga. In truth, I feel like a bear myself. You say that the souls of warriors have gone into the bears about us, and it may be that the soul of a bear has come into me."

"It may be," said Tayoga, gravely. "It is at least a wise thought, since, for a while, we must live like bears."

Robert would have chafed, any other time, at a stay that amounted to imprisonment, but peace and shelter were too welcome now to let him complain. Moreover, there were many little but important household duties to do. They made needles of bone, and threads of sinew and repaired their clothing. Tayoga had stored suitable wood and bone and he turned out arrow after arrow. He also made another bow, and Robert, by assiduous practice, acquired sufficient skill to help in these tasks. They did not drive themselves now, but the hours being filled with useful and interesting labour, they were content to wait.

For three or four days, while the snow still fell, they ate cold food, but when the clouds at last floated away, and the air was free from the flakes, they went outside and by great effort—the snow being four or five feet deep—cleared a small space near the entrance, where they cooked a good dinner from their stores and enjoyed it extravagantly. Meanwhile the days passed. Robert was impatient at times, but never a long while. If the mental weariness of waiting came to him he plunged at once into the tasks of the day.

There was plenty to do, although they had prepared themselves so well before the great snowfall came. They made rude shovels of wood and enlarged the space they had cleared of snow. Here, they fitted stones together, until they had a sort of rough furnace which, crude though it was, helped them greatly with their cooking. They also pulled more brushwood from under the snow, and by its use saved the store they had heaped up for impossible days. Then, by continued use of the bone needles and sinews, they managed to make cloaks for themselves of the bearskins. They were rather shapeless garments, and they had little of beauty save in the rich fur itself, but they were wonderfully warm and that was what they wanted most.

Tayoga, after a while, began slow and painstaking work on a pair of snowshoes, expecting to devote many days to the task.

"The snow is so deep we cannot pass through it," he said, "but I, at least, will pass upon it. I cannot get the best materials, but what I have will serve. I shall not go far, but I want to explore the country about us."

Robert thought it a good plan, and helped as well as he could with the work. They still stayed outdoors as much as possible, but the cold became intense, the temperature going almost to forty degrees below zero, the surface of the snow freezing and the boughs of the big trees about the valley becoming so brittle that they broke with sharp crashes beneath the weight of accumulated snow. Then they paused long enough in the work on the snowshoes to make themselves gloves of buckskin, which were a wonderful help, as they laboured in the fresh air. Ear muffs and caps of bearskin followed.

"I feel some reluctance about using bearskin so much," said Robert, "since the bears about us are inhabited by the souls of great warriors and are our friends."

"But the bears that we killed did not belong here," said Tayoga, "and were bears and nothing more. It was right for us to slay them because the bear was sent by Manitou to be a support for the Indian with his flesh and his pelt."

"But how do you know that the bears we killed were just bears and bears only?"

"Because, if they had not been we would not have killed them."

Thus were the qualms of young Lennox quieted and he used his bearskin cap, gloves and cloak without further scruple. The snowshoes were completed and Tayoga announced that he would start early the next morning.

"I may be gone three or four days, Dagaeoga," he said, "but I will surely return. I shall avoid danger, and do you be careful also."

"Don't fear for me," said Robert. "I'm not likely to go farther than the brook, since there's no great sport in breaking your way through snow that comes to your waist, and which, moreover, is covered with a thick sheet of ice. Don't trouble your mind about me, Tayoga, I won't roam from home."

The Onondaga took his weapons, a supply of food, and departed, skimming over the snow with wonderful, flying strokes, while Robert settled down to lonely waiting. It was a hard duty, but he again found solace in work, and at intervals he contemplated the mouths of the bears' caves, now almost hidden by the snow. Tayoga's belief was strong upon him, for the time, and he concluded that the warriors who inhabited the bodies of the bears must be having some long and wonderful dreams. At least, they had plenty of time to dream in, and it was an extraordinary provision of nature that gave them such a tremendous sleep.

Tayoga returned in four days, and Robert, who had more than enough of being alone, welcomed him with hospitable words to a fire and a feast.

"I must first put away my spoils," said the Onondaga, his dark eyes glittering.

"Spoils! What spoils, Tayoga?"

"Powder and lead," he replied, taking a heavy bundle wrapped in deerskin from beneath his bearskin overcoat. "It weighs a full fifty pounds, and it made my return journey very wearisome. Catch it, Dagaeoga!"

Robert caught, and he saw that it was, in truth, powder and lead.

"Now, where did you get this?" he exclaimed. "You couldn't have gone to any settlement!"

"There is no settlement to go to. I made our enemies furnish the powder and lead we need so much, and that is surely the cheapest way. Listen, Dagaeoga. I remembered that to the east of us, about two days' journey, was a long valley sheltered well and warm, in which Indians who fight the Hodenosaunee often camp. I thought it likely they would be there in such a winter as this, and that I might take from them in the night the powder and lead we need so much.

"I was right. The savages were there, and with them a white man, a Frenchman, that Charles Langlade, called the Owl, from whom we fled. They had an abundance of all things, and they were waxing fat, until they could take the war path in the spring. Then, Dagaeoga, I played the fox. At night, when they dreamed of no danger, I entered their biggest lodges, passing as one of them, and came away with the powder and lead."

"It was a great feat, Tayoga, but are you sure none of them will trail you here?"

"The surface of the snow and ice melts a little in the noonday sun, enough to efface all trace of the snowshoes, and my trail is no more than that made by a bird in its flight through the air. Nor can we be followed here while we are guarded by the bears, who sleep, but who, nevertheless, are sentinels."

Tayoga took off his snowshoes, and sank upon a heap of furs in the cave, while Robert brought him food and inspected the great prize of ammunition he had brought. The package contained a dozen huge horns filled with powder, and many small bars of lead, the latter having made the weight which had proved such a severe trial to the Onondaga.

"Here's enough of both lead and powder to last us throughout the winter, whatever may happen," said Robert in a tone of intense satisfaction. "Tayoga, you're certainly a master freebooter. You couldn't have made a more useful capture."

Each, after the invariable custom of hunters and scouts, carried bullet moulds, and they were soon at work, melting the lead and casting bullets for their rifles, then pouring the shining pellets in a stream into their pouches. They continued at the task from day to day until all the lead was turned into bullets and then they began work on another pair of snowshoes, these intended for Robert.

Despite the safety and comfort of their home in the rock, both began to chafe now, and time grew tremendously long. They had done nearly everything they could do for themselves, and life had become so easy that there was leisure to think and be restless, because they were far away from great affairs.

"When my snowshoes are finished and I perfect myself in the use of them," said Robert, "I favour an attempt to escape on the ice and snow to the south. We grow rusty, you and I, here, Tayoga. The war may be decided in our absence and I want to see Dave, too. I want to hear him tell how he got through the savage cordon to the lake."

"Have no fear about the war, Dagaeoga," said the Onondaga. "It will not be ended this winter nor the next. Before there is peace between the French king and the British king you will have a chance to make many speeches. Yet, like you, I think we should go. It is not well for us to lie hidden in the ground through a whole winter."

"But when we leave our good home here I shall leave many regrets behind."

He looked around at the cave and its supplies of skins and furs, its stores of wood and food. Fortune had helped their own skill and they had made a marvellous change in the place. Its bleakness and bareness had disappeared. In the cold and bitter wilderness it offered more than comfort, it was luxury itself.

"So shall I," said Tayoga, appreciatively, "but we will heap rocks up to the very top of the door, so that only a little air and nothing else can enter, and leave it as it is. Some day we may want to use it again."

Having decided to go, they became very impatient, but they did not skimp the work on the snowshoes, knowing how much depended on their strength, but that task too, like all the others, came to an end in time. Robert practiced a while and they selected a day of departure. They were to take with them all the powder and bullets, a large supply of food and their heavy bearskin overcoats. They had also made for themselves over-moccasins of fur and extra deerskin leggings. They would be bundled up greatly, but it was absolutely necessary in order to face the great cold, that hovered continuously around thirty to forty degrees below zero. The ear muffs, the caps and the gloves, too, were necessities, but they had the comfort of believing that if the fierce winter presented great difficulties to them, it would also keep their savage enemies in their lodges.

"The line that shut us in in the autumn has thinned out and gone!" exclaimed Robert in sanguine tones, "and we'll have a clear path from here to the lake!"

Then they rolled stones, as they had planned, before the door to their home, closing it wholly except a few square inches at the top, and ascended on their snowshoes to the crest of the ridge.

"Our cave will not be disturbed, at least not this winter," said Tayoga confidently. "The bears that sleep below are, as I told you, the silent sentinels, and they will guard it for us until we come again."

"At least, they brought us good luck," said Robert. Then, with long, gliding strokes they passed over the ridge, and their happy valley was lost to sight. They did not speak again for hours, Tayoga leading the way, and each bending somewhat to his task, which was by no means a light one, owing to the weight they carried, and the extremely mountainous nature of the country. The wilderness was still and intensely cold. The deep snow was covered by a crust of ice, and, despite vigorous exertion and warm clothing, they were none too warm.

By noon Robert's ankle, not thoroughly hardened to the snowshoes, began to chafe, and they stopped to rest in a dense grove, where the searching north wind was turned aside from them. They were travelling by the sun for the south end of Lake George, but as they were in the vast plexus of mountains, where their speed could not be great, even under the best of conditions, they calculated that they would be many days and nights on the way.

They stayed fully an hour in the shelter of the trees, and an hour later came to a frozen lake over which the travelling was easy, but after they had passed it they entered a land of close thickets, in which their progress was extremely slow. At night, the cold was very great, but, as they scooped out a deep hollow in the snow, though they attempted no fire, they were able to keep warm within their bearskins. A second and a third day passed in like fashion, and their progress to the south was unimpeded, though slow. They beheld no signs of human life save their own, but invariably in the night, and often in the day, they heard distant wolves howling.

On the fourth day the temperature rose rapidly and the surface of the snow softened, making their southward march much harder. Their snowshoes clogged so much and the strain upon their ankles grew so great that they decided to go into camp long before sunset, and give themselves a thorough rest. They also scraped away the snow and lighted a fire for the first time, no small task, as the snow was still very deep, and it required much hunting to find the fallen wood. But when the cheerful blaze came they felt repaid for all their trouble. They rejoiced in the glow for an hour or so, and then Tayoga decided that he would go on a short hunting trip along the course of a stream that they could see about a quarter of a mile below.

"It may be that I can rouse up a deer," he said. "They are likely to be in the shelter of the thick bushes along the water's edge, but whether I find them or not I will return shortly after sundown. Do you await me here, Dagaeoga."

"I won't stir. I'm too tired," said Robert.

The Onondaga put on his snowshoes again, and strapped to his back his share of the ammunition and supplies—it had been agreed by the two that neither should ever go anywhere without his half, lest they become separated. Then he departed on smooth, easy strokes, almost like one who skated, and was soon out of sight among the bushes at the edge of the stream. Robert settled back to the warmth and brightness of the fire, and awaited in peace the sound of a shot telling that Tayoga had found the deer.

He had been so weary, and the blaze was so soothing that he sank into a state, not sleep, but nevertheless full of dreams. He saw Willet again, and heard him tell the tale how he had reached the lake and the army with Garay's letter. He saw Colonel Johnson, and the young English officer, Grosvenor, and Colden and Wilton and Carson and all his old friends, and then he heard a crunch on the snow near him. Had Tayoga come back so soon and without his deer? He did not raise his drooping eyelids until he heard the crunch again, and then when he opened them he sprang suddenly to his feet, his heart beating fast with alarm.

A half dozen dark figures rushed upon him. He snatched at his rifle and tried to meet the first of them with a bullet, but the range was too close. He nevertheless managed to get the muzzle in the air and pull the trigger. He remembered even in that terrible moment to do that much and Tayoga would hear the sharp, lashing report. Then the horde was upon him. Someone struck him a stunning blow on the side of the head with the flat of a tomahawk, and he fell unconscious.

When he returned to the world, the twilight had come, the hole in the snow had been enlarged very much, and so had the fire. Seated around it were a dozen Indians, wrapped in thick blankets and armed heavily, and one white man whose attire was a strange compound of savage and civilized. He wore a three-cornered French military hat with a great, drooping plume of green, an immense cloak of fine green cloth, lined with fur, but beneath it he was clothed in buckskin.

The man himself was as picturesque as his attire. He was young, his face was lean and bold, his nose hooked and fierce like that of a Roman leader, his skin, originally fair, now tanned almost to a mahogany colour by exposure, his figure of medium height, but obviously very powerful. Robert saw at once that he was a Frenchman and he felt instinctively that it was Langlade. But his head was aching from the blow of the tomahawk, and he waited in a sort of apathy.

"So you've come back to earth," said the Frenchman, who had seen his eyes open—he spoke in good French, which Robert understood perfectly.

"I never had any intention of staying away," replied young Lennox.

The Frenchman laughed.

"At least you show a proper spirit," he said. "I commend you also for managing to fire your rifle, although the bullet hit none of us. It gave the alarm to your comrade and he got clean away. I can make a guess as to who you are."

"My name is Robert Lennox."

"I thought so, and your comrade was Tayoga, the Onondaga who is not unknown to us, a great young warrior, I admit freely. I am sorry we did not take him."

"I don't think you'll get a chance to lay hands on him. He'll be too clever for you."

"I admit that, too. He's gone like the wind on his snowshoes. It seems queer that you and he should be here in the mountain wilderness so far north of your lines, in the very height of a fierce winter."

"It's just as queer that you should be here."

"Perhaps so, from your point of view, though it's lucky that I should have been present with these dark warriors of mine when you were taken. They suffered heavily in the battle by Andiatarocte, and but for me they might now be using you as fuel. Don't wince, you know their ways and I only tell a fact. In truth, I can't make you any promise in regard to your ultimate fate, but, at present, I need you alive more than dead."

"You won't get any military information out of me."

"I don't know. We shall wait and see."

"Do you know the Chevalier de St. Luc?"

"Of course. All Frenchmen and all Canadians know him, or know of him, but he is far from here, and we shall not tell him that we have a young American prisoner. The chevalier is a great soldier and the bravest of men, but he has one fault. He does not hate the English and the Bostonnais enough."

Robert was not bound, but his arms and snowshoes had been taken and the Indians were all about him. There was no earthly chance of escape. With the wisdom of the wise he resigned himself at once to his situation, awaiting a better moment.

"I'm at your command," he said politely to Langlade.

The French leader laughed, partly in appreciation.

"You show intelligence," he said. "You do not resist, when you see that resistance is impossible."

Robert settled himself into a more comfortable position by the fire. His head still ached, but it was growing easier. He knew that it was best to assume a careless and indifferent tone.

"I'm not ready to leave you now," he said, "but I shall go later."

Langlade laughed again, and then directed two of the Indians to hunt more wood. They obeyed. Robert saw that they never questioned his leadership, and he saw anew how the French partisans established themselves so thoroughly in the Indian confidence. The others threw away more snow, making a comparatively large area of cleared ground, and, when the wood was brought, they built a great fire, around which all of them sat and ate heartily from their packs.

Langlade gave Robert food which he forced himself to eat, although he was not hungry. He judged that the French partisan, who could be cruel enough on occasion, had some object in treating him well for the present, and he was not one to disturb such a welcome frame of mind. His weapons and the extra rifle of Garay that they had brought with them, had already been divided among the warriors, who, pleased with the reward, were content to wait.

The night was spent at the captured camp, and in the morning the entire party, Robert included, started on snowshoes almost due north. The young prisoner felt a sinking of the heart, when his face was turned away from his own people, and he began an unknown captivity. He had been certain at first of escape, but it did not seem so sure now. In former wars many prisoners taken on raids into Canada had never been heard of again, and when he reflected in cold blood he knew that the odds were heavy against a successful flight. Yet there was Tayoga. His warning shot had enabled the Onondaga to evade the band, and his comrade would never desert him. All his surpassing skill and tenacity would be devoted to his aid. In that lay his hope.

They pressed on toward the north as fast as they could go, and when night came they were all exhausted, but they ate heavily again and Robert received his share. Langlade continued to treat him kindly, though he still had the feeling that the partisan, if it served him, would be fully as cruel as the Indians. At night, although they built big fires, Langlade invariably posted a strong watch, and Robert noticed also that he usually shared it, or a part of it, from which habit he surmised that the partisan had received the name of the Owl. He had hoped that Tayoga might have a chance to rescue him in the dark, but he saw now that the vigilance was too great.

He hid his intense disappointment and kept as cheerful a face as he could. Langlade, the only white man in the Indian band, was drawn to him somewhat by the mere fact of racial kinship, and the two frequently talked together in the evenings in what was a sort of compulsory friendliness, Robert in this manner picking up scraps of information which when welded together amounted to considerable, being thus confirmed in his belief that Willet with the letter had reached the lake in time. St. Luc with a formidable force had undertaken a swift march on Albany, but the town had been put in a position of defence, and St. Luc's vanguard had been forced to retreat by a large body of rangers after a severe conflict. As the success of the chevalier's daring enterprise had depended wholly on surprise, he had then withdrawn northward.

But Robert could not find out by any kind of questions where St. Luc was, although he learned that Garay had never returned to Albany and that Hendrik Martinus had made an opportune flight. Langlade, who was thoroughly a wilderness rover, talked freely and quite boastfully of the French power, which he deemed all pervading and invincible. Despite the battle at Lake George the fortunes of war had gone so far in favour of France and Canada and against Britain and the Bostonnais. When the great campaign was renewed in the spring more and bigger victories would crown French valour. The Owl grew expansive as he talked to the youth, his prisoner.

"The Marquis de Montcalm is coming to lead all our armies," he said, "and he is a far abler soldier than Dieskau. You really did us a great service when you captured the Saxon. Only a Frenchman is fit to lead Frenchmen, and under a mighty captain we will crush you. The Bostonnais are not the equal of the French in the forest. Save a few like Willet, and Rogers, the English and Americans do not learn the ways of woods warfare, nor do you make friends with the Indians as we do."

"That is true in the main," responded Robert, "but we shall win despite it. Both the English and the English Colonials have the power to survive defeat. Can the French and the Canadians do as well?"

Langlade could not be shaken in his faith. He saw nothing but the most brilliant victories, and not only did he boast of French power, but he gloried even more in the strength of the Indian hordes, that had come and that were coming in ever increasing numbers to the help of France. Only the Hodenosaunee stood aloof from Québec, and he believed the Great League even yet would be brought over to his side.

Robert argued with the Owl, but he made no impression upon him. Meanwhile they continued to march north by west.

Chapter 8

Before Montcalm

The Owl, with his warriors and captive, descended in time into the low country in the northwest. They, too, had been on snowshoes, but now they discarded them, since they were entering a region in which little snow had fallen, the severity of the weather abating greatly. Robert was still treated well, though guarded with the utmost care. The Indians, who seemed to be from some tribe about the Great Lakes, did not speak any dialect he knew, and, if they understood English, they did not use it. He was compelled to do all his talking with the Owl who, however, was not at all taciturn. Robert saw early that while a wonderful woodsman and a born partisan leader, he was also a Gascon, vain, boastful and full of words. He tried to learn from him something about his possible fate, but he could obtain no hint, until they had been travelling more than three weeks, and Langlade had been mellowed by an uncommonly good supper of tender game, which the Indians had cooked for him.

"You've been trying to draw that information out of me ever since you were captured," he said. "You were indirect and clever about it, but I noticed it. I, Charles Langlade, have perceptions, you must understand. If I do live in the woods I can read the minds of white men."

"I know you can," said Robert, smilingly. "I observed from the first that you had an acute intellect."

"Your judgment does you credit, my young friend. I did not tell you what I was going to do with you, because I did not know myself. I know more about you than you think I do. One of my warriors was with Tandakora in several of his battles with you and Willet, that mighty hunter whom the Indians call the Great Bear, and Tayoga, the Onondaga, who is probably following on our trail in the hope of rescuing you. I have also heard of you from others. Oh, as I tell you,

I, Charles Langlade, take note of all things. You are a prisoner of importance. I would not give you to Tandakora, because he would burn you, and a man does not burn valuable goods. I would not send you to St. Luc, because, being a generous man, he might take some foolish notion to exchange you, or even parole you. I would not give you to the Marquis Duquesne at Quebec, because then I might lose my pawn in the game, and, in any event, the Marquis Duquesne is retiring as Governor General of New France."

"Is that true? I have met him. He seemed to me to be a great man."

"Perhaps he is, but he was too haughty and proud for the powerful men who dwelt at Quebec, and who control New France. I have heard something of your appearance at the capital with the Great Bear and the Onondaga, and of what chanced at Bigot's ball, and elsewhere. Ah, you see, as I told you, I, Charles Langlade, know all things! But to return, the Marquis Duquesne gives way to the Marquis de Vaudreuil. Oh, that was accomplished some time ago, and perhaps you know of it. So, I do not wish to give you to the Marquis de Vaudreuil. I might wait and present you to the Marquis de Montcalm when he comes, but that does not please me, either, and thus I have about decided to present you to the Dove."

"The Dove! Who is the Dove?"

Langlade laughed with intense enjoyment.

"The Dove," he replied, "is a woman, none other than Madame de Langlade herself, a Huron. You English do not marry Indian women often—and yet Colonel William Johnson has taken a Mohawk to wife—but we French know them and value them. Do not think to have an easy and careless jailer when you are put in the hands of the Dove. She will guard you even more zealously than I, Charles Langlade, and you will notice that I have neither given you any opportunity to escape nor your friend, Tayoga, the slightest chance to rescue you."

"It is true, Monsieur Langlade. I've abandoned any such hope on the march, although I may elude you later."

"The Dove, as I told you, will attend to that. But it will be a pretty play of wits, and I don't mind the test. I'm aware that you have intelligence and skill, but the Dove, though a woman, possesses the wit of a great chief, and I'll match her against you."

There was a further abatement of the weather, and they reached a region where there was no snow at all. Warm winds blew from the direction of the Great Lakes and the band travelled fast through a land in which the game almost walked up to their rifles to be killed, such plenty causing the Indians, as usual, now that they were not on the war path, to feast prodigiously before huge fires, Langlade often joining them, and showing that he was an adept in Indian customs.

One evening, just as they were about to light the fire, the warrior who had been posted as sentinel at the edge of the forest gave a signal and a few moments later a tall, spare figure in a black robe with a belt about the waist appeared. Robert's heart gave a great leap. The wearer of the black robe was an elderly man with a thin face, ascetic and high. The captive recognized him at once. It was Father Philibert Drouillard, the priest, whose life had already crossed his more than once, and it was not strange to see him there, as the French priests roamed far through the great wilderness of North America, seeking to save the souls of the savages.

Langlade, when he beheld Father Drouillard, sprang at once to his feet, and Robert also arose quickly. The priest saw young Lennox, but he did not speak to him just yet, accepting the food that the Owl offered him, and sitting down with his weary feet to the fire that had now been lighted.

"You have travelled far, Father?" said Langlade, solicitously.

"From the shores of Lake Huron. I have converts there, and I must see that they do not grow weak in the faith."

"All men, red and white, respect Philibert Drouillard. Why are you alone, Father?"

"A runner from the Christian village came with me until yesterday. Then I sent him back, because I would not keep him too long from his people. I can go the rest of the way alone, as it will be but a few days before I meet a French force."

Then he turned to Robert for the first time.

"And you, my son," he said, "I am sorry it has fared thus with you."

"It has not gone badly, Father," said Robert. "Monsieur de Langlade has treated me well. I have naught to complain of save that I'm a prisoner."

"It is a good lad, Charles Langlade," said the priest to the partisan, "and I am glad he has suffered no harm at your hands. What do you purpose to do with him?"

"It is my present plan to take him to the village in which Madame Langlade, otherwise the Dove, abides. He will be her prisoner until a further plan develops, and you know how well she watches."

A faint smile passed over the thin face of the priest.

"It is true, Charles Langlade," he said. "That which escapes the eyes of the Dove is very small, but I would take the lad with me to Montreal."

"Nay, Father, that cannot be. I am second to nobody in respect for Holy Church, and for you, Father Drouillard, whose good deeds are known to all, and whose bad deeds are none, but those who fight the war must use their judgment in fighting it, and the prisoners are theirs."

Father Drouillard sighed.

"It is so, Charles Langlade," he said, "but, as I have said, the prisoner is a good youth. I have met him before, as I told you, and I would save him. You know not what may happen in the Indian village, if you chance to be away."

"The Dove will have charge of him. She can be trusted."

"And yet I would take him with me to Montreal. He will give his parole that he will not attempt to escape on the way. It is the custom for prisoners to be ransomed. I will send to you from Montreal five golden louis for him."

Langlade shook his head.

"Ten golden louis," said Father Drouillard.

"Nay, Father, it is no use," said the partisan. "I cannot be tempted to exchange him for money."

"Fifteen golden louis, Charles Langlade, though I may have to borrow from the funds of the Church to send them to you."

"I respect your motive, Father, but 'tis impossible. This is a prisoner of great value and I must use him as a pawn in the game of war. He was taken fairly and I cannot give him up."

Again Father Drouillard sighed, and this time heavily.

"I would save you from captivity, Mr. Lennox," he said, "but, as you see, I cannot."

Robert was much moved.

"I thank you, Father Drouillard, for your kind intentions," he said. "It may be that some day I shall have a chance to repay them. Meanwhile, I do not dread the coming hospitality of Madame Langlade."

The priest shook his head sadly.

"It is a great and terrible war," he said, "though I cannot doubt that France will prevail, but I fear for you, my son, a captive in the vast wilderness. Although you are an enemy and a heretic I have only good feeling for you, and I know that the great Chevalier, St. Luc, also regards you with favour."

"Know you anything of St. Luc?" asked Robert eagerly.

"Only that the expedition he was to lead against Albany has turned back and that he has gone to Canada to fight under the banner of Montcalm, when he comes with the great leaders, De Levis, Bourlamaque and the others."

"I thought I might meet him."

"Not here, with Charles Langlade."

The priest spent the night with them and in the morning, after giving them his blessing, captors and captive alike, he departed on his long and solitary journey to Montreal.

"A good man," said Robert, as he watched his tall, thin figure disappear in the surrounding forest.

"Truly spoken," said the Owl. "I am little of a churchman myself, the forest and the war trail please me better, but the priests are a great prop to France in the New World. They carry with them the authority of His Majesty, King Louis."

A week later they reached a small Indian village on Lake Ontario where the Owl at present made his abode, and in the largest lodge of which his patient spouse, the Dove, was awaiting him. She was young, much taller than the average Indian woman, and, in her barbaric fashion, quite handsome. But her face was one of the keenest and most alert Robert had ever seen. All the trained observation of countless ancestors seemed stored in her and now he understood why Langlade had boasted so often and so warmly of her skill as a guard. She regarded him with a cold eye as she listened attentively to her husband's instructions, and, for the remainder of that winter and afterward, she obeyed them with a thoroughness beyond criticism.

The village included perhaps four hundred souls, of whom about a hundred were warriors. Langlade was king and Madame Langlade, otherwise the Dove, was queen, the two ruling with absolute sovereignty, their authority due to their superior intelligence and will and to the service they rendered to the little state, because a state it was, organized completely in all its parts, although composed of only a few hundred human beings. In the bitter weather that came again, Langlade directed the hunting in the adjacent forest and the fishing conducted on the great lake. He also made presents from time to time of gorgeous beads or of huge red or yellow blankets that had been sent from Montreal. Robert could not keep from admiring his diplomacy and tact, and now he understood more thoroughly than ever how the French partisans made themselves such favourites with the wild Indians.

His own position in the village was tentative. Langlade still seemed uncertain what to do with him, and held him meanwhile for a possible reward of great value. He was never allowed to leave the cluster of tepees for the forest, except with the warriors, but he took part in the fishing on the lake, being a willing worker there, because idleness grew terribly irksome, and, when he had nothing to do, he chafed over his long captivity. He slept in a small tepee built against that of Monsieur and Madame Langlade, and from which there was no egress save through theirs.

He was enclosed only within walls of skin, and he believed that he might have broken a way through them, but he felt that the eyes of the Dove were always on him. He even had the impression that she was watching him while he slept, and sometimes he dreamed that she was fanged and clawed like a tigress.

Langlade went away once, being gone a long time, and while he was absent the Dove redoubled her watchfulness. Robert's singular impression that her eyes were always on him was strengthened, and these eyes were increased to the hundred of Argus and more. It became so oppressive that he was always eager to go out with the warriors in their canoes for the fishing. On Lake Ontario he was sure the eyes of the Dove could not reach him, but the work was arduous and often perilous. The great lake was not to be treated lightly. Often it took toll of the Indians who lived around its shores. Winter storms came up suddenly, the waves rolled like those of the sea, freezing spray dashed over them, and it required a supreme exertion of both skill and strength to keep the light canoes from being swamped.

Yet Robert was always happier on water than on land. On shore, confined closely and guarded zealously, his imaginative temperament suffered and he became moody and depressed, but on the lakes, although still a captive, he felt the winds of freedom. When the storms came and the icy blasts swept down upon them he responded, body and soul. Relief and freedom were to be found in the struggle with the elements and he always went back to shore refreshed and stronger of spirit and flesh. He also had a feeling that Tayoga might come by way of the lake, and when he was with the little Indian fleet he invariably watched the watery horizon for a lone canoe, but he never saw any.

The absence of news from his friends, and from the world to which they belonged, was the most terrible burden of all. If the Indians had news they told him none. He seemed to have vanished completely. But, however numerous may have been his moments of despondency, he was not made of the stuff that yields. The flexible steel always rebounded. He took thorough care of his health and strength. In his close little tepee he flexed and tensed his muscles and went through physical exercises every night and morning, but it was on the lake in the fishing, where the Indians grew to recognize his help, that he achieved most. Fighting the winds, the water and the cold, he felt his muscles harden and his chest enlarge, and he would say to himself that when the spring came and he escaped he would be more fit for the life of a free forest runner than he had ever been before. Langlade, when he returned, took notice of his increased size and strength and did not withhold approval.

"I like any prisoner of mine to flourish," he laughed. "The more superior you become the greater will be the reward for me when I dispose of you. You have found the Dove all I promised you she should be, haven't you, Monsieur Lennox?"

"All and more," replied Robert. "Although she may be out of sight I feel that her eyes are always on me, and this is true of the night as well as the day."

"A great woman, the Dove, and a wife to whom I give all credit. If it should come into the king's mind to call me to Versailles and bestow upon me some kind of an accolade perhaps Madame Langlade would not feel at home in the great palace nor at the Grand Trianon, nor even at the Little Trianon, and maybe I wouldn't either. But since no such idea will enter His Majesty's mind, and I have no desire to leave the great forests, the Dove is a perfect wife for me. She is the true wilderness helpmate, accomplished in all the arts of the life I live and love, and with the eye and soul of a warrior. I repeat, young Monsieur Lennox, where could I find a wife more really sublime?"

"Nowhere, Monsieur Langlade. The more I see you two together the more nearly I think you are perfectly matched."

The Owl seemed pleased with the recognition of his marital felicity, and grew gracious, dropping some crumbs of information for Robert. He had been to Montreal and the arrival of the great soldier, the Marquis de Montcalm, with fresh generals and fresh troops from France, was expected daily at Quebec. The English, although their fleets were larger, could not intercept them, and it was now a certainty that the spring campaign would sweep over Albany and almost to New York. He spoke with so much confidence, in truth with such an absolute certainty, that Robert's heart sank and then came back again with a quick rebound.

After a winter that had seemed to the young captive an age, spring came with a glorious blossoming and blooming. The wilderness burst into green and the great lake shining in the sun became peaceful and friendly. Warm winds blew out of the west and the blood flowed more swiftly in human veins. But spring passed and summer came. Then Langlade announced that he would depart with the best of the warriors, and that Robert would go with him, although he refused absolutely to say where or for what purpose.

Robert's joy was dimmed in nowise by his ignorance of his destination. He had not found the remotest chance to escape while in the village, but it might come on the march, and there was also a relief and pleasant excitement in entering the wilderness again. He joyously made ready, the Dove gave her lord and equal, not her master, a Spartan farewell, and the formidable band, Robert in the centre, plunged into the forest.

When the great mass of green enclosed them he felt a mighty surge of hope. His imaginative temperament was on fire. A chance for him would surely come. Tayoga might be hidden in the thickets. Action brought renewed courage. Langlade, who was watching him, smiled.

"I read your mind, young Monsieur Lennox," he said. "Have I not told you that I, Charles Langlade, have the perceptions? Do I not see and interpret everything?"

"Then what do you see and interpret now?"

"A great hope in your heart that you will soon bid us farewell. You think that when we are deep in the forest it will not be difficult to elude our watch. And yet you could not escape when we were going through this same forest to the village. Now why do you think it will be easier when you are going through it again, but away?"

"The Dove is not at the end of the march. Her eyes will no longer be upon me."

The Owl laughed deeply and heartily.

"You're a lad of sense," he said, "when you lay such a tribute at the feet of that incomparable woman, that model wife, that true helpmate in every sense of the word. Why should you be anxious to leave us? I could have you adopted into the tribe, and you know the ceremony of adoption is sacred with the Indians. And let me whisper another little fact in your ear which will surely move you. The Dove has a younger sister, so much like her that they are twins in character if not in years. She will soon be of marriageable age, and she shall be reserved for you. Think! Then you will be my brother-in-law and the brother-in-law of the incomparable Dove."

"No! No!" exclaimed Robert hastily.

Now the laughter of the Owl was uncontrollable. His face writhed and his sides shook.

"A lad does not recognize his own good!" he exclaimed, "or is it bashfulness? Nay, don't be afraid, young Monsieur Lennox! Perhaps I could get the Dove to intercede for you!"

Robert was forced to smile.

"I thank you," he said, "but I am far from the marriageable age myself."

"Then the Dove and I are not to have you for a brother-in-law?" said Langlade. "You show little appreciation, young Monsieur Lennox, when it is so easy for you to become a member of such an interesting family."

Robert was confirmed in his belief that there was much of the wild man in the Owl, who in many respects had become more Indian than the Indians. He was a splendid trailer, a great hunter, and the hardships of the forest were nothing to him. He read every sign of the wilderness and yet he retained all that was French also, lightness of manner, gayety, quick wit and a politeness that never failed. It is likely that the courage and tenacity of the French leaders were never shown to better advantage than in the long fight they made for dominion in North America. Despite the fact that he was an enemy, and his belief that Langlade could be ruthless, on occasion, Robert was compelled to like him.

The journey, the destination yet unknown to him, was long, but it was not tedious to the young prisoner. He watched the summer progress and the colours deepen and he was cheered continually by the hope of escape, a fact that Langlade recognized and upon which he commented in a detached manner, from time to time. Now and then the leader himself went ahead with a scout or two and one morning he said to Robert:

"I saw something in the forest last night."

"The forest contains much," said Robert.

"But this was of especial interest to you. It was the trace of a footstep, and I am convinced it was made by your friend Tayoga, the Onondaga. Doubtless he is seeking to effect your escape."

Robert's heart gave a leap, and there was a new light in his eyes, of which the shrewd Owl took notice.

"I have heard of the surpassing skill of the Onondaga," he continued, "but I, Charles Langlade, have skill of my own. It will be some time before we arrive at the place to which we are going, and I lay you a wager that Tayoga does not rescue you."

"I have no money, Monsieur Langlade," said Robert, "and if I had I could not accept a wager upon such a subject."

"Then we'll let it be mental, wholly. My skill is matched against the combined knowledge of Tayoga and yourself. He'll never be able, no matter how dark the night, to get near our camp and communicate with you."

Although Robert hoped and listened often in the dusk for the sound of a signal from Tayoga, Langlade made good his boast. The two were able to establish no communication. It was soon proved that he was in the forest near them, one of the warriors even catching a sufficient glimpse of his form for a shot, which, however, went wild. The Onondaga did not reply, and, despite the impossibility of reaching him, Robert was cheered by the knowledge that he was near. He had a faithful and powerful friend who would help him some day, be it soon or late.

The summer was well advanced when Langlade announced that their journey was done.

"Before night," he said triumphantly, "we will be in the camp of the Marquis de Montcalm, and we will meet the great soldier himself. I, Charles Langlade, told you that it would be so, and it is so."

"What, Montcalm near?" exclaimed Robert, aflame with interest.

"Look at the sky above the tops of those trees in the east and you will see a smudge of smoke, beneath which stand the tents of the French army."

"The French army here! And what is it doing in the wilderness?"

"That, young Monsieur Lennox, rests on the knees of the gods. I have some curiosity on the subject myself."

An hour or two later they came within sight of the French camp, and Robert saw that it was a numerous and powerful force for time and place. The tents stood in rows, and soldiers, both French and Canadian, were everywhere, while many Indian warriors were on the outskirts. A large white marquee near the centre he was sure was that of the commander-in-chief, and he was eager to see at once the famous Montcalm, of whom he was hearing so much. But to his intense disappointment, Langlade went into camp with the Indians.

"The Marquis de Montcalm is a great man," he said, "the commander-in-chief of all the forces of His Majesty, King Louis, in North America, and even I, Charles Langlade, will not approach him without ceremony. We will rest in the edge of the forest, and when he hears that I have come he will send for me, because he will want to know many things which none other can tell him. And it may be, young Monsieur Lennox, that, in time, he will wish to see you also."

So Robert waited with as much patience as he could muster, although he slept but little that night, the noises in the great French camp and his own curiosity keeping him awake. What was Montcalm doing so far from the chief seats of the French power in Canada, and did the English and Americans know that he was here?

Curiously enough he had little apprehension for himself, it was rather a feeling of joy that he had returned to the world of great affairs. Soon he would know what had been occurring during the long winter when he was buried in an Indian village, and he might even hear of Willet. Toward dawn he slept a little, and after daylight he was awakened by Langlade who was as assured and talkative as usual.

"It may be, my gallant young prisoner," he said, ruffling and strutting, "that I am about to lose you, but if it is so it will be for value received. I, Charles Langlade, have seen the great Marquis de Montcalm, but it was an equal speaking to an equal. It was last night in his grand marquee, where he sat surrounded by his trusted lieutenants, De Levis, St. Luc, Bourlamaque, Coulon de Villiers and the others. But I was not daunted at all. I repeat that it was an equal speaking to an equal, and the Marquis was pleased to commend me for the work I have already done for France."

"And St. Luc was there?"

"He was. The finest figure of them all. A brave and generous man and a great leader. He stood at the right hand of the Marquis de Montcalm, while I talked and he listened with attention, because the Chevalier de St. Luc is always willing to learn from others. No false pride about him! And the Marquis de Montcalm is like him. I gave the commander-in-chief much excellent advice which he accepted with gratitude, and in return for you, whom he expects to put to use, he has raised me in rank, and has extended my authority over the western tribes. Ah, I knew that you were a prize when I captured you, and I was wise to save you as a pawn."

"How can I be of any value to the Marquis de Montcalm?"

"That is to be seen. He knows his own plans best. You are to come with me at once into his presence."

Robert was immediately in a great stir. He straightened out, and, with his hands, brushed his own clothing, smoothed his hair, intending, with his usual desire for neatness, to make the best possible appearance before the French leader.

After breakfast Langlade took him to the great marquee in which Montcalm sat, as the morning was cool, and when their names had been taken in a young officer announced that they might enter, the officer, to Robert's great surprise, being none other than De Galissonnière, who showed equal amazement at meeting him there. The Frenchman gave him a hearty grasp of the hand in English fashion, but they did not have time to say anything.

Robert, walking by the side of Langlade, entered the great tent with some trepidation, and beheld a swarthy man of middle years, in the uniform of a general of France, giving orders to two officers who stood respectfully at attention. Neither of the officers was St. Luc, nor were they among those whom Robert had seen at Quebec. He surmised, however, that they were De Levis and Bourlamaque, and he learned soon that he was right. Langlade paused until Montcalm was ready to speak to him, and Robert stood in silence at his side. Montcalm finished what he had to say and turned his eyes upon the young prisoner. His countenance was mild, but Robert felt that his gaze was searching.

"And this, Captain Langlade," he said, "is the youth of whom you were speaking?"

So the Owl had been made a captain, and the promotion had been one of his rewards. Robert was not sorry.

"It is the one, sir," replied Langlade, "young Monsieur Robert Lennox. He has been a prisoner in my village all the winter, and he has as friends some of the most powerful people in the British Colonies."

Montcalm continued to gaze at Robert as if he would read his soul.

"Sit down, Mr. Lennox," he said, not unkindly, motioning him to a little stool. Robert took the indicated seat and so quick is youth to warm to courtesy that he felt respect and even liking for the Marquis, official and able enemy though he knew him to be. De Levis and Bourlamaque also were watching him with alert gaze, but they said nothing.

"I hear," continued Montcalm, with a slight smile, "that you have not suffered in Captain Langlade's village, and that you have adapted yourself well to wild life."

"I've had much experience with the wilderness," said Robert. "Most of my years have been passed there, and it was easy for me to live as Captain Langlade lived. I've no complaint to make of his treatment, though I will say that he has guarded me well."

Montcalm laughed.

"It agrees with Captain Langlade's own account," he said. "I suppose that one must be born, or at least pass his youth in it, to get the way of this vast wilderness. We of old Europe, where everything has been ruled and measured for many centuries, can have no conception of it until we see it, and even then we do not understand it. Although with an army about me I feel lost in so much forest. But enough of that. It is of yourself and not of myself that I wish to speak. I have heard good reports of you from one of my own officers, who, though he has been opposed to you many times, nevertheless likes you."

"The Chevalier de St. Luc!"

"Aye, the Chevalier de St. Luc. I know, also, that you have been in the councils of some of the Colonial leaders. You are a friend of Sir William Johnson."

"Colonel William Johnson?"

"No, Sir William Johnson. In reward for the affair at Lake George, in which our Dieskau was unfortunate, he has been made a baronet by the British king."

"I am glad."

"And doubtless Sir William is also. You know him well, I understand, and he was still at the lake when you left on the journey that led to your capture."

Robert was silent.

"I have not asked you to answer," continued Montcalm, "but I assume that it is so. His army, although it was victorious in the battle there, did not advance. There was much disagreement among the governors of the British Colonies. The provinces could not be induced to act together?"

Robert was still silent.

"Again I say I am not asking you to answer, but your silence confirms the truth of our reports."

Robert flushed, and a warm reply trembled on his lips, but he restrained the words. A swift smile passed over the dark face of Montcalm.

"You see, Mr. Lennox," he continued, "I am not asking you to say anything, but there was great disappointment among the British Colonials because there was no advance after the battle at the lake. It has also cooled the enthusiasm of the Iroquois, many of whom have gone home and who perhaps will take no further part in the war as the allies of the English."

Again Robert flushed and again he bit back the hot reply. He looked uneasily at De Levis and Bourlamaque, but their faces expressed nothing. Then Montcalm suddenly changed the subject.

"I am going to make you a very remarkable offer," he said, "and do not think for a moment it is going to imply any change of colours on your part, or the least suspicion of treason, which I could not ask of the gentleman you obviously are. I request of you your parole, your word of honour that you will not take any further part in this war."

"I can't do it! As I have often told Captain Langlade, I intend to escape."

"That is impossible. If you could not do so when you were in Captain Langlade's village, you have no chance at all now that you are surrounded by an army. But since you will not give me your parole it will become necessary to keep you as a prisoner of war, and to send you to a safe place."

"Many of our people in this and former wars with the French have been held prisoners in the Province of Quebec. I know somewhat of the city of Quebec, and it is not wholly an unpleasant place."

"I did not have Quebec, either the province or the city, in mind so far as concerns you, Mr. Lennox. Three of our ships are to return shortly to France, and, not wishing to give us your parole, you are to go to France."

"To France?"

"Yes, to France. Where else? And you should rejoice. It is a fair and glorious land. And I have heard there is a spirit in you, Mr. Lennox, which is almost French, a kindred touch, a Gallic salt and savour, so to speak."

"I'm wholly American and British."

"Perhaps there are others who know you better than you know yourself. I repeat, there is about you a French finish. Why should you deny it? You should be proud of it. We are the oldest of the great civilized nations, and the first in culture. Your stay in France should be very pleasant. You can drink there at the fountain of ancient culture and glory. The wilderness is magnificent in its way, but high civilization is magnificent also in its own and another way. You can see Paris, the city of light, the centre of the world, and you can behold the splendid court of His Majesty, King Louis. That should appeal to a young man of taste and discernment."

Robert felt a thrill and his pulses leaped, but the thrill lasted only a moment. It was clearly impossible that he should go even as a prisoner, though a willing one, to France, and he did not see any reason why the Marquis de Montcalm should take any personal interest in his future. But responding invariably to the temperature about him his manner was now as polite as that of the French general.

"You have my thanks, sir," he said, "for the kindly way in which you offer to treat a prisoner, but it is impossible for me to go to France, unless you should choose to send me there by sheer force."

The slight smile passed again over the face of the Marquis de Montcalm.

"I fancied, young sir," he said, "that this would be your answer, and, being what it is, I cannot say that it has lowered you aught in my esteem. For the present, you abide with us."

Robert bowed. Montcalm inspired in him a certain liking, and a decided respect. Then, still under the escort of Langlade, he withdrew.

Chapter 9

The Sign of the Bear

Robert returned with Langlade to the partisan's camp at the edge of the forest adjoining that of the main French army, where the Indian warriors had lighted fires and were cooking steaks of the deer. He was disposed to be silent, but Langlade as usual chattered volubly, discoursing of French might and glory, but saying nothing that would indicate to his prisoner the meaning of the present military array in the forest.

Robert did not hear more than half of the Owl's words, because he was absorbed in those of Montcalm, which still lingered in his mind. Why should the Marquis wish to send him to France, and to have him treated, when he was there, more as a guest than as a prisoner? Think as he would he could find no answer to the question, but the Owl evidently had been impressed by his reception from Montcalm, as he treated him now with distinguished courtesy. He also seemed particularly anxious to have the good opinion of the lad who had been so long his prisoner.

"Have I been harsh to you?" he asked with a trace of anxiety in his tone. "Have I not always borne myself toward you as if you were an important prisoner of war? It is true I set the Dove as an invincible sentinel over you, but as a good soldier and loyal son of France I could do no less. Now, I ask you, Monsieur Robert Lennox, have not I, Charles Langlade, conducted myself as a fair and considerate enemy?"

"If I were to escape and be captured again, Captain Langlade, it is my sincere wish that you should be my captor the second time, even as you were the first."

The Owl was gratified, visibly and much, and then he announced a visitor. Robert sprang to his feet as he saw St. Luc approaching, and his heart throbbed as always when he was in the presence of this man. The chevalier was in a splendid uniform of white and silver unstained by the forest. His thick, fair hair was clubbed in a queue and powdered neatly, and a small sword, gold hilted, hung at his belt. He was the finest and most gallant figure that Robert had yet seen in the wilderness, the very spirit and essence of that brave and romantic France with which England and her colonies were fighting a duel to the death. And yet St. Luc always seemed to him too the soul of knightly chivalry, one to whom it was impossible for him to bear any hostility that was not merely official. His own hand went forward to meet the extended hand of the chevalier.

"We seem destined to meet many times, Mr. Lennox," said St. Luc, "in battle, and even under more pleasant conditions. I had heard that you were the prisoner of our great forest ranger, Captain Langlade, and that you would be received by our commander-in-chief, the Marquis de Montcalm."

"He made me a most extraordinary offer, that I go as a prisoner of war to Paris, but almost in the state of a guest."

"And you thought fit to decline, which was unwise in you, though to be expected of a lad of spirit. Sit down, Mr. Lennox, and we can have our little talk in ease and comfort. It may be that I have something to do with the proposition of the Marquis de Montcalm. Why not reconsider it and go to France? England is bound to lose the war in America. We have the energy and the knowledge. The Indian tribes are on our side. Even the powerful Hodenosaunee may come over to us in time, and at the worst it will become neutral. As a prisoner in France you will have no share in defeat, but perhaps that does not appeal to you."

"It does not, but I thank you, Chevalier de St. Luc, for your many kindnesses to me, although I don't understand them. Your solicitude for my welfare cannot but awake my gratitude, but it has been more than once a source of wonderment in my mind."

"Because you are a young and gallant enemy whom I would not see come to harm."

Robert felt, however, that the chevalier was not stating the true reason, and he felt also with equal force that he would keep secret in the face of all questions, direct or indirect, the motives impelling him. St. Luc asked him about his life in the Indian village with Langlade, and then came back presently to Paris and France, which he described more vividly than even Montcalm had done. He seemed to know the very qualities that would appeal most to Robert, and, despite himself, the lad felt his heart leap more than once. Paris appeared in deeper and more glowing colours than ever as the city of light and soul, but he was firm in his resolution not to go there as a prisoner, if choice should be left to him. St. Luc himself became enamoured of his own words as he spoke. His eyes glowed, and his tone took on great warmth and enthusiasm. But presently he ceased and when he laughed a little his laugh showed a slight tone of disappointment.

"I do not move you, Mr. Lennox," he said. "I can see by your eye that your will is hardening against my words, and yet I could wish that you would listen to me. You will believe me when I say I mean you only good."

"I am wholly sure of it, Monsieur de St. Luc," said Robert, trying to speak lightly, "but a long while ago I formed a plan to escape, and if I should go to France it would interfere with it seriously. It would not be so easy to leave Paris, and come back to the province of New York, and while I am in North America it is always possible. I informed Captain Langlade that I meant to escape, and now I repeat it to you."

The chevalier laughed.

"Time will tell," he said. "Your ambition to leave is a proper and patriotic motive on your part, and I should be the last to accuse it. But 'tis not easy of accomplishment. I betray no military secret when I say our army marches quickly and you will, of necessity, march with us. Captain Langlade will still keep a vigilant watch over you, and you may be in readiness to depart tomorrow morning."

Robert slept that night in Langlade's little section of the camp, but, before he went to sleep, he spent much time wondering which way they would go when the dawn came. Evidently no attack upon Albany was meant, as they were too far west for such a venture, and he had reason to believe, also, that with the coming of spring the Colonials would be in such posture of defence that Montcalm himself would hesitate at such a task. He made another attempt to draw the information from Langlade, but failed utterly. Garrulous as he was otherwise, the French partisan would give no hint of his general's plans. Yet he and his warriors made obvious preparations for battle, and, before Robert went to sleep, a gigantic figure stalked into the firelight and regarded him with a grim gaze. The young prisoner's back was turned at the moment, but he seemed to feel that fierce look, beating like a wind upon his head, and, turning around, he looked full into the eyes of Tandakora.

The huge Ojibway was more huge than ever. Robert was convinced that he was the largest man he had ever seen, not only the tallest, but the broadest, and the heaviest, and his very lack of clothing—he wore only a belt, breech cloth, leggings and moccasins—seemed to increase his size. His vast shoulders, chest and arms were covered with paint, and the scars of old wounds, the whole giving to him the appearance of some primeval giant, sinister and monstrous. He carried a fine, new rifle of French make and two double barrelled pistols; a tomahawk and knife swung from his belt.

Robert, nevertheless, met that full gaze firmly. He shut from his mind what he might have had to suffer from Tandakora had the Ojibway held him a captive in the forest, but here he was not Tandakora's prisoner, and he was in the midst of the French army. Centring all his will and soul into the effort he stared straight into the evil eyes of the Indian, until those of his antagonist were turned away.

"The Owl has a prisoner whom I know," said Tandakora to Langlade.

"Aye, a sprightly lad," replied the partisan. "I took him before the winter came, and I've been holding him at our village on Lake Ontario."

"It was he who, with the Onondaga, Tayoga, and the hunter, Willet, whom we call the Great Bear, carried the letters from Corlear at New York to Onontio at Quebec. The nations of the Hodenosaunee call him Dagaeoga, and he is a danger to us. I would buy him from you. I will send to you for him fifty of the finest buffalo robes taken from the great western plains."

"Not for fifty buffalo robes, Tandakora, no matter how fine they are."

"Ten packs of the finest beaver skins, fifty in each pack."

"It's no use to bid for him, Tandakora. I don't sell captives. Moreover, he has passed out of my hands. I have had my reward for him. His fate rests now with the Chevalier de St. Luc and the Marquis de Montcalm."

The Ojibway's face showed foiled malice. "It is a snake that the Owl warms in his bosom," he said, and strode away. The partisan followed him with observant eyes.

"It is evident that the Ojibway chief bears you no love, young Monsieur Lennox," he said. "Now that you have served the purposes for which I held you I wish you no harm, and so I bid you beware of Tandakora."

"Your advice is good and well meant, and for it I thank you," said Robert; "but I've known Tandakora a long time. My friends and I have met him in several encounters and we've not had the worst of them."

"I judged so by his manner. All the more reason then why you should beware of him. I repeat the warning."

Robert was not bound, and he was permitted to roll himself in a blanket and sleep with his feet to the fire, an Indian on either side of him. Save where a space had been cleared for the French army, the primeval forest, heavy in the foliage of early spring, was all about them, and the wind that sang through the leaves united with the murmuring of a creek, beside which Langlade had pitched his camp.

Slumber was slow in coming to Robert. Too much had occurred for his faculties to slip away at once into oblivion. His interview with Montcalm, his meeting with St. Luc, and the appearance of Tandakora at the camp fire, stirred him mightily. Events were certainly marching, and, while he tried to coax slumber to come, he listened to the noises of the camp and the forest. Where the French tents were spread, men were softly singing songs of their ancient land, and beyond them sentinels in neat uniforms were walking back and forth among trees that had never beheld uniforms before.

The sounds sank gradually, but Robert did not yet sleep. He found a peculiar sort of interest in detaching these murmurs from one another, the stamp of impatient horses, the moving of arms, the last dying, notes of a song, the whisper of the creek's waters, and then, plainly separate from the others, he heard a faint, unmistakable swish, a noise that he knew, that of an arrow flying through the air. Langlade knew it too, and sprang up with an angry cry.

"Now, has some warrior got hold of whiskey to indulge in this madness?" he exclaimed.

The faint swish came a second time, and Robert, who had risen to his feet, saw two arrows standing upright in the earth not twenty feet away. Langlade saw them also and swore.

"They must have come in a wide curve overhead," he said, "or they would not be standing almost straight up in the earth, and that does not seem like the madness of liquor."

He looked suspiciously at the forest, in which Indian sentinels had been posted, but which, nevertheless, was so dark that a cunning form might pass there unseen.

"There is more in this than meets the eye," muttered the partisan, and drawing the arrows from the earth he examined them by the light of the fire. Robert stood by, silent, but his eyes fell on fresh marks with a knife, near the barb on each weapon, and the great pulse in his throat leaped. The yellow flame threw out in distinct relief what the knife had cut there, and he saw on each arrow the rude but unmistakable outline of a bear.

The Owl might not determine the meaning of the picture, but the captive comprehended it at once. It was the pride of Tayoga that he was of the clan of the Bear, of the nation Onondaga, of the great League of the Hodenosaunee, and here upon the arrows was his totem or sign of the Bear. It was a message and Robert knew that it was meant for him. Had ever a man a more faithful comrade? The Onondaga was still following in the hope of making a rescue, and he would follow as long as Robert was living. Once more the young prisoner's hopes of escape rose to the zenith.

"Now what do these marks mean?" said the partisan, looking at the arrows suspiciously.

"It was merely an intoxicated warrior shooting at the moon," replied Robert, innocently, "and the cuts signify nothing."

"I'm not so sure of that. I've lived long enough among the Indians to know they don't fire away good arrows merely for bravado, and these are planted so close together it must be some sort of a signal. It may have been intended for you."

Robert was silent, and the partisan did not ask him any further questions, but, being much disturbed, sent into the forest scouts, who returned presently, unable to find anything.

"It may or it may not have been a message," he said, speaking to Robert, in his usual garrulous fashion, "but I still incline to the opinion that it was, though I may never know what the message meant, but I, Charles Langlade, have not been called the Owl for nothing. If it refers to you then your chance of escape has not increased. I hold you merely for tonight, but I hold you tight and fast. Tomorrow my responsibility ceases, and you march in the middle of Montcalm's army."

Robert made no reply, but he was in wonderful spirits, and his elation endured. His senses, in truth, were so soothed by the visible evidence that his comrade was near that he fell asleep very soon and had no dreams. The French and Indian army began its march early the next morning, and Robert found himself with about a dozen other prisoners, settlers who had been swept up in its advance. They had been surprised in their cabins, or their fields, newly cleared, and could tell him nothing, but he noticed that the march was west.

He believed they were not far from Lake Ontario, and he had no doubt that Montcalm had prepared some fell stroke. His mind settled at last upon Oswego, where the Anglo-American forces had a post supposed to be strong, and he was smitten with a fierce and commanding desire to escape and take a warning. But he was compelled to eat his heart out without result. With French and Indians all about him he had not the remotest chance and, helpless, he was compelled to watch the Marquis de Montcalm march to what he felt was going to be a French triumph.

Swarms of Indian scouts and skirmishers preceded the army and

Canadian axmen cut a way for the artillery, but to Robert's great amazement these operations lasted only a short time. Almost before he could realize it they had emerged from the deep woods and he looked again upon the vast, shining reaches of Lake Ontario. Then he learned for the first time that Montcalm's army had come mostly in boats and in detachments, and was now united for attack. As he had surmised, Oswego, which the English and Americans had intended to be a great stronghold and rallying place in the west, was the menaced position.

Robert from a hill saw three forts before the French force, the largest standing upon a plateau of considerable elevation on the east bank of the river, which there flowed into the lake. It was shaped like a star, and the fortifications consisted of trunks of trees, sharpened at the ends, driven deep into the ground, and set as close together as possible. On the west side of the river was another fort of stone and clay, and four hundred yards beyond it was an unfinished stockade, so weak that its own garrison had named it in derision Rascal Fort. Some flat boats and canoes lay in the lake, and it was a man in one of these canoes who had been the first to learn of the approach of Montcalm's army, so slender had been the precautions taken by the officers in command of the forts.

"We have come upon them almost as if we had dropped from the clouds," said Langlade, exultingly, to Robert. "When they thought the Marquis de Montcalm was in Montreal, lo! he was here! It is the French who are the great leaders, the great soldiers and the great nation! Think you we would allow ourselves to be surprised as Oswego has been?"

Robert made no reply. His heart sank like a plummet in a pool. Already he heard the crackling fire of musketry from the Indians who, sheltered in the edge of the forest, were sending bullets against the stout logs of Fort Ontario, but which could offer small resistance to cannon. And while the sharpshooting went on, the French officers were planting the batteries, one of four guns directly on the strand. The work was continued at a great pace all through the night, and when Robert awoke from an uneasy sleep, in the morning, he saw that the French had mounted twenty heavy cannon, which soon poured showers of balls and grape and canister upon the log fort. He also saw St. Luc among the guns directing their fire, while Tandakora's Indians kept up an incessant and joyous yelling.

The defenders of the stockade maintained a fire from rifles and several small cannon, but it did little harm in the attacking army and Robert was soldier enough to know that the log walls could not hold.

While St. Luc sent in the fire from the batteries faster and faster, a formidable force of Canadians and Indians led by Rigaud, one of the best of Montcalm's lieutenants, crossed the river, the men wading in the water up to their waists, but holding their rifles over their heads.

Tandakora was in this band, shouting savagely, and so was Langlade, but Robert and the other prisoners, left under guard on the hill, saw everything distinctly. They had no hope whatever that the chief fort, or any of the forts, could hold out. Fragments of the logs were already flying in the air as the stream of cannon balls beat upon them. The garrison made a desperate resistance, but the cramped place was crowded with women—settlers' wives—as well as men, the commander was killed, and at last the white flag was hoisted on all the forts.

Then the Indians, intoxicated with triumph and the strong liquors they had seized, rushed in and began to ply the tomahawk. Montcalm, horrified, used every effort to stop the incipient butchery, and St. Luc, Bourlamaque and, in truth, all of his lieutenants, seconded him gallantly. Tandakora and his men were compelled to return their tomahawks to their belts, and then the French army was drawn around the captives, who numbered hundreds and hundreds.

It was another French and Indian victory like that over Braddock, though it was not marked by the destruction of an army, and Robert's heart sank lower and lower. He knew that it would be appalling news to Boston, to Albany and to New York. The Marquis de Montcalm had justified the reputation that preceded him. He had struck suddenly with lightning swiftness and with terrible effect. Not only this blow, but its guarantee of others to come, filled Robert's heart with fear for the future.

The sun sank upon a rejoicing army. The Indians were still yelling and dancing, and, though they were no longer allowed to sink their tomahawks in the heads of their defenceless foes, they made imaginary strokes with them, and shouted ferociously as they leaped and capered.

Robert was on the strand near the shore of the lake, and wearied by his long day of watching that which he wished least in the world to see, he sat down on a sand heap, and put his head in his hands. Peculiarly sensitive to atmosphere and surroundings, he was, for the moment, almost without hope. But he knew, even when he was in despair, that his courage would come back. It was one of the qualities of a temperament such as his that while he might be in the depths at one hour he would be on the heights at the next.

Several of the Indians, apparently those who had got at the liquor, were careering up and down the sands, showing every sign of the blood madness that often comes in the moment of triumph upon savage minds. Robert raised his face from his hands and looked to see if Tandakora was among them, but he caught no glimpse of the gigantic Ojibway. The French soldiers who were guarding the prisoners gazed curiously at the demoniac figures. They were of the battalions Bearn and Guienne and they had come newly from France. Plunged suddenly into the wilderness, such sights as they now beheld filled them with amazement, and often created a certain apprehension. They were not so sure that their wild allies were just the kind of allies they wanted.

The sun set lower upon the savage scene, casting a dark glow over the ruined forts, the troops, the leaping savages and the huddled prisoners. One of the Indians danced and bounded more wildly than all the rest. He was tall, but slim, apparently youthful, and he wore nothing except breech cloth, leggings and moccasins, his naked body a miracle of savage painting. Robert by and by watched him alone, fascinated by his extraordinary agility and untiring enthusiasm. His figure seemed to shoot up in the air on springs, and, with a glittering tomahawk, he slew and scalped an imaginary foe over and over again, and every time the blade struck in the air he let forth a shout that would have done credit to old Stentor himself. He ranged up and down the beach, and presently, when he was close to Robert, he grew more violent than ever, as if he were worked by some powerful mechanism that would not let him rest. He had all the appearance of one who had gone quite mad, and as he bounded near them, his tomahawk circling about his head, the French guards shrank back, awed, and, at the same time, not wishing to have any conflict with their red allies, who must be handled with the greatest care.

The man paused a moment before the young prisoner, whirled his tomahawk about his head and uttered a ferocious shout. Robert looked straight into the burning eyes, started violently and then became outwardly calm, though every nerve and muscle in him was keyed to the utmost tension. "To the lake!" exclaimed the Indian under his breath and then he danced toward the water.

Robert did not know at first what the words meant, and he waited in indecision, but he saw that the care of the guards, owing to the confusion, the fact that the battle was over, and the rejoicing for victory, was relaxed. It would seem, too, that escape at such a time and place was impossible, and that circumstance increased their inattention.

The youth watched the dancing warrior, who was now moving toward the water, over which the darkness of night had spread. But the lake was groaning with a wind from the north, and several canoes near the beach were bobbing up and down. The dancer paused a moment at the very edge of the water, and looked back at Robert. Then he advanced into the waves themselves.

All the young prisoner's indecision departed in a flash. The signal was complete and he understood. He sprang violently against the French soldier who stood nearest him and knocked him to the ground. Then with three or four bounds he was at the water's edge, leaping into the canoe, just as Tayoga settled himself into place there, and, seizing a paddle, pushed away with powerful shoves.

Robert nearly upset the canoe, but the Onondaga quickly made it regain its balance, and then they were out on the lake under the kindly veil of the night. The fugitive said nothing, he knew it was no time to speak, because Tayoga's powerful back was bending with his mighty efforts and the bullets were pattering in the water behind them. It was luck that the canoe was a large one, partaking more of the nature of a boat, as Robert could remain concealed on the bottom without tipping it over, while the Onondaga continued to put all his nervous power and skill into his strokes. It was equally fortunate, also, that the night had come and that the dusk was thick, as it distracted yet further the hasty aim of the French and Indians on shore. One bullet from a French rifle grazed Robert's shoulder, another was deflected from Tayoga's paddle without striking it from his hand, but in a few minutes they were beyond the range of those who stood on the bank, although lead continued to fall in the water behind them.

"Now you can rise, Dagaeoga," said the Onondaga, "and use the extra paddle that I took the precaution to stow in the boat. Do not think because you are an escaped prisoner that you are to rest in idleness and luxury, doing no work while I do it all."

"God bless you, Tayoga!" exclaimed Robert, in the fullness of his emotion. "I'll work a week without stopping if you say so. I'm so glad to see you that I'll do anything you say, and ask no questions. But I want to tell you you're the most wonderful dancer and jumper in America!"

"I danced and jumped so well, Dagaeoga, because your need made me do so. Necessity gives a wonderful spring to the muscles. Behold how long and strong you sweep with the paddle because the bullets of the enemy impel you."

"Which way are we going, Tayoga? What is your plan?"

"Our aim at this moment, Dagaeoga, is the middle of the lake, because the sons of Onontio and the warriors of Tandakora are all along the beach, and would be waiting for us with rifle and tomahawk should we seek to land. This is but a small boat in which we sit and it could not resist the waves of a great storm, but at present it is far safer for us than any land near by."

"Of course you're right, Tayoga, you always are, but we're in the thick of the darkness now, so you rest awhile and let me do the paddling alone."

"It is a good thought, Dagaeoga, but keep straight in the direction we are going. See that you do not paddle unconsciously in a curve. We shall certainly be pursued, and although our foes cannot see us well in the dark, some out of their number are likely to blunder upon us. If it comes to a battle you will notice that I have an extra rifle and pistol for you lying in the bottom of the canoe, and that I am something more than a supple dancer and leaper."

"You not only think of everything, Tayoga, but you also do it, which is better. I shall take care to keep dead ahead."

Robert in his turn bent forward and plied the paddle. He was not only fresh, but the wonderful thrill of escape gave him a strength far beyond the normal, and the great canoe fairly danced over the waters toward the dusky deeps of the lake, while the Onondaga crouched at the other end of the canoe, rifle in hand, intently watching the heavy pall of dusk behind them.

Their situation was still dangerous in the extreme, but the soul of Tayoga swelled with triumph. Tandakora, the Ojibway, had rejoiced because he had expected a great taking of scalps, but the purer spirit of the Onondaga soared into the heights because he had saved his comrade of a thousand dangers. He still saw faintly through the darkness the campfires of the victorious French and Indian army, and he heard the swish of paddles, but he did not yet discern any pursuing canoe. He detached his eyes for a moment from the bank of dusk in front of him, and looked up at the skies. The clouds and vapours kept him from seeing the great star upon which his patron saint, Tododaho, sat, but he knew that he was there, and that he was watching over him. He could not have achieved so much in the face of uttermost peril and then fail in the lesser danger.

The canoe glided swiftly on toward the wider reaches of the lake, and the Onondaga never relaxed his watchfulness, for an instant. He was poised in the canoe, every nerve and muscle ready to leap in a second into activity, while his ears were strained for the sounds of paddles or oars. Now he relied, as often before, more upon hearing than sight. Presently a sound came, and it was that of oars. A boat parted the wall of dusk and he saw that it contained both French and Indians, eight in all, the warriors uttering a shout as they beheld the fugitive canoe.

"Keep steadily on, Dagaeoga," said the Onondaga. "I have my long barrelled rifle, and it will carry much farther than those of the foe. In another minute it will tell them they had best stop, and if they will not obey its voice then I will repeat the command with your rifle."

Robert heard the sharp report of Tayoga's weapon, and then a cry from the pursuing boat, saying the bullet had found its mark.

"They still come, though in a hesitating manner," said Tayoga, "and I must even give them a second notice."

Now Robert heard the crack of the other rifle, and the answering cry, signifying that its bullet, too, had sped home.

"They stop now," said Tayoga. "They heed the double command." He rapidly reloaded the rifles, and Robert, who saw an uncommonly thick bank of dusk ahead, paddled directly into the heart of it. They paused there a few moments and neither saw nor heard any pursuers. Tayoga put down the rifles, now ready again for his deadly aim, and the two kept for a long time a straight course toward the centre of the lake.

Chapter 10

The Flight of the Two

Tayoga, into whose hands Robert had entrusted himself with the uttermost faith, at last said stop, and drawing the paddles into the canoe they took long, deep breaths of relief. Around them was a world of waters, silver under the moon and stars now piercing the dusk, and the Onondaga could see the vast star on which sat the mighty chieftain who had gone away four hundred years ago to eternal life.

"O Tododaho," he murmured, "thou hast guarded us well."

"Where do you think we are, Tayoga?" asked Robert.

"Perhaps twenty miles from land," replied the Onondaga, "and the farther the better."

"True, Tayoga. Never before did I see a big lake look so kindly. If it didn't require so much effort I'd like to go to the very centre of it and stay there for a week."

"Even as it is, Dagaeoga, we will wait here a while and take the long rest we need."

"And while we're doing nothing but swing in our great canoe, Tayoga, I want to thank you for all you've done for me. I'd been a prisoner much longer than I wished."

"It but repays my debt, Dagaeoga. You will recall that you helped to save me from the hands of Tandakora when he was going to burn me at the stake. My imprisonment was short, but I have been in the forest the whole winter and spring seeking to take you from Langlade."

"All of which goes to show, Tayoga, that we must allow only one of us to be captured at a time. The other must go free in order to rescue the one taken."

Although Robert's tone was light, his feeling was far from frivolous, but he had been at extreme tension so long that he was compelled to seek relief.

"How did you manage it, Tayoga?" he asked.

"In the confusion of the attack on the forts and the rejoicing that followed it was easy," replied the Onondaga. "When so many others were dancing and leaping it attracted no attention for me to dance and leap also, and I selected, without interference, the boat, the extra paddle, weapons and ammunition that I wished. Areskoui and Tododaho did the rest. Do you feel stronger now, Dagaeoga?"

"Aye, I'm still able to handle the paddle. I suppose we'd better seek a landing. We can't stay out in the lake forever. Tayoga, you've taken the part of Providence itself. Now did it occur to you in your infinite wisdom, while you were storing paddles, weapons and ammunition in this boat, to store food also?"

The Onondaga's smile was wide and satisfying.

"I thought of that, too, Dagaeoga," he replied, "because I knew our journey, if we should be so fortunate as to have a journey, would take us out on the lake, and I knew, also, that no matter how many hardships and dangers Dagaeoga might pass through, the time would come when he would be hungry. It is always so with Dagaeoga."

He took a heavy knapsack from the bottom of the canoe and opened it. "It is a French knapsack," he said, "and it contains both bread and meat, which we will enjoy."

They ate in great content, and their spirits rose to an extraordinary degree, though Tayoga regretted the absence of clothing which his disguise had made necessary. Having been educated with white lads, and having associated with white people so much, he was usually clad as completely as they, either in their fashion or in his own full Indian costume.

"My infinite wisdom was not so infinite that it told me to take a blanket," he said, "and the wind coming down from the Canadian shore is growing cold."

"I'm surprised to hear you speak of such trifles as that, Tayoga, when we've been dealing with affairs of life and death."

"We are cold or we are warm, Dagaeoga, and peril and suffering do not alter it. But lo! the wind is bringing the great mists with it, and we will escape in them."

They turned the canoe toward a point far to the east of the Indian camp and began to paddle, not hastily but with long, slow, easy strokes that sent the canoe over the water at a great rate. The fogs and vapours were thick and close about them, but Tayoga knew the direction. Robert asked him if he had heard of Willet, and the Onondaga said he had not seen him, but he had learned from a Mohawk runner that the Great Bear had reached Waraiyageh with the news of St. Luc's prospective advance, and Tayoga had also contrived to get news through to him that he was lying in the forest, waiting a chance to effect the rescue of Robert.

Toward morning they landed on a shore, clothed in deep and primeval forest, and with reluctance abandoned their canoe.

"It is an Abenaki craft," said Tayoga. "It is made well, it has served us well, and we will treat it well."

Instead of leaving it on the lake to the mercy of storms they drew it into some bushes at the mouth of a small creek, where it would stay securely, and probably serve some day some chance traveller. Then they plunged into the deep forest, but when they saw a smoke Robert remained hidden while Tayoga went on, but with the intention of returning.

The Onondaga was quite sure the smoke indicated the presence of a small village and his quest was for clothes.

"Let Dagaeoga rest in peace here in the thicket," he said, "and when I come back I shall be clad as a man. Have no fears for me. I will not enter the village Until after dark."

He glided away without noise, and Robert, having supreme confidence in him, lay down among the bushes, which were so dense that the keenest eyes could not have seen him ten feet away. His frame was relaxed so thoroughly after his immense exertions and he felt such utter thankfulness at his escape that he soon fell into a deep slumber rather than sleep, and when he awoke the dark had come, bringing with it Tayoga.

"Lo, Dagaeoga," said the Onondaga, in a tone of intense satisfaction, "I have done well. It is not pleasant to me to take the property of others, but in this case what I have seized must have been captured from the English. No watch was kept in the village, as they had heard of their great victory and the warriors were away. I secured three splendid blankets, two of green and one of brown. Since you have a coat, Dagaeoga, you can have one green blanket and I will take the other two, one to wear and the other to sleep in. I also took away more powder and lead, and as I have my bullet moulds we can increase our ammunition when we need it. I have added, too, a supply of venison to our beef and bread."

"You're an accomplished burglar, Tayoga, but I think that in this case your patron saint, Tododaho, will forgive you. I'm devoutly glad of the blanket. I feel stiff and sore, after such great exertions, and I find I've grown cold with the coming of the dark."

"It is a relapse," said Tayoga with some anxiety. "The strain on mind and body has been too great. Better wrap yourself in the blanket at once, and lie quiet in the thicket."

Robert was prompt to take his advice, as his body was hot and his sight was wavering. He felt that he was going to be ill and he might get it over all the quicker by surrendering to it at once. He rolled the blanket tightly about himself and lay down on the softest spot he could find. In the night he became delirious and talked continually of Langlade, St. Luc and Montcalm. But Tayoga watched by him continually until late, when he hunted through the forest by moonlight for some powerful herbs known to the Indians. In the morning he beat them and bruised them and cooked them as best he could without utensils, and then dropped the juices into his comrade's mouth, after which he carefully put out the fire, lest it be seen by savage rovers.

Robert was soon very much better. He had a profuse perspiration and came out of his unconscious state, but was quite weak. He was also thoroughly ashamed of himself.

"Nice time for me to be breaking down," he said, "here in the wilderness near an Indian village, hundreds of miles from any of our friends, save those who are captured. I make my apologies, Tayoga."

"They are not needed," said the Onondaga. "You defended me with your life when I was wounded and the wolves sought to eat me, now I repay again. There is nothing for Dagaeoga to do but to keep on perspiring, see that the blanket is still wrapped around him, and tonight I will get something in which to cook the food he needs."

"How will you do that?"

"I will go again to my village. I call it mine because it supplies what we need and I will return with the spoil. Bide you in peace, Dagaeoga. You have called me an accomplished burglar. I am more, I am a great one."

Robert had the utmost confidence in him, and it was justified. When he awoke from a restless slumber, Tayoga stood beside him, holding in his hand a small iron kettle made in Canada, and a great iron spoon.

"They are the best they had in the village," he said. "It is not a large and rich village and so its possessions are not great, but I think these will do. I have also brought with me some very tender meat of a young deer that I found in one of the lodges."

"You're all you claimed to be and more, Tayoga," said Robert earnestly and gratefully.

The Onondaga lighted a fire in a dip, and cutting the deer into tiny bits made a most appetizing soup, which Robert's weak stomach was able to retain and to crave more.

"No," said Tayoga, "enough for tonight, but you shall have twice as much in the morning. Now, go to sleep again."

"I haven't been doing anything but sleep for the last day or two. I want to get up and walk."

"And have your fever come back. Besides, you are not strong enough yet to walk more than a few steps."

Robert knew that he would be forced to obey, and he passed the night partly in dozing, and partly in staring at the sky. In the morning he was very hungry and showed an increase of strength. Tayoga, true to his word, gave him a double portion of the soup, but still forbade sternly any attempt at walking.

"Lie there, Dagaeoga," he said, "and let the wind blow over you, and I'll go farther into the forest to see if friend or enemy be near."

Robert, feeling that he must, lay peacefully on his back after the Onondaga left him. He was free from fever, but he knew that Tayoga was right in forbidding him to walk. It would be several days yet before he could fulfil his old duties, as an active and powerful forest runner. Yet he was very peaceful because the soreness of body that had troubled him was gone and strength was flowing back into his veins. Despite the fact that he was lying on his back alone in the wilderness, with savage foes not far away, he believed that he had very much for which to be grateful. He had been taken almost by a miracle out of the hands of his foes, and, when he was ill and in his weakness might have been devoured by wild beasts or might have starved to death, the most loyal and resourceful of comrades had been by his side to save him.

He saw the great star on which Tayoga's Tododaho lived, and he accepted so much of the Iroquois theology, believing that it was in spirit and essence the same as his own Christian belief, that he almost imagined he could see the great Onondaga chieftain who had gone away four centuries ago. In any event, it was a beneficent star, and he was glad that it shone down on him so brilliantly.

Tayoga before his departure had loaned him one of his blankets and now he lay upon it, with the other wrapped around him, his loaded pistol in his belt and his loaded rifle lying by his side. The fire that the Onondaga had built in the dip not far away had been put out carefully and the ashes had been scattered.

Although it was midsummer, the night, as often happened in that northern latitude, had come on cool, and the warmth of the blankets was not unwelcome. Robert knew that he was only a mote in all that vast wilderness, but the contiguity of the Indian village might cause warriors, either arriving or departing, to pass near him. So he was not surprised when he heard footsteps in the bushes not far away, and then the sound of voices. Instinctively he tried to press his body into the earth, and he also lifted carefully the loaded rifle, but second thought told him he was not likely to be seen.

Warriors presently came so near that they were visible, and to his surprise and alarm he saw the huge figure of Tandakora among them. They were about a dozen in number, walking in the most leisurely manner and once stopped very close to him to talk. Although he raised himself up a little and clutched the rifle more tightly he was still hopeful that they would not see him. The Ojibway chieftain was in full war paint, with a fine new American rifle, and also a small sword swinging from his belt. Both were undoubtedly trophies of Oswego, and it was certain that after carrying the sword for a while as a prize he would discard it. Indians never found much use for swords.

Robert always believed that Tayoga's Tododaho protected him that night, because for a while all the chances were against him. As the warriors stood near talking a frightened deer started up in the thicket, and Tandakora himself brought it down with a lucky bullet, the unfortunate animal falling not thirty yards from the hidden youth. They removed the skin and cut it into portions where it lay, the whole task taking about a half hour, and all the time Robert, lying under the brush, saw them distinctly.

He was in mortal fear lest one of them wander into the dip where Tayoga had built the fire, and see traces of the ashes, but they did not do so. Twice warriors walked in that direction and his heart was in his mouth, but in neither case did the errand take them so far. Tandakora was not alone in bearing Oswego spoils. Nearly all of them had something, a rifle, a pistol or a sword, and two wore officers' laced coats over their painted bodies. The sight filled Robert with rage. Were his people to go on this way indefinitely, sacrificing men and posts in unrelated efforts? Would they allow the French, with inferior numbers, to beat them continuously? He had seen Montcalm and talked with him, and he feared everything from that daring and tenacious leader.

While the Indians prepared the deer the moon and stars came out with uncommon brilliancy, filling the forest with a misty, silver light. Robert now saw Tandakora and his men so clearly that it seemed impossible for them not to see him. Once more he had the instinctive desire to press himself into the earth, but his mind told him that absolute silence was the most necessary thing. As he lay, he could have picked off Tandakora with a bullet from his rifle, and, so far as the border was concerned, he felt that his own life was worth the sacrifice, but he loved his life and the Ojibway might be put out of the way at some other time and place.

Tayoga's Tododaho protected him once more. Two of the Indians wanted water and they started in search of a brook which was never far away in that region. It seemed for a moment or two that they would walk directly into the dip, where scattered ashes lay, but the great Onondaga turned them aside just in time and they found at another point the water they wished. Robert's extreme tension lasted until they were back with the others. Nevertheless their harmless return encouraged him in the belief that the star was working in his behalf.

The Indians were in no hurry. They talked freely over their task of dressing and quartering the deer, and often they were so near that Robert could hear distinctly what they said, but only once or twice did they use a dialect that he could understand, and then they were speaking of the great victory of Oswego, in which they confirmed the inference, drawn from the spoils, that they like Tandakora had taken a part. They were in high good humour, expecting more triumphs, and regarded the new French commander, Montcalm, as a great and invincible leader.

Robert was glad, then, that he was such an insignificant mote in the wilderness and had he the power he would have made himself so small that he would have become invisible, but as that was impossible he still trusted in Tayoga's Tododaho. The Indian chief gave two of the warriors an order, and they started on a course that would have brought them straight to him. The lad gave himself up for lost, but, intending to make a desperate fight for it, despite his weakness, his hand crept to the hammer and trigger of his rifle. Something moved in the thicket, a bear, perhaps, or a lynx, and the two Indians, when they were within twenty feet of him, turned aside to investigate it. Then they went on, and it was quite clear again to Robert that he had been right about the friendly intervention of Tododaho.

Nor was it long until the truth was demonstrated to him once more, and in a conclusive manner. The entire party departed, taking with them the portions of the deer, and they passed so very close to him that their wary eyes, which always watched on all sides, would have been compelled to see him, if Tododaho, or perhaps it was Areskoui, or even Manitou, had not seen fit just at that moment to draw a veil before the moon and stars and make the shadow so deep under the bush where young Lennox lay that he was invisible, although they stepped within fifteen feet of him. They went on in their usual single file, disappearing in the direction of the village, while he lay still and gave thanks.

They had not been gone more than fifteen minutes when there was a faint rustle in the thicket, and Tayoga stood before him.

"I was hid in a clump of weeds not far away and I saw," said the Onondaga. "It was a narrow escape, but you were protected by the great powers of the earth and the air. Else they would have seen you."

"It is so," said Robert, devoutly, "and it makes me all the more glad to see you, Tayoga. I hope your journey, like all the others, has been fruitful."

The Onondaga smiled in the dusk.

"It is a good village to which I go," he replied in his precise fashion. "You will recall that they had in Albany what they call in the English tongue a chemist's shop. It is such that I sought in the village, and I found it in one lodge, the owners of which were absent, and which I could reach at my leisure. Here is a gourd of Indian tea, very strong, made from the essence of the *sassafras* root. It will purge the impurities from your blood, and, in another day, your appetite will be exceedingly strong. Then your strength will grow so fast that in a short time you will be ready for a long journey. I have also brought a small sack filled with *samp*."

Robert uttered a little cry of joy. He craved bread, or at least something that would take its place, and *samp*, a variation of which is known as hominy, was a most acceptable substitute.

"You are, in truth, a most efficient burglar, Tayoga," he said.

"I obtained also information," continued the Onondaga. "While I lay in one of the lodges, hidden under furs, I heard two of the old men talking. They believe since they have taken Oswego that all things are possible for them and the French. Montcalm appears to them the greatest of all leaders and he will take them from one victory to another. Their defeat by Andiatarocte is forgotten, and they plan a great advance toward the south. But they intend first to sweep up all the scouts and bands of the Americans and English. Their first attack will be upon Rogers, him whom we call the Mountain Wolf."

"Rogers! Is he somewhere near us?" exclaimed Robert eagerly.

"Far to the east toward Andiatarocte, but they mean to strike him. The Frenchmen De Courcelles and Jumonville will join with Tandakora, then St. Luc will go too and he will lead a great force against the Mountain Wolf, with whom, I suspect, our friend the Great Bear now is, hoping perhaps, as they hunt through the forest, to discover some traces of us."

"I knew all along, Tayoga, that Dave would seek me and rescue me if you didn't, or if I didn't rescue myself, provided I remained alive, as you see I did."

"The Great Bear is the most faithful of all comrades. He would never desert a friend in the hands of the enemy."

"You think then that we should try to meet the Mountain Wolf and his rangers?"

"Of a certainty. As soon as Dagaeoga is strong enough. Now lie still, while I scout through the forest. If no enemy is near I will heat the tea, and then you must drink, and drink deep."

He made a wide circuit, and, coming back, lighted a little fire on which he warmed the tea in the pot that he had taken from the village on an earlier night. Then, under the insistence of Tayoga, Robert drank a quantity that amounted to three cups, and soon fell into a deep sleep, from which he awoke the next day with an appetite so sharp that he felt able to bite a big piece out of a tree.

"I think I'll go hunt a buffalo, kill him and eat him whole," he said in a large, round voice.

"If so Dagaeoga will have to roam far," said Tayoga sedately. "The buffalo is not found east of the Alleghanies, as you well know."

"Of course I know it, but what are time and distance to a Samson like me? I say I will go forth and slay a buffalo, unless I am fed at once and in enormous quantities."

"Would a haunch of venison and a gallon of *samp* help Dagaeoga a little?"

"Yes, a little, they'd serve as appetizers for something real and substantial to come."

"Then if you feel so strong and are charged so full of ambition you can help cook breakfast. You have had an easy time, Dagaeoga, but life henceforth will not be all eating and sleeping."

They had a big and pleasant breakfast together and Robert rejoiced in his new vigour. It was wonderful to be so strong after having been so weak, it was like life after death, and he was eager to start at once.

"It is a good thing to have been ill," he said, "because then you know how fine it is to be well."

"But we will not depart before tomorrow," said the Onondaga decisively.

"And why?"

"Because you have lived long enough in the wilderness, Dagaeoga, to know that one must always fight the weather. Look into the west, and you will see a little cloud moving up from the horizon. It does not amount to much at present, but it contains the seed of great things. It has been sent by the Rain God, and it will not do yet for Dagaeoga, despite his new strength, to travel in the rain."

Robert became anxious as he watched the little cloud, which seemed to swell as he looked at it, and which soon assumed an angry hue. He knew that Tayoga had told the truth. Coming out of his fever it would be a terrible risk for him to become drenched.

"We will make a shelter such as we can in the dip where we built the fire," said Tayoga, "and now you can use your new strength as much as you will in wielding a tomahawk."

They cut small saplings with utmost speed and speedily accomplished one of the most difficult tasks of the border, making a rude brush shelter which with the aid of their blankets would protect them from the storm. By the time they had finished, the little cloud which had been at first a mere signal had grown so prodigiously that it covered the whole heavens, and the day became almost as dark as twilight. The lightning began to flash in great, blazing strokes, and the thunder was so nearly continuous that the earth kept up an incessant jarring. Then the rain poured heavily and Robert saw Tayoga's wisdom. Although the shelter and his blanket kept the rain from him he felt cold in the damp, and shivered as if with a chill.

"When the storm stops, which will not be before dark," said Tayoga, "I shall go to the village and get you a heavy buffalo robe. They have some, acquired in trade from the Indians of the western plains, and one of them belongs to you. So, Dagaeoga, I will get it."

"Tayoga, you have taken too much risk for me already. I can make out very well as I am, and suppose we start tonight in search of Rogers and Willet."

"I mean to have my way, because in this case my way is right. We work together as partners, and the partnership becomes ineffective when one member of it cannot endure the hardships of a long march, and perhaps of battle. And has not Dagaeoga said that I am an accomplished burglar? I prove it anew tonight. As soon as the rain ceases I will go to the village, the great storehouse of our supplies."

The Onondaga spoke in a light tone with a whimsical inflection, but Robert saw that he was intensely in earnest, and that it was not worth while for him to say more. The great storm passed on to the southward, the rain sank to a drizzle, but it was very cold in the forest, and Robert's teeth chattered, despite every effort to control his body.

"I go, Dagaeoga," said Tayoga, "and I shall return with the great, warm buffalo robe that belongs to you."

Then he melted without noise into the darkness and Robert was alone. He knew the mission of the Onondaga to be a perilous one, but he did not doubt his success. The cold drizzle fell on the shelter of brush and saplings, and some of it seeped through. Now and then a drop found its way down his neck, and it felt like ice. Physically he was very miserable, and it began to depress his spirit. He hoped that Tayoga would not be long in obtaining the buffalo robe.

The thunder moaned a little far to the south, and then died down entirely. There were one or two stray flashes of lightning and then no more. He sank into a sort of doze that was more like a stupor, from which he was awakened by a dusky figure in the doorway of the little shelter. It was Tayoga, and he bore a heavy dark bundle over his arm.

"I have brought the buffalo robe that belongs to you, Dagaeoga," he said cheerfully. "It was in the lodge of the head chief of the village and I had to wait until he went forth to greet Tandakora, who came with a band of his warriors to claim shelter, food and rest. Then I took what was your own and here it is, one of the finest I have ever seen."

He held up the great buffalo robe, tanned splendidly and rich in fur and the sight of it made Robert's teeth stop chattering. He wrapped it around his body and sufficient warmth came back.

"You're a marvel, Tayoga," he said. "Does the village contain anything else that belongs to us?"

"Nothing that I can think of now. The rain will cease entirely in an hour, and then we will start."

His prediction was right, and they set forth in the dark forest, Robert wearing the great buffalo robe which stored heat and consequent energy in his frame. But the woods were so wet, and it was so difficult to find a good trail that they did not make very great progress, and when dawn came they were only a few miles away. Robert's strength, however, stood the test, and they dared to light a fire and have a warm breakfast. Much refreshed they plunged on anew, hunting for friends who could not be much more than motes in the wilderness. Robert hoped that some chance would enable him to meet Willet, to whom he owed so much, and who stood in the place of a father to him. It did not seem possible that the Great Bear could have fallen in one of the numerous border skirmishes, which must have been fought since his capture. He could not associate death with a man so powerful and vital as Willet.

The day was bright and warm, and he took off the buffalo robe. It was quite a weight to be carried, but he knew he would need it again when night came and particularly if there were other storms. They saw many trails in the afternoon and Tayoga was quite sure they were made by war bands. Nearly all of them led southeast.

"The savages in the west and about the Great Lakes," he said, "have heard of the victory at Oswego, and so they pour out to the French standard, expecting many scalps and great spoils. Whenever the French win a triumph it means more warriors for them."

"And may not some of the bands going to the war stumble on our own trail?"

"It is likely, Dagaeoga. But if it comes to battle see how much better it is that you should be strong and able."

"Yes, I concede now, Tayoga, that it was right for us to wait as long as we did."

The trails grew much more numerous as they advanced. Evidently swarms of warriors were about them and before midday Tayoga halted.

"It will not be wise for us to advance farther," he said. "We must seek some hiding place."

"Hark to that!" exclaimed Robert.

A breeze behind them bore a faint shout to his ear. Tayoga listened intently, and it was repeated once.

"Pursuit!" he said briefly. "They have come by chance upon our trail. It may be Tandakora himself and it is unfortunate. They will never leave us now, unless they are driven back."

"Then we'd better turn back towards the north, as the thickest of the swarms are sure to be to the south of us."

"It is so. Again the longest of roads becomes the safest for us, but we will not make it wholly north, we will bear to the east also. I once left a canoe, hidden in the edge of a lake there, and we may find it."

"What will we do with it if we find it?"

"Tandakora will not be able to follow the trail of a canoe. But now we must press forward with all speed, Dagaeoga. See, there is a smoke in the south and now another answers it in the north. They are talking about us."

Robert saw the familiar signals which always meant peril to them, and he was willing to go forward at the uttermost speed. He had become hardened in a measure to danger, though it seemed to him that he was passing through enough of it to last a lifetime. But his soul rose to meet it.

They used all the customary devices to hide their traces, wading when there was water, walking on stones or logs when they were available, but they knew these stratagems would only delay Tandakora, they could not throw him off the trail entirely. They hoped more from the coming dark, and, when night came, it found them going at great speed. Just at twilight they heard a faint shout again and the faint shout in reply, telling them the pursuit was maintained, but the night fortunately proved to be very dark, and, an hour or two later, they came to a heavy windrow, the result of some old hurricane into which they drew for shelter and rest. They knew that not even the Indian trailers could find them there in such darkness, and for the present they were without apprehension.

"Do you think they will pass us in the night?" asked Robert.

"No," replied Tayoga. "They will wait until the dawn and pick up the trail anew."

"Then we'd better start again about midnight."

"I think so, too."

Meanwhile, lying comfortably among the fallen trees and leaves, they waited in silence.

Chapter 11

The Mystic Voyage

The long stay in the windrow served Robert well, more than atoning for the drain made upon his strength by their rapid flight. In three or four hours he was back in his normal state, and he felt proudly that he was now as good as he had ever been. The night, as they had expected, was cold, and he was thankful that he had hung on to the buffalo robe, in which he wrapped himself once more, while Tayoga was snug between two big blankets.

Robert dozed, but he was awakened by something stirring near them, and he sat up with his finger on the trigger of his rifle. The Onondaga was already listening and watching, ready with his weapon. Presently the white youth heard his companion laughing softly, and his own tension relaxed, as he knew Tayoga would not laugh without good cause.

"It is a bear," said Tayoga, "and he has a lair in the windrow, not more than twenty feet away. He has been out very late at night, too late for a good, honest home-keeping bear, but he is back at last, and he smells us."

"And alarmed by the odour he does not know whether to enter his home or not. Well, I hope he'll conclude to take his rest. We eat bear at times, Tayoga, but just now I wouldn't dream of harming one."

"Nor would I, Dagaeoga, and maybe the bear will divine that we are harmless, that is, Tododaho or Areskoui will tell him in some way of which we know nothing that his home is his own to be entered without fear."

"I think I hear him moving now, and also puffing a little."

"You hear aright, Dagaeoga. Tododaho has whispered to him, even as I said, and he is going into his den which I know is snug and warm, in the very thickest part of the windrow. Now he is lying down in it with the logs and branches about him, and soon he will be asleep, dreaming happy dreams of tender roots and wild honey with no stings of bees to torment him."

"You grow quite poetical, Tayoga."

"Although foes are hunting us, I feel the spirit of the forest and of peace strong upon me, Dagaeoga. Moreover, Tododaho, as I told you, has whispered to the animals that we are not to be feared tonight. Hark to the tiny rustling just beyond the log against which we lie!"

"Yes, I hear it, and what do you make of it, Tayoga?"

"Rabbits seeking their nests. They, too, have snuffed about, noticing the man odour, which man himself cannot detect, and once they started away in alarm, but now they are reassured, and they have settled themselves down to sleep in comfort and security."

"Tayoga, you talk well and fluently, but as I have told you before, you talk out of a dictionary."

"But as I learned my English out of a dictionary I cannot talk otherwise. That is why my language is always so much superior to yours, Dagaeoga."

"I'll let it be as you claim it, you boaster, but what noise is that now? I seem to hear the light sound of hoofs."

The Onondaga raised himself to his full height and peered over the dense masses of trunks and boughs, his keen eyes cutting the thick dusk. Then he sank back, and, when he replied, his voice showed distinct pleasure.

"Two deer have come into a little open space, around which the arms of the windrow stretch nearly all the way, and they have crouched there, where they will rest, indifferent to the nearness of the bear. Truly, O Dagaeoga, we have come into the midst of a happy family, and we have been accepted, for the night, as members of it."

"It must be so, Tayoga, because I see a figure much larger than that of the deer approaching. Look to the north and behold that shadow there under the trees."

"I see it, Dagaeoga. It is the great northern moose, a bull. Perhaps he has wandered down from Canada, as they are rare here. They are often quarrelsome, but the bull is going to take his rest, within the shelter of the windrow, and leave its other people at peace. Now he has found a good place, and he will be quiet for the night."

"Suppose you sleep a while, Tayoga. You have done all the watching for a long time, and, as I'm fit and fine now, it's right for me to take up my share of the burden."

"Very well, but do not fail to awaken me in about three hours. We must not be caught here in the morning by the warriors."

He was asleep almost instantly, and Robert sat in a comfortable position with his rifle across his knees. Responsibility brought back to him self-respect and pride. He was now a full partner in the partnership, and will and strength together made his faculties so keen that it would have been difficult for anything about the windrow to have escaped his attention. He heard the light rustlings of other animals coming to comfort and safety, and flutterings as birds settled on up-thrust boughs, many of which were still covered with leaves. Once he heard a faint shout deep in the forest, brought by the wind a great distance, and he was sure that it was the cry of their Indian pursuers. Doubtless it was a signal and had connection with the search, but he felt no alarm. Under the cover of darkness Tayoga and he were still motes in the wilderness, and, while the night lasted, Tandakora could not find them.

When he judged that the three hours had passed he awoke the Onondaga and they took their silent way north by east, covering much more distance by dawn. But both were certain that warriors of Tandakora would pick up their traces again that day. They would spread through the forest, and, when one of them struck the trail, a cry would be sufficient to call the others. But they pressed on, still adopting every possible device to throw off their pursuers, and they continued their flight several days, always through an unbroken forest, over hills and across many streams, large and small. It seemed, at times, to Robert that the pursuit must have dropped away, but Tayoga was quite positive that Tandakora still followed. The Ojibway, he said, had divined the identity of the fugitives and every motive would make him follow, even all the way across the Province of New York and beyond, if need be.

They came at last to a lake, large, beautiful, extending many miles through the wilderness, and Tayoga, usually so calm, uttered a little cry of delight, which Robert repeated, but in fuller volume.

"I think lakes are the finest things in the world," he said. "They always stir me."

"And that is why Manitou put so many and such splendid ones in the land of the Hodenosaunee," said Tayoga. "This is Ganoatohale, which you call in your language Oneida, and it is on its shores that I hid the canoe of which I spoke to you. I think we shall find it just as I left it."

"I devoutly hope so. A canoe and paddles would give me much pleasure just now, and Ganoatohale will leave no trail."

They walked northward along the shore of the lake, and they came to a place where many tall reeds grew thick and close in shallow water. Tayoga plunged into the very heart of them and Robert's heart rose with a bound, when he reappeared dragging after him a large and strong canoe, containing two paddles.

"It has rested in quiet waiting for us," he said. "It is a good canoe, and it knew that I would come some time to claim it."

"Before we go upon our voyage," said Robert, "I think we shall have to pay some attention to the question of food. My pouch is about empty."

"And so is mine. We shall have to take the risk, Dagaeoga, and shoot a deer. Tandakora may be so far behind that none of his warriors will hear the shot, but even so we cannot live without eating. We will, however, hunt from the canoe. Since the war began, all human beings have gone away from this lake, and the deer should be plentiful."

They launched the canoe on the deep waters, and the two took up the paddles, sending their little craft northward, with slow, deliberate strokes. They had the luck within the hour to find a deer drinking, and with equal luck Robert slew it at the first shot. They would have taken the body into the canoe, but the burden was too great, and Tayoga cut it up and dressed it with great dispatch, while Robert watched. Then they made room for the four quarters and again paddled northward. Fearing that Tandakora had come much nearer, while they were busy with the deer, they did not dare the wide expanse of the lake, but remained for the present under cover of the overhanging forest on the western shore.

"If we put the lake between Tandakora and ourselves," said Robert, "we ought to be safe."

"It is likely that they, too, have canoes hidden in the reeds," said Tayoga. "Since the French and their allies have spread so far south they would provide for the time when they wanted to go upon the waters of Ganoatohale. It is almost a certainty that we shall be pursued upon the lake."

They continued northward, never leaving the dark shadow cast by the dense leafage, and, as they went slowly, they enjoyed the luxury of the canoe. After so much walking through the wilderness it was a much pleasanter method of travelling. But they did not forget vigilance, continually scanning the waters, and Robert's heart gave a sudden beat as he saw a black dot appear upon the surface of the lake in the south. It was followed in a moment by another, then another and then three more.

"It is the band of Tandakora, beyond a doubt," said Tayoga with conviction. "They had their canoes among the reeds even as we had ours, and now it is well for us that water leaves no trail."

"Shall we hide the canoe again, and take to the woods?"

"I think not, Dagaeoga. They have had no chance to see us yet. We will withdraw among the reeds until night comes, and then under its cover cross Ganoatohale."

Keeping almost against the bank, they moved gently until they came to a vast clump of reeds into which they pushed the canoe, while retaining their seats in it. In the centre they paused and waited. From that point they could see upon the lake, while remaining invisible themselves, and they waited.

The six canoes or large boats, they could not tell at the distance which they were, went far out into the lake, circled around for a while, and then bore back toward the western shore, along which they passed, inspecting it carefully, and drawing steadily nearer to Robert and Tayoga.

"Now, let us give thanks to Tododaho, Areskoui and to Manitou himself," said the Onondaga, "that they have been pleased to make the reeds grow in this particular place so thick and so tall."

"Yes," said Robert, "they're fine reeds, beautiful reeds, a greater bulwark to us just now than big oaks could be. Think you, Tayoga, that you recognize the large man in the first boat?"

"Aye, Dagaeoga, I know him, as you do also. How could we mistake our great enemy, Tandakora? It is a formidable fleet, too strong for us to resist, and, like the wise man, we hide when we cannot fight."

Robert's pulses beat so hard they hurt, but he would not show any uneasiness in the presence of Tayoga, and he sat immovable in the canoe. Nearer and nearer came the Indian fleet, partly of canoes and partly of boats, and he counted in them sixteen warriors, all armed heavily. Now he prayed to Manitou, and to his own God who was the same as Manitou, that no thought of pushing among the reeds would enter Tandakora's head. The fleet soon came abreast of them, but his prayers were answered, as Tandakora led ahead, evidently thinking the fugitives would not dare to hide and lie in waiting, but would press on in flight up the western shore.

"I could pick him off from here with a bullet," said Robert, looking at the huge, painted chest of the Ojibway chief.

"But our lives would be the forfeit," the Onondaga whispered back.

"I had no intention of doing it."

"Now they have passed us, and for the while we are safe. They will go on up the lake, until they find no trace of us there, and then Tandakora will come back."

"But how does he know we have a canoe?"

"He does not know it, but he feels sure of it because our trail led straight to the lake, and we would not purposely come up against such a barrier, unless we knew of a way to cross it."

"That sounds like good logic. Of course when they return they'll make a much more thorough search of the lake's edge, and then they'd be likely to find us if we remained here."

"It is so, but perhaps the night will come before Tandakora, and then we'll take flight upon the lake."

They pushed their canoe back to the edge of the reeds, and watched the Indian boats passing in single file northward, becoming smaller and smaller until they almost blended with the water, but both knew they would return, and in that lay their great danger. The afternoon was well advanced, but the sun was very brilliant, and it was hot within the reeds. Great quantities of wild fowl whirred about them and along the edges of the lake.

"No warriors are in hiding near us," said Tayoga, "or the wild fowl would fly away. We can feel sure that we have only Tandakora and his band to fear."

Robert had never watched the sun with more impatience. It was already going down the western arch, but it seemed to him to travel with incredible slowness. Far in the north the Indian boats were mere black dots on the water, but they were turning. Beyond a doubt Tandakora was now coming back.

"Suppose we go slowly south, still keeping in the shadow of the trees," he said. "We can gain at least that much advantage."

Fortunately the scattered fringe of reeds and bushes, growing in the water, extended far to the south, and they were able to keep in their protecting shadow a full hour, although their rate of progress was not more than one-third that of the Indians, who were coming without obstruction in open water. Nevertheless, it was a distinct gain, and, meanwhile, they awaited the coming of the night with the deepest anxiety. They recognized that their fate turned upon a matter of a half hour or so. If only the night would arrive before Tandakora! Robert glanced at the low sun, and, although at all times, it was beautiful, he had never before prayed so earnestly that it would go over the other side of the world, and leave their own side to darkness.

The splendour of the great yellow star deepened as it sank. It poured showers of rays upon the broad surface of the lake, and the silver of the waters turned to orange and gold. Everything there was enlarged and made more vivid, standing out twofold against the burning western background. Nothing beyond the shadow could escape the observation of the Indians in the boats, and they themselves in Robert's intense imagination changed from a line of six light craft into a great fleet.

Nevertheless the sun, lingering as if it preferred their side of the world to any other, was bound to go at last. The deep colours in the water faded. The orange and gold changed back to silver, and the silver, in its turn, gave way to gray, twilight began to draw a heavy veil over the east, and Tayoga said in deep tones:

"Lo, the Sun God has decided that we may escape! He will let the night come before Tandakora!"

Then the sun departed all at once, and the brilliant afterglow soon faded. Night settled down, thick and dark, with the waters, ruffled by a light wind, showing but dimly. The line of Tandakora became invisible, and the two youths felt intense relief.

"Now we will start toward the north-eastern end of the lake," said Tayoga. "It will be wiser than to seek the shortest road across, because Tandakora will think naturally that we have gone that way, and he will take it also."

"And it's paddling all night for us," said Robert "Well, I welcome it."

They were interrupted by the whirring of the wild fowl again, though on a much greater scale than before. The twilight was filled with feathered bodies. Tayoga, in an instant, was all attention.

"Something has frightened them," he said.

"Perhaps a bear or a deer," said Robert.

"I think not. They are used to wild animals, and would not be startled at their approach. There is only one being that everything in the forest generally fears."

"Man?"

"Even so, Dagaeoga."

"Perhaps we'd better pull in close to the bank and look."

"It would be wise."

Robert saw that the Onondaga, with his acute instincts, was deeply alarmed, and he too felt that the wild fowl had given warning. They sent the canoe with a few silent strokes through the shallow water almost to the edge of the land, and, as it nearly struck bottom, two dusky figures rising among the bushes threw their weight upon them. The light craft sank almost to the edges with the weight, but did not overturn, and both attackers and attacked fell out of it into the lake.

Robert for a moment saw a dusky face above him, and instinctively he clasped the body of a warrior in his arms. Then the two went down together in the water. The Indian was about to strike at him with a knife, but the lake saved him. As the water rushed into eye, mouth and nostril the two fell apart, but Robert was able to keep his presence of mind in that terrible moment, and, as he came up again, he snatched out his own knife and struck almost blindly.

He felt the blade encounter resistance, and then pass through it. He heard a choked cry and he shuddered violently. All his instincts were for civilization and against the taking of human life, and he had struck merely to save his own, but almost articulate words of thankfulness bubbled to his lips as he saw the dark figure that had hovered so mercilessly over him disappear. Then a second figure took the place of the first and he drew back the fatal blade again, but a soft voice said:

"Do not strike, Dagaeoga. I also have accounted for one of the warriors who attacked us, and no more have yet come. We may thank the wild fowl. Had they not warned us we should have perished."

"And even then we had luck, or your Tododaho is still watching over us. I struck at random, but the blade was guided to its mark."

"And so was mine. What you say is also proved to be true by the fact that the canoe did not overturn, when they threw themselves upon us. The chances were at least ninety-nine out of a hundred that it would do so."

"And our arms and ammunition and our deer?"

"All in the canoe, except the weapons that are in our belts."

"Then, Tayoga, it is quite sure that your Tododaho has been watching over us. But where is the canoe?"

Robert was filled with alarm and horror. They were standing above their knees in the water, and they no longer saw the little craft, which had become a veritable ship of refuge to them. They peered about frantically in the dusk and then Tayoga said:

"There is a strong breeze blowing from the land and waves are beginning to run on the water. They have taken the canoe out into the lake. We must swim in search of it."

"And if we don't find it?"

"Then we drown, but O Dagaeoga, death in the water is better than death in the fires that Tandakora will kindle."

"We might escape into the woods."

"Warriors who have come upon our trail are there, and would fall upon us at once. The attack by the two who failed proves their presence."

"Then, Tayoga, we must take the perilous chance and swim for the canoe."

"It is so, Dagaeoga."

Both were splendid swimmers, even with their clothes on, and, wading out until the water was above their waists, they began to swim with strong and steady strokes toward the middle of the lake, following with exactness the course of the wind. All the time they sought with anxious eyes through the dusk for a darker shadow that might be the canoe. The wind rose rapidly, and now and then the crest of a wave dashed over them. Less expert swimmers would have sunk, but their muscles were hardened by years of forest life—all Robert's strength had come back to him—and an immense vitality made the love of life overwhelming in them. They fought with all the powers of mind and body for the single chance of overtaking the canoe.

"I hope you see it, Tayoga," said Robert.

"Not yet," replied the Onondaga. "The darkness is heavy over the lake, and the mists and vapours, rising from the water, increase it."

"It was a fine canoe, Tayoga, and it holds our rifles, our ammunition, our deer, my buffalo robe, and all our precious belongings. We have to find it."

"It is so, Dagaeoga. We have no other choice. We truly swim for life. One could pray at this time to have all the powers of a great fish. Do you see anything behind us?"

Robert twisted his head and looked over his shoulder.

"I see no pursuit," he replied. "I cannot even see the shore, as the mists and vapours have settled down between. In a sense we're out at sea, Tayoga."

"And Ganoatohale is large. The canoe, too, is afloat upon its bosom and is, as you say, out at sea. We and it must meet or we are lost. Are you weary, Dagaeoga?"

"Not yet. I can still swim for quite a while."

"Then float a little, and we can take the exact course of the wind again. The canoe, of course, will continue to go the way the wind goes."

"Unless it's deflected by currents which do not always follow the wind."

"I do not notice any current, and to follow the wind is our only hope. The mists and vapours will hide the canoe from us until we are very close to it"

"And you may thank Tododaho that they will hide something else also. Unless I make a great mistake, Tayoga, I hear the swish of paddles."

"You make no mistake, Dagaeoga. I too hear paddles, ten, a dozen, or more of them. It is the fleet of Tandakora coming back and it will soon be passing between us and the shore. Truly we may be thankful, as you say, for the mists and vapours which, while they hide the canoe from us, also hide us from our enemies."

"I shall lie flat upon my back and float, and I'll blend with the water."

"It is a wise plan, Dagaeoga. So shall I. Then Tandakora himself would not see us, even if he passed within twenty feet of us."

"He is passing now, and I can see the outlines of their boats."

The two were silent as the fish themselves, sustained by imperceptible strokes, and Robert saw the fleet of Tandakora pass in a ghostly line. They looked unreal, a shadow following shadows, the huge figure of the Ojibway chief in the first boat a shadow itself. Robert's blood chilled, and it was not from the cold of the water. He was in a mystic and unreal world, but a world in which danger pressed in on every side. He felt like one living back in a primeval time. The swish of the paddles was doubled and tripled by his imagination, and the canoes seemed to be almost on him.

The questing eyes of Tandakora and his warriors swept the waters as far as the night, surcharged with mists and vapours, would allow, but they did not see the two human figures, so near them and almost submerged in the lake. The sound of the swishing paddles moved southward, and the line of ghostly canoes melted again, one by one, into the darkness.

"They're gone, Tayoga," whispered Robert in a tone of immense relief.

"So they are, Dagaeoga, and they will seek us long elsewhere. Are you yet weary?"

"I might be at another time, but with my life at stake I can't afford to grow tired. Let us follow the wind once more."

They swam anew with powerful strokes, despite the long time they had been in the water, and no sailors, dying of thirst, ever scanned the sea more eagerly for a sail than they searched through the heavy dusk for their lost canoe. The wind continued to rise, and the waves with it. Foam was often dashed over their heads, the water grew cold to their bodies, now and then they floated on their backs to rest themselves and thus the singular chase, with the wind their only guide, was maintained.

Robert was the first to see a dim shape, but he would not say anything until it grew in substance and solidity. Nevertheless hope flooded his heart, and then he said:

"The wind has guided us aright, Tayoga. Unless some evil spirit has taught my eyes to lie to me that is our canoe straight ahead."

"It has all the appearance of a canoe, Dagaeoga, and since the only canoe on this part of the lake is our canoe, then our canoe it is."

"And none too soon. I'm not yet worn out, but the cold of the water is entering my bones. I can see very clearly now that it's the canoe, our canoe. It stands up like a ship, the strongest canoe, the finest canoe, the friendliest canoe that ever floated on a lake or anywhere else. I can hear it saying to us: 'I have been waiting for you. Why didn't you come sooner?'"

"Truly when Dagaeoga is an old, old man, nearly a hundred, and the angel of death comes for him, he will rise up in his bed and with the rounded words pouring from his lips he will say to the angel: 'Let me make a speech only an hour long and then I will go with you without trouble, else I stay here and refuse to die.'"

"I'm using words to express my gratitude, Tayoga. Look, the canoe is moving slowly toward the centre of the lake, but it stays back as much as the wind will let it and keeps beckoning to us. A few more long, swift strokes, Tayoga, and we're beside it."

"Aye, Dagaeoga, and we must be careful how we climb into it. It is no light task to board a canoe in the middle of a lake. Since Tododaho would not let it be overturned, when we fell out of it, we must not overturn it ourselves when we get back into it, else we lose all our arms, ammunition and other supplies."

The canoe was now not more than fifty feet in front of them, moving steadily farther and farther from land before the wind that blew out of the west, but, sitting upright on the waters like a thing of life, bearing its precious freight. The mists and vapours had closed in so much now that their chance of seeing it had been only one in a thousand, and yet that lone chance had happened. The devout soul of Tayoga was filled with gratitude. Even while swimming he looked up at the great star that he could not see beyond the thick veil of cloud, but, knowing it was there, he returned thanks to the mighty Onondaga chieftain who had saved them so often.

"The canoe retreats before us, Dagaeoga," he said, "but it is not to escape us, it is to beckon us on, out of the path of Tandakora's boats which soon may be returning again and which will now come farther out into the lake, thinking that we may possibly have made a dash under the cover of the mists."

"What you predict is already coming true, Tayoga," said Robert, "because I hear the first faint dip of their paddles once more, and they can't be more than two hundred yards behind us."

The regular swishing grew louder and came closer, but the courage of the two youths was still high. They had been drawn on so steadily by the canoe, apparently in a predestined course, and they had been victors over so many dangers, that they were confident the boats of Tandakora would pass once more and leave them unseen.

"They're almost abreast of us now, Tayoga," said Robert.

"Aye, Dagaeoga," said the Onondaga, looking back. "They do not appear through the mist and we hear only the paddles, but we know the threat is there, and we can follow them as well with ear as with eye. They keep straight on, going back toward the north. Nothing tells them we are here, as our canoe beckons to us, nothing guides them to that for which they are looking. Now the sound of their paddles becomes less, now it is faint and now it is gone wholly. They have missed us once more! Let us summon up the last of our strength and overtake the canoe."

They put all their energy into a final effort and presently drew up by the side of the canoe. Tayoga steadied it with his hands while Robert was the first to climb into it. The Onondaga followed and the two lay for a few minutes exhausted on the bottom. Then Tayoga sat up and said in a full voice:

"Lo, Dagaeoga, let us give thanks to Manitou for our wonderful escape, because we have looked into the face of death."

Robert, awed by time and circumstance, shared fully the belief of Tayoga that their escape was a miracle. His nature contained much that was devout and spiritual and he, too, with his impressionable imagination, peopled earth and air almost unconsciously with spirits, good and bad. The good and bad often fought together, and sometimes the good prevailed as they had just done. There lay in the canoe the paddles, which they had lifted out of the water in their surprise at the sudden attack, and beside them were the rifles and everything else they needed.

They were content to let the canoe travel its own course for a long time, and that course was definite and certain, as if guided by the hand of man. The wind always carried it toward the northeast and farther and farther away from the fleet of Tandakora. But they took off their clothing, wrung out as much water as they could, and wrapped themselves in the dry blankets from their packs. Robert's spirits, stimulated by the reaction, bubbled up in a wonderful manner.

"We'll see no more of Tandakora for a long time, at least," he exclaimed, "and now, ho! for our wonderful voyage!"

They drew the wet charges from their pistols and reloaded them, they polished anew their hatchets and knives and then, these tasks done, they still sat for a long time in the canoe, idle and content. Their little boat needed no help or guidance from their hands. That favouring wind always carried it away from their enemies and in the direction in which they wished it to go. And yet the wind did not blow away the mists and vapours, that grew thicker and thicker around them, until they could not see twenty feet away.

Robert's feeling that they were protected, his sense of the spiritual and mystic, grew, and he saw that the mind of Tayoga was under the same spell. The waters of the lake were friendly now. As they lapped around the canoe they made a soothing sound, and the wind that guided and propelled them sang a low but pleasant song.

"We are in the arms of Tododaho," said Tayoga in a reverential tone, "and Hayowentha, the great Mohawk, also looks on and smiles. What need for us to strive when the gods themselves take us in their keeping?"

Hours passed before they spoke again. They had been at the uttermost verge of exhaustion when they climbed into the canoe, and perhaps physical weakness had made their minds more receptive to the belief that they were in hands mightier than their own, but even as strength came back the conviction remained in all its primitive force. Warmth returned to their bodies, wrapped in the blankets, and they felt an immense peace. Midnight passed and the boat bore steadily on with its two silent occupants.

CHAPTER 12

The Marvellous Trailer

"Where are we, Tayoga?"

Robert stirred from a doze and the words were involuntary. He looked upon water, covered with mists and vapours, and the driving wind was still behind them.

"I know not, Dagaeoga," replied the Onondaga in devout tones. "I too have dozed for a while, and awoke to find nothing changed. All I know is that we are yet on the bosom of Ganoatohale, and that the west wind has borne us on. I have always loved the west wind, Dagaeoga. Its breath is sweet on my face. It comes from the setting sun, from the greatest of all seas that lies beyond our continent, it blows over the vast unknown plains that are trodden by the buffalo in myriads, it comes across the mighty forests of the great valley, it is loaded with all the odours and perfumes of our immense land, and now it carries us, too, to safety."

"You talk in hexameters, Tayoga, but I think your rhapsody is justified. I also have plenty of cause now to love the west wind. How long do you think it will be until we feel the dawn on our faces?"

"Two hours, perhaps, but we may reach land before then. While I cannot smell the dawn I seem to perceive the odour of the forest. Now it grows stronger, and lo, Dagaeoga, there is another sign! Do you not notice it?"

"No, what is it?"

"The west wind that has served us so well is dying. *Gaoh*, which in our language of the Hodenosaunee is the spirit of the winds, knows that we need it no more. Surely the land is near because *Gaoh* after being a benevolent spirit to us so long would not desert us at the last moment."

"I think you must be right, Tayoga, because now I also notice the strong, keen perfume of the woods, and our west wind has sunk to almost nothing."

"Nay, Dagaeoga, it is more than that. It has died wholly. *Gaoh* tells us that having brought us so near the land we can now fend for ourselves."

The air became absolutely still, the swell ceased, the surface of the lake became as smooth as glass, and, as if swept back by a mighty, unseen hand, the mists and vapours suddenly floated away toward the east. Tayoga and Robert uttered cries of admiration and gratitude, as a high, green shore appeared, veiled but not hidden in the dusk.

"So Tododaho has brought us safely across the waters of Ganoatohale," said the Onondaga.

"Have you any idea of the point to which we have come?" asked Robert.

"No, but it is sufficient that we have come to the shore anywhere. And see, Dagaeoga, the mists and vapours still hang heavily over the western half of the lake, forming an impenetrable wall that shuts us off from Tandakora and his warriors. Truly we are for the time the favourites of the gods."

"Even so, Tayoga, you see, too, that we have come to land just where a little river empties into the lake, and we can go on up it."

They paddled with vigorous arms into the mouth of the stream, and did not stop until the day came. It was a beautiful little river, the massed vegetation growing in walls of green to the very water's edge, the songs of innumerable birds coming out of the cool gloom on either side. Robert was enchanted. His spirits were still at the high key to which they had been raised by the events of the night. Both he and Tayoga had enjoyed many hours of rest in the canoe, and now they were keen and strong for the day's work. So, it was long after dawn when they stopped paddling, and pushed their prow into a little cove.

"And now," said Robert, "I think we can land, dress, and cook some of this precious deer, which we have brought with us in spite of everything."

Their clothing had been dried by the sun, and they resumed it. Then, taking all risks, they lighted a fire, broiled tender steaks and ate like giants who had finished great labours.

"I think," said Tayoga, "that when we proceed a few miles farther it will be better to leave the canoe. It is likely that as we advance the river will become narrower, and we would be an easy target for a shot from the bank."

"I don't like to abandon a canoe which has brought us safely across the lake."

"We will put it away where it can await our coming another time. But I think we can dare the river for some distance yet."

Robert had spoken for the sake of precaution, and he was easily persuaded to continue in the river some miles, as travelling by canoe was pleasant, and after their miraculous escape or rather rescue, as it seemed to them, their spirits, already high, were steadily rising higher. The lone little river of the north, on which they were travelling, presented a spectacle of uncommon beauty. Its waters flowed in a clear, silver stream down to the lake, deeper in tint on the still reaches, and, flashing in the sunlight, where it rushed over the shallows.

All the time they moved between two lofty, green walls, the forest growing so densely on either shore that they could not see back into it more than fifty yards, while the green along its lower edges was dotted with pink and blue and red, where the delicate wild flowers were blooming. The birds in the odorous depths of the foliage sang incessantly, and Robert had never before heard them sing so sweetly.

"I don't think any of our foes can be in ambush along the river," he said. "It's too peaceful and the birds sing with too much enthusiasm. You remember how they warned us of danger once by all going away?"

"True, Dagaeoga, and at any time now they may leave. But, like you, I am willing to take the risk for several hours more. Most of the warriors must be far south of us unless the rangers are in this region, and a special force has been sent to meet them."

They came by and by to a long stretch of rippling shallows, and they were compelled to carry the canoe with its load through the woods and around them, the task, owing to the density of the forest and thicket and the weight of their burden, straining their muscles and drawing perspiration from their faces. But they took consolation from the fact that game was amazingly plentiful. Deer sprang up everywhere, and twice they caught glimpses of bears shambling away. Squirrels chattered over their heads and the little people of the forest rustled all about them.

"It shows that no human being has been through here recently," said Tayoga, "else the game, big and little, would not have been stirring abroad with so much confidence."

"Then as soon as we make the portage we can return to the river with the canoe."

"Dagaeoga grows lazy. Does he not know that to do the hard thing strengthens both mind and body? Has he forgotten what Mynheer Jacobus Huysman told us so often in Albany? Now is a splendid opportunity for Dagaeoga to harden himself a great deal."

"I realize it, Tayoga, but I don't want my mind and body to grow too hard. When one is all steel one ceases to be receptive. Can you see the river through the trees there?"

"I catch the glitter of sunlight on the water."

"I hope it looks like deep water."

"It is sufficient to float the canoe and the lazy Dagaeoga can take to his paddle again."

They put their boat back into the stream, uttering great sighs of relief, and resumed the far more pleasant travel by water, the day remaining golden as if doing its best to please them. They had another long stretch of good water, and they did not stop until they were well into the afternoon. Then Tayoga proposed that they make a fire and cook all of the deer.

"It seems that the risk here is not great," he said, "and we may not have the chance later on."

Robert, who still felt that they were protected and that for a day or two no harm could come to them under any circumstances, was more than willing, and they spent the remainder of the day in their culinary task. After dark he slept three hours, to be followed by Tayoga for the same length of time, and about midnight they started up the stream again, with their food cooked and ready beside them.

Although the Onondaga shared Robert's feeling that they were protected for the time, both exercised all their usual caution, believing thoroughly in the old saying that heaven helps those who help themselves. It was this watchfulness, particularly of ear, that caused them to hear the dip of paddles approaching up the stream. Softly and in silence, they lifted the canoe out of water and hid with it in the greenwood. Then they saw a fleet of eight large canoes go by, all containing warriors, armed heavily and in full war paint.

"Hurons," whispered Tayoga. "They go south for a great taking of scalps, doubtless to join Montcalm, who is surely meditating another sudden and terrible blow."

"And he will strike at our forts by Andiatarocte," rejoined Robert. "I hope we can find Willet and Rogers soon and take the news. All the woods must be full of warriors going south to Montcalm."

"They have French guns, and good ones too, and they are wrapped in French blankets. Onontio does not forget the power of the warriors and draws them to him."

The silent file of war canoes passed on and out of sight, and, for a space, Robert's heart was heavy within him. He felt the call of battle, he ought to be in the south, giving what he could to the defence against the might of Montcalm, but to go now would be merely a dash in the dark. They must continue to seek Willet and Rogers.

When the last Indian canoe was far beyond hearing they re-launched their own and paddled until nearly daybreak, coming to a place where bushes and tall grass grew thick in the shallow water at the edge of the river.

"Here," said Tayoga, "we will leave the canoe. A good hiding place offers itself, and with the dawn it will be time for us to take to the woods."

They concealed with great art the little boat that had served them so well, sinking it in the heart of the densest growth and then drawing back the bushes and weeds so skilfully that the keenest Indian eye would not have noticed that anyone had ever been there.

"I hope," said Robert sincerely, "that we'll have the chance to return here some time or other and use it again."

"That rests in the keeping of Manitou," said the Onondaga, "and now we will take up our packs and go eastward toward Oneadatote."

"But we won't go fast, because my pack, with all this venison in it, is by no means light."

"It is no heavier than mine, Dagaeoga, but, as you say, we will not hasten, lest we pass the Great Bear and the Mountain Wolf in the forest and not know it. But I think we are safe in going toward Oneadatote, as Rogers and his rangers usually operate in the region of George and Champlain."

They travelled two days and two nights and came once more among the high ridges and peaks. They saw many Indian trails and always they watched for another. On the third day Tayoga discovered traces in moss and he said with great satisfaction to his comrade:

"Lo, Dagaeoga, we, too, be wise in our time. The print here speaks to me like the print on the page of a book. It says that the Great Bear has passed this way."

"I can tell that the traces were made by the feet of a white man," said Robert, "but how do you know they are Dave's?"

"I have noticed that the Great Bear's feet are more slender than the average. Also he bears less upon the heel. He poises himself more upon the toe, like the great swordsman we saw him to be that time in Quebec."

"The distinctions are too fine for me, Tayoga, but I don't question your own powers of observation. I accept your statement with gratitude and joy, too, because now we know that Dave is alive, and somewhere in the great northern forest of the Province of New York. I knew he could not be dead, but it's a relief anyhow to have the proof. But as I see no other traces, how is it, do you think, that he happens to be alone?"

"The Great Bear may have been making a little scout by himself. I still think that he is with Rogers and the rangers, and when we follow his trail we are likely to find soon that he has rejoined them."

The traces led north and east until they came to rocky ground, where they were lost, and Tayoga assumed from the fact that they were several days old, otherwise he could have made them out even in the more difficult region. But when the path, despite all his searching, vanished in the air, he began to look higher than the earth. Soon he smiled and said:

"Ah, the Great Bear is as wise as the fox and the serpent combined. He knows that a little chance may lead to great results, and so he neglects none of the little chances."

"I don't understand you," said Robert, puzzled.

The Onondaga bent over a bush and showed where a twig had been cut off.

"See the wound made by his knife," he said, "and look! here is another on a bush farther on. Both wounds are partly healed, showing that the cut of the knife was made several days ago. It occurred to the Great Bear that we might strike his trail some time or other, and when he came to the stony uplift upon which his moccasins would leave no sign, he made traces elsewhere. He knew the chance of our ever seeing them was slight, and he may have made thousands of other traces that we never will see, but the possibility that we would see some one of the many became a probability."

"As you present it, it seems simple, Tayoga, but what an infinity of pains he must have taken!"

"The Great Bear is that kind of a man."

The hard, rocky ground extended several miles and their progress over it was, of necessity, very slow, as Tayoga was compelled to look with extreme care for the signs the hunter might have left. He found the cut twigs five times and twice footprints where softer soil existed between the rocks, making the proofs conclusive to both, and when they emerged into a normal region beyond they picked up his defined and clear trail once more.

"I shall be glad to see the Great Bear," said the Onondaga, "and I think he will be as pleased to know certainly that we are alive as we are to be assured that he is."

"He'd never desert us, and if you hadn't come to the Indian village I think he'd have done so later on."

"The Great Bear is a man such as few men are. Now, his trail leads on, straight and bold. He took no trouble to hide it, which proves that he had friends in this region, and was not afraid to be followed. Here he sat on a fallen log and rested a while."

"How do you know that, Tayoga?"

"See the prints in front of the log. They were made by the heels of his moccasins only. He tilted his feet up until they rested merely on the heels. The Great Bear could not have been in that attitude while standing. Nay, there is more. The Great Bear sat down here not to rest but to think."

"It's just supposition with you, Tayoga."

"It is not supposition at all, Dagaeoga, it is certainty. Look, several little pieces of the bark on the dead log where the Great Bear sat, are picked off. Here are the places from which they were taken, and here are the fragments themselves lying on the ground. The Great Bear must have been thinking very hard and he must have been in great doubt to have had uneasy hands, because, as you and I know, Dagaeoga, his mind and nerves are of the calmest."

"What, then, do you think was on his mind?"

"He was undecided whether to go on towards Oneadatote or to turn back and seek us anew. Here are three or four traces, a short and detached trail leading in the direction from which we have come. Then the traces suddenly turn. He sat down again and thought it over a second time."

"You can't possibly know that he resumed his seat on the log!"

"Oh, yes, I can, Dagaeoga. I wish all that we had to see was as easy, because here is the second place on the log where he picked at the bark. Mighty as the Great Bear is he cannot sit in two places at once. Not Tododaho himself could do that."

"It's conclusive, and I find here at the end of the log his trail, leading on toward the east."

"And he went fast, because the distance between his footprints lengthens. But he did not do so long. He became very slow suddenly. The space between the footprints shortens all at once. He turned aside, too, from his course, and crept through the bushes toward the south."

"How do you know that he crept?"

"Because for many steps he rested his weight wholly on his toes. The traces show it very clearly. The Great Bear was stalking something, and it was not a foe."

"That, at least, is supposition, Tayoga."

"Not supposition, Dagaeoga, and while not absolute certainty it is a great probability. The toe prints lead straight toward the tiny little lake that you see shining through the foliage. It was game and not a foe that the Great Bear was seeking. He wished to shoot a wild fowl. Look, the edge of the lake here is low, and the tender water grasses grow to a distance of several yards from the shore. It is just the place where wild ducks or wild geese would be found, and the Great Bear secured the one he wanted. If you will look closely, Dagaeoga, you will see the faint trace of blood on the grass. Blood lasts a long time. Manitou has willed that it should be so, because it is the life fluid of his creatures. It was a wild goose that the Great Bear shot."

"And why not a wild duck?"

"Because here are two of the feathers, and even Dagaeoga knows they are the feathers of a goose and not of a duck. It was, too, the fattest goose in the flock."

"Which you have no possible way of knowing, Tayoga."

"But I do, Dagaeoga. It was the fattest goose of the flock, because the fattest goose of the flock was the one that so wise and skilful a hunter as the Great Bear would, as a matter of course, select and kill. Learn, O, Dagaeoga, to trail with your mind as well as with your eye, and ear. The day may come when the white man will equal the red man in intellect, but it is yet far off. The Great Bear was very, very hungry, and we shall soon reach the place where he cleaned and cooked his goose."

"Come, come, Tayoga! You may draw good conclusions from what you see, but there are no prophets nowadays. You don't know anything about the state of Dave's appetite, when he shot that goose, and you can't predict with certainty that we'll soon come to the place where he made it ready for the eating."

"I cannot, Dagaeoga! Why, I am doing it this very instant. Mind! Mind! Did I not tell you to use your mind? O, Dagaeoga, when will you learn the simpler things of life? The Great Bear would not have risked a shot at a wild goose in enemy country, if he had not been very hungry. Otherwise he would have waited until he rejoined the rangers to obtain food. And, having risked his shot, and having obtained his goose, which was the fattest in the flock, he became hungrier than ever. And having risked so much he was willing to risk more in order to complete the task he had undertaken, without which the other risks that he had run would have been all in vain."

"Tayoga, I can almost believe that you have your dictionary with you in your knapsack."

"Not in my knapsack, Dagaeoga, but in my head, where yours also ought to be. Ah, here is where the Great Bear began to make preparations to cook his goose! His trail wanders back and forth. He was looking for fallen wood to build the fire. And there, in the little sink between the hills, was where he built it. Even you, Dagaeoga, can see the ashes and burnt ends of sticks. The Great Bear must have been as hungry as a wolf to have eaten a whole goose, and the fattest goose of the flock, too. How do I know he ate it all? Look in the grass and leaves and you will find enough bones to make the complete frame of a goose, and every bone is picked clean. Wild animals might have gleaned on them, you say? No. Here is the trail of a wolf that came to the dip after the Great Bear had gone, drawn by the savoury odours, but he turned back. He never really entered the dip. Why? When he stood at the edge his acute and delicate senses told him no meat was left on the bones, and a wolf neither makes idle exertion, nor takes foolish risk. He went back at once. And if the wolf had not come, there is another reason why I knew the Great Bear ate all the goose. He would not have thrown away any of the bones with flesh still on them. He is too wise a man to waste. He would have taken with him what was left of the goose. Having finished his most excellent dinner, the Great Bear looked for a brook."

"Why a brook?"

"Because he was thirsty. Everyone is thirsty after a heavy meal. He turned to the right, as the ground slopes down in that direction. Even you, Dagaeoga, know that one is more likely to find a brook in a valley than on a hilltop. Here is the brook, a fine, clear little stream with a sandy bottom, and here is where the Great Bear knelt and drank of the cool water. The prints of his strong knees show like carving on a wall. Finding that he was still thirsty he came back for another drink, because the second prints are a little distance from the first.

"Then, after rejoicing over the tender goose and his renewed strength, he suddenly became very cautious. The danger from the warriors, which he had forgotten or overlooked in his hunger, returned in acute form to his mind. He came to the brook a third time, but not to drink. He intended to wade in the stream that he might hide his trail, which, as you well know, Dagaeoga, is the oldest and best of all forest devices for such purposes. How many millions of times must the people of the wilderness have used it!

"Now the Great Bear had two ways to go in the water, up the stream or down the stream, and you and I, Dagaeoga, think he went down the stream, because the current leads on the whole eastward, which was the way in which he wished to go. At least, we will choose that direction and I will take one side of the bank and you the other."

They followed the brook more than a mile with questing eyes, and Tayoga detected the point at which Willet had emerged, plunging anew into the forest.

"Warriors, if they had picked up his trail, could have followed the brook as we did," said Robert.

"Of course," said Tayoga, "but the object of the Great Bear was not so much to hide his flight as to gain time. While we went slowly, looking for the emergence of his trail, he went fast. Now I think he meant to spend the night in the woods alone. The rangers must still have been far away. If they had been near he would not have felt the need of throwing off possible pursuit."

They followed the dim traces several hours, and then Tayoga announced with certainty that the hunter had slept alone in the forest, wrapped in his blanket.

"He crept into this dense clump of bushes," he said, "and lay within their heart, sheltered and hidden by them. You, Dagaeoga, can see where his weight has pressed them down. Why, here is the outline of a human body almost as clear and distinct as if it were drawn with black ink upon white paper! And the Great Bear slept well, too. The bushes are not broken or shoved aside except in the space merely wide enough to contain his frame. Perhaps the goose was so very tender and his nerves and tissues had craved it so much that they were supremely happy when he gave it to them. That is why they rested so well.

"In the morning the Great Bear resumed his journey toward the east. He had no breakfast and doubtless he wished for another goose, but he was refreshed and he was very strong. The traces are fainter than they were, because the Great Bear was so vigorous that his feet almost spurned the earth."

"Don't you think, Tayoga, that he'll soon turn aside again to hunt? So strong a man as Dave won't go long without food, especially when the forest is full of it. We've noticed everywhere that the war has caused the game to increase greatly in numbers."

"It will depend upon the position of the force to which the Great Bear belongs. If it is near he will not seek game, waiting for food until he rejoins the rangers, but if they are distant he will look for a deer or another goose, or maybe a duck. But by following we will see what he did. It cannot be hidden from us. The forest has few secrets from those who are born in it. Ah, what is this? The Great Bear hid in a bush, and he leaped suddenly! Behold the distance between the footprints! He saw something that alarmed him. It may have been a war party passing, and of which he suddenly caught sight. If so we can soon tell."

A hundred yards beyond the clump of bushes they found a broad trail, indicating that at least twenty warriors had gone by, their line of march leading toward the southeast.

"They were in no hurry," said the Onondaga, "as they had no fear of enemies. Their steps are irregular, showing that sometimes they stopped and talked. Doubtless they meant to join Montcalm, but as they can travel much faster than an army they were taking their time about it. We will now return to the bushes in which the Great Bear lay hidden while he watched. The traces of his footsteps in the heart of the clump are much deeper than usual, which proves that he stood there quite a while. It is also another proof that the warriors stopped and talked when they were near him, else he would not have remained in the clump so long. It is likely, too, that the Great Bear followed them when they resumed their journey. Yes, here is his trail leading from the bushes. But it is faint, the Great Bear was stepping lightly and here is where it merges with the trail of the warriors. He could not have been more than three or four hundred yards behind them. The Great Bear was very bold, or else they were very careless. He will not follow them long, as he merely wishes to get a general idea of their course, it being his main object to rejoin the rangers."

"And at this point he turned away from their trail," said Robert, after they had followed it about a mile. "He is now going due east, and his traces lead on so straight that he must have known exactly where he intended to go."

"Stated with much correctness," said Tayoga in his precise school English. "Dagaeoga is taking to heart my assertion that the mind is intended for human use, and he is beginning to think a little. But we shall have to stop soon for a while, because the night comes. We, too, will sleep in the heart of the bushes as the Great Bear did."

"And glad am I to stop," said Robert. "My burden of buffalo robe and deer and arms and ammunition is beginning to weigh on me. A buffalo robe doesn't seem of much use on a warm, summer day, but it is such a fine one and you took so much trouble to get it for me, Tayoga, that I haven't had the heart to abandon it."

"It is well that you have brought it, in spite of its weight," said the Onondaga, "as the night, at this height, is sure to be cold, and the robe will envelop you in its warmth. See, the dark comes fast."

The sun sank behind the forest, and the twilight advanced, the deeper dusk following in its trail, a cold wind began to blow out of the north, and Robert, as Tayoga had predicted, was thankful now that he had retained the buffalo robe, despite its weight. He wrapped it around his body and sat on a blanket in a thicket. Tayoga, by his side, used his two blankets in a similar manner, and they ate of the deer which they had had the forethought to cook, and make ready for all times.

The dusk deepened into the thick dark, and the night grew colder, but they were warm and at ease. Robert was full of courage and hope.

The elements and all things had served them so much that he was quite sure they would succeed in everything they undertook. By and by, he stretched himself on the blanket, and clothed from head to foot in the great robe he slept the deep sleep of one who had toiled hard and well. An hour later Tayoga also slept, but in another hour he awoke and sat up, listening with all the marvellous powers of hearing that nature and cultivation had given him.

Something was stirring in the thicket, not any of the wild animals, big or little, but a human being, and Tayoga knew the chances were a hundred to one that it was a hostile human being. He put his ear to the earth and the sound came more clearly. Now his wonderful gifts of intuition and forest reasoning told him what it was. Slowly he rose again, cleared himself of the blankets, and put his rifle upon them. Then, loosening the pistol in his belt, but drawing his long hunting knife, he crept from the thicket.

Tayoga, despite his thorough white education and his constant association with white comrades, was always an Indian first. Now, as he stole from the thicket in the dark, knife in hand, he was the very quintessence of a great warrior of the clan of the Bear, of the nation Onondaga, of the great League of the Hodenosaunee. He was what his ancestors had been for unnumbered generations, a primeval son of the wilderness, seeking the life of the enemy who came seeking his.

He kept to his hands and knees, and made no sound as he advanced, but at intervals he dropped his ear to the ground, and heard the faint rustling that was drawing nearer. He decided that it was a single warrior who by some chance had struck their trail in the dusk, and who, with minute pains and with slowness but certainty, was following it.

His course took him about thirty yards among the bushes and then through high grass growing luxuriantly in the open. In the grass his eye also helped him, because at a point straight ahead the tall stems were moving slightly in a direction opposed to the wind. He took the knife in his teeth and went on, sure that bold means would be best.

The stalking warrior who in his turn was stalked did not hear him until he was near, and then, startled, he sprang to his feet, knife in hand. Tayoga snatched his own from his teeth and stood erect facing him. The warrior, a Huron, was the heavier though not the taller of the two, and recognizing an enemy, a hated Iroquois, he stared fiercely into the eyes that were so close to his. Then he struck, but, agile as a panther, Tayoga leaped aside, and the next instant his own blade went home. The Huron sank down without a sound, and the Onondaga stood over him, the spirit of his ancestors swelling in fierce triumph.

But the feeling soon died in the heart of Tayoga. His second nature, which was that of his white training and association, prevailed. He was sorry that he had been compelled to take life, and, dragging the heavy body much farther away, he hid it in the bushes. Then, making a circle through the forest to assure himself that no other enemies were near, he went swiftly back to the thicket and lay down again between his blankets. He had a curious feeling that he did not want Robert to know what had happened.

Tayoga remained awake the remainder of the night, and, although he did not stir again from the thicket, he kept a vigilant watch. He would hear any sound within a hundred yards and he would know what it was, but there was none save the rustlings of the little animals, and dawn came, peaceful and clear. Robert moved, threw off the buffalo robe and stood up among the bushes.

"A big sleep and a fine sleep, Tayoga," he said.

"It was a good time for Dagaeoga to sleep," said the Onondaga.

"I was warm, and your Tododaho watched over me."

"Aye, Dagaeoga, Tododaho was watching well last night."

"And you slept well, too, Tayoga?"

"I slept as I should, Dagaeoga. No man can ask more."

"Philosophical and true. It's breakfast now, slices of deer, and water of a brook. Deer is good, Tayoga, but I'm beginning to find I could do without it for quite a long time. I envy Dave the fat goose he had, and I don't wonder that he ate it all at one time. Maybe we could find a juicy goose or duck this morning."

"But we have the deer and the Great Bear had nothing when he sought the goose. We will even make the best of what we have, and take no risk."

"It was merely a happy thought of mine, and I didn't expect it to be accepted. My happiest thoughts are approved by myself alone, and so I'll keep 'em to myself. My second-rate thoughts are for others, over the heads of whom they will not pass."

"Dagaeoga is in a good humour this morning."

"It is because I slept so well last night. Now, having had a sufficiency of the deer I shall seek a brook. I'm pretty sure to find one in the low ground over there."

He started to the right, but Tayoga immediately suggested that he go to the left—the hidden body of the warrior lay in the bushes on the right—and Robert, never dreaming of the reason, tried the left where he found plenty of good water. Tayoga also drank, and with some regret they left the lair in the bushes.

"It was a good house," said Robert. "It lacked only walls, a roof and a floor, and it had an abundance of fresh air. I've known worse homes for the night."

"Take up your buffalo robe again," said the Onondaga, "because when another night comes you will need it as before."

They shouldered their heavy burdens and resumed the trail of the hunter, expecting that it would soon show a divergence from its straight course.

"The rangers seem to be farther away than we thought," said Tayoga, "and the Great Bear must eat. One goose, however pleasant the memory, will not last forever. It is likely that he will turn aside again to one of the little lakes or ponds that are so numerous in this region."

In two hours they found that he had done so, and this time his victim was a duck, as the feathers showed. They saw the ashes where he had cooked it, and as before only the bones were left. Evidently he had lingered there some time, as Tayoga announced a distinctly fresher trail, indicating that they were gaining upon him fast, and they increased their own speed, hoping that they would soon overtake him.

But the traces led on all day, and the next morning, after another night spent in the thickets, Tayoga said that the Great Bear was still far ahead, and it was possible they might not overtake him until they approached the shores of Champlain.

"But if necessary we'll follow him there, won't we, Tayoga?" said Robert.

"To Oneadatote and beyond, if need be," said the Onondaga with confidence.

CHAPTER 13

Reading the Signs

On the third day the trail of the Great Bear was well among the ranges and Tayoga calculated that they could not be many hours behind him, but all the evidence, as they saw it, showed conclusively that he was going toward Lake Champlain.

"It seems likely to me," said the Onondaga, "that he left the rangers to seek us, and that Rogers meanwhile would move eastward. Having learned in some way or other that he could not find us, he will now follow the rangers wherever they may go."

"And we will follow him wherever he goes," said Robert.

An hour later the Onondaga uttered an exclamation, and pointed to the trail. Another man coming from the south had joined Willet. The traces were quite distinct in the grass, and it was also evident from the character of the footsteps that the stranger was white.

"A wandering hunter or trapper? A chance meeting?" said Robert.

Tayoga shook his head.

"Then a ranger who was out on a scout, and the two are going on together to join Rogers?"

"Wrong in both cases," he said. "I know who joined the Great Bear, as well as if I saw him standing there in the footprints he has made. It was not a wandering hunter and it was not a ranger. You will notice, Dagaeoga, that these traces are uncommonly large. They are not slender like the footprints of the Great Bear, but broad as well as long. Why, I should know anywhere in the world what feet made them. Think, Dagaeoga!"

"I don't seem to recall."

"Willet is a great hunter and scout, among the bravest of men, skilful on the trail, and terrible in battle, but the man who is now with him is all these also. A band attacking the two would have no easy task to conquer them. You have seen both on the trail in the forest and you have seen both in battle. Try hard to think, Dagaeoga!"

"Black Rifle!"

"None other. It is far north for him, but he has come, and he and the Great Bear were glad to see each other. Here they stood and shook hands."

"There is not a possible sign to indicate such a thing."

"Only the certain rules of logic. Once again I bid you use your mind. We see with it oftener than with the eye. White men, when they are good friends and meet after a long absence, always shake hands. So my mind tells me with absolute certainty that the Great Bear and Black Rifle did so. Then they talked together a while. Now the eye tells me, because here are footsteps in a little group that says so, and then they walked on, fearless of attack. It is an easy trail to follow."

He announced in a half hour that they were about to enter an old camp of the two men.

"Any child of the Hodenosaunee could tell that it is so," he said, "because their trails now separate. Black Rifle turns off to the right, and the Great Bear goes to the left. We will follow Black Rifle first. He wandered about apparently in aimless fashion, but he had a purpose nevertheless. He was looking for firewood. We need not follow the trail of the Great Bear, because his object was surely the same. They were so confident of their united strength that they built a fire to cook food and take away the coldness of the night. Although Great Bear had no food it was not necessary for him to hunt, because Black Rifle had enough for both. The fact that the Great Bear did not go away in search of game proves it.

"I think we will find the remains of their fire just beyond the low hill on the crest of which the bushes grow so thick. Once more it is mind and not eye that tells me so, Dagaeoga. They would build a fire near because they had begun to look for firewood, which is always plentiful in the forest, and they would surely choose the dip which lies beyond the hill, because the circling ridge with its frieze of bushes would hide the flames. Although sure of their strength they did not neglect caution."

They passed over the hill, and found the dead embers of the fire.

"After they had built it Black Rifle sat on that side and the Great Bear on this," said Tayoga, "and while they were getting it ready the Great Bear concluded to add something on his own account to the supper."

"What do you mean, Tayoga? Is this mind or eye?"

"A combination of the two. The Great Bear is a wonderful marksman, as we know, and while sitting on the log that he had drawn up before the fire, he shot his game out of the tall oak on our right."

"This is neither eye nor mind, Tayoga, it is just fancy."

"No, Dagaeoga, it is mostly eye, though helped by mind. My conclusion that he was sitting, when he pulled the trigger is mind chiefly. He would not have drawn up the log unless he had been ready to sit down, and everything was complete for the supper. The Great Bear never rests until his work is done, and he is so marvellous with the rifle that it was not necessary for him to rise when he fired. Wilderness life demands so much of the body that the Great Bear never makes needless exertion. There mind works, Dagaeoga, but the rest is all eye. The squirrel was on the curved bough of the oak, the one that projects toward the north."

"You assume a good deal to say that it was a squirrel and surely mind not eye would select the particular bough on which he sat."

"No, Dagaeoga, eye served the whole purpose. All the other branches are almost smothered in leaves, but the curved one is nearly bare. It is only there that the casual glance of the Great Bear, who was not at that time seeking game, would have caught sight of the squirrel. Also, he must have been there, otherwise his body could not have fallen directly beneath it, when the bullet went through his head."

"Now tell me how your eye knows his body fell from the bough."

"Ah, Dagaeoga! Your eye was given to you for use as mine was given to me, then you should use it; in the forest you are lost unless you do. It was my eye that saw the unmistakable sign, the sign from which all the rest followed. Look closely and you will detect a little spot of red on the grass just beneath the bare bough. It was blood from the squirrel."

"You cannot be sure that it was a squirrel. It might have been a pigeon or some other bird."

"That, O, Dagaeoga, would be the easiest of all, even for you, if you could only use your eyes, as I bid you. Almost at your feet lies a slender bone that cannot be anything but the backbone of a squirrel. Beyond it are two other bones, which came from the same body. We know as certainly that it was a squirrel as we know that the Great Bear ate first a wild goose, and then a wild duck. But it is a good camp that those two great men made, and, as the night is coming, we will occupy it."

They relighted the abandoned fire, warmed their food and ate, and Robert was once more devoutly glad that he had kept the heavy buffalo robe. Deep fog came over the mountain soon after dark, and, after a while, a fine cold, and penetrating rain was shed from the heart of it. They kept the fire burning and wrapped, Tayoga in his blankets, and, Robert in the robe, crouched before it. Then they drew the logs that the Great Bear and Black Rifle had left, in such position that they could lean their backs against them, and slept, though not the two at the same time. They agreed that it was wise to keep watch and Robert was sentinel first.

Tayoga, supported by the log, slept soundly, the flames illuminating his bronze face and showing the very highest type of the Indian. Robert sat opposite, his rifle across his knees, but covered by his blanket to protect it from the fine rain, which was not only cold but insidious, trying to insert itself beneath his clothing and chill his body. But he kept himself covered so well that none reached him, and the very wildness of his surroundings increased his sense of intense physical comfort.

He did not stir, except now and then to put a fresh chunk of wood on the fire, and the red blaze between Tayoga and himself was for a time the centre of the world. The cold, white fog was rolling up everywhere thick and impenetrable, and the fine rain, like a heavy dew that was distilled from it, fell incessantly. Robert knew that it was moving up the valleys and clothing all the peaks and ridges. He knew, too, that it would hide them from their enemies and his sense of comfort grew with the knowledge. But his conviction that they were safe did not make him relax caution, and, since eye was useless in the fog, he made extreme call upon ear.

It seemed to him that the fog was a splendid conductor of sound. It brought him the rustling of the foliage, the moaning of the light wind through the ravines, and, at last, another sound, sharp, distinct, a discordant note in the natural noises of the wilderness, which were always uniform and harmonious. He heard it a second time, to his right, down the hill, and he was quite sure that it indicated the presence of man, man who in reality was near, but whom the fog took far away. The vapours, however, would lift, then man might come close, and he felt that it was his part to discover who and what he was.

Still wrapped in the buffalo robe, he rose and took a few steps from the fire. Tayoga did not stir, and he was proud that his tread had been without noise. Beyond the rim of firelight, he paused and listening again heard the clank twice, not very loud but coming sharp and definite as before through the vapoury air. He parted the bushes very carefully and went down the side of a ravine, the wet boughs and twigs making no noise as they closed up after his passage.

But his progress was very slow, purposely so, as he knew that any mistake or accident might be fatal, and he intended that no fault of his should precipitate such a crisis. Once or twice he thought of going back, deeming his a foolish quest, lost in a wilderness of bushes and blinding fog, but the sharp, clear clank stirred his purpose anew, and he went on down the slope, until he saw a red glow in the heart of the fog. Then he sank down among the bushes and listened with intentness. Presently the faint hum of voices came to his ear, and he was quite sure that many men were not far away.

He resumed his slow advance, but now he was glad the bushes were soaked with water, as they did not crackle or snap with the passage of his body, and the luminous glow in front of him broadened and deepened steadily. Near the bottom of a deep valley he stopped and from his covert saw where great fires had driven the fog away. Around the fires were many warriors, some of them sleeping in their blankets, while others were eating prodigiously, after their manner. Rifles and muskets were stacked in French fashion and the clank, clank that Robert had heard had been made by the warriors as they put up their weapons.

Many were talking freely and seemed to rejoice in the food and fires. It was Robert's surmise that they had arrived but recently and were weary. Their numbers were large, they certainly could not be less than four or five hundred, and his experience was great enough now to tell him that half of them, at least, were Canadian Indians. All were in war paint, and they had an abundance of arms.

Robert's eager eye sought Tandakora, but did not find him. He had no doubt, however, that this great body of warriors was moving against Rogers and his rangers, and that it would soon be joined by the Ojibway chief. Tandakora, anxious for revenge upon the Great Bear and the Mountain Wolf, would be willing to leave Montcalm for a while if he thought that by doing so he could achieve his purpose. His gaze wandered from the warriors to the stacked rifles and muskets, and he saw that many of them were of English or American make, undoubtedly spoil taken at the capture of Oswego. His heart swelled with anger that the border should have its own weapons turned against it by the foe.

It did not take him long to see enough. It was a powerful force, equipped to strike, and now he was more anxious than ever to overtake Willet. The fog was still thick and wet, distilling the fine rain, but he had forgotten discomfort, and, turning back on his path, he sought the dip in which he had left Tayoga sleeping. He felt a certain pride that it had been his fortune to discover the band, and, as he had marked carefully the way by which he had come, it was not a difficult task to retrace his steps.

The Onondaga was still sleeping, his back against the log, but he awoke instantly when Robert touched him gently on the shoulder.

"What is it, Dagaeoga?" he whispered. "You have seen something! Your face tells me so!"

"My face tells you the truth," replied Robert. "There is a valley only a few hundred yards from us, and, in it, are about four hundred warriors, armed for battle. All the signs indicate that they are going eastward in search of our friends."

"You have done well, Dagaeoga. You have used both eye and mind. Was Tandakora there?"

"No, but I'm convinced he soon will be."

"It appears likely. They think, perhaps, they are strong enough to annihilate the rangers."

"Maybe they are, unless the rangers are warned. We ought to move at once."

"But the fog is too thick. We could not tell which way we were going. We must not lose the trail of the Great Bear and Black Rifle, and, if the fog lifts, we can regain it in the morning, going ahead of the war band."

"And then the warriors may pursue us."

"What does it matter, if we keep well ahead of them and overtake the Great Bear and Black Rifle, who are surely going toward the rangers? We will put out the fire, Dagaeoga, and stay here. The fog protects us. Now, you sleep and I will watch."

His calmness was reassuring, and it was true that the fog was an almost certain protection, while it lasted. They smothered the fire carefully, and then, Robert was sufficient master of his nerves, to go to sleep, wrapped in the invaluable buffalo robe. The Onondaga kept vigilant watch. His own ear, too, heard the occasional sound made by human beings in the valley below, but he did not stir from his place. He had absolute confidence in Robert's report, and he would not take any unnecessary risk.

An hour or two before dawn a wind began to rise, and Tayoga knew by feeling rather than sight that the fog was beginning to thin. If the wind held, it would all blow away by sunrise, and the rain with it. He awakened Robert at once.

"I think we would better move now," he said. "We shall soon be able to see our way, and a good start ahead of the war band is important."

They made a northward curve, passing around the valley, in which the camp of the warriors lay, and, when the sun showed its first luminous edge over the horizon, they were several miles ahead. The steady wind had carried all the fog and rain to the southward, but the forest was still wet and dripping.

"And now," said Tayoga, "we must pick up anew the trail of the Great Bear and Black Rifle. We are sure they were continuing east, and by ranging back and forth from north to south and from south to north we can find it."

It was a full two hours before they discovered it, leading up a narrow gorge, and Robert grew anxious lest the war band was already on their own traces, which the warriors were sure to see in time. So they hastened their own pursuit and very soon came to a thicket in which the two redoubtable scouts had passed the night. The trail leading from it was comparatively fresh and Tayoga was hopeful that they might overtake them before the next sunset.

"They do not hurry," he said. "The Great Bear has been telling Black Rifle of us, and now and then it was their thought to go back into the west to make another hunt for us. My certainty about it is based on nothing in the trail. It is just mind once more. It is exactly the idea that a valiant and patient man like the Great Bear would have, and it would appeal too, to the soul of such a great warrior as Black Rifle. But after thinking well upon it, they have decided that the search would be vain for the present, and once more they go on, though the wish to find us puts weights on their feet."

Before noon they came to a place where Black Rifle shot a deer. The useless portions of the body that the two had left behind spoke a language none could fail to understand, and they were sure it was Black Rifle who had fired the shot, because his broader footprints led to the place where the body had fallen.

"It proves," said Tayoga, "that the rangers are still well ahead, else two such wise men as the Great Bear and Black Rifle would not take the trouble to kill a deer here and carry so much weight with them. It is likely that the Mountain Wolf and his men are on the shores of Oneadatote itself."

All that afternoon the trail went upward higher and higher among the ranges and peaks, but the infallible eye of Tayoga never lost it for a moment. "We will not overtake them today, as I had hoped," he said, "but we shall certainly do so tomorrow before noon."

"And the coming night is going to offer a striking contrast to the one just passed," said Robert. "It will be crystal clear."

"So it will, Dagaeoga, and we will seek a camp among the rocks. It is best to leave no traces for the warriors."

They travelled a long distance on the stony uplift before they stopped for the night, and they did not build any fire, dividing the time into two watches, each kept with great vigilance. But the pursuit which they were so sure was now on did not overtake them, and early in the morning they were once more on the traces of the two hunters.

"It is now sure we shall reach them before noon," said Tayoga, "but in what manner we shall first see them I do not know. The trail has become wonderfully fresh. Ah, they turned suddenly from their course here, and soon they came back to it, at a point not more than ten feet away. We need not follow them on their loop to see where they went. We know without going. They climbed the steep little peak we see on the right, from the crest of which they had a splendid view over an immense stretch of country behind us. They looked in that direction because that was the point from which pursuit or danger would come. The band behind us built a fire, and the Great Bear and Black Rifle saw its smoke. They saw the smoke because they could see nothing else so far behind them. After a good look, they went on at their leisure. They had no fear. It was easy for such as they to leave the band well in the rear, if they wished."

"If they haven't changed greatly since we last saw 'em," said Robert, "they'll go all the more slowly because of the pursuit, and we may catch 'em in a couple of hours. Won't Dave be surprised when he sees us?"

"It will be a pleasant surprise for him. Here, they have stopped again, and one of them climbed the tall elm for another view, while the other stood guard by the trunk. I think, Dagaeoga, that the Great Bear and Black Rifle were beginning to think less of flight than of battle."

"You don't mean that knowing the presence of the band behind us they intended to meet it?"

"Not to stop it, of course, but spirits such as theirs might have a desire to harm it a little, and impede its advance. In any event, Dagaeoga, we shall soon see. Here is where the climber came down, and then the two went on, walking slowly. They walked slowly, because the traces indicate that they turned back often, and looked toward the point at which they had seen the smoke rising. My mind tells me that the Great Bear thought it better to continue straight ahead, but that Black Rifle was anxious to linger, and get a few shots at the enemy. It is so, because the Great Bear, as we know, is naturally cautious and would wish to do what is of the most service in the campaign, while it is always the desire of Black Rifle to injure the enemy as much as he can."

"Your reasoning seems conclusive to me."

"Did I not tell you, Dagaeoga, that you had the beginnings of a mind? Use it sedulously, and it will grow yet more."

"And the time may come when I can talk out of a dictionary as you do, Tayoga."

"Which merely proves, Dagaeoga, that those who learn a language always talk it better than those who are born to it. Ah, they have turned once more, and the trail leads again to the crest of a hill, where they will take another long look backward. It seems that the wishes of Black Rifle are about to prevail. Now we are at the top of the hill, and they stood here several minutes talking and moving about, as the traces show very clearly. But look, Dagaeoga, they saw something very much closer at hand than smoke. Their talk was interrupted with great suddenness, and they took to ambush. They crouched among these bushes, and you and I know they were a very dangerous pair with their rifles ready. Still, Dagaeoga, instead of their taking the battle to the warriors the battle was brought to them."

"You think, then, an encounter occurred?"

"I know it. They did not stay crouched here until the enemy went away, but moved off down the hill, their course on the whole leading away from the lake. The enemy was before them, because they kept among the bushes, always in the densest part of them. Here they knelt. The bent grass stems indicate the pressure of knees. The warriors must have been very close.

"Now the trail divides. Look, Dagaeoga! Black Rifle went to the right and the Great Bear to the left. They formed a plan to flank the enemy and to assail him from two sides. I should judge then that the warriors did not number more than five or six. We will follow the Great Bear, who made the slender traces, and if necessary we will come back and follow also those of Black Rifle. But I think we can read the full account of the contest which most certainly occurred from the evidence that the Great Bear left."

"You feel quite sure then that there was fighting?"

"Yes. It is not an opinion formed from the signs yet seen, but it is drawn from the characters of the Great Bear and Black Rifle. They would not have taken so much care unless there was the certainty of conflict. Here the Great Bear knelt again, and took a long look at his enemy or at least at the place where his enemy was lying. They were coming to close quarters or he would not have knelt and waited. Perhaps he held his fire because Black Rifle was making the wider circuit, and they meant to use their rifles at the same time."

The Onondaga was on his own knees now, examining the faint trail intently, his eyes alight with interest.

"The event will not be delayed long," he said, "because the Great Bear stopped continually, seeking an opportunity for a shot. Here he pulled the trigger."

He picked up a minute piece of the burned wadding of the muzzle-loading rifle.

"The warrior at whom he fired was bound to have been in the thicket beyond the open space," he said, "and it was there that he fell. He fell because at such a critical time the Great Bear would not have fired unless he was sure of his aim. We will look into the thicket"

They found several spots of blood among the bushes and at another point about twenty feet away they saw more.

"Here is where the warrior fell before Black Rifle's bullet," said Tayoga. "He and the Great Bear must have fired almost at the same time. Undoubtedly the warriors retreated at once, carrying their dead with them. Let us see if they did not unite, and leave the thicket at the farthest point from our two friends."

The trail was very clear at the place the Onondaga had indicated, and also many more red spots were there leading away toward the east.

"We will not follow them." said Tayoga, "because they do not interest us any more. They have retreated and they do not longer enter into your campaign and mine, Dagaeoga. We will go back and see where the left wing of our army, that was the Great Bear, reunited with the right wing, that was Black Rifle."

They found the point of junction not far away, and then the deliberate trail led once more toward Champlain, the two pursuing it several hours in silence and both noticing that it was rapidly growing fresher. At length Tayoga stopped on the crest of a ridge and said:

"We no longer need to seek their trail, Dagaeoga, because I will now talk with the Great Bear and Black Rifle."

"Very good, Tayoga. I am anxious to hear what you will say and how you will say it."

A bird sang at Robert's side. It was Tayoga trilling forth a melody, wonderfully clear and penetrating, a melody that carried far up the still valley beyond. "You will remember, Dagaeoga," he said, "that we have often used this call with the Great Bear. The reply will soon come."

The two listened and Robert's heart beat hard. He owed much to Willet. Their relationship was almost that of son and father, and the two were about to meet after a long parting. He never doubted for a moment that the Onondaga had always read the trail aright, and that Willet was with Black Rifle in the valley below them.

Full and clear rose the song of a bird out of the dense bushes that filled the valley. When it was finished Tayoga sang again, and the reply came as before. The two went rapidly down the slope and the stalwart figures of the hunter and Black Rifle rose to meet them. The four did not say much, but in every case the grasp of the hand was strong and long.

"I went west in search of you, Robert," said the hunter, "but I was compelled to come back, because of the great events that are forward here. I felt, however, that Tayoga was there looking for you and would do all any number of human beings could do."

"He found me and rescued me," said Robert, "and what of yourself, Dave?"

"I'm attached, for the present, to the rangers under Rogers. He's on the shores of Champlain, and he's trying to hold back a big Indian army that means to march south and join Montcalm for an attack on Fort William Henry or Fort Edward."

"And there's a great Indian war band behind you, too, Dave."

"We know it. We saw their smoke. We also had an encounter with some scouting warriors."

"We know that, too, Dave. You ambushed 'em and divided your force, one of you going to the right and the other to the left. Two of their warriors fell before your bullets, and then they fled, carrying their slain with them."

"Correct to every detail. I suppose Tayoga read the signs."

"He did, and he also told me when he rescued me that you had carried the text of the letter we took from Garay to Colonel Johnson in time, and that the force of St. Luc was turned back."

"Yes, the preparations for defence made an attack by him hopeless, and when his vanguard was defeated in the forest he gave up the plan."

They did not stop long, as they knew the great war band behind them was pressing forward, but they felt little fear of it, as they were able to make high speed of their own, despite the weight of their packs, and for several days and nights they travelled over peaks and ridges, stopping only at short intervals for sleep. They had no sign from the band behind them, but they knew it was always there, and that it would probably unite at the lake with the force the rangers were facing.

It was about noon of a gleaming summer day when Robert, from the crest of a ridge, saw once more the vast sheet of water extending a hundred and twenty-five miles north and south, that the Indians called Oneadatote and the white men Champlain, and around which and upon which an adventurous part of his own life had passed. His heart beat high, he felt now that the stage was set again for great events, and that his comrades and he would, as before, have a part in the war that was shaking the Old World as well as the New.

In the afternoon they met rangers and before night they were in the camp of Rogers, which included about three hundred men, and which was pitched in a strong position at the edge of the lake. The Mountain Wolf greeted them with great warmth.

"You're a redoubtable four," he said, "and I could wish that instead of only four I was receiving four hundred like you."

He showed intense anxiety, and soon confided his reasons to Willet.

"You've brought me news," he said, "that a big war band is coming from the west, and my scouts had told me already that a heavy force is to the northward, and what is worst of all, the northern force is commanded by St. Luc. It seems that he did not go south with Montcalm, but drew off an army of both French and Indians for our destruction. He remembers his naval and land defeat by us and naturally he wants revenge. He is helped, too, by the complete command of the lake, that the French now hold. Since we've been pressed southward we've lost Champlain."

"And of course St. Luc is eager to strike," said Willet. "He can recover his lost laurels and serve France at the same time. If we're swept away here, both the French and the Indians will pour down in a flood from Canada upon the Province of New York."

Robert did not hear this talk, as he was seeking in the ranger camp the repose that he needed so badly. He had brought with him some remnants of food and the great buffalo robe that Tayoga had secured for him with so much danger from the Indian village. Now he put down the robe, heaved a mighty sigh of relief and said to the Onondaga:

"I'm proud of myself as a carrier, Tayoga, but I think I've had enough. I'm glad the trail has ended squarely against the deep waters of Lake Champlain."

"And yet, Dagaeoga, it is a fine robe."

"So it is. I should be the last to deny it, but now that we're with the rangers I mean to carry nothing but my arms and ammunition. To appreciate what it is to be without burdens you must have borne them."

The hospitable rangers would not let the two youths do any work for the present, and so they took a luxurious bath in the lake, which they commanded as far as the bullets from their rifles could reach. They rejoiced in the cool waters, after their long flight through the wilderness.

"It's almost worth so many days and nights of danger to have this," said Robert, swimming with strong strokes.

"Aye, Dagaeoga, it is splendid," said the Onondaga, "but see that you do not swim too far. Remember that for the time Oneadatote belongs to Onontio. We had it, but we have lost it."

"Then we'll get it back again," said Robert courageously. "Champlain is too fine a lake to lose forever. Wait until I've had a big sleep. Then my brain will be clear, and I'll tell how it ought to be done."

The two returned to land, dressed, and slept by the campfire.

Chapter 14

St. Luc's Revenge

When Robert awoke from a long and deep sleep he became aware, at once, that the anxious feeling in the camp still prevailed. Rogers was in close conference with Willet, Black Rifle and several of his own leaders beside a small fire, and, at times, they looked apprehensively toward the north or west, a fact indicating to the lad very clearly whence the danger was expected. Most of the scouts had come in, and, although Robert did not know it, they had reported that the force of St. Luc, advancing in a wide curve, and now including the western band, was very near. It was the burden of their testimony, too, that he now had at least a thousand men, of whom one-third were French or Canadians.

Tayoga was sitting on a high point of the cliff, watching the lake, and Robert joined him. The face of the young Onondaga was very grave.

"You look for an early battle, I suppose," said Robert.

"Yes, Dagaeoga," replied his comrade, "and it will be fought with the odds heavily against us. I think the Mountain Wolf should not have awaited Sharp Sword here, but who am I to give advice to a leader, so able and with so much experience?"

"But we beat St. Luc once in a battle by a lake!"

"Then we had a fleet, and, for the time, at least, we won command of the lake. Now the enemy is supreme on Oneadatote. If we have any canoes on its hundred and twenty-five miles of length they are lone and scattered, and they stay in hiding near its shores."

"Why are you watching its waters now so intently, Tayoga?"

"To see the sentinels of the foe, when they come down from the north. Sharp Sword is too great a general not to use all of his advantages in battle. He will advance by water as well as by land, but, first he will use his eyes, before he permits his hand to strike. Do you see anything far up the lake, Dagaeoga?"

"Only the sunlight on the waters."

"Yes, that is all. I believed, for a moment or two, that I saw a black dot there, but it was only my fancy creating what I expected my sight to behold. Let us look again all around the horizon, where it touches the water, following it as we would a line. Ah, I think I see a dark speck, just a black mote at this distance, and I am still unable to separate fancy from fact, but it may be fact. What do you think, Dagaeoga?"

"My thought has not taken shape yet, Tayoga, but if 'tis fancy then 'tis singularly persistent. I see the black mote too, to the left, toward the western shore of the lake, is it not?"

"Aye, Dagaeoga, that is where it is. If we are both the victims of fancy then our illusions are wonderfully alike. Think you that we would imagine exactly the same thing at exactly the same place?"

"No, I don't! And as I live, Tayoga, the mote is growing larger! It takes on the semblance of reality, and, although very far from us, it's my belief that it's moving this way!"

"Again my fancy is the same as yours and it is not possible that they should continue exactly alike through all changes. That which may have been fancy in the beginning has most certainly turned into fact, and the black mote that we see upon the waters is in all probability a hostile canoe coming to spy upon us."

They watched the dark dot detach itself from the horizon and grow continuously until their eyes told them, beyond the shadow of a doubt, that it was a canoe containing two warriors. It was moving swiftly and presently Rogers and Willet came to look at it. The two warriors brought their light craft on steadily, but stopped well out of rifle shot, where they let their paddles rest and gazed long at the shore.

"It is like being without a right arm to have no force upon the lake," said Rogers.

"It cripples us sorely," said Willet. "Perhaps we'd better swallow our pride, bitter though the medicine may be, and retreat at speed."

"I can't do it," said Rogers. "I'm here to hold back St. Luc, if I can, and moreover, 'tis too late. We'd be surrounded in the forest and probably annihilated."

"I suppose you're right. We'll meet him where we stand, and when the battle is over, whatever may be its fortunes, he'll know that he had a real fight."

They walked away from the lake, and began to arrange their forces to the most advantage, but Robert and Tayoga remained on the cliff. They saw the canoe go back toward the north, melt into the horizon line, and then reappear, but with a whole brood of canoes. All of them advanced rapidly, and they stretched into a line half way across the lake. Many were great war canoes, containing eight or ten men apiece.

"Now the attack by land is at hand," said Tayoga. "Sharp Sword is sure to see that his two forces move forward at the same time. Hark!"

They heard the report of a rifle shot in the forest, then another and another. Willet joined them and said it was the wish of Rogers that they remain where they were, as a small force was needed at that point to prevent a landing by the Indians. A fire from the lake would undoubtedly be opened upon their flank, but if the warriors could be kept in their canoes it could not become very deadly. Black Rifle came also, and he, Willet, Robert, Tayoga and ten of the rangers lying down behind some trees at the edge of the cliff, watched the water.

The Indian fleet hovered a little while out of rifle shot. Meanwhile the firing in the forest grew. Bullets from both sides pattered on leaves and bark, and the shouts of besieged and besiegers mingled, but the members of the force on the cliff kept their eyes resolutely on the water.

"The canoes are moving again," said Tayoga. "They are coming a little nearer. I see Frenchmen in some of them and presently they will try to sweep the bank with their rifles."

"Our bullets will carry as far as theirs," said the hunter.

"True, O, Great Bear, and perhaps with surer aim."

In another moment puffs of white smoke appeared in the fleet, which was swinging forward in a crescent shape, and Robert heard the whine of lead over his head. Then Willet pulled the trigger and a warrior fell from his canoe. Black Rifle's bullet sped as true, and several of the rangers also found their targets. Yet the fleet pressed the attack. Despite their losses, the Indians did not give back, the canoes came closer and closer, many of the warriors dropped into the water behind their vessels and fired from hiding, bullets rained around the little band on the cliff, and presently struck among them. Two of the rangers were slain and two more were wounded. Robert saw the Frenchmen in the fleet encouraging the Indians, and he knew that their enemies were firing at the smoke made by the rifles of the defenders. Although he and his comrades were invisible to the French and Indians in the fleet, the bullets sought them out nevertheless. Wounds were increasing and another of the rangers was killed. Theirs was quickly becoming an extremely hot corner.

But Willet, who commanded at that point, gave no order to retreat. He and all of his men continued to fire as fast as they could reload and take aim. Yet to choose a target became more difficult, as the firing from the fleet made a great cloud of smoke about it, in which the French and Indians were hidden, or, at best, were but wavering phantoms. Robert's excited imagination magnified them fivefold, but he had no thought of shirking the battle, and he crept to the very brink, seeking something at which to fire in the clouds of smoke that were steadily growing larger and blacker.

The foes upon the lake fought mostly in silence, save for the crackle of their rifles, but Robert became conscious presently of a great shouting behind him. In his concentration upon their own combat he had forgotten the main battle; but now he realized that it was being pressed with great fury and upon a half circle from the north and west. He looked back and saw that the forest was filled with smoke pierced by innumerable red flashes; the rattle of the rifles there made a continuous crash, and then he heard a tremendous report, followed by a shout of dismay from the rangers.

"What is it?" he cried. "What is it?"

Willet, who was crouched near him, turned pale, but he replied in a steady voice.

"St. Luc has brought a field piece, a twelve-pounder, I think, and they've opened fire with grape-shot. They'll sweep the whole forest. Who'd have thought it?"

The battle sank for a moment, and then a tremendous yell of triumph came from the Indians. Presently, the cannon crashed again, and its deadly charge of grape took heavy toll of the rangers. Then the lake and the mountains gave back the heavy boom of the gun in many echoes, and it was like the toll of doom. The Indians on both water and shore began to shout in the utmost fury, and Robert detected the note of triumph in the tremendous volume of sound. His heart went down like lead. Rogers crept back to Willet and the two talked together earnestly.

"The cannon changes everything," said the leader of the rangers. "More than twenty of my men are dead, and nearly twice as many are wounded. 'Tis apparent they have plenty of grape, and they are sending it like hail through the forest. The bushes are no shelter, as it cuts through 'em. Dave, old comrade, what do you think?"

"That St. Luc is about to have his revenge for the defeat we gave him at Andiatarocte. The cannon with its grape turns the scale. They come on with uncommon fury! It seems to me I hear a thousand rifles all together."

St. Luc now pressed the attack from every side save the south. The French and Indians in the fleet redoubled their fire. The twelve-pounder was pushed forward, and, as fast as the expert French gunners could reload it, the terrible charges of grape-shot were sent among the rangers. More were slain or wounded. The little band of defenders on the high cliff overlooking the lake at last found their corner too hot for them and were compelled to join the main force. Then the French and Indians in the fleet landed with shouts of triumph and rushed upon the Americans.

Robert caught glimpses of other Frenchmen as he faced the forest. Once an epaulet showed behind a bush and then a breadth of tanned face which he was sure belonged to De Courcelles. And so this man who had sought to make him the victim of a deadly trick was here! And perhaps Jumonville also! A furious rage seized him and he sought eagerly for a shot at the epaulet, but it disappeared. He crept a little farther forward, hoping for another view, and Tayoga noticed his eager, questing gaze.

"What is it, Dagaeoga?" he asked. "Whom do you hate so much?"

"I saw the French Colonel, De Courcelles, and I was seeking to draw a bead on him, but he has gone."

"Perhaps he has, but another takes his place. Look at the clump of bushes directly in front of us and you will see a pale blue sleeve which beyond a doubt holds the arm of a French officer. The arm cannot be far away from the head and body, which I think we will see in time, if we keep on looking."

Both watched the bushes with a concentrated gaze and presently the head and shoulders, following the arm, disclosed themselves. Robert raised his rifle and took aim, but as he looked down the sights he saw the face among the leaves, and a shudder shook him. He lowered his rifle.

"What is it, Dagaeoga?" whispered the Onondaga.

"The man I chose for my target," replied Robert, "was not De Courcelles, nor yet Junonville, but that young De Galissonnière, who was so kind to us in Quebec, and whom we met later among the peaks. I was about to pull trigger, and, if I had done so, I should be sorry all my life."

"Is he still there?"

Robert looked again and De Galissonnière was gone. He felt immense relief. He thought it was war's worst cruelty that it often brought friends face to face in battle.

The French and Indian horde from the lake landed and drove against the rangers on the eastern flank with great violence, firing their rifles and muskets, and then coming on with the tomahawk. The little force of Rogers was in danger of being enveloped on all sides, and would have been exterminated had it not been for his valour and presence of mind, seconded so ably by Willet, Black Rifle and their comrades.

They formed a barrier of living fire, facing in three directions and holding back the shouting horde until the main body of the surviving rangers could gather for retreat. Robert and Tayoga were near Willet, all the best sharpshooters were there, and never had they fought more valiantly than on that day.

Robert crouched among the bushes, peering for the faces of his foes, and firing whenever he could secure a good aim.

"Have you seen Tandakora?" he asked Tayoga.

"No," replied the Onondaga.

"He must be here. He would not miss such a chance."

"He is here."

"But you said you hadn't seen him."

"I have not seen him, but O, Dagaeoga, I have heard him. Did not we observe when we were in the forest that ear was often to be trusted more than eye? Listen to the greatest war shout of them all! You can hear it every minute or two, rising over all the others, superior in volume as it is in ferocity. The voice of the Ojibway is huge, like his figure."

Now, in very truth, Robert did notice the fierce triumphant shout of Tandakora, over and above the yelling of the horde, and it made him shudder again and again. It was the cry of the man-hunting wolf, enlarged many times, and instinct with exultation and ferocity. That terrible cry, rising at regular intervals, dominated the battle in Robert's mind, and he looked eagerly for the colossal form of the chief that he might send his bullet through it, but in vain; the voice was there though his eyes saw nothing at which to aim.

Farther and farther back went the rangers, and the youth's heart was filled with anger and grief. Had they endured so much, had they escaped so many dangers, merely to take part in such a disaster? Unconsciously he began to shout in an effort to encourage those with him, and although he did not know it, it was a reply to the war cries of Tandakora. The smoke and the odours of the burned gunpowder filled his nostrils and throat, and heated his brain. Now and then he would stop his own shouting and listen for the reply of Tandakora. Always it came, the ferocious note of the Ojibway swelling and rising above the war whoop of the other Indians.

"Dagaeoga looks for Tandakora," said the Onondaga.

"Truly, yes," replied Robert. "Just now it's my greatest wish in life to find him with a bullet. I hear his voice almost continuously, but I can't see him! I think the smoke hides him."

"No, Dagaeoga, it is not the smoke, it is Areskoui. I know it, because the Sun God has whispered it in my ear. You will hear the voice of Tandakora all through the battle, but you will not see him once."

"Why should your Areskoui protect a man like Tandakora, who deserves death, if anyone ever did?"

"He protects him, today merely, not always. It is understood that I shall meet Tandakora in the final reckoning. I told him so, when I was his captive, and he struck me in the face. It was no will of mine that made me say the words, but it was Areskoui directing me to utter them. So, I know, O, my comrade, that Tandakora cannot fall to your rifle now. His time is not today, but it will come as surely as the sun sets behind the peaks."

Tayoga spoke with such intense earnestness that Robert looked at him, and his face, seen through the battle smoke, had all the rapt expression of a prophet's. The white youth felt, for the moment at least, with all the depth of conviction, the words of the red youth would come true. Then the tremendous voice of Tandakora boomed above the firing and yelling, but, as before, his body remained invisible. Tandakora's Indians, many of whom had come with him from the far shores of the Great Lakes, showed all the cunning and courage that made them so redoubtable in forest warfare. Armed with good French muskets and rifles they crept forward among the thickets, and poured in an unceasing fire. Encouraged by the success at Oswego, and by the knowledge that the great St. Luc, the best of all the French leaders, was commanding the whole force, their ferocity rose to the highest pitch and it was fed also by the hope that they would destroy all the hated and dreaded rangers whom they now held in a trap.

Robert had never before seen them attack with so much disregard of wounds, and death. Usually the Indian was a wary fighter, always preferring ambush, and securing every possible advantage for himself, but now they rushed boldly across open spaces, seeking new and nearer coverts. Many fell before the bullets of the rangers but the swarms came on, with undiminished zeal, always pushing the battle, and keeping up a fire so heavy that, despite the bullets that went wild, the rangers steadily diminished in numbers.

"It's a powerful attack," said Robert.

"It's because they feel so sure of victory," said Tayoga, "and it's because they know it's the Mountain Wolf and his men whom they have surrounded. They would rather destroy a hundred rangers than three hundred troops."

"That's so," said Willet, who overheard them in all the crash of the battle. "They won't let the opportunity escape. Back a little, lads! This place is becoming too much exposed."

They withdrew into deeper shelter, but they still fired as fast, as they could reload and pull the trigger. Their bullets, although they rarely missed, seemed to make no impression on the red horde, which always pressed closer, and there was a deadly ring of fire around the rangers, made by hundreds of rifles and muskets.

Robert and Tayoga were still without wounds. Leaves and twigs rained around them, and they heard often the song of the bullets, they saw many of the rangers fall, but happy fortune kept their own bodies untouched. Robert knew that the battle was a losing one, but he was resolved to hold his place with his comrades. Rogers, who had been fighting with undaunted valour and desperation, marshalling his men in vain against numbers greatly superior, made his way once more to the side of Willet and crouched with him in the bushes.

"Dave, my friend," he said, "the battle goes against us."

"So it does," replied the hunter, "but it is no fault of yours or your men. St. Luc, the best of all the French leaders, has forced us into a trap. There is nothing left for us to do now but burst the trap."

"I hate to yield the field."

"But it must be done. It's better to lose a part of the rangers than to lose all. You've had many a narrow escape before. Men will come to your standard and you'll have a new band bigger than ever."

The dark face of the ranger captain brightened a little. But he looked sadly upon his fallen men. He was bleeding himself from two slight wounds, but he paid no attention to them. The need to flee pierced his soul, but he saw that it must be done, else all the rangers would be destroyed, and, while he still hesitated a moment or two, the silver whistle of St. Luc, urging on a fresh and greater attack, rose above all the sounds of combat. Then he knew that he must wait no longer, and he gave the command for ordered flight.

Not more than half of the rangers escaped from that terrible converging attack. St. Luc's triumph was complete. He had won full revenge for his defeat by Andiatarocte, and he pushed the pursuit with so much energy and skill that Rogers bade the surviving rangers scatter in the wilderness to reassemble again, after their fashion, far to the south.

Black Rifle remained with the leader, but Robert, Tayoga and Willet continued their flight together, not stopping until night, when they were safe from pursuit. As the three went southward through the deep forest, they saw many trails that they knew to be those of hostile Indians, and nowhere did they find a sign of a friend. All the wilderness seemed to have become the country of the enemy. When they looked once more from the lofty shores upon the vivid waters of George, they beheld canoes, but as they watched they discovered that they were those of the foe. A terrible fear clutched at their hearts, a fear that Montcalm, like St. Luc, had struck already.

"The tide of battle has flowed south of us," said Tayoga. "All that we find in the forest proclaims it."

"I would you were not right, Tayoga," said the hunter, "but I fear you are."

They came the next day to the trail of a great army, soldiers and cannon. Night overtook them while they were still near the shores of Lake George, following the road, left by the French and Indian host as it had advanced south, and the three, wearied by their long flight, drew back into the dense thickets for rest. The darkness had come on thicker and heavier than usual, and they were glad of it, as they were well hidden in its dusky folds, and they wished to rest without apprehension.

They had food with them which they ate, and then they wrapped their blankets about their bodies, because a wind was coming from the lake, and its touch was damp. Clouds also covered all the skies, and, before long, a thin, drizzling rain fell. They would have been cold, and, in time, wet to the bone, but the blankets were sufficient to protect them.

"Areskoui, after smiling upon us for so long, has now turned his face from us," said Tayoga.

"What else can you expect?" said the valiant Willet. "It is always so in war. You're up and then you're down. We were masters of the peaks for a while, and by our capture of Garay's letter we kept St. Luc from attacking Albany, but the stars never fight for you all the time. We couldn't do anything that would save the rangers from defeat."

The Onondaga looked up. The others could not see his face, but it was reverential, and the cold rain that fell upon it had then no chill for him. Instead it was soothing.

"Tododaho is on his great star beyond the clouds," he said, "and he is looking down on us. We have done wrong or he and Areskoui would not have withdrawn their favour from us, but we have done it unknowingly, and, in time, they will forgive us. As long as the Onondagas are true to him Tododaho will watch over them, although at times he may punish them."

That Tododaho was protecting them even then was proved conclusively to Tayoga before the night was over. A great war party passed within a hundred yards of them, going swiftly southward, but the three, swathed in their blankets, and, hidden in the dark thickets, had no fear. They were merely three motes in the wilderness and the warriors did not dream that they were near. When the last sound of their marching had sunk into nothingness, Tayoga said:

"It was not the will of Tododaho that they should suspect our presence, but I fear that they go to a triumph."

They rose from the thicket early the following morning, and resumed their flight, but it soon came to a halt, when the Onondaga pointed to a trail in the forest, made apparently by about twenty warriors. The hawk eye of Tayoga, however, picked out one trace among them which all three knew was made by a white man.

"I know, too," said the red youth, "the white man who made it."

"Tell us his name," said the hunter, who had full confidence in the wonderful powers of the Onondaga.

"It is the Frenchman, Langlade, who held Dagaeoga a prisoner in his village so long. I know his traces, because I followed them before. His foot is very small, and it has been less than an hour since he passed here. They are ahead of us, directly in our path."

"What do you think we ought to do, Dave?" asked Robert, anxiously. "You know we want to go south as fast as we can."

"We must try to go around Langlade," replied Willet. "It's true, we'll lose time, but it's better to lose time and be late a little than to lose our lives and never get there at all."

"The Great Bear is a very wise man," said Tayoga.

They made at once a sharp curve toward the east, but just when they thought they were passing parallel with Langlade's band, they were fired upon from a thicket, the bullet singing by Robert's ear. The three took cover in the bushes, and a long and trying combat of sharpshooters took place.

Two warriors were slain and both Willet and Tayoga were grazed by the Indian fire, but they were not hurt. Robert once caught sight of Langlade, and he might have dropped the partisan with his bullet, but his heart held his hand. Langlade had shown him many a kindness, during his long captivity and, although he was a fierce enemy now, the lad was not one to forget. As he had spared De Galissonnière, so would he spare Langlade, and, in a moment or two, the Frenchman was gone from his sight.

Another dark and rainy night came, and, protected by it, they crept in silence past the partisan's band soon leaving this new danger far behind them. Tayoga was very grateful, and accepted their escape as a sign.

"While Manitou, who rules all things, has decreed that we must suffer much before victory," he said, "yet, as I see it, he has decreed also that we three shall not fall, else why does he spread so many dangers before us, and then take us safely through them?"

"It looks the same way to me," said Willet. "The dark and rainy night that he sent enabled us to pass by Langlade and his band."

"A second black night following a first," said Tayoga, devoutly. "I do not doubt that it was sent for our benefit by Manitou, who is lord even over Tododaho and Areskoui."

They made good speed near the shores of Andiatarocte and now and then they caught glimpses once more through the heavy green foliage of the lake's glittering waters. But they saw anew the canoes of the French and Indians upon its surface, and they realized with increasing force that Andiatarocte, so vital in the great struggle, belonged, for the time at least, to their enemies. Yet the three themselves were favoured. The rain ceased, a warm wind out of the south dried the forest, and their flight became easy. A fat deer stood in their path and fairly asked to be shot, furnishing them all the food they might need for days to come, and they were able to dress and prepare it at their leisure.

"It is clear, as I have already surmised and stated," said Tayoga in his precise language, "that the frown of Manitou is not for us three. The way opens before us, and we shall rejoin our friends."

"If we have any friends left," said the hunter. "I fear greatly, Tayoga, that Montcalm will have struck before we arrive. He has a powerful force with plenty of cannon, and we know he acts with decision and speed."

"He has struck already and he has struck terribly," said Tayoga with great gravity.

"How do you know that?" asked Robert, startled.

"I do not know it because of anything that has been told to me in words," replied the Onondaga, "but O, Dagaeoga, the mind, which is often more potent than eye or ear, as I have told you so many times, is now warning me. We know that our people farther south have been in disagreement. The governors of the provinces have not acted together. Everyone is of his own mind, and no two minds are alike. No effort was made to profit by the great victory last year on the shores of Andiatarocte. Waraiyageh, sore in body and mind, rests at home, so it is not possible that our people have been ready and vigorous."

"While the French and Indians are all that we are not?"

"Even so. Montcalm advances with great speed, and knows precisely what he intends to do. He has had plenty of time to reach our forts below. His force is overwhelming, though more so in preparation and decision, than in numbers. He has had time to strike, and being Montcalm, therefore he has struck. There is no chance of error, O, Dagaeoga and Great Bear, when I tell you a heavy blow has fallen upon us."

"I don't want to believe you, Tayoga," said the hunter, "but I do. The conclusion seems inevitable to me."

"I'm hoping when hope's but faint," said Robert.

They swung again into the great trail, left by the army of Montcalm, or at least a part of it, and the Onondaga and the hunter told its tale with precision.

"Here passed the cannon," said Tayoga. "I judge by the size of the ruts the wheels made that a battery of twelve pounders went this way. What do you say, Great Bear?"

"You're right, of course, Tayoga, and there were eight guns in the battery; a child could tell their number. They had other batteries too."

"And the wooden walls of our forts wouldn't stand much chance against a continuous fire of twelve and eighteen pounders," said Robert.

"No," said Willet. "The forts could be saved only by enterprising and skilful commanders who would drive away the batteries."

"Here went the warriors," said Tayoga. "They were on the outer edges of the great trail, walking lightly, according to their custom. See the traces of the moccasins, scores and scores of them. We will come very soon to a place where the whole army camped for the night. How do I know, O, Dagaeoga? Because numerous trails are coming in from the forest and converging upon one point. They do that because it is time to gather for food and the night's rest. Some of the warriors went into the forest to hunt game, and they found it, too. Look at the drops of blood, still faintly showing on the grass, leading here, and here, and here into the main trail, drops that fell from the deer they had slain. Also they shot birds. Behold feathers hanging on the bushes, blown there by the wind, which proves that the site of their camp is very near, as I said."

"It's just over the hill in that wide, shallow valley," said Willet.

They entered the valley which had been marked by the departed army with signs as clear as the print of a book for the Onondaga and the hunter to read.

"Here at the northern end of the valley is where the warriors cooked and ate the deer they had slain," said Tayoga. "The bones are scattered all about, and we see the ashes of their fires, but they kept mostly to themselves, because few footprints of white men lead to the place they set aside as their own. Just beyond them the cannon were parked. All this is very simple. An Onondaga child eight years old could read what is written in this camp. Here are the impressions made by the cannon wheels, and just beside them the artillery horses were tethered, as the numerous hoofprints show."

"And here, I imagine," said Robert, who had walked on, "the Marquis de Montcalm and his lieutenants spent the night. Tents were pitched for them. You can see the holes left by the pegs."

"Spoken truly, O, Dagaeoga. You are using eye and mind, and lo! you are showing once more the beginnings of wisdom. Four tents were pitched. The rest of the army slept in the open. Montcalm and his lieutenants themselves would have done so, but the setting up of the tents inspired respect in the warriors and even in the troops. The French leaders have mind and they profit by it. They neglect no precaution, no detail to increase their prestige and maintain their authority."

"It is so, Tayoga," said Willet, "and I can wish that our own officers would do the same. The French are marvellously expert in dealing with Indians. They can handle them all, except the Hodenosaunee. But don't you think they held a short council here by this log, after they had eaten their suppers?"

"It cannot be doubted, Great Bear. Montcalm and his captains sat on the log. The Indian chiefs sat in a half circle before it, and they smoked a pipe. See, the traces of the ashes on the grass. They were planning the attack upon the fort. It is bound to be William Henry, because the trail leads in that direction."

"And these marks on the log, Tayoga, show that there was some indecision, at first, and much talking. Two or three of the French officers had their hunting knives in their hands, and they carved nervously at the log, just as a man will often whittle as he argues."

"Well stated, O, Great Bear. After the conference, the chiefs went back in single file to their own part of the camp. Here goes their trail, and you can nearly fancy that all stepped exactly in the footprints of the first."

"The straight, decisive line proves too, Tayoga, that the plan was completed and everything ready for the attack. The chiefs would not have gone away in such a manner if they had not been satisfied."

"Well stated again, Great Bear. The Marquis de Montcalm also went directly back to his tent. See, where the boot heels pressed."

"But you have no way of knowing," said Robert, "that the traces of boot heels indicate the Marquis."

"O, Dagaeoga, after all my teaching, you forget again that mind can see where the eye cannot. Train the mind! Train the mind, and you will get much profit from it. The traces of these boot heels lead directly to the place where the largest tent stood. We know it was the largest, because the holes left by the tent pegs are farthest apart. And we know it belonged to the Marquis de Montcalm, because, always having that keen eye for effect, the French Commander-in-Chief would have no tent but the largest."

"True as Gospel, Tayoga," said the hunter, "and the French officers themselves had a little conference in the tent of the Marquis, after they had finished with the Indian chiefs. Here, within the square made by the pegs, are the prints of many boot heels and they were not all made by the Marquis, since they are of different sizes. Probably they were completing some plans in regard to the artillery, since the warriors would have nothing to do with the big guns. Here are ashes, too, in the corner near one of the pegs. I think it likely that the Marquis smoked a thoughtful pipe after all the others had gone."

"Aye, Dave," said Robert, "and he had much to think about. The officers from Europe find things tremendously changed when they come from their open fields into this mighty wilderness. We know what happened to Braddock, because we saw it, and we had a part in it. I can understand his mistake. How could a soldier from Europe read the signs of the forest, signs that he had never seen before, and foresee the ambush?"

"He couldn't, Robert, lad, but while countries change in character men themselves don't. Braddock was brave, but he should have remembered that he was not in Europe. The Marquis de Montcalm remembers it. He made no mistake at Oswego and he is making none here. He took the Indian chiefs into council, as we have just seen. He placates them, he humours their whims, and he draws out of them their full fighting power to be used for the French cause."

Tayoga ranged about the shallow valley a little, and announced that the whole force had gone on together the morning after the encampment.

"The artillery and the infantry were in close ranks," he said, "and the warriors were on either flank, scouting in the forest, forming a fringe which kept off possible scouts of the English and Americans. There was no chance of a surprise attack which would cut up the forces of Montcalm and impede his advance."

Willet sighed.

"The Marquis, although he may not have known it," he said, "was in no danger from such an enterprise. We have read the signs too well, Tayoga. Our own people have been lying in their forts, weak of will, waiting to defend themselves, while the French and their allies have had all the wilderness to range over, and in which they might do as they pleased. It is easy to see where the advantage lies."

"And we shall soon learn what has happened," said Tayoga, gravely.

The next morning they met an American scout who told them the terrible news of the capture of Fort William Henry, with its entire garrison, by Montcalm, and the slaughter afterward of many of the prisoners by the Indians.

Robert was appalled.

"Is Lake George to remain our only victory?" he exclaimed.

"It's better to have a bad beginning and a good ending than a good beginning and a bad ending," said the scout.

"Remember," said Tayoga, "how Areskoui watched over us, when we were among the peaks. As he watched over us then so later on he will watch over our cause."

"It was only for a moment that I felt despair," said Robert. "It is certain that victory always comes to those who know how to work and wait."

Courage rose anew in their hearts, and once more they sped southward, resolved to make greater efforts than any that had gone before.

ALSO FROM LEONAUR

AVAILABLE IN SOFTCOVER OR HARDCOVER WITH DUST JACKET

GARRETT P. SERVISS' SCIENCE FICTION *by Garrett P. Serviss*—Three Interplanetary Adventures including the unauthorised sequel to H. G.Wells' *War of the Worlds--Edison's Conquest of Mars, A Columbus of Space, The Moon Metal.*

JUNK DAY by *Arthur Sellings*—". . . . his finest novel was his last, *Junk Day,* a post-holocaust tale set in the ruins of his native London and peopled with engrossing character types . . . . perhaps grimmer than his previous work but pointedly more energetic." *The Encyclopedia of Science Fiction.*

KIPLING'S SCIENCE FICTION by *Rudyard Kipling*—Science Fiction & Fantasy stories by a Master Storyteller including 'As East As A,B,C' 'With The Night Mail'.

THE COLLECTED SCIENCE FICTION AND FANTASY OF STANLEY G. WEINBAUM: THE BLACK HEART by *Stanley G. Weinbaum*—Classic Strange Tales Including: the Complete Novel The Dark Other, Plus Proteus Island and Others Stories included in this Volume The Dark Other (novel) Proteus Island The Adaptive Ultimate Pymalion's Spectacles.

THE COLLECTED SCIENCE FICTION AND FANTASY OF STANLEY G. WEINBAUM: STRANGE GENIUS by *Stanley G. Weinbaum*—Classic Tales of the Human Mind at Work Including the Complete Novel The New Adam, the 'van Manderpootz' Stories and Others Stories included in this Volume The New Adam (novel) The Brink of Infinity The Circle of Zero Graph The Worlds of If The Ideal The Point of View.

THE COLLECTED SCIENCE FICTION AND FANTASY OF STANLEY G. WEINBAUM OTHER EARTHS by *Stanley G. Weinbaum*—Classic Futuristic Tales Including: Dawn of Flame & its Sequel The Black Flame, plus The Revolution of 1960 & Others.

THE COLLECTED SCIENCE FICTION AND FANTASY OF STANLEY G. WEINBAUM INTERPLANETARY ODYSSEYS by *Stanley G. Weinbaum*—Classic Tales of Interplanetary Adventure Including: A Martian Odyssey, its Sequel Valley of Dreams, the Complete 'Ham' Hammond Stories and Others Stories included in this Volume Mars A Martian Odyssey Valley of Dreams Venus Parasite Planet The Lotus Eaters Uranus The Planet of Doubt Titan Flight on Titan Pluto The Red Peri Io The Mad Moon Europa Redemption Cairn Ganymede Tidal Moon.

SUPERNATURAL BUCHAN by *John Buchan*—Stories of Ancient Spirits, Uncanny Places & Strange Creatures.

AVAILABLE ONLINE AT

www.leonaur.com

AND OTHER GOOD BOOK STORES

SF-1

Printed in the United States
217427BV00001B/107/P

9 781846 775871